To Louise:

— Best wishes to you and your family this holiday season!

I hope that you find this book to be an enjoyable read in this Sgt. Markie series.

Have a safe & healthy 2022!

Best wishes,

Anthony Allen

1

Author Bio:

ANTHONY CELANO is a former Detective and Detective Squad Commander who served twenty-two years in the NYPD. His expertise in organized crime led to assignments in the Queens District Attorney's Office Squad and the Colombo Organized Crime Task Force during the Colombo Wars of the 1990's. Other assignments included, the Office of the Special State Prosecutor-Nursing Home Investigation, the Drug Enforcement Administration Joint Task Force and several detective squads in Manhattan and Brooklyn. He was the Co-Founder/Owner/CEO of Full Security Incorporated, a Midtown Manhattan based investigative firm, for seventeen years. Now retired, he resides in New York City with his family and devotes his time to writing Sergeant Markie Mystery novels. His first, "The Case of Two in the Trunk" was published in 2019 by Significance Press. His second, "The Case of the Cross-Eyed Strangler" was published in 2020 by Boulevard Books. Both offerings are available on Amazon. A visit to the website, anthonycelano.com, will enable the reader to find links to several author interviews.

This book is dedicated to the loving memory of Thomas Kavanagh Sr., Helen O'Connor Kavanagh, Thomas Kavanagh Jr., and to our law enforcement officers and military who keep us safe.

Boulevard Books

The New Face of Publishing

www.BoulevardBooks.org

THE CASE OF THE ONE EARED WOLF

Anthony Celano

1

Armory Animosity (The Early '70s)

FRIDAY NIGHT WAS PARTY NIGHT for the young mob associates. It would be accurate to say that attending weekend drills at the Park Slope armory was problematic for the sibling privates. Having slept only an hour, Jasper was hung over and in a foul mood. His twin brother, Chris, who drank moderately, was far better prepared to meet the demands that awaited them at the armory. The National Guardsmen were scheduled to be in uniform on the armory drill floor by 6:00 a.m.

"C'mon, hurry up, will ya?" Chris called to his brother as he tapped on the bathroom door. "We were late last month, so let's try not to make it three in a row."

Jasper lowered the razor. Looking upward, he responded in frustration at being rushed. "Okay . . . keep your shirt on," hollered Jasper. He decided to take a chance and not shave his soul patch.

Assimilating to army life on a military base in another part of the country was one thing, but once back in Brooklyn, adherence to rules became far less palatable. The twins considered having to rise at such a crazy hour of the morning to attend a weekend drill to be pure insanity. Jasper especially regretted having signed on for the six-year commitment. He cursed himself for having listened to his brother, who felt that enlisting in the National Guard was the only sure way to avoid combat in Vietnam.

"They're already lined up in formation," whispered Chris.

"So they're lined up," replied Jasper.

The tardiness of Cristofaro and Gaspare Stanlee drew attention. Jasper's pronounced yawn only made their late arrival on the drill floor more conspicuous. The pair took their place among what they liked to refer to as the chorus line. Those standing formation were predominantly men who were several years older than the brothers. Practically all shared the belief that they were a cut above the leadership they were required to serve under. In private life, a number of those in the lower ranks were accomplished professionals with high-paying jobs. For them, the Guard represented a viable option once their college deferment ceased to apply. Electricians, plumbers, carpenters, and civil servants were also represented in ample numbers. Both spectrums shared one common denominator. They had signed on with the National Guard in order to duck the draft. Their weekend ruined, the grim-faced soldiers stood shoulder to shoulder, waiting to be ordered about. Aware of the negative attitude of the troops, Sergeant Cornell Mathis felt the need to remind those standing in formation that it was *he* who held the power. Even if only for the brief period of a weekend, Mathis would never let them forget that they answered to him.

"Settle down and open ranks . . . and straighten out those lines!" ordered Sergeant Mathis. "Prepare for inspection."

The sergeant was a squat man with a bull neck. In compliance with regulations, he sported a neatly manicured mustache that didn't extend beyond the corners of his mouth. The hair on his upper lip was contoured in a way that projected a sinister look, reminiscent of the *Rocky and Bullwinkle* cartoon spy Boris Badinov. The sergeant's black hair was cut short with some whiteness visible at the sides. After ordering the ranks to open, he began inspecting he troops. Mathis came to an abrupt halt after he noticed Jasper. The Alabama-born Mathis began licking his lower lip as he stared at Jasper's face. There was an evilness that seemed to come over him. He acted as if he'd made a great discovery by noticing the tiny patch of hair beneath the center of Jasper's lower lip.

"What's that dirt you got under your lip?" Mathis demanded to know.

Jasper touched the offending area with his fingers. "I must have missed a spot shaving, Sarge."

"Get that hand down and remain at attention!" hissed the sergeant. "I didn't say at ease! Fall out and get rid of those whiskers pronto, and then report back to me! Now, move it!"

Jasper's mouth was taut as he restrained himself from reacting. He left the formation, walking slowly to his locker, where he kept a razor. The look on his face suggested to his brother, Chris, that there might be a problem afoot. Mathis continued along the line inspecting the troops. Try as he might, he found nothing out of order with Chris, whom he also had an unmistakable animosity toward.

"You and your brother are staying behind with me, so don't disappear," advised Mathis.

The sergeant's behavior was perplexing to Chris, who wondered why Mathis was looking for trouble. The animosity Mathis had for the twins stemmed from a scar the sergeant carried that dated back to his horrid sexual victimization as a youth.

An hour after inspection, the noise of truck motors began echoing throughout the vast drill floor. Mathis watched as the trucks lined up to depart the armory. This was an unusual weekend that called for everyone to camp out in the field overnight in tents left over from World War Two. The battle to be fought was against a mosquito army hell-bent on feasting off soldiers.

"Hey, you two, what are you doing, waiting for a bus? Snap into it and follow me," ordered Mathis.

"What's with this guy?" whispered Jasper to his brother.

"Who knows with this friggin' hillbilly," replied Chris. "C'mon, let's see what he has up his sleeve."

The brothers followed the sergeant into the arms room. "You two are staying back at the armory with me. It'll be just the three of us assigned to the cleanup detail," advised the sergeant.

Since Chris he was susceptible to mosquito bites, he was delighted at the prospect of not having to sleep in the woods after all. "We got lucky," he commented to his brother,

"Lucky? I'll show you how lucky you are." The tone used by Mathis clearly indicated a problem.

##########

CORNELL ALVIN MATHIS ORIGINALLY HAILED FROM Mobile, Alabama. He moved to New York City with his wife after taking a new job. With this relocation came a transfer to the 187th Field Artillery at the 14th Regiment Armory in Brooklyn's Park Slope. Mathis arrived in Brooklyn with a troubled past. Sexually abused as a child at the hands of Billy Weaver, his late stepfather, he carried deep psychological wounds. In answer to his long ago victimization he tended to lash out at anyone who reminded him of Weaver. Unfortunately for the Stanlee twins, they bore a striking physical resemblance to Billy Weaver. They shared the same eye coloring, high cheekbones, and straight hair. Jasper even had the same cleft chin as Weaver. The similarities were enough to trigger a reaction in the transplanted sergeant.

The departure of the last vehicle left Mathis in total command. For the sergeant, this presented a golden opportunity to harass the Billy Weaver lookalikes

"You with the hole in your chin, I want you to give this arms room a fresh coat of green paint," directed Mathis. "And you," he bellowed, now addressing Chris, "get your ass up in the balcony and police the floor up there. When that's done, I want you come down and do the same on the drill floor."

When finished with these chores, the brothers took a break. Mathis, who had been looking for them, approached them in a huff. "This ain't a vacation," he shouted. "You men follow me."

Chris looked directly at the sergeant with a slight smile. "Sure, Sarge," he said in a calm voice. "Whatever you say is okay with me." Remaining visibly calm, Chris was biding his time until he could figure out a way to neutralize the sergeant.

Although he said nothing, Jasper was seething. He stared coldly at Mathis, thinking of what he'd like to do to him. The malice in Jasper's expression wasn't lost on Mathis.

"What's the matter, does *Casper* the friendly ghost not feel like working today?" taunted Mathis, reducing the private's name to that of a popular cartoon character.

The hotheaded Jasper was hard pressed to maintain his cool. "I don't mind work," he answered through the side of his mouth. "Friggin' jerk-off," he angrily added under his breath.

"Good. Now, you and *Chris-the-fairy* follow me."

"My name is Cristofaro," corrected Chris, taking a stand in response to the assault on his name.

"Oh, excuse me, my mistake, *Sister-faro*," the sergeant replied before turning to walk away.

In answer to these provocations, Chris made a calculated decision to say nothing. Adept at plotting, he intended to bide his time until the proper opportunity to get even presented itself. Chris became alarmed when he noticed Jasper tightening his grip on the handle of the open gallon can of paint he held. He feared that the sergeant was about to be the recipient of a fresh coat of Army green.

"Jasper," whispered Chris, "ignore him. Can't you see what he's trying to do? Don't give him a reason to do a number on us. Give it time; I'll figure out a way to pay this guy off."

"I ain't waiting, Chris. I'll be laying for this prick when we get outta here later," threatened Jasper.

"Let it go, bro. After tomorrow, we don't have to see him for another month. We've got plenty of time to square the account. I'm thinking maybe we fill the inside of his car one night with concrete."

"I'm not gonna wait; he gets his right after the drill. I'm parting the cocksucker's hair with a pipe." At this point, Chris knew trouble was inevitable.

Hearing voices behind him, Mathis looked over his shoulder. He returned to where the brothers were standing. "Hey, what are you two jawing about? I said get moving!"

"Listen to this moron," muttered Jasper, wanting things to come to a head at this point.

Mathis couldn't believe what he heard. "What did you say?" he asked, not expecting a reply. "You two go grab a couple of flashlights. I've got some work for you to do down in The Deep Six."

Jasper's eyes met those of his brother. Receiving a subtle nod, Chris knew that there was a good chance that things would get ugly down in The Deep Six.

2

Payback Brooklyn Style

SERGEANT MATHIS LED THE TWINS TO THE DEEP SIX, a subterranean section two levels below the armory basement. People rarely ventured there because, as legend had it, the location was believed to be haunted. Be that true or not, between the cobwebs and dankness, The Deep Six was a spooky place.

"Where is this guy going?"

"I got no idea," whispered Chris.

"Nobody ever comes down here," complained Jasper.

The privates watched Mathis carefully. He walked around the Deep Six with a flashlight in hand as if searching for something. Eventually it became clear to the brothers what the sergeant was up to.

"I know what he's doing," whispered Chris. "He's hunting for something lousy for us to do."

"Here we go," declared Mathis, finding what he was looking for. He stopped at the sealed entrance to an underground tunnel that the soldiers used years ago. "Behind this wall is an escape route that leads all the way into Prospect Park."

"Escape from what?" asked Jasper sarcastically. He had no actual interest in a history lesson.

"Escape from the enemy, stupid!" Mathis answered tartly. After the sergeant turned toward Jasper, his mouth dropped open. In the dim lighting, Jasper looked even more like Billy Weaver.

"Why did they seal it up?" asked Chris, who was curious to know.

Mathis turned to answer Chris. "When they did the construction for the underground trains, they caved in parts of the tunnel. You live in Brooklyn and you don't know that?"

"I must have missed that day in school," replied Chris, shrugging.

Mathis shined his light on the floor by the entranceway of the tunnel. Several of the aged bricks had loosened and fallen to the ground, leaving a gaping hole.

"Go upstairs and see what we've got to patch this wall," ordered Mathis. "Then I want you to clean up down here so that you can eat off the floor." The twins held their ground. "Did you hear me? I said go get what you need and patch this wall!" he thundered. "Then, make this place sparkle!"

"Sparkle?" asked Chris, perplexed by the ridiculousness of the order.

"You heard what I said. Now, get going."

Finally, Chris took a stand. "How far do you think you can push us?" he asked.

Mathis was taken aback, thinking he misheard what was said. "What?" he asked.

"You heard him!" jumped in Jasper.

"Are you addressing me, *Private*?" asked Mathis, pulling rank. His tone was clearly derisive.

"Oooooo, again with this 'Private.' . . . Who do you think you're talking to over here, a couple of jerk-offs?" shot back Jasper, who was working himself up to a dangerous state.

Mathis took a step back, assuming a defensive stance. A robust man, the sergeant wasn't intimidated from a physical standpoint. On the contrary, he seemed to welcome a showdown. "Well, well, well. Aren't things getting interesting," declared Mathis, sounding pleased.

"Hold up a second, Sarge," said Chris, looking to deescalate things. "Before things get crazy down here, can you just explain to us what we ever did to you?"

"You expect *me* to explain to *you*?"

"Yeah, *if* you don't mind, tell us what the big problem is over here."

"I don't have to tell *you* shit! *You* answer to *me*, *Private*!" said Mathis, again pulling rank.

When Mathis faced Chris, he made the fatal mistake of turning his back on Jasper, who was itching to take a piece of the sergeant. Mathis neglected to see Jasper pick up one of the bricks off the floor.

"HERE'S AN ORDER FOR YOU, ASSHOLE!" Jasper shouted as he viciously pounded the brick down on the skull of the sergeant. His legs buckling, Mathis struggled to remain on his feet. Now staggering, he took a second and third pounding before finally dropping to the ground.

At this point even Chris knew there was no turning back. The mob-connected brothers pummeled the sergeant with bricks, punches, and kicks until the man with the stripes drew his last breath. It was the first time the twins had ever killed anyone. They themselves were surprised at how easy it was for them to perform the dastardly deed. Acutely aware of the ramifications of their actions, the brothers nervously pondered what to do.

"I'm thinking maybe we should call Silky," said Jasper, unsure of what steps to take.

"Are you crazy?" answered Chris. "He'll want no part of this. It'll be the federal government or the state or whoever the hell it is that'll be coming after us. Silky will give us worse than this hump got."

"What are we supposed do, then?"

"You should have thought about that before you caved his skull in," chastised Chris.

"C'mon, Chris . . . you know he had it coming. . . ."

"Yeah, I suppose he *was* asking for it. Let me think a minute."

"Let's just take off," suggested Jasper. "We can lam it to Canada. . . ."

"Easy, not so fast," said Chris. "I'm not so sure we need to go anyplace."

"Huh? I'm telling you right now, I ain't sticking around to face no music over this prick!" declared Jasper vehemently. He then kicked the corpse in frustration.

Out of the blue, Chris brightened, suddenly becoming whimsical. "How about we eat his heart, Jasper? It'll probably taste better than the rabbits," he said. Chris was alluding to an active-duty training moment in which they witnessed a Green Beret remove the heart of a live rabbit and eat it.

"C'mon, this is serious," said the concerned Jasper. "We gotta split!"

"Relax, bro, we're not booking. I got us a plan. Think about it. Nobody is in this armory but us, right?"

"Yeah. . . "

"And nobody will be back from the field until late tomorrow, right?"

"Yeah. . . "

"So we got plenty of time to stash him way the hell back in the tunnel. Nobody ever comes down here. Once we get him on the other side of the wall, we'll seal him in, and that'll be that."

Jasper pondered the proposed solution. A silly smile of approval soon formed on his face. "That's a brilliant plan! There ain't nobody gonna be coming down into this rat-infested shithole to look for him."

After going upstairs to gather the appropriate tools to work with, the twins returned. They removed enough loose bricks to create an opening wide enough for them to get in and out of the tunnel.

"Let me get the money out of his poke before we tuck him in," said Chris, removing the sergeant's wallet. "He's got 178 bucks on him."

"I'm surprised this bum has that much," commented Jasper. "What kind of watch is he wearing?"

"Not too shabby; it's an Omega."

"How about we do this, Chris? Let's split the money and you keep the watch. I'll take his pinkie ring."

Chris looked at the wolf head ring with the emerald eyes. "The wolf has only one ear," noted Chris.

"I know. That's why I like it. . . . It's different."

"Alright, Jasper, if you want it, you take the ring."

Jasper ran into difficulty when trying to remove the ring from the victim's pinkie. "I had my eye on this baby since I first saw it on this prick's finger," he stated. "Now, if I could only get the damn thing off."

"Keep working on it. I'll take his car keys and watch."

Jasper continued his efforts at trying to remove the pinkie ring without success.

"This son-of-a-bitching ring ain't coming, Chris. I'm gonna go get a bolt cutter," said Jasper.

Upon his return, Jasper snipped the sergeant's pinkie off and took the ring

"It's a good fit," declared Jasper, after putting the ring on his pinkie. "WHAT DO YOU SAY TO THAT, SARGE?" Jasper asked loudly, looking down at the dead man.

"What are you yelling for, Jasper?"

"Dead people can hear you right after they die. So you gotta talk to them."

Chris looked down at the dead body. "Did you see John Wayne in *True Grit*, Sarge?" he asked casually. "Jasper said I should talk to you. What do you make of the Frank Sinatra–Mia Farrow situation?"

After sharing a buffoonish chortle, the brothers toted the dead body and the detached digit a hundred yards into the tunnel. Dropping their cargo to the ground with a thud, they then doubled back to exit the tunnel.

"We have to get to a hardware store," said Chris.

"There is one on Seventh Avenue," advised Jasper.

"We need to go to one outside of this neighborhood. C'mon, get what we'll need to seal up the wall." The twins returned with enough mortar cement to brick up the opening they'd created. They then did a thorough job of cleaning up. The Deep Six darkness was to their advantage. Their work would go unnoticed unless someone came down to specifically inspect. The killers were on solid ground in assuming that it would be a long, long time before anyone would find the murdered sergeant, if ever.

"C'mon, Jasper, let's wash up and put on clean uniforms."

Once they were cleaned up, the brothers went outside to find the sergeant's gold Chevrolet that was parked someplace on the street. They took along their recently purchased materials. After finding the sergeant's car, they drove to the foot of Columbia Street in Red Hook, where they tossed the materials off the pier.

"Take me back to my car," said Chris. "I'll follow you to Lemon's Brownsville lot."

##########

LEMON WAS AN UNASSUMING MAN who could be found working in his used car lot six days a week. Based on outward appearances, one would think he was a typical business owner. His habit was to leave his Staten Island home each morning at the same time dressed in a sport jacket, tie, and black pants. He maintained a locker inside his office trailer where he kept work clothes for when he had to get his hands dirty. Before going home, he'd clean up and leave the lot after again donning his street clothes. In addition to legally selling cars, Lemon traded in stolen vehicles. He worked closely with his wife's brother Monte, the shady owner of a Bayonne, New Jersey chop shop.

Lemon was surprised to see Chris and Jasper pull into his lot. He knew the brothers as young thieves.

Their business transactions were usually arranged by appointment. He had become friendly enough with them to nickname the duo the James Brothers, after the famed western outlaws Frank and Jesse James.

"Hey, look who it is . . . the James Brothers!" declared Lemon as he stood on the steps leading to his trailer. "What's with the uniforms? What are you looking to do, sell me a jeep?"

"We need a favor, Lemon," said Chris.

Lemon detected an unmistakable graveness in his voice. "Come on into the office, boys."

"You have to take this Chevy off our hands."

Lemon looked out the window of the trailer at the Chevrolet. "You know I don't take in cars unannounced like this. You have to let me know in advance so I can make arrangements."

"This is a special thing, Lemon," advised Chris. "We need this car to disappear."

"Yeah, but—"

"No fucking buts, Lemon," injected Jasper excitedly. "You gotta take this car and make it do a Houdini."

Left without wiggle room for discussion, Lemon sensed that something bad must have gone down. He tried distancing himself. "Look, boys, why don't you just dump it or torch it someplace?"

"That's not gonna work," replied Chris. "We need *you* to make it *disappear*."

"I hear you, but—"

Jasper's volatility again surfaced. "Listen, the owner of this car gave us grief *too*, Lemon. . . ."

The implied threat was an effective argument that convinced Lemon to cooperate.

"Jasper!" barked Chris harshly. "Take that damn ring off!"

"Oh shit! I forgot," answered Jasper, removing the ring from his pinkie.

Lemon didn't need a diagram drawn for him at this point. When he saw the emerald eyes of the wolf, he assumed the twins had committed a robbery. Seeing Jasper and Chris dressed in army fatigues now made Lemon more than a little curious. But under the circumstances, he kept his curiosity to himself.

Lemon removed the Chevy to the rear of his lot. He opened the front doors to a three-sided garage that was large enough to house two cars. The back of the garage abutted an abandoned building with a carved-out hole in the wall. Lemon drove the Chevy through the garage and parked it inside the building. The owner of record for the property was a dummy corporation Lemon created in the name of a long-dead Norwegian fish store owner. The building was home to much of Lemon's stolen property.

############

THE OVERWEIGHT CHOP SHOP OWNER picked up the telephone on the third ring. The several steps Monte took to reach the telephone left him winded.

"Yeah?" he asked.

"Monte, it's me. I need you to make a pickup over here at the lot," said his brother-in-law.

"What have ya got?"

"I got a set of wheels that needs to go down south."

"I'll get someone over there tomorrow."

"This can't wait," protested Lemon. "This is a *special* job."

Monte immediately understood the urgency in having the vehicle disappear right away.

"Okay, sit tight. I'll send someone over now."

Lemon removed the license plates to the Chevy and waited.

############

THE PRECINCT DETECTIVES COMMENCED THEIR PROBE into the whereabouts of Sergeant Mathis by first conducting a cursory search of the armory. After coming up dry, they then looked for the missing man's vehicle. When this met with negative results, they began conducting interviews. When the detectives got around to speaking to Chris and Jasper, they were given a concise account that seemed plausible. They told the detectives that Mathis went out to buy a sandwich and never returned to the armory.

With the twins having no prior arrest records, there was no reason for the law to doubt the statements provided. With no evidence to the contrary, the sequence of events conveyed was deemed plausible.

The mysterious disappearance of Sergeant Mathis drew great media interest even though there wasn't any indication of foul play. The unsolved mystery was covered on television, on the radio, and in the newspapers. Numerous theories emerged as to what had become of Sergeant Mathis. The most generally accepted explanation was that Mathis fled to be free of an unhappy home life.

After Lemon learned about the missing sergeant, a satisfied look came over him. While he didn't have direct knowledge that Mathis had been murdered, his gut feeling led him to that conclusion. His suspicion was the reason why he held on to the license plates of the car he received from the twins. He had taken the tags home as a sort of insurance policy, a bargaining chip of sorts to be used in negotiating with the law if he were ever to get into real trouble. Lemon was a lot shrewder than many people ever gave him credit for.

3

Silky Steps In (The Early '60s)

THE STANLEE HOUSEHOLD WAS NO different from that of any of the other working class Brooklyn family during the 1950s and 1960s. The early years in the life of Chris and Jasper were pleasant ones. This normalcy disappeared after their mother died unexpectedly after surgery. Left without the support of his Italian-born wife, Jim Stanlee began drinking excessively as a way to cope with his responsibilities. His alcoholism led the television repairman to recklessly enter into a marriage with a Coney Island fortune teller, whose daily consumption of alcohol exceeded his own. Their drunken marathons prompted the twelve-year-old twins to spend as much time as possible away from home. Hanging out in the street unsupervised, they were drawn to a youth gang known as the Deadly Diamonds. With the brothers under the influence of these unsavory role models, their ability to distinguish right from wrong became blurred. They began relying on criminal undertakings to gain social acceptance. Petty theft came to replace athletics and studies. Poker and dice trumped more wholesome pastimes such as Monopoly and Scrabble. To put it plainly, misbehavior had become their new norm.

The wayward siblings reached a crossroads at sixteen. By this time the twins were used to having cash in their pocket. Wanting more, they no longer had time for school. Over an ice cream soda in a candy store, they smoked cigarettes and discussed the matter.

"So what do you say, Jasper?" asked Chris. "Are you going along with me on this or what?"

"Yeah, I've had enough of school," replied Jasper.

"What do you want to tell the old man?"

"Why tell him anything? Let his wife look in her crystal ball and find out."

In addition to dropping out of school, they were in agreement that the quicker they divorced themselves from the man who had sired them the better. While they conversed, a dapper man in a gray suit and white open-collared shirt entered the store to purchase cigars. The man became interested in the twins after overhearing part of their conversation. Assuming correctly that the brothers were a couple of neighborhood kids, the organized crime soldier injected himself into their conversation.

"What's the matter with school?" asked the gangster, speaking through the side of his mouth that wasn't stiff. A slender man, he spoke in a clear, somewhat mechanical voice that lacked any semblance of emotion. There was the slightest trace of an accent in his speech.

"Who wants to know?" asked Jasper, who didn't realize he was addressing the local Mafia power.

"You don't know me?"

"Are we supposed to?" asked Chris, backing up his brother.

"Some people would advise that," replied the gangster, who began fingering the white silk pocket square that was protruding from the breast pocket of his suit jacket. The gesture wasn't lost on Chris. The clue provided was enough information for him to identify the stranger.

"We're just not interested in school," answered Chris in a much more respectful tone. "Sorry, I didn't know who you were at first."

The stranger accepted the reply he received. "You seem like a bright boy. Why quit school?"

"We didn't want to get ahead of our father!" said Jasper, still unaware of the stranger's identity.

The mobster found Jasper's smart-alecky remark less than amusing. "What kind of thing is that to say?" he asked softly. The racketeer believed in showing respect to a family patriarch.

"Are you two brothers?"

"We're twins but not identical," advised Chris.

"So why are you dropping out of school?"

"We want to make money," answered Chris. "We figure that putting an available dollar in our pocket now is better than waiting for two bucks down the road that might never come."

The logic was impressive to the mobster. "I can see that you're the smart one."

Jasper took exception to the remark. "Say, who are you?"

"You know the Palsy-Walsy around the corner?" asked the stranger.

"Yeah . . ."

"It's *my* club."

"This is Silky Seggio, Jasper," alerted Chris.

Jasper's mouth dropped. He now stood in awe of the man before him. "I didn't know. . . ."

"Forget it, kid. If school ain't for you, it ain't for you," he said. "What do your people say about this?"

"We have nobody but each other," answered Chris.

"That's too bad," said the gangster, nodding understandingly. "Maybe I can do something for you two. How would you like a break and go to work for me?"

"We'd love it, Mr. Seggio," answered Chris, jumping at the opportunity being offered.

"Call me Silky," said the gangster.

Their association with Silky Seggio began with the organized crime figure giving the twins errands to run in order to put money in their pockets. As they matured, more responsible tasks came their way. To impress their boss, they made sure to carry out their assignments to perfection. When Silky understood their home situation, he allowed Chris and Jasper to move into a two-bedroom apartment over the gangster's Palsy-Walsy Social Club. The digs also served as Silky's storage area for swag and a place for meetings when he had serious business to discuss with other members of the crime family he belonged to. In return for practically living rent free, the brothers watched over stolen property, cartons of untaxed cigarettes, fireworks, and whatever else Silky wanted them to keep an eye on.

It wasn't long before Chris impressed Silky by introducing a scheme in which he forged autographed photos of athletes and sold them to those gullible enough to believe his convoluted explanations as to how he acquired them. Seeing real potential in Chris as an earner, Silky fast-tracked the twins. As they came to appreciate the value of having Silky's name behind them, the brothers pursued a life of criminality with vigor. When it came to money, it was understood that a tax was to be paid to Silky on whatever the brothers earned

21

on the street. They began stealing cars after making the acquaintance of a man who owned a used car lot in Brownsville. It was at the annual Christmas party at the Palsy-Walsy that they first met Lemon. It was after the twins delivered a Cadillac stolen from the driveway of a criminal court judge that Lemon dubbed them the James Brothers, after the notorious outlaws. The nickname struck. After seeing that Silky received his taste of their money, the brothers made sure to hang onto the rest of their cash. The motivation behind acquiring wealth had nothing to do with saving for their old age. Their incentive was to start their own loan-sharking operation. As they began to flourish, Chris and Jasper became more and more entrepreneurial. Soon it became common knowledge that they were no poltroons when it came to taking a chance on business ventures.

##########

SHELDON TEPPER WASN'T BROUGHT up to be a criminal. He hailed from a nice family who saw to it that he took his schooling seriously. He became knowledgeable in business by working in his father's Brownsville furniture store on Livonia Avenue. After a stint in the army during World War Two, he entered Baruch College, where he studied accounting at night. By all accounts, he appeared to have a promising future. Unfortunately, the year 1950 proved to be the beginning of bad times. Sheldon was an only child, and his first setback came with the tragic death of his father, who was murdered during an argument with a homeless man who periodically urinated against the front glass of their store. The passing of his brokenhearted mother a short time later left Sheldon in dire need of bolstering. He found his crutch in the form of a neighborhood girl whom he hastily married. Rising poverty in Brownsville, along with a spiking crime rate, had a devastating effect on the furniture business. Things came to a head when weekend break-ins at the store became the norm. Disgusted, Sheldon closed the business but kept the building. It was one of three Brownsville properties he inherited from his parents. At the urging of his wife, he got involved with her successful but shady brother Monte. Sheldon opened a used car lot in Brownsville that complemented Monte's chop shop in Bayonne, New Jersey. Monte was Sheldon's initial entrée into Silky Seggio and the world of organized crime. Thanks to the substandard cars that were sometimes sold off the lot, Sheldon found himself saddled with the nickname of Lemon. With Silky Seggio's blessing, Chris and Jasper began taking the cars they stole to Lemon's Brownsville lot with regularity. The hot cars would later be picked up and transported to Monte's Bayonne chop shop, where the vehicle identification number would be altered in preparation for resale. Sometimes the vehicles were dismantled and the parts sold off. The twins, who were limited in terms of business principles, listened closely whenever Lemon imparted nuggets of information pertaining to the fundamentals of operating an enterprise. It could be said that in some respects, Lemon was their business professor. The brothers, especially Chris, proved to be diligent students.

4

Birthday Blues

LIKE OTHER MEN OF DRAFT AGE DURING THE VIETNAM WAR, the twins sat in front of their television waiting for the US Selective Service System to commence the drawing for its national draft lottery. They soothed their nerves by drinking beer as they waited to see what their number was going to be.

"So how is this gonna work?" asked Jasper.

"They go by date of birth," explained Chris. "If they pull our date of birth first, then we go first."

"What is this, something new?"

"They did this last year, Jasper," answered Chris. "Maybe we'll get lucky and draw a good number."

When the first capsule drawn reflected their date of birth, Jasper's outrage could be heard from the street as he began cursing at the top of his lungs. In his anger, he fired a folded *Playboy* magazine, tomahawk style, at the television screen.

Chris sat quietly, shaking his head. When he spoke, he was barely audible. "I'll be a son of a bitch!" he repeated several times.

"CAN YOU BELIEVE IT? WE HIT THE FRIGGIN' JACKPOT!" shouted the peeved Jasper. The very idea that he and his brother might be sent to Vietnam incensed him. "Go figure the odds of that jerk-off picking our birthday right off the bat!"

"Take it easy, Jasper. This ain't the last word."

"What are ya talking about? We drew number one! There ain't a second chance in this shit."

"We still got a card to play," said Chris.

"Yeah, like what? Shoot off a toe?"

"C'mon, get a grip on yourself."

"What then?" asked Jasper. "How can you be so calm? What, all of a sudden we're gonna be rah-rah boys and go to college to get out of this thing? We didn't even get out of high school!"

"No, no college."

"What's left, then? We gotta lam it someplace."

"We may not have to go no place," said Chris. "Listen, I spoke to Silky about this yesterday, figuring we might need some insurance just in case we got unlucky. He said that if it comes down to it, he knows somebody who may be able to pull a wire for us."

Jasper perked up at this ray of hope. "You mean we won't have to go in the army?"

"Not for long," answered Chris. "We'll have to enlist in the National Guard." Jasper's face became distorted at the very thought of enlisting anyplace. "Look, Jasper, this war ain't going away anytime soon. Listen to me; why take a chance and risk getting hurt?"

"But what the hell is the National Guard?" asked Jasper.

"It's a weekend thing." Chris could see that his brother needed convincing, so he painted a graver picture. "In Nam you could get shot in the wrong place and lose something a lot *worse* than your life!"

"Alright, alright," said Jasper, "I get it." The argument made by Chris was too compelling to discount.

##########

ARRANGEMENTS WERE MADE FOR THE TWINS to meet Monte at Itchy's Panama Inn on Staten Island. The brothers were the first to arrive. They stood at the bar nursing their drinks. The Panama was a convenient place to meet up with Lemon's brother-in-law because it was centrally located between Brooklyn and Bayonne. It was a no-frills venue frequented primarily by men whose attention rarely strayed to the affairs of others. Aside from privacy, the Panama offered cheap whiskey, long-necked bottled beer, peanuts, and hard-boiled eggs. A color television sat high on an overhead shelf wedged in a corner behind the bar. Anyone looking closely could see the bullet holes in the black tin ceiling. They were reminders of Prohibition, when bootleggers muscled bar owners to sell their product. For Chris, this made for interesting conversation.

"Silky told me he knew the bootlegger who put those holes in the ceiling," said Chris. "He said the guy's beer tasted awful, but everyone out here peddled it anyway."

Jasper wasn't interested in hearing any of this. Nursing his beer, he glanced down at his foot as he made pathways out of the sawdust on the floor. His thoughts were on what it was costing him to get into the National Guard.

"Who gives a rat's ass about that?" Jasper said. "All I care about is the ten grand we're pissing away."

"Things could be worse. Look at this poor bastard," he added, pointing to the television, where the news was reporting on a military officer on trial by court-martial.

"What did he do?" asked Jasper, who rarely read a newspaper or listened to the news.

"They're saying he knocked off over a hundred civilians in Nam last year."

"Hey, I got my own problems." Jasper then reverted back to the issue at hand. "It seems like Monte's being a glutton about this. He's getting too much money," he complained.

"Be reasonable, will ya? They got us over a barrel. What choice have we got?" asked Chris, who was beginning to grow frustrated by his brother's harping on the payout. "Either he gets what he wants or we get drafted. It's as simple as that."

"I hear ya, Chris. But still, ten G's and we *still* have to suit up and play GI Joe once a month on weekends for six years? What kind of a deal is that?"

"It'll be okay," assured Chris. "Don't forget, while we're away, Silky said he'll help us collect the vig on whatever money we got out in the street."

"Yeah, and Silky will be making out as well. What can you do? They got us coming and going."

"Don't forget, Jasper, the ten grand is for *both* of us to jump the waiting list. Silky said he got the price knocked down. Monte originally asked for *fifteen* grand."

"Yeah, so he says. What's his end on this, I wonder?" asked Jasper.

##########

26

THE CIGAR-CHOMPING MONTE WAS a short man who looked boxy in the wrinkled sport jacket he wore. At fifty-eight, he ate high-calorie meals, which kept him heavier than what was probably healthy. His income came from a wide variety of sources, both legal and illegal. One particularly timely revenue stream pertained to facilitating the entry of draft-eligible men into the National Guard. Since getting into the Guard was exceedingly challenging due to the war, there was no lack of want for his intervention. When Silky informed him that he wanted a couple of his people taken care of, Monte was naturally receptive. Yet he remained cautious enough to reach out Lemon before moving on the request.

"How well do you know these two kids?"

"I've known them for a few years," replied Lemon. "They're with Silky. In fact, I was the one who nicknamed them the James Brothers."

"So you're telling me that they can be trusted?"

"They have my stamp of approval."

The following afternoon, Monte and Lemon again spoke telephonically. "I'm meeting those two kids," advised Monte. "When I'm done, I'll stop by your place, okay?"

"No problem. I'll be home."

Monte's in at the armory was a sergeant who controlled the waiting list of those desperately looking to get into the National Guard. Once cash made it into the right hands, a name was catapulted to the top of the list. This stroke-of-the-pen adjustment eliminated any concern about being drafted into the regular army. For parents worried about a son facing the prospect of battle, Monte was a godsend. The chop shop owner was paid handsomely in cash by people of means looking to protect their loved ones.

########

AS SOON AS MONTE ENTERED ITCHY'S PANAMA INN, he observed two young men at the bar. He seemed to be sweating and short of breath. He correctly assumed that the two men were Chris and Jasper. He approached them to confirm his suspicion.

"Are you the James Brothers?" he asked while at the same time pulling the seat of his pants out.

"Yeah, that's us," replied Chris.

"I'm Monte, you have something for me, I believe. . . ."

Chris removed an envelope containing one-hundred-dollar bills from his jacket pocket. Monte smiled as he extended his hand just under the bar. Instead of reaching to shake, Monte left his hand open, palm up, to receive. Chris discreetly passed the envelope. Jasper turned away. It pained him to look at Monte's grubby fingers clamping down on the money-filled envelope. Monte nodded, acknowledging the payoff. He then put the envelope in his ample waistband and closed his sport jacket.

"It's fortunate for you that we both happen to know the right people," stated Monte.

"Yeah, it is," agreed Chris.

"Scratch your full name, Social Security number, date of birth, and telephone number on this paper; then go home and start packing," said Monte with an assuredness that suggested that such transactions were routine. "You'll get a call sometime tomorrow from the armory advising you when to go fill out the papers and get sworn in. You'll be shipping out by the end of the month."

"Where to?" asked Jasper.

"Could be anyplace," replied Monte. "What's the difference? Wherever they send you, you'll be back around Christmas." Monte left the bar smiling.

5

Army Days

CHRIS AND JASPER WALKED OFF THE PLANE with a handful of other recruits. They were met by soldiers, who escorted them to an army base reception center. While they hadn't any idea of what to expect, they steeled themselves for an experience that they assumed wouldn't be pleasant. They were taken to a barracks where the beds were spaced a comfortable distance apart. The twins were instructed to write a letter informing a loved one that they had safely made it to the base. Chris took charge of this task. He penned a short note to Silky Seggio. It read:

> We're here, skipper, thanks to you. Count on our love and loyalty when we get back.
> The James Brothers.

Jasper began exploring his surroundings. When he got to the latrine, he couldn't believe his eyes "Hey, Chris, come in here," he called out to his brother. "Get a load of this setup. What do they expect us to do, hold hands every time we take a crap?" he asked, pointing to the toilets that were lined up side by side without partitions for privacy.

Having to jump when addressed by someone of a higher rank was another thing that took some getting used to. This reality became evident the following morning.

The drill sergeant took a final drag from his Camel cigarette before entering the barracks at precisely 5:00 a.m. He was a wiry man of average height with chiseled features. After turning the overhead lights on, the sergeant woke everyone up by shouting at the top of his lungs.

"WAKE UP!" the man with the stripes bellowed. "I WANT EVERY SWINGING DICK OUT OF BED! YOU'RE IN THE ARMY NOW, SOLDIER!" he roared. The strain of his hollering reddened his face and caused a vein to pop from his neck.

Jasper was sleeping soundly on his back. Unsure if he'd heard something, he opened one eye. The dazzle of the ceiling lights caused him to squint and then reclose his eye. Seconds later, the booming voice again interrupted his slumber, this time from a distance of just a few feet.

"GET YOUR LAZY ASS OUT OF BED, BOY!" ordered the sergeant, zeroing in on Jasper.

The verbal blast was forceful enough to roust Jasper from his bed. Now sitting up, he yawned loudly. Once he recognized his surroundings, a frown formed on his face.

"What am I doing here?" he asked himself, again closing his eyes.

The call of sleep was so potent that his head began drifting down toward his pillow, similar to the way a drug addict nods off. Catching himself midway, he began to tap the side of his head with the heel of his hand in an effort to clear the cobwebs. Swinging his legs around, he sat up on the side of the bed. He looked over at Chris, who had gotten to his feet on the first call.

"This was a great idea, wasn't it?" Jasper asked his brother sarcastically.

Chris tossed a fresh white towel over his shoulder. "C'mon, get what you need. We gotta clean up," he said, holding up his shaving gear.

The walking alarm clock with the stripes on his arm was a roughhouse sort with little patience. Taking Jasper's procrastination personally, he took a step closer to the private's bunk and lifted the bed upward, knocking Jasper to the floor. Chris braced himself for the worst as he watched Jasper scurry to his feet. Brushing himself off, Jasper surprised Chris with the self-control he exhibited. The incendiary brother threw his shoulders back and gave them a quick shake, as if loosening them from something restrictive.

"Thank you, Sergeant," Jasper said loudly. On his way to the latrine with Chris, he whispered, "One day I'm gonna get this prick."

"Take it easy, Jasper. Don't forget, we're in the army," said Chris, trying to calm his brother.

"Yeah, I know. It cost me a bundle for an admission ticket."

Much of the military training bored the young thugs. What did stimulate their attentiveness was being issued an M-16 rifle. They remained focused

30

throughout the hours spent aligning their sights so that they could shoot accurately. During the process of zeroing their weapon, the twins made sure to pay attention to every shooting tip they received. Shooting was a skill that the twins believed would be valuable in the eyes of Silky.

At the end of basic training, the twins ran into some minor difficulty when the time came to turn in their rifles. The M-16s were expected to be returned to the arms room perfectly clean. After their efforts were met with several rejections, they grew frustrated.

"What's it take to turn this gun in?" asked Jasper, looking for an explanation from the examiner.

The examining sergeant shook his head. "The barrel of this weapon is filthy," he replied. "Remember something; this is your weapon," he said, shaking the M-16 in the air before returning it to Jasper. "And this is your gun," he added, grabbing at his own crotch area. "*One* is for killing and *the other* for fun . . . and they *both* have to be in good working order!"

"What are we going to do about this, Chris?" asked Jasper once they were alone. "If they keep rejecting our rifles, we'll be here forever."

"Relax. I'll figure something out," assured Chris.

"These guys are gonna find a problem no matter what we do."

Chris looked over at a towering soldier who had successfully turned in his rifle hours ago. "Let me go talk to the big farm boy over there, Jasper. Maybe I can get him to clean the rifles for us."

"Good idea, Chris. See how much he wants to do it." After a short conversation with the soldier, Chris could be seen giving him money.

"You owe me ten bucks," said Chris upon his return.

"Ten bucks?" asked Jasper, surprised at the amount demanded. "How come he's so cheap?"

"Here is the deal. If we want him to clean the guns, he's looking for twenty-five bucks for *each* rifle. For a flat twenty, he agreed to go into the arms room and take a flop. He'll fall over the inspection desk. When he goes down, there will be enough confusion to distract everyone's attention."

"So?"

"So we slip in the back door, go to the rack, and take out two clean rifles and replace them with our dirty ones. The inspection tags are only attached by rubber band. We'll put the pass tags on our dirty rifles. Then, when the smoke settles, we'll go around front and submit the clean rifles for inspection."

The scheme worked perfectly. It was planning such as this that set Chris apart from his brother. Once their active duty obligation was satisfied, the twins returned to their Brooklyn apartment tanned, lean and in condition. When Silky summoned them to his social club office his intention was to determine if the service had poisoned them. The gangster put them through a test to find out.

"I have a job for you two," said Silky as he struck a match to light his cigar. "Now that the vacation is over, are you boys ready to step up and do a little heavy lifting?"

"Sure, Silky. Whatever you need, just say the word," Jasper piped up energetically.

"What do you want us to do, Silky?" asked Chris, proceeding more cautiously.

"You know that guy with the black glasses who they call Bug Eyes?"

"Yeah," answered Jasper. "I know him. He comes from Sixty-Ninth Street."

"He's no friend of *yours*, is he?"

Jasper gathered that Bug Eyes had a problem. "No, I never liked that guy! He's been wearing that same black vest for years."

"Good. This motherless junkie piece of shit has been using the schoolyard opposite my apartment house as a shooting gallery. My tenants don't need to see that. I want you should put him out of commission. You think you could accomplish that?"

"You want we should talk to him first?" suggested Chris.

"That was tried with no luck. *Now* I want him out of commission," clarified the gangster.

"No problem, Silky," answered Jasper.

"How much out of commission do you want him?" inquired Chris.

"I'm not asking you to plant him. But if he happens to die, he dies. Nobody's gonna care."

"So you basically want him sidelined for a long time. . . ." stated Chris.

"That's right," answered gangster.

"Consider it done."

The brothers caught up with Bug Eyes in the schoolyard the following evening. This was the opportunity they had been looking for. They crept up behind their man slowly. The unsuspecting junkie was so intent on getting the needle in his arm that he never heard them approaching. Directly in front of where Bug Eyes stood was a four-foot-high iron rail that overlooked a twenty-five-foot drop to the basement level of the school. As the junkie fished for a vein, Jasper took hold of him by the collar and the back of his belt. With the help of Chris, Bug Eyes was swiftly flipped over the railing. The brothers looked down to watch their victim bounce off the cement. Bug Eyes sustained multiple injuries, including a broken back. The sight of the junkie's smashed body was proof enough that he'd be out of commission for a long time. Chris and Jasper walked off, leaving the pained man's nasal-sounding pleas for help behind them.

"Jesus, just listen to that guy whine," said Chris.

"He always was a crybaby," noted Jasper, who began crooning bandleader Guy Lombardo's New Year's Eve standard "Boo-Hoo."

6

Every Dog Has His Day

SILKY WAS PLEASED WITH THE WAY THE BROTHERS corrected the situation involving Bug Eyes. Since the drug addict never actually saw who had tossed him over the rail, there were no legal repercussions. Impressed by this, Silky rewarded the twins by incorporating them into his gambling operation. Their new responsibilities included taking bets and paying off winning gamblers. In terms of recognition, the move was considered a step up because not everyone possessed the finesse necessary to cultivate and interact with the betters.

"Who do we have to see?" asked Jasper.

"We got one winner to pay off, replied Chris, "the butcher in the supermarket."

"Which guy won?"

"The big guy with the eye patch won."

"That pirate won again?"

"He's a lucky guy," commented Chris. "I don't know how he does it."

##########

THE SUPERMARKET BUTCHERS WERE considered special. From the perspective of other store employees, it was the higher wages they received that set them apart. For the store manager, respect came from their membership in the powerful meat cutters union. This affiliation enabled the butchers to work more or less independently in their meat department. On the final day of the workweek the meat cutters worked unsupervised. The butchers took advantage of this when it suited them.

The butchers had stepped up their pace throughout the morning in order to have the afternoon free to party. The men in the bloody aprons were in a celebratory mood because one of them won money and was expecting the delivery of a cash payoff. Folding chairs were placed around a table after they cleaned up their work area. When a diminutive senior citizen nicknamed Dime Bread entered the work area carrying a loaf of pumpernickel, the butcher with the eye problem graciously waved to him.

"C'mon in, Dime," said the meat cutter. "What do you need?" he asked cordially.

Dime's hair was a thick steel gray. He wore it plastered down on both sides of the part that crossed the center of his head. Regardless of the weather, the retired salesman could usually be seen wearing a gray winter sport jacket, dark pants, an olive or blue collared button-down shirt, and a matching bowtie. His footwear alternated between black and brown bucks. At eighty-five, Dime was usually a couple of days behind in shaving. A penny watcher, the butchers nicknamed him Dime Bread because of his penchant for buying day-old bread that the store regularly marked down to ten cents.

"Do me a favor. Change the price on the pumpernickel for me," asked the senior citizen. There was a trace of frailness in Dime's voice.

The meat cutter with the eye patch was a powerfully built, bald-headed man in his early fifties. He smiled at the octogenarian. "Sure, no problem, I can take care of that. How about you do me a favor?"

"What favor?" asked the old man suspiciously.

"Go across the street to the liquor store and get me two bottles of Fleischmann's."

Agreeing to run the errand, the old man took the butcher's money. "Alright, but make sure you mark down the bread," he reminded the meat cutter before leaving for the liquor store.

The party got underway once Dime Bread returned with the bottles of rye. "Did you mark down the pumpernickel for me?" he asked.

"What's the rush? Sit down and have a shot with us," replied the butcher with the problem eye.

"What shot? I don't want any shot," said the exasperated Dime Bread. "I want the mark down."

Dime watched openmouthed as the butcher with the eye patch passed one of the bottles of rye to his work partner, a functional alcoholic in his late forties.

"Here, you do the honors," he said. He then turned up the volume on the radio to listen to the race results.

"Do you think they'll get here soon with the money?" asked the alcoholic butcher, who began filling their cups.

"The James Brothers are usually early. Besides, they know I take good care of them whenever I win."

Dime Bread stood by with a loaf of pumpernickel in his hand. Feeling ignored, he became increasingly agitated. The old man removed his eyeglasses and began feverishly wiping them clean with the paper napkin he removed from his jacket pocket. A few minutes later he finally blew a gasket.

"I got you the damn rye, didn't I?" he shouted in a voice that cracked with emotion. "Now, stop fooling around, will ya? Mark down this bread so I can get the hell outta here!"

"Alright, relax," said the butcher with the eye covering. "Give me the bread." The butcher took the bread and marked the price down with a black magic marker.

"Thank you," said the relieved customer, letting out a deep sigh.

Dime, who had a sweet tooth, noticed small chocolate candy kisses in a bowl next to a slicing machine that rested on top of a nearby table. The candy pieces were actually dog treats that the meat cutters fed to a stray hound that would come to the back door of the meat department. The alcoholic butcher noticed Dime's interest in the contents of the bowl.

"Help yourself, Dime. Take some home with you," suggested the butcher.

"Maybe just one or two," the old man said, taking him up on the offer. After putting a treat in his mouth, he began to squint as he chewed. "Say, this tastes very bitter," Dime commented, his face now contorted. When the two butchers burst out laughing, it dawned on the unwitting senior that he had been duped by the pranksters. "Awwww, who do you think you are . . . a couple of comedians?" said Dime, storming out of the meat department in a huff.

The stench of alcohol permeated the meat department by the time Chris and Jasper arrived to pay the butcher off on his big win. Trailing behind them with a head of lettuce, grapes, and cherries was the sixty-one-year-old manager of the produce department.

"Congratulations, big guy!" said Chris cheerily as he entered the work area unannounced.

"Here you go," said Jasper, acting like Santa Claus on Christmas. "Count out the money with me." The butcher counted along with Jasper as each bill was placed into his hand.

After kicking back some thank-you money, the fortunate winner held up the open bottle of Fleishmann's. "Now, everybody, let's have a drink on me. Grab a Dixie cup."

The produce manager was the first to reach for a cup. Reasonably handsome for a man his age, his features were fine. He was clean-shaven with snow-white wavy hair that was neatly combed back. His complexion was pinkish. The produce manager wore a white button-down collared shirt, black pants, and black work shoes with thick white socks. He spoke with a smoker's rasp.

The butcher with the eye covering looked over at his partner. Knowing that bad blood existed between the men, he wanted to see his reaction to the produce manager being the first to reach for the bottle. There was none.

The ill will was based entirely on the fruit and vegetable man's tendency to tease the butcher with the drinking problem. While the alcoholic meat cutter could dish it out, he wasn't one to take it well. The produce manager ran his hand through his hair as he drank. After refilling his Dixie cup with rye, he settled back in his chair and began running his mouth.

"You made a great score," he said to the winning butcher. Then, flicking his head toward the other butcher, he added, "He gets potatoes . . . heh, heh, heh." The produce manager's laughter was such that it inspired irritation.

"Why don't you go back to your apples? You've exhausted your welcome," said alcoholic butcher.

"What? I'm just saying . . . don't catch an attitude with me because you're a loser."

It was at this point that things began to turn ugly between the two men. A session of belittling ensued that culminated with the produce manager challenging the meat cutter to an arm wrestling contest. Everyone in the room looked to see if the issued challenge was going to be met. Chris turned to look at Jasper. He tossed his chin in the direction of the angered butcher, indicating that he should be watched. Jasper acknowledged with a nod. Suddenly, the alcoholic butcher rose from his seat.

"You want to arm wrestle?" he asked, addressing the produce manager.

"I know I'd have no chance against your partner. He's a bull. But you, my friend, are a piece of cake. How much do you want to lose?" asked the unpopular guest, reaching into his pocket.

The alcoholic butcher began rubbing his hands confidently against his pants. He walked over to the drawer where the knives were stored. He removed two large cutting instruments and slammed the point of each knife into a butcher block table. The blades were distanced approximately twenty inches apart, with the cutting sides facing each other. The butcher rested his elbow between the business end of the knives, prepared to arm wrestle the produce man.

"Come on, let's go!" challenged the butcher, beckoning the produce manager to join him at the table.

The produce manager turned ghost white. Visibly shaken, his entire demeanor was altered. His words were now voiced with an unusual humbleness. "C'mon, man . . . you know how I feel about knives," he said timidly. "They give me the willies."

Jasper and Chris were appalled at the response of the deflated loudmouth. They found his backpedaling astoundingly unmanly. Thoroughly humiliated, the produce manager removed himself from the meat department to avoid further embarrassment. The alcoholic butcher, having called out the produce manager, felt that he had solidified his reputation as a man in full view of the others. In his delight, he exhibited a rarely seen openmouthed grin that revealed he was missing a couple of front teeth.

"Now, that calls for another drink!" said the money winner, proud of his coworker. "Pour them for the boys, partner, while I let the dog in. I hear him scratching at the back door. I got a package of baloney for him."

"No more for me," said Chris. "I still have a couple of stops to make. You can stay, Jasper. I'll finish making the rounds."

Jasper was in no rush to stop drinking. "Thanks, Chris. I'll hang out awhile."

Ninety minutes later, the imbibers, who by now were feeling no pain, could still be heard rehashing the great triumph they'd witnessed over the produce manager.

"What a wimp he turned out to be," said Jasper.

"He's always been all talk," commented the victorious butcher. "He won't be trying that again with me."

Jasper, who hadn't eaten a thing, felt the need to get food into his stomach Noticing the slicer, he decided to cut up a log of salami. His inexperience with the slicing machine, coupled with his alcohol intake, resulted in a freak accident that cost Jasper his pinkie finger.

"Jesus Christ! What the hell did you do?" shouted the eye-patch-wearing butcher, reacting to Jasper's scream. He watched as Jasper began hopping about as he cradled his injured hand.

Jasper's foot came down heavily on the detached pinkie finger that had fallen to the ground. The contact caused his foot to slide, propelling the digit across the floor to the other side of the room. Realizing that his job was now at risk, the butcher with the eye covering quickly sobered up. He rose from his seat to render assistance to the injured Jasper. He rushed to a cabinet where there were clean aprons. Taking two, he tossed an apron to his partner.

"Pick up his finger while I wrap his hand," he shouted to his fellow butcher.

The alcoholic butcher rose slowly to follow his partner's directive. Somewhat unsteady on his feet, he began looking for the detached pinkie. Unable to locate it, a peculiar look came over him after he heard a belch coming from the stray dog. The meat cutter wasn't drunk enough not to realize that it would be futile to search further.

"Don't just stand there; go find the finger!" shouted the more sober butcher.

"Ya gonna have to wait for the mutt to take a dump."

"You mean that . . .?"

"What do you want from me?" asked the intoxicated butcher defensively.

"You gotta get me to a hospital," said Jasper.

"Don't worry, Jasper," said the butcher wearing the eye patch. "I'll get you to a hospital." Holding on to the injured man's arm, he guided Jasper through the back door to where the meat cutter's car was parked nearby.

########

JASPER WAS AT HOME RECOVERING from his injury. Depressed, he had been spending most of his time watching television. During the commercials, his mind returned to his missing pinkie. He never realized how important the tiny digit was in balancing things he held or gripped.

Back at the supermarket, the incident was receiving wide attention. At 8:00 a.m. on Monday morning, the meat department manager walked into two waiting camps of authority looking for answers. Lawyers were on hand to represent the corporation, and officials from the union turned out to protect the interest of the butchers.

As the two sides tried to establish what had occurred, an unassuming part-time meat wrapper named Wayna Garcia was performing her duties. The young woman noticed that there was a ring on the floor not far from where the men were standing. She discreetly opened a storage door to secure a broom and dustpan. As she began to casually sweep the floor, she brushed the ring into the dustpan. Once taking charge of the ring, she went to the ladies' room, where she could inspect her booty. After seeing the emerald eyes on the one-eared wolf, she felt as if she'd hit the lotto. She couldn't help but think of what a wonderful present the ring would make for her father's birthday. She placed the ring inside her bra for safekeeping. The piece remained close to her bosom throughout the employee questioning that occurred that day. The meat wrapper sincerely hoped that the meat cutters weren't going to be terminated. They had always been nice to her, even going so far as sharing their rye once in a while. She was especially fond of the butcher with the eye patch. He was the one who had turned her on to the certified nursing assistant training program she was enrolled in. She had no use for the produce manager, however, who was prone to becoming too familiar without an invitation.

##########

A WEEK AFTER THE ACCIDENT, CHRIS CONVINCED JASPER to go for a drink at a small local bar they frequented. He felt that being outdoors among people would be the best therapy for his brother until he got used to the idea of having nine fingers.

"Two beers?" asked the bartender.

"Yeah, make mine Michelob," answered Chris.

"And you?"

Jasper was still thinking about what he was going to have. "Let me have a Budweiser," he finally said.

The bartender placed the drinks in front of the men. As he gathered the money off the bar, he noticed Jasper's hand. "What happened to you, Jasper?" he asked innocently.

"I bite my nails," answered Jasper in a clipped fashion. He was making it clear that he wasn't in the mood for entertaining questions. Realizing that he might have spoken out of turn, the bartender walked off without saying anything further. After he left, Jasper turned to speak to his brother.

"I never did like that nosy bastard," he said.

Chris shrugged and changed the subject. "So how is the finger today?"

"What finger? All I got left is a stub."

"Look at the bright side, bro. This might get you out of the National Guard!"

"You think so?"

"I don't know. . . . It might. What does the doctor say?"

"He said it'll heal. My real problem isn't the finger; it's money. What am I supposed to do for money?"

"Don't worry about the money. We'll be fine," assured Chris. "What did Silky have to say?"

"What do you think he said? He's pissed off. He blames me for losing the supermarket action."

"What exactly did he say?"

"He said I should think about taking the test for the sanitation department."

"That's it?"

"No. . . . He also said for me to tell my twin brother to do the same."

The news wasn't exactly surprising to Chris. "Well, forget about it. That's just the way he is. His attitude will pass."

"You know what, Jasper? I think Silky did us a favor."

"How is that?"

"The James Brothers are going into a new business."

"What new business?"

"We are going to run our own gambling operation . . . but with a twist."

"You mean run in opposition to Silky?" asked Jasper. "Are you nuts?"

"The only thing that's going to matter is that the old man gets his taste. Once that's understood, we'll get his blessing. The money will shield us like lead protects Superman from kryptonite."

"What have you got in mind?"

"There is a game about baseball that kids play. It's all based on statistics. We are gonna form leagues, and everybody who buys in gets to run his own team. We'll have the teams play each other over the course of a season. We'll book bets on the outcome of every game."

"It sounds complicated," commented Jasper.

"Just listen. We'll form a James Brothers pool that we pay out on just before the holidays. All we need are degenerate gamblers willing to buy into the pool for a big number, then we—"

Jasper saw value in the plan Chris outlined. "I think you really got something with this, Chris."

"I know I do, Jasper. We're going for the brass ring this time."

"Talk about rings . . . did I tell you that somebody walked off with my wolf ring?"

"It has to be somewhere in the butcher's work area. Did you go back and talk to the butchers?"

"I couldn't. Everybody got fired. I really loved that ring," said Jasper, sounding a little sad. "Where am I ever going to get another?"

"Ah, forget it. You'll get another ring."

"Not like that one. It had emerald eyes and just one ear. It was special."

"So get one with two ears and bigger emeralds," suggested Jasper's brother.

"You don't understand. That one had . . . sentimental value."

"What sentimental value?"

"It was a souvenir from our first work," explained Jasper, referring to the Mathis homicide as work.

###########

THE MEAT WRAPPER'S FATHER lived in the city of Milagro, Guayas Province, in Ecuador. Seated at the head of the table, the family patriarch was celebrating his fiftieth birthday with his loved ones. He waited for the full complement of relatives to be assembled before he opened up the package that his twenty-one-year-old daughter had sent from America. The father read aloud with pride the note wishing him a happy birthday. He closely examined the one-eared wolf head ring with the emerald eyes. Impressed by the uniqueness of the piece, he immediately began searching for the finger that fit the ring best. He held up his hand proudly for all to see the beautiful present he'd received from his thoughtful daughter.

7

<u>Captains Of Industry (1990s)</u>

THE JAMES BROTHERS GREW THEIR BASEBALL-THEMED GAMBLING operation to where the enterprise enabled the brothers to donate a healthy amount of money to Silky and still have plenty remaining to expand their interests. Remembering one of the business teachings of Lemon in Brownsville, the brothers set out to diversify. They looked to acquire already-established entities that dealt primarily in cash. Chris began investigating the various Brooklyn neighborhoods for possible opportunities. As a result of his due diligence, he noticed an emerging trend. He shared his insight with his brother.

"Jasper, these poor neighborhoods are being infiltrated by young people," noted Chris.

"Where else are they gonna go?" asked Jasper. "The rents are cheap."

"Ever notice how *dirty some of their clothes are?*"

"So people don't wash their clothes a lot. . . ."

"They don't wash clothes because there aren't a lot of places to wash them. If they live in an apartment, they probably have no washing machine. They need someplace to go."

"I get it," said Jasper, now seeing the point.

The discussion was concluded with the twins agreeing to open a Laundromat. Their decision was wise.

After tasting success in their first *legitimate* venture, the duo remained loyal to the formula. They began opening up similar places in neighborhoods undergoing gentrification. As their money stockpiled, they branched out to purchase a pizzeria, another cash business. Twenty years later, they found themselves owning businesses that went beyond the cash-only blueprint. Their portfolio now included an auto glass replacement business, a lumberyard, and a two-floor sporting goods store.

The earning capacity of the James Brothers rejuvenated the now-aging Silky. The gangster, who was receiving a cut of each business, saw the twins as inspirational. No longer satisfied with just receiving tribute envelopes, the mobster had ideas on how to profit further off the backs of the James Brothers. Silky launched an initiative to purify the reputation of Chris and Jasper. He began by spreading a false narrative that Jasper was a disabled war hero. He and the twins, in the name of their legitimate businesses, began making donations to select politicians and worthy causes. Silky was correct in assuming that once a reputation for spreading money around took hold, few would look further than the checks. The smoke screen was thick enough to enable the brothers to segue onto the other side of the tracks without raising too many eyebrows.

After the political arena had been penetrated, the brothers began a campaign to cultivate those directly connected to the mayor's office. Once the wining and dining took hold, Silky partnered with the James Brothers to form a concrete company named Silk-James Incorporated. The gangster recruited a bricklayer relative to front as the owner of record for the new entity. In exchange for a few points in Silk-James, the bricklayer agreed to run the business. The role of the James Brothers in the enterprise was to compromise those with the authority to approve city asphalt contracts. Silky's job was to collude with competitors so that Silk-James was guaranteed to be the low bid on proposals for city contracts. Once Silk-James was awarded the work, the losing bidders were retained as subcontractors. This amicable arrangement left Silk-James as the dominant vendor in the city asphalt industry.

##########

JASPER WAS DESIGNATED AS THE PERSON tasked with delivering money to Silky at his social club. Chris preferred it that way so that his brother was made to feel more important than he actually was. Jasper welcomed the opportunity to run this errand, thinking it would endear himself to the gangster.

The amount of the payments fluctuated depending on how well their businesses were doing. The brothers sat in their office at the Brooklyn C & J Windshield Replacement Company discussing the decline in revenue at this particular business as of late.

"The numbers here have been slipping, Jasper," said Chris. "We got Silky's birthday coming up, and the old man will be expecting a little extra."

"Do you think maybe we should crack the whip?" asked Jasper.

"We may have to."

"I'll bounce out some of the deadwood we got over here right now," offered Jasper.

"Before we do anything, let's see how we make out after tonight. I got that kid Spanky going out to drum up some business for us."

"You know, I was never crazy about that kid, Chris."

"Why is that?"

"Nothing I can put my finger on. There is just something about him that I don't trust."

"You can't condemn a man without evidence," reminded Chris.

"He's a punk," declared Jasper in no uncertain terms. "The word on him is that he'll run scared when the chips are down."

"People talk a lot of crap. That kid was raised by his grandmother. He came up like us, the hard way."

"Nobody cried for us, brother of mine," pointed out Jasper.

"Anyway, he's going out tonight to bust up some windshields. In a couple of days, we'll compare the number of cars he tells us he damaged against the number of glass repairs we get in," said Chris. If the new jobs don't come close to what was busted up, then we'll look at our inventory to make sure it ain't less than what it should be."

"If we come up short, then we know we got somebody in need of a tuning up," added Jasper. "We should think about busting windshields quarterly."

"Yeah, we could do that," agreed Chris.

"What do you want to do with the two guys from Chinatown looking to buy the lumberyard?"

"Let's stall them. As long as it's profitable for us, we can afford to wait it out."

"Are you sure, Chris? Those guys from Williamsburg also have an interest. We could play one against the other to get the number up."

"I know they're both hot for it. Let's wait and see if we can loosen up the property owner. If we can grab the building, we'll swing a better deal."

Jasper nodded his concurrence. "I got asked by our friends at the club if we want fireworks."

"What did you tell them?"

"I told them we're passing. After losing the whole load last Fourth of July, why take a chance on it happening again? Those cops didn't just stumble on that abandoned building. Somebody snitched."

"What did Silky have to say about us declining?" asked Chris with a trace of concern in his voice.

"He didn't say one way or the other. He just said we should find out who the stoolie is."

"I still think it was probably some nosy neighbor," speculated Chris.

"It wouldn't surprise me. I bet it was the old guy who always sits outside on his stoop."

"I don't think so, Jasper. His grandson set off Roman candles last year in front of the house."

"That's right; I forgot. Anyway, Silky got over it once I told him that I knew someone who would take a truckload of bicycles off his hands."

When the office phone rang, Chris picked it up. After a few seconds, he said, "Okay, send him in."

"Who is it?" asked Jasper.

"Spanky."

Jasper rolled his eyes but said nothing.

Spanky Ritzland was approximately twenty years younger than the James Brothers. A handsome man with a full head of long blond hair, he maintained a good physical appearance thanks to his passion for playing handball. Ritzland was a small-time wannabe who snorted cocaine recreationally when partying with one of his many lady friends. He entered the office wearing a black track suit and white sneakers.

"Are you squared away for tonight, Spanky?" asked Chris.

"Yeah, no problem," replied Ritzland. "We'll bust up about fifteen or twenty windshields"

"Be sure to break the front *and* back glass," Jasper reminded him.

"No sweat."

"Hey, I heard that you got married," said Chris.

The younger man shook his head. "I had to. She got knocked up."

"What do you mean, you *had* to? You were planning on getting married anyway, weren't you?"

"Yeah," Spanky answered unenthusiastically, "but the situation sort of rushed it, Chris."

"What's the matter with you? Kids are a blessing. You should be thrilled."

"Yeah, I know. I'm not *un-thrilled* about it, but I'm having problems with my father-in-law."

"What happened?" asked Jasper, anxious to hear more.

"We had a big blowout at the reception."

"What was the beef about?"

"He wanted to take charge of the money we collected at the hall until after we returned from our honeymoon," explained Spanky. "Can you believe that? Like I'm gonna give somebody my money!"

"You don't trust him?" asked Jasper.

"I don't trust anybody when it comes to my money!" The remark made sense to the James Brothers.

"So what was the windup?"

"We got into a fistfight. I clocked him one and knocked out his front tooth with one shot!" said Spanky proudly, believing that assaulting a man forty years his senior was a testament to his toughness. "It's been downhill with him ever since."

"It happens," commented Jasper.

"So do we have anything else to talk about?" asked Chris, looking to send Spanky on his way.

"Well, actually there is. I got a proposition to make."

"What proposition is that?"

"I have an idea for a business. It requires financing and partners with the right connections."

"What kind of business?" asked Chris.

"I'm talking coke."

"What, are you looking to buy a soda route?" asked Jasper.

"No, I'm talking *cocaine*. . . ."

"That's an idea?" asked Chris, underwhelmed at the prospect of being a drug trafficker.

"I have the connections to move kilos," advised Spanky. "I just don't have the in or the financing to get rolling with that kind of demand."

"You sure you aren't talking to undercover cops?" asked Jasper suspiciously.

"There are no cops in this. I got a friend who plugged me into people who have a need for product."

"Why is it that all of a sudden *now* they need you?" asked Chris.

"Their connection got busted."

"Go on. . . . Keep talking," said Chris. "Your audience is listening."

Jasper sat up and paid attention. He still disliked Spanky, but business *was* business.

########

CHRIS MADE ARRANGEMENTS TO MEET SILKY at the front bar in the famed Sardi's Restaurant on West Forty-Fourth Street. The purpose of the meeting was to propose the opportunity that had been presented to them by Spanky. Jasper looked at his watch. Growing impatient, he turned to Chris.

"Do you think something happened?"

"Nah, he'll be here," said Chris. "You have to figure on Manhattan traffic."

"What made you make the meet over here?"

"It was Silky's idea to have dinner in Sardi's. Silky loves the food here, the atmosphere and the idea of the celebrity caricatures on the walls."

"I never knew he was into that showbiz stuff."

"Silky ain't no stargazer. You want to know another reason why he picked this joint?"

"Yeah. . . ."

"He wants to see if they got Frankie Laine's picture hanging on the wall someplace. He loves the guy."

"Frankie Laine the singer?"

"He likes him more than he likes Sinatra."

"Is Frankie Laine still alive?" asked Jasper.

"Who the heck knows?"

Silky entered the restaurant alone, leaving his driver outside to wait in the car. A secretive man, the mobster preferred to keep the topic of his business dealings on a need-to-know basis. After the standard greeting, which included a respectful peck on the gangster's cheek, Chris ordered a round of drinks to be sent to the table he'd reserved.

Once seated, the men got right down to business. The James Brothers were unsure whether or not they'd be able to entice the mobster to join them on their cocaine-trafficking odyssey. Chris delicately broached the subject of a joint venture. He thought his pitch was effective because Silky heard him out until he was finished speaking. Silky's response came with a grave tone.

"Have you ever heard me talk about being in the drug racket?" asked the gangster, using a stern voice.

"Not that I recall," replied Chris.

"Didn't I tell you that I want you to maintain a clean image?" asked the mobster. "You guys are positioned perfectly to know what moves these politicians are thinking about making."

"There's a lot of money in this shit, Silky," said Jasper.

"It's against the rules!" barked Silky. "Where do you get the balls to make such a proposal to *me*?" asked Silky, feigning outrage. "I hate everything about that filthy business!"

"We only brought this to you out of respect, Silky," explained Chris. "We've been with you since we were kids. You were good to us, so we feel like we'll always owe you. Without you, where would we be? We saw this as a chance to show our gratitude. The last thing in the world we want to do is offend you."

Silky seemed to calm down after hearing this. "You know the rules, don't you?

"Yeah, we know them," admitted Chris.

"Yet you come to me with this?"

"You're like a father to us, Silky. We would do nothing without your blessing."

Truth be told, the James Brothers didn't have a narcotics connection that could meet the cocaine demand. They were looking to Silky in the hope that he could identify a reliable resource to do business with. Once Silky permitted his indignation to subside, to the surprise of the twins, he came around.

"What do you two know about narcotics anyway?" asked the gangster with all signs of umbrage apparently vanishing.

Chris instinctively knew that the racketeer was now thinking the proposition over. "Not a thing," Chris answered honestly, "other than we got an in with people wanting to buy kilos of coke."

"You know that going against the family rules when it comes to drugs is a death sentence, right? Yet you come to me with such a proposal. . . ."

Jasper spoke up bluntly. "Look, Silky, we recognize the risk, but the return on investment makes it worth all the risk in the world. Me and Chris got ideas that could make this the long ball."

Silky couldn't discount the track record of the brothers for making money. The twins had proven themselves to have the golden touch in that department. That and their trustworthiness influenced his decision to reconsider their deal. What was unknown to the twins was that the gangster needed no education in the vast amount of profit to be made in trafficking narcotics.

"Let's jump to the main event," said the gangster. "Why come to me? You got plenty of money."

"We're hoping that you could turn us on to the right connection for the product," said Chris.

"What makes you think I'm capable of that?" asked Silky suspiciously.

"Silky, we go back a long time with you. You can part the waters if you want to. And there is nobody better to have in this as a partner than you," added Chris.

Silky let out a deep breath as he thought things over. He knew well that the money was too potent an incentive to turn his back on. "So you need a reliable supplier just to load you up with product, right?"

"Yeah, that's it in a nutshell," answered Chris.

"Are you sure you got kilo customers?" asked Silky. "It wouldn't be good for you if you don't."

"I hear you, Silky," said Chris. "Our man Spanky can definitely move the shit. We believe in him. All we need is access to the product in order to meet the demand."

Again Silky thought prior to speaking. "You realize the danger if my involvement were to come out? Exposure would mean curtains for all of us." The James Brothers nodded, waiting to hear more. "I suppose that this is in the cards for us," said Silky. "I know of someone in Toronto who can supply you with all you can sell . . . *as long as I'm your partner.*"

"At what price to us?" asked Jasper.

Silky scoffed at the remark. "Don't underestimate what partnership with me means. Don't worry about a price. Toronto will front the powder *and* tell *you* what to charge. *After* you guys make the sale, you turn in the money to me. I'll pay off Toronto, and we whack up the rest. But remember this: if you don't collect or get ripped off, then we're the ones on the hook for the money."

"That works for us," said Chris, turning to Jasper. Jasper nodded his agreement.

"There are two things for you to remember going into this. First off, I'm a *silent* partner. When it comes to the narcotics business, my name is never to be uttered . . . ever. Always front this kid Spanky, understood?" Both Chris and Jasper again nodded their heads. "Good. The second thing is the split. We go forty–sixty. Forty for me and you two spilt the sixty. Agreed?"

"What do we do about Spanky?" asked Jasper.

"He'll be the face of the business. Give him a 10 percent commission on every deal he puts over," replied Silky. "We split his cost three ways."

Jasper and Chris looked at each other. Knowing that there was little they could do to restructure the deal more favorably to themselves, they went along. "Whatever you say, Silky," said Chris.

"Don't ever let Spanky know *my* involvement in this. All he needs to know about me is that my role is to protect you in the event somebody starts shaking you down."

When the men were finished talking business, they shook hands and toasted to the future success of their new venture. After finishing dinner, Chris asked for the bill. As the waiter was taking payment, Silky raised his finger, indicating that he wanted to have a word with him.

"Yes sir?" asked the waiter, lowering his ear to Silky's mouth in order to hear.

"You got a picture of Frankie Laine hanging in this joint?" asked the gangster.

########

CHRIS LOST HIS VISION IN ONE EYE shortly after having lunch at home. The shock of losing his sight scared him enough to have his wife drive him to the nearest hospital. While en route his sight returned. With his vision corrected, he instructed his wife to turn the car around and take him home. The aversion Chris had for doctors foolishly prevented him from following up with a physician. He fooled himself into believing that his prosperity came along with a destiny of a long, healthy life.

It was a pleasant Sunday afternoon as the brothers sat in Jasper's yard. As the twins smoked and chatted, their wives were inside preparing for dinner.

"You know, Chris, even though the taxes out here are through the roof and I'm bored to death half the time, I'm still glad we moved out of Brooklyn," said Jasper.

"It's the best thing we ever did," replied Chris as he inhaled the smoke from his cigar, a Cohiba Mini. "At least out here you see where your money goes. The schools are good, everybody works, and there is none of the New York bullshit to contend with."

Jasper nodded his head in agreement. As he lit up a Marlboro, he noticed that Chris was inhaling the draws he was taking from his cigar.

"You shouldn't be inhaling those suckers."

"What can I tell ya?" answered Chris dismissively. "How about we go partners on a boat?" he asked.

Jasper had to laugh. "You want a boat? What are we gonna do with a boat?"

"I don't know. We could sail up the Hudson. Go fishing, maybe."

"C'mon, will ya, Chris? There's no money in that. A boat will just bleed us dry. Besides, it's a lot of work to maintain those suckers. And don't forget, you have to be a half-ass mechanic on the water to boot."

Chris blew smoke rings as he contemplated his brother's reaction to purchasing a boat. He then suddenly began coughing furiously. His eyes bulged and then rolled back into his head.

"Chris, you alright?" asked Jasper, alarmed at what he was witnessing.

When he received no response, Jasper immediately dialed 911. Chris was gone before the ambulance reached the house.

When a respectable amount of time had passed, Jasper sat down with his sister-in-law to talk. Since her knowledge was limited concerning her late husband's affairs, she relied on Jasper to see her through a fair and equitable distribution of their assets. Jasper restricted the conversation to their legal concerns. His intent was not to gain a financial edge. He was just certain that his brother would have wanted the criminal aspect of their lives kept in the shade.

"Why don't we go and talk to that lawyer in your family?"

"You know I trust you, Jasper. But perhaps having my cousin involved would be beneficial."

"Let's hold off on making any decision until I kick things around with your cousin. We'll figure a way to whack up the businesses evenly."

########

SILKY'S CONVERSATION WITH JASPER was brief. "I'm sorry about Chris. He was a very bright boy businesswise. You capable of handling everything alone?" asked the gangster.

"Yeah," answered Jasper. "I'm good."

"Good. Next time I see you, you can drop off the ziti," said the gangster cryptically, referring to the tribute money due him.

With Chris gone, Jasper was left to assume his dead brother's role in the businesses as well as his own. Fortunately, the cocaine enterprise was set up to run in a relatively uncomplicated fashion, so Jasper was able to handle things.

Spanky filled customer orders and was responsible for the delivery of the product to customers and the collection of payment. A dimwitted street thug known as Q-Ball Otto served as Spanky's backup during these hand-to-hand transactions. Sufficient product was kept in Spanky's Brooklyn bachelor apartment to meet the demand.

An agreement arranged by Silky resulted in the Canadian supplier being paid once the goods were sold. Whenever inventory ran low, Spanky notified Jasper, who called Silky, who in turn sent word to Toronto. Toronto would then dispatch an upstate New York transport team to replenish the apartment stash. Having their own apartment key, the transporters made their deliveries when Spanky wasn't present. This eliminated the chance of a potential facial identification in the event of a bust or someone turning snitch. Upon consummation of every transaction, Spanky turned in the money he received directly over to Jasper. After giving Spanky his cut, Jasper handed over the remaining money to Silky with an accounting. Silky paid Jasper his end of the money and kept the rest. It was the responsibility of the organized crime soldier to straighten out with the Canadian supplier.

"Okay," acknowledged Jasper, "next time I'll bring the ziti."

"By the way, there is a bar up for sale in the neighborhood if you have an interest to go in with me. I can get us a good deal on it."

Jasper was flattered. "You want to go partners with me in a bar?" he asked.

"Sure," replied Silky. "That's a business that needs the attention of a younger man . . . like you."

"What bar is it?"

"It called Lau's Lucky Lounge. It's on Third Avenue."

"I know that place. It's a pretty big joint. Why is the guy selling?"

"He wants to retire and move to Arizona with his wife. He's no kid anymore."

"Do you know what he wants for the bar?"

"I don't exactly know," replied Silky. "But whatever it is, you don't need to worry about it. I'll get his price down. I loaned him the money to open the joint years ago," he added.

After a minute of thought, Jasper went for the offer. "I'm in."

"I figured you would be," said the mobster. "Remember, with a bar, there is the state liquor authority to deal with. Those guys are like cops. We'll use my man Johnny to front as the owner on paper. He has a clean record. Remember, like everything else, I'm in the shadows on this deal."

"Johnny Blondell has no record?"

"No really smart guy has a record. I don't have one; do you?"

"No, I was never busted for anything. Neither was my brother, rest his soul."

"See what I mean?"

8

Las Vegas Lucy

AS THINGS PROGRESSED, JASPER's CONFIDENCE as a businessman grew. Astute enough not to overrate his ability, he proceeded cautiously as he sought out new opportunities. To his credit, at least when it came to his drug business, he was honest with himself. Jasper knew that without Spanky, the future of the illicit enterprise would be a question mark. As a result, he afforded Spanky enough latitude to avoid disrupting a successful formula. This wasn't easy for the surviving twin, whose basic dislike for his underling remained firm. Jasper's suspicious nature reached a new plateau when Spanky asked for a few minutes in private with him to *talk about the business.*

"You got some time?" asked Spanky, approaching Jasper inside the James Brothers Saloon.

Recognizing that Spanky had something on his mind, Jasper knew that a meeting was going to be inevitable. "I gotta run a couple of errands. I'll swing by your place in a couple of hours. We'll talk then."

"Okay. I'll be at the apartment waiting for you."

At the heart of the matter was Spanky's belief that he was undervalued and being shortchanged. Not being an equal partner in a business that he had brought to the table never sat well with the drug dealer. Unaware of Silky's involvement, Spanky felt entitled to equity in the business. He naively justified his position by citing the passing of Jasper's brother, Chris, whose death he believed had created a partnership vacancy. However delusional his thinking, Spanky nevertheless realized that he couldn't expect the same stake in the drug enterprise that Chris once held. Spanky's strategy called for his taking baby steps, inching his way to a sizable business interest. Their conversation took place in the bachelor apartment Spanky maintained in Brooklyn. Spanky's opening statement was all it took to light a fire.

"I wanted to talk to you about my end," said Spanky with surprising confidence.

"What about your end?" The edge in Jasper's voice spoke volumes.

"I was thinking that with your brother gone now, you got room for me to get a piece of the business."

"Are you kidding me or what?" asked Jasper, taken aback.

"Seriously, it's only right that I get a cut," replied Spanky. "Let's face it; you *need* me. I'm the guy drumming up all the business."

Spanky could see Jasper's eyes narrow. He recognized this as a dangerous reaction. Lacking the intestinal fortitude to stand up to Jasper physically, Spanky felt his stomach grow queasy.

"If you think I'm letting you hold me up, think again," Jasper declared, going on the offensive. Spanky instinctively backed up a step, distancing himself from Jasper. "If you're smart, you'll stay happy with your 10 percent. You gotta be on crack to think that you could get away with shaking me down!"

"Jasper, be reasonable. I'm only asking for relief. I can even live with a little raise, maybe."

Seeing Spanky's lips tremble alerted Jasper that he had him scared. Capitalizing on Spanky's weakness, Jasper pressed his advantage. "What's going on with you?"

"There's nothing going on. . . ."

"Come out with it," demanded Jasper. "Why are you coming at me with this shit?"

"I got money issues, Jasper. Between the new house, this apartment, and my wife and kids, my girlfriend . . . I'm always strapped for cash."

"Maybe you gotta start living within your means."

"Maybe I do," conceded Spanky. "Anyway, I was thinking the time might be right just to ask."

"You want relief?"

"I'm just asking for a larger slice of the pie, that's all. I mean, it's just me and you now. There's plenty of extra gravy going your way."

Jasper remembered that Spanky wasn't aware of Silky's role. "Let's understand each other. It's *never* been me and you. It was always me and my brother. . . . *You never* figured in. You're just a footnote."

Used to such crudeness, Spanky hardly flinched. "I know that I'm working for you, Jasper."

Jasper eased up now that Spanky was falling back in line. *What would Chris do in a spot like this?* he asked himself, trying to arrive at a graceful resolution. Jasper put himself in Spanky's shoes. He concluded that if he were Spanky, he'd start stealing from the business in order to get what he wanted.

"Look, Spanky, let me mull this over for a couple of days. I'll get back to you."

"Thanks, Jasper," replied Spanky. He took Jasper's apparent change of heart as a good sign.

Jasper saw Silky the following day at his social club. "How do you want me to handle this kid, Silky?" he asked.

"We need him, right?"

"Yeah, we do. He brings in the deals. To be honest, in that respect he's been doing a good job."

"Alright then, since you're pulling in more cabbage anyway, keep him happy."

"What do you think his end should be upped to?"

"You're the guy who inherited what Chris was getting, so you'll have to pay the added tax on this kid. That makes it your call."

"No problem, Silky. I'm just asking your opinion on how much to give him. What would you suggest?"

"Bring him up to 20 percent on his commission, but spread it over three years. Give him 2 percent now, 2 percent next year, and then 6 percent the last year. By that time, make sure you got somebody groomed to take his place for 10 percent. We can't have the little prick coming around with his hand out every three years."

The formula impressed Jasper. "That makes sense. Thanks, Silky."

"Never let anyone feel too important. If you do, they'll start believing it and put the arm on you."

"I hear you," agreed Jasper. "Let me ask you something else, Silky. What do you think of us expanding our business out of town?"

"Where out of town?"

"I was thinking of Las Vegas."

Silky smiled approvingly. "Go see what's out there. But be sure to talk to me before you do anything."

"Will do," said Jasper without revealing that branching out to Vegas was the last idea his brother, Chris, had had before passing on.

Jasper was willing to put aside his personal feelings. Like it or not, Spanky was a necessary component if he were to expand to Vegas. Jasper picked up the telephone to make nice. "Spanky, it's me, Jasper."

"What's up, Jasper?"

"I got some good news for you. We're taking a trip to Las Vegas."

"What's in Vegas?"

"Opportunity," replied Jasper. "It'll be my treat. We'll do a little partying, and I'll amend our financial arrangement. You'll be happy."

"Are you serious?" asked Spanky, flabbergasted at Jasper's sudden turnaround.

"I'm very serious. We're gonna discuss your future."

"That's great, Jasper. I'll pack a bag anytime you say." Spanky was overjoyed. The prospect of a free trip to the land of delightful temptations only sweetened the pot for him.

"I'll make all the arrangements; bring enough to cover your gambling and extracurricular activities."

"No problem." Spanky envisioned good things coming to him in the foreseeable future.

The night before his trip to Las Vegas all Spanky could think of was the delight to be derived amidst the ambrosial scents produced at the Ride-Em Ranch in Sin City. When the time finally came to rise from bed, he did so to the aroma of bacon coming from the downstairs kitchen. As he stood at the top of the stairs taking in a stronger whiff, he could hear the sizzling. He could also hear his wife talking on the kitchen phone. Curious, he returned to his bedroom to listen in on the extension. Hearing his mother-in-law's voice caused him to monitor the conversation.

"You already knew that he sometimes has to travel for work."

"But he's going to be gone for three days this time, Ma," said Spanky's wife.

"Where is he going?"

"He never tells me. All he ever says is that he has to go away on a business trip."

"Don't you ask him where?"

"All I got from him is that he's going out West someplace. Maybe Daddy is right when he says—"

"Just a minute," interrupted the mother. "What's the difference where he goes? He's providing?"

"Yeah, that's the one thing he does do. Actually, he is pretty regular with the money. When I ask where he gets it, his answer is that it comes from hard work. He calls himself a rainmaker."

"Well, look . . . I don't know what to tell you."

"I'm thinking of leaving him, Ma." she said.

The statement stunned the older woman. "Is he being physically abusive to you or the children?"

"No, I'm just upset over these absences," said the unhappy wife. "I get lonely."

"Will you stop already," said the older woman, sounding frustrated. "You think I've always been happy with your father? If you want happy, you should have stayed single like your aunt."

"You think she's happy, Ma?"

"All I know is that you don't ruin a good thing. Look at the house you live in. Look out the window at the manicured lawn, the nice yard, and nice schools. These are things to consider," said the mother. "My advice is to suck it up or go for counseling."

"He'd never go for counseling. Besides, even Daddy isn't thrilled with him, Ma."

"Your father hasn't had a thrill since his honeymoon!" barked the mother. "He hates his boss and most of the time he hates me, but he still goes to work for that boss and comes home to me. People learn to persevere in this life."

"But Spanky isn't my boss. . . ."

"Of course he's not," agreed the mother, who was tiring of the conversation, "but sometimes we have to be careful not to bite our nose to spite our face."

Spanky silently nodded in agreement as he listened to his mother-in-law. "The old lady knows who butters the bread," he said after softly hanging up the phone. "I'll give her that."

##########

JASPER EMERGED FROM THE OFFICE BUILDING with an unlit cigarette dangling from his lips. He had been visiting his accountant. He proceeded to where Spanky was parked on the street. As he neared the vehicle, he suddenly stopped walking. He raised his hand, signaling Spanky to stand by. Jasper's attention was drawn to a young boy on his knees looking down into a sidewalk grating.

"What's the problem?" called out Jasper. "What happened? Did you drop something down there, kid?" he asked after approaching the youth.

"Yeah, I dropped my house key," answered the boy.

"Do you know how to get it up from down there?"

"Chewing gum?" guessed the youth.

Jasper expressed scorn at the notion of using chewing gum. "C'mon, where do you get chewing gum from, kid? I'll show you a trick that works in any weather."

Spanky exited the car, curious as to what all the talk was about. "We gotta get going, Jasper. We got a plane to catch," he said.

"Relax. We got time," answered Jasper, intent on doing what he perceived to be a good deed.

Spanky stood by quietly as Jasper reached into his pocket for some money. "Here, take this and go to that Rite Aid over there and come back with a jar of Vaseline and some string."

The youth took the money and did as instructed. When he returned, Jasper took the Vaseline and string, allowing the youth to keep the change.

"Watch this," Jasper instructed, producing a multi-tool Swiss Army knife from his pocket.

Jasper cut a long length of string. He then took the lid off the Vaseline and punched a hole in it. He passed the string through the hole, looped it around the lid several times, and tied it off, leaving enough length to reach the key. Jasper then handed the makeshift retriever to the boy.

"Grease the lid heavy with the Vaseline and pass it through the hole in the grating," instructed Jasper. "Drop the lid on the key. It'll stick, and you'll be able to pull it up. How is that, kid?"

The youth recovered his key on the second try. Proud of himself, he looked at Jasper with a smile.

"Keep what you learned to yourself, kid," advised Jasper. "There is no percentage in educating the competition. Check the gratings regular. You can grab whatever falls down there for yourself."

"I don't get it. . . . What's the big lesson you taught this kid, Jasper? How to spend ten bucks to get a key or a quarter?" asked Spanky once they were in the car.

"Today it was peanuts; tomorrow it could be some sucker's diamond ring."

"Where did you learn that trick anyway?"

"I saw a bum on the Bowery do it one time. So are we going to the airport today or not?" asked Jasper, now in a rush to get going.

Jasper and Spanky sat in their seats on the plane waiting for the rest of the passengers to board. Since Jasper couldn't have been friendlier, Spanky felt their relationship was advancing.

"I've been meaning for us to spend time together for a while now," fibbed Jasper.

"You have?"

"We're going to see if it makes sense to plant a flag in Vegas."

"You want we should do business in Vegas?"

"That's right. I want to see if we can make some moves."

Spanky was thrilled at the prospect. "Vegas is perfect for us. It's a party town. It's all about people gambling, having a good time, and doing things they'd have a hard time getting away with at home. You know the formula . . . sex, drugs, and rock and roll. Our customers are drawn to places like Vegas."

"That's just what I figured."

"But about my end . . . did you put any thought into it?"

"Yeah, plenty," replied Jasper. "I'm bumping up your commission from 10 to 20 percent."

"Twenty percent works," replied Spanky, finding the increase acceptable. It was actually more than he'd figured on. However, his euphoria was destined to be short-lived.

"That'll be spread over three years," added Jasper. "It'll be an increase of 2, 2, and 6 percent for a total of 20 percent after the third year. After that, we'll sit down and talk again."

Spanky hadn't expected a staggered payout. He tried countering with an offer of his own. "How about we make it more like 5 and 5 over two years?"

Not anticipating a counterproposal, Jasper gave Spanky a hard stare. "Look, Spanky," he said in a serious tone, "go with the flow, will ya? If we can make something happen in Vegas, I promise you, you'll be fatter than you ever dreamed of."

Having little choice, Spanky accepted the deal. "I got a question," he said.

"Shoot."

"I know you have to kick in to the boys in New York for protection. Does that cover Vegas as well?"

"That's my worry," replied Jasper abruptly, making it clear that the topic was off the table.

##########

JASPER AND SPANKY'S FIRST NIGHT in Sin City was spent casino hopping. They focused on tables and bars frequented by high rollers. Spanky was searching for a specific type. Spanky identified someone of interest who had just left the blackjack table. He appeared to be someone who seemed to know everyone. As the stranger made his way to the closest bar Spanky and Jasper followed. Taking a seat near the man at the bar, Spanky initiated a conversation while Jasper watched from afar. Through their chitchat, Spanky learned that the stranger was a heavy gambler who had gotten stranded in Vegas after going broke several years prior. He indicated that he now sustained himself by earning his living as a cabdriver. The drug dealer from Brooklyn ended the conversation feeling that there might be a place for his new acquaintance in their drug initiative.

"He could be useful, Jasper," said Spanky. "He definitely knows his way around out here."

"What makes you think that?"

"He told me where to go if I wanted to cop some drugs."

"He did?"

"Why don't I call him tomorrow and see what I can do to maybe work something out with him."

"Let's not jump the gun," said Jasper, taking a page from his late brother's book. "We're in no rush."

Once back at their casino hotel, the two men took seats at one of the bars for a nightcap. A distance from where they sat was semicircular seating around small cocktail tables. Spanky noticed two women in their thirties sitting alone. They were chatting quietly over drinks.

"Look at those two," Spanky said, drawing Jasper's attention to the women.

"What about them?"

"Unless I'm mistaken, they're available."

"What, are they wearing a sign?"

"Trust my radar, Jasper. I have a nose for this."

"So go talk to them."

"I'm gonna do just that."

Spanky, considered handsome by most standards, was exceedingly confident when it came to the opposite sex. He slowly rose from his station at the bar and sashayed his way to the men's room. On his way, he took the opportunity to roguishly smile at the two ladies. The blond woman exhibited similar interest by returning his smile as he swaggered past them. The brunette, who was the more attractive of the two, remained reserved. On his return trip from the restroom, Spanky went all out by flashing the broad smile that had netted him many a past conquest. Again the blond reciprocated without hesitation, thus confirming that a mutual attraction existed. Upon returning to the bar, Spanky took a sip of bourbon, after which he elbowed his older companion.

"Jasper, I think the blond is a cinch for me."

"You think so?" asked Jasper. "What is she, a hooker?"

"Nah, she's no hooker. I'm not too sure about the other one, though."

After taking another glance from a distance, Jasper rose to conduct his own survey. He returned shortly. "I'll take the one with dark hair," he announced. "You okay with whacking them up that way?"

"No problem. I can live with the blond," answered Spanky.

"Go on over and do them a favor," said Jasper.

##########

THE BLOND SHOWED MUCH MORE interest in meeting the two strangers than her friend. "The young one likes me," she said. "He checked me out when he passed by."

"I saw that," answered the less enthusiastic brunette.

"Look at them. I think they're talking about us. Do you think they'll come by?"

"If they're looking, they'll come," replied the brunette with certainty.

"If things work out, don't forget what we agreed on."

"Don't worry, Dotty," assured Lucy. "If it comes down to that, I'll see you at breakfast."

"What do you think of the older one with the potbelly? Is he your type?"

"We'll see," replied Lucy. "I can't say I'd cut him from the team just yet."

"Don't stare. . . . Mine is coming over!" The two women looked at each other. After holding their look for a couple of seconds, they turned to face Spanky as he neared them.

"Hello, ladies. Glad to see you were paroled," said Spanky.

"Paroled from where?" asked Dotty, puzzled by the remark.

"Heaven," replied Spanky, flashing the wise-guy smirk that had proven successful in the past. "My friend and I would love to buy you girls a drink," he said. Spanky displayed perfectly aligned teeth, which added to his already appealing appearance.

The two women graciously accepted the drink offer. After introducing himself, Spanky confidently slipped in to sit beside Dotty. He raised his arm, signaling Jasper to join them. After being introduced, Jasper assumed a seat alongside Lucy. The four, sitting side by side, conversed on those getting-to-know-you topics that are commonly discussed after a pickup. After the consumption of a couple of rounds, things progressed nicely for Spanky and Dotty. Spanky was a fast worker. He snuggled closer to Dotty as they spoke. She conveyed her receptiveness by staring deeply into his eyes and nodding understandingly at his every fabrication. After she uttered the word *really* with great emphasis, the drug dealer felt like a rock star partying with a groupie. Jasper, who could overhear the talk, thought that Spanky would've made a great pimp. He lifted his eyebrows in disbelief at the tripe being dished. When Jasper turned for a closer look at Lucy, he decided that she was too icy to be a working prostitute.

"I like your hair that way," Dotty could be overheard stating softly.

"And I just *love* your overbite," replied Spanky, who was not shy about being naughty.

The suggestive remark was well received. A short time later, they stood in unison to make their good nights. Spanky winked at Jasper as he retreated to his room with Dotty, who smiled at Lucy.

Now alone with Lucy, Jasper began fishing to see if he could stimulate some interest on her part. He noticed for the first time how Lucy's eyes tended to slightly bulge when speaking. Unsure of what that meant, he forged ahead to see if he could penetrate her armor.

"So where did you say you're from?" Jasper asked.

"Boulder City," answered Lucy.

"That's close to here, isn't it?"

"It's about a forty-five-minute drive," she replied, not giving him anything to work with.

Jasper resorted to letting his money do his talking. He lifted his sleeve to check the time on his Rolex watch. Judging by Lucy's facial expression, he could see that he had secured her interest.

"How long are you here for?" she asked, initiating conversation after spotting the watch.

Sure, now she wants to talk, thought Jasper, having her number. He pressed his advantage by laying it on thick. "We're here for a few days. Spanky works for me back East in *one* of the businesses I own," he said, making it clear he was the more substantial of the two men.

Lucy's thawing out came quickly. "So what type of *businesses* are you in?" she asked.

The more Jasper expanded on his holdings, the more appealing Lucy found him to be. She justified her newfound attraction by considering Jasper a novelty rather than just another of the multitude of available handsome men. His age was now equated with wisdom, his thinning hair an indication of a superior intellect, and an expanded waistline attributable to a sophisticated palate. As Jasper spoke of his assets, Lucy mentally calculated his worth. She began getting aggressive, telegraphing her interest by looking deeply into *his* eyes. Several times she leaned forward to brush against him. To a thug like Jasper, Lucy was becoming an easy read. He saw her for what she was . . . as streetwise as he. Jasper now viewed Lucy as not merely a potential plaything but rather as possibly the right associate in his Vegas initiative. For him, getting close to Lucy had become part of a business plan.

"What do you do again?" he asked.

"I work at Sellover's Finest," replied Lucy.

"What's Sellover's Finest?"

"It's a high-end jewelry store."

Jasper nodded. "What else have you done other than push jewelry? I *know* you've been around."

Lucy saw Jasper differently after he made that statement. They were in many ways the same. For a long time, Lucy had been in the market for a fat cat. Had Jasper been a man of modest means, her involvement with someone closing in on fifty would have been out of the question. What never occurred to her was that Jasper had motives that weren't restricted to intimacy.

Without blinking an eye, she answered his question in a direct fashion. "Before Sellover's, I rode with the Vengeful Kings. That was back in the days when I used to get in trouble."

"What's the Vengeful Kings?"

"The VKs are a biker gang." Lucy noted that Jasper didn't express surprise. "Doesn't that surprise you?"

"Not in the least," replied Jasper. He then offered her a cigarette, which she immediately accepted. In doing so, she revealed herself further. As he lit her smoke, he nodded knowingly.

"I figured you for having a whole other side."

"You did?"

"Yeah, and I find the dark side reassuring. Now, tell me about your trouble."

"Why?"

"Because I'm interested," he answered. "You know, I was afraid that you two girls might be cops."

"Yeah, and I have my handcuffs with me," said Lucy suggestively.

The wheels in Jasper's head began to turn at an accelerated pace. The great Venetian seducer Giacomo Casanova couldn't have sped up the pace any quicker. They concluded their talking and decided to retreat to Jasper's room, where they wasted no time engaging. During the intermissions, Jasper did his best to learn all he could about Lucy's past as they blew cigarette smoke up at the ceiling.

##########

PERHAPS THE REBELLIOUSNESS OF BEATRIZ LUCIA SWEETAPPLE was attributable to poor parenting. Whatever the causation factor, she was problematic from an early age. When she made it known that she detested the name Beatriz, her parents agreed to never call her that or any variation of the name. Their daughter wanted to be known as Lucy, and forevermore she was. The spoiled child found dissatisfaction in just about everything that fell into the parameters of normal. A fun after-school activity for the ten-year-old Lucy was placing worms in an envelope and mailing them to her teacher. At fourteen she began experimenting with drugs and became sexually active. Not surprisingly, Lucy was attracted to bad boys, with bikers heading her list of ideal beaus. She viewed tattooed motorcycle gang members as knight-like figures, men who could liberate her from the restrictiveness of societal norms.

Spotting a row of motorcycles lined up outside a Burger King, the sixteen-year-old Lucy found herself intrigued. She stared at the tough-looking gang members, and their women, as they wolfed down burgers while standing alongside their bikes. She was captivated by the thought of one day being a biker chick. She found thrilling the thought of tightly holding on to the waist of her very own macho man as they tore up the roads on his wheels. The teenager made it her business to meet the one seemingly unattached biker. He happened to be the leader of the pack.

"Nice wheels," she commented, walking up to the head biker. He was her senior by twenty years.

"You like them, honey lamb?" he asked.

"You bet. How about taking me for a ride?"

Amused by her directness, the biker looked the young girl over from head to toe. After she passed muster, he signaled Lucy to get on his bike. He never bothered to ask how old she was.

"You can learn a lot from me, honey lamb," advised the biker when they returned.

"I know," she answered, staring unabashedly into his face.

All it took was a few more spins on his Harley and some additional exposure to the macho side of the biker for Lucy to be convinced to travel with the gang. On the road, she became the recipient of a dubious education. She willingly engaged in the biker way when it came to relationships and making money, which included narcotics trafficking. Unbeknownst to Lucy, her new boyfriend was the target of a Drug Enforcement Administration investigation.

When they were rounded up by the federal narcotics agents, Lucy was pregnant. The father of the child was slapped with enough jail time that made any notion of seeing the street again a fantasy. Lucy found herself jailed, pregnant, and alone. While Lucy was serving a sentence on drug charges, her baby came. Fortunately, the care of the child was assumed by her parents, who remained supportive..

After her release from prison, Lucy returned home to live in the house of her parents. She landed a job at a jewelry store thanks to the intervention of a relative. While her pay was enough to maintain, it was insufficient compensation for what she wanted for her family. Everyday expenses, along with her having to contribute to the household she lived in, often left her stretching her dollars. The free hotel stays at the casino came courtesy of her employer, who as an established high roller was able to get comp rooms. When Jasper came along, she came to recognize his potential as a lifeline. At that point, she wasted no time latching on to him.

##########

JASPER WALKED OUT OF THE BATHROOM with a white towel wrapped around his waist. His face was clean-shaven, with the scent of cologne strong enough for Lucy to smell from several feet away.

"So, Lucy, what's it gonna be?" asked Jasper, who had just come out of the shower. "Are we getting together on this or what?"

"I'm still thinking about it," she answered.

"C'mon, what's to think about?" he asked. "I'm only here a couple of more days."

Jasper had a one-track mind when it came to what he wanted. He had been working on her ever since she confided that she was once the girlfriend of a drug-dealing biker. Jasper was determined to sign her up for a role in his own drug operation. Her credentials were impeccable by his standards. She knew the business, her way around Vegas *and* had a proven track record when it came to keeping her mouth shut when facing incarceration. In short, she was about as low a risk as could be expected.

"This is a big step for me," she said, holding out.

"You'll be making real money with me. Didn't you say that you could use an injection of funds?"

Lucy, who was already dressed, looked at him seriously. "I don't know," she said, pretending to have reservations. "I was lucky to get the job that I have. I'd need some guarantees."

"What guarantees can I give you?" he replied. "I'll tell you what; keep that job you got and work part time for me. You're no cherry. You know the kind of people we need to do business with."

"I don't want to get myself fired."

"What fired? Will you just listen to me? You have friends and connections in Vegas. If you can get the ball rolling, you'll be able to light your joints with twenty-dollar bills." Jasper's talk was persuasive.

Lucy's main reservation was whether or not she wanted back into the drug scene. Her craving for money ultimately overrode any reluctance. Thinking practically about it, she admitted to herself that pushing drugs was the only way someone with her history could get ahead financially.

"The only people I'll be involved with are you and Spanky?"

Jasper assured her by nodding as he spoke. "That's correct, just me and Spanky. Look, it'll be easy. You just line up the customers, get Spanky in front of them, and he'll do the rest."

"You won't do ounces?"

"Strictly kilos; and that's it."

Lucy understood. She mulled things over for another few minutes. "What is my cut again?"

"Five percent goes to you on each kilo sold."

"What if I can do a deal on my own without Spanky?"

Jasper thought about the question before answering. "Look, Lucy . . ."

"No, you look, Jasper," Lucy replied, now sounding more like someone in charge. "All this sounds good . . . but who's finding the customers out here?"

The question caused Jasper to pull his head back. "So what do you want?"

"I want to be an equal partner with you in Vegas, fifty-fifty."

"You want *50* percent?" Jasper asked in a shocked voice. "If you want that kind of equity, *you* put up the money and come up with the product, lady."

"Alright, so let's get real. Make it 20 percent."

After taking a moment to think, Jasper made a counteroffer. "Take 15 percent on everything you put over on your own and 5 percent if Spanky is involved. Deal?"

"You got a deal."

Jasper put out his hand to seal the arrangement. "Oh, there is one stipulation. I get a good *friend* out of this."

Lucy had expected to see his lecherous side resurface at some point. She smiled a straight-line smile. "Alright, you have yourself a friend," said Lucy, "with benefits. Can I ask you a personal question?"

"Go ahead."

"Where did you leave your pinkie?"

"A war wound," he replied. "Now, how about giving me my due, *smarty-pants*?"

Lucy went along. From where she stood, she'd be working for a boss who'd be too far away to really check on her. What she wasn't able to worm out of Jasper in commission, she intended to steal from him. Her new lover was going to pay one way or the other.

"Come over here . . . friend," she purred.

9

Squeezing Lemon

THE TWO VETERAN POLICE OFFICERS HAD BEEN patrolling the streets of
Brownsville for close to twenty-five years. The radio car partners adhered to a
time-tested formula that enabled them to navigate the needs of the community
with few complications. Their methodology, a simple one, called for minimizing
their involvement with the public. One tactic they employed was to delay their
response to calls for service. Such procrastination often resulted in incidents
having self-corrected or being long over by the time they arrived at the scene.
Neither officer had been involved in an arrest situation in recent memory. It was
late in the afternoon when the division dispatcher summoned their sector.

"Seven-Three Adam," called the voice over the radio.

"Adam standing by," acknowledged the recording officer, who sat in the
passenger seat.

"Respond to a dispute on the street at Saratoga and Sutter; two men fighting,
one armed with a hammer. Be advised that the man with the hammer is
wearing a white t-shirt and jeans."

"Ten-four, on the way," acknowledged the recorder, jotting down the
information.

The operator of the police vehicle reacted to the call by casually puffing on his
cigar. "Did you see that game last night?" he asked his partner. "They should
have taken the pitcher out in the fifth inning."

"I'd have taken him out long before that."

After more cigar puffs and additional discussion of the game, the operator
sluggishly drove in the direction of the incident.

"Seven-Three-Adam to Central," called in the recorder after finally arriving at
the scene.

"Go ahead, Adam."

"Ten-ninety," advised the recorder. "There is nothing here."

"Ten-four," replied the dispatcher, acknowledging that the job was unfounded.

The operator wasted no time in pulling away from the location. He wanted to gain distance from the puddle of blood on the sidewalk. Both officers were stocky men who looked cramped in their seats. Out of the blue the recorder did something out of character. . . . He made a street observation.

"Look over to your right. You seeing what I see?"

His partner chomped down on his cigar. "What are you doing, looking for trouble?" he asked.

"I can't believe this dummy is driving that El Dorado in broad daylight like he owns it!"

The operator shook his head disapprovingly. He also was appalled at the daringness of the car thief. "What are you looking to do . . . make a collar?" he asked.

The recorder thought for a few seconds before responding. "You know, maybe I should take him in. I got a wedding coming up, and I could use the overtime."

"What do you want me to do if he makes a run for it?"

"Just let him go. There is no sense in us chasing after him."

The driver of the police car chuckled. "I can just see the desk sergeant's face when we bring in this collar," said the operator. "Call in the plate to make sure the car is hot."

Once confirmation was received that the vehicle was stolen, the operator tapped the siren as a signal for the El Dorado to pull over. The twenty-five-year-old car thief looked in his rearview mirror.

"Shit!" said the thief, recognizing the officers. "It's the senior citizen cops."

The felon didn't make a run for it because he knew he was known to the officers. Even if he got away today, they'd be sure to get him another day. The thief complied with the authority behind the yelp and pulled over. The patrol car pulled up behind the El Dorado. The veteran cops, although not exactly arrest oriented, were not lax. They carefully approached the stolen car with their guns drawn.

"Shut off the engine and step out of the car," ordered the operator. The thief did as he was told. "You know the routine—up against the car and assume the position," commanded the officer.

"But Officer, I'm just doing someone a solid. . . ."

"Get those hands on top of the hood and spread."

After patting his man down, the operator rear cuffed him without incident. He then put the prisoner in the back seat of the radio car. While he was doing this, the recording officer searched the stolen vehicle.

"C'mon, let me explain the situation," said the prisoner. "A dude asked me to drop his car off. . . ."

The operator expressed no interest in what the prisoner was saying.

"You don't care, man," said the prisoner, who was foolishly trying to lay a guilt trip on the veteran officer. It was an exercise in futility.

The operator looked at the thief coldly. "Did *you* care when you stole the car?" The officer was met with a blank stare in answer to his question. "If I took that watch you're wearing, put it in my pocket, and kept it, how would you feel? Well, that's how the owner of the stolen car feels."

After some back and forth with the officers the thief advised that he was taking the stolen vehicle to Lemon's car lot, which was located nearby.

"Since when is Lemon taking in stolen cars?" asked the recording officer.

"I don't know, man. But you can drive through the garage in the rear of the lot and straight into the abandoned building behind it."

After hearing this, the two officers left their prisoner cuffed in the back seat of their police car so that they could discuss the matter over in private.

"What do we do now?" asked the operator. "Lemon's been good to the precinct for a lot of years." "Yeah, I know. I took my nephew there for a car," commented the recorder. "We can't just go in there and knock him over," he added, now angry at himself for getting involved.

After a short conversation, the officers decided to voucher the stolen car as found property and kick the car thief in his Fruit of the Looms, sending him on his way.

"I'll drop a dime to the auto crime squad anonymously," said the recorder. "Let them handle Lemon."

"Sounds like a plan," agreed the operator. "This is what we get for being too ambitious."

##########

74

THE AUTO CRIME SQUAD TOOK THE INFORMATION they received from the anonymous tipster seriously. Their subsequent investigation was one of little difficulty. The investigators entered the abandoned building behind Lemon's yard late in the evening and verified that there were stolen vehicles there. Their investigation established that the only way the stolen vehicles could have entered the building was via Lemon's lot. There was enough available evidence to secure a search warrant of Lemon's business. The day after securing the warrant the authorities executed a morning raid of the lot. Lemon, a man in his late seventies, no sooner sat at his desk in the trailer office when half a dozen auto crime investigators, led by a lieutenant, came swarming in to take him at gunpoint.

"What the . . .?" asked the stunned business owner.

"Be quiet and get up against the wall," shouted the closest investigator.

"What's this all about?" asked Lemon as he felt hands about his body searching for a weapon.

Noticing that the person being arrested was a man of advanced years, the lieutenant intervened in the apprehension. "Ease up, guys. Just empty his pockets, cuff him and sit him down," ordered the boss.

"I got aspirin there in my pocket," advised Lemon. "I got a bad headache. Can I take a couple?"

"You need to go to a hospital?" asked the lieutenant.

"No, I just need some aspirin. There is some water in my refrigerator."

The lieutenant got the water and front cuffed his prisoner. As Lemon took the aspirin and drank the water, the lieutenant could see that his hand was trembling.

"Relax," said the supervisor. "This is nothing to work yourself up over."

Lemon was read his rights by one of the investigators. The prisoner felt increasing unease with each Miranda warning. Every police utterance of "You have the right to . . ." was counseling that only deepened the aged prisoner's distress. Noticing how exceedingly nervous Lemon seemed to be, the lieutenant became concerned that the business owner just might drop dead on him.

"Don't get excited. This isn't a murder charge you're facing," said the lieutenant. "Have you ever been arrested before?"

"No. I've never been arrested."

"Then relax. There is nothing for you to worry about. This is no big deal. All the detectives are going to do is talk to you. If you don't want to talk to them, you don't have to." The words that were meant to calm the senior citizen were limited in their effectiveness.

It all came to a head after Lemon's worst nightmare materialized. An investigator unearthed half a dozen loaded guns and multiple knives that were secreted in an old file cabinet buried under some blankets. The business owner had amassed these weapons from the stolen cars he had received over the years. Lemon never quite understood why a car thief would neglect to search a vehicle they took to him. He capitalized on their lack of thoroughness by selling the weapons from time to time. The discovery of the guns was particularly devastating to Lemon because he didn't know their history. Since his fingerprints were on each gun, his greatest fear was that there might be a murder attached to some of the firearms.

Lemon was a practical man who realized that he was likely facing incarceration. Regardless of how distasteful, he pondered the feasibility of striking a deal with the law. His mind became made up when the police discovered yet another gun. The loaded German Luger he kept in his desk drawer had been given to him by his brother-in-law for protection. Knowing Monte, there was no telling the history connected to the Luger.

"So where did you get all these guns from?" asked the lieutenant.

"They aren't mine," replied Lemon.

"Whose are they, then?" asked the lieutenant. "Mine? You'll have plenty of time to remember when you're spending your golden years doing a stretch rather than in the Florida sunshine."

Lemon turned his head away when he overheard the loud voices of several investigators coming through the open door.

"Don't worry about finding a VIN on that Porsche in the back. Just take a look at the leather under the door handle," shouted the first voice. "See that cigarette burn?"

"Perfect!" said the second voice. "No Porsche owner is gonna forget that imperfection. We'll check the FBI list for every stolen black Porsche and call every owner. Whoever this car belongs to will definitely remember the burn mark and identify his car."

After hearing this conversation, Lemon asked to speak to the lieutenant privately.

"What's up, Lemon?" asked the lieutenant.

"Can we talk?"

"Talk," answered the supervising officer.

A puzzled look came over the prisoner when it dawned on him that the lieutenant knew his nickname.

"How do you know I'm called Lemon?"

"That was the information we received. Someone dropped a dime on you."

" Look, Lieutenant, jail isn't exactly on my bucket list. Can I get a straight answer from you?"

"Ask your question."

"If I decided to join your team . . . would it *really* do me any good? I don't want to go to jail."

"That depends on what you have to say."

"I got plenty to say," noted Lemon, adding, "Enough to get me killed if I'm found out by *some* people."

"Life is a risk."

"I know that. I just don't want to die in the jail."

The lieutenant could tell that Lemon wasn't really a hardened criminal. "Let me be as truthful as possible. You'll be at the mercy of a judge who may or may not take into consideration your age."

Lemon's face dropped. "So what are you telling me to do?"

"I'm not *telling* you anything. I'm saying that if you cooperate, you'll have a shot at their going easy."

"No jail?"

"I can't answer that with accuracy because I really don't know. It'll depend on the information."

"Don't worry about that. I got *good* information for you if I sign on."

"You'll have to do better than keeping me happy," said the lieutenant. "I'm not the person who you need to satisfy. Frankly, nobody gets too excited over what we do over at auto crime."

Lemon's face tightened at hearing this news. "I'm not talking about auto crimes. I have information about a murder that rocked this town."

"Now, that's singing in the right key. What have you got?"

"Yeah, I figured that would get your attention. Can I ask you another question, Lieutenant?"

"What?"

"How did you find out about me? I was always pretty careful."

"I already told you; somebody dropped a dime on you," answered the lieutenant. "You must have pissed someone off."

"I don't get it. I make it a point to never piss anyone off. I'm even good to the guys in the precinct here."

"Never mind about that," said the lieutenant, cutting him off. He didn't want to hear anything about Lemon's relationship with the local precinct. "Talk to me about the murder."

Lemon shook his head with disgust. "What a choice I have . . . jail if I don't talk and bullets if I do!"

"Bullets?" asked the lieutenant. "If mob guys are involved, it'll be all the better for you."

Lemon took a moment to think. He sized up the lieutenant closely, arriving at the decision that he could probably be trusted. "You may be too young, but did you ever hear about that soldier who went missing years ago? They called him the man who went on the drill of no return."

"I know of the case. There are missing person posters still hanging in the precincts. I wasn't even on the force when that guy took off."

"Well, he didn't exactly take off, Lieutenant. He was *knocked* off . . . and I know who did it."

The lieutenant looked at Lemon seriously. "You do?"

"Lieutenant, my life is at stake here. I'm prepared to go all the way with you *if* it's in my interest."

"Are we talking mob guys?"

"Yeah, I'm talking important people."

"Sit tight," said the lieutenant. "I want to reach out to someone I know."

The lieutenant picked up the phone and dialed police headquarters to speak with Lieutenant Wright.

After Wright learned that Lemon could provide information on the missing soldier, he immediately reached out to Chief of Detectives Harry McCoy. McCoy was thrilled at the prospect of solving the decades-long mystery. Closing the case with positive results would certainly be a feather in the cap of his detective division. Politically inclined, McCoy knew that cracking such a newsworthy case would play big in the press. After he directed Lieutenant Wright to put Markie and Von Hess on the case he sat back in his chair and smiled with satisfaction. He was envisioning e himself publicly announcing that "We always get our man."

########

BACK AT THE BROWNSVILLE CAR LOT, Lemon and the lieutenant waited patiently for Markie and Von Hess to arrive. Knowing that it would be a long wait, they made themselves as comfortable as possible while the auto crime investigators continued with their work in the lot.

"You play rummy?" asked Lemon.

"No, I never really learned to play cards," replied the lieutenant.

"You want to learn?"

"Not really. I'm not a gambler. How about we put on the television?"

10

Let's Make A Deal

MARKIE BEGAN TO HEAR HIS CAR RATTLE after he reached a certain speed. The strain on the engine concerned him but not enough for him to slow down. Anxious to begin work on his new assignment, he was determined to get home from Myrtle Beach as soon as possible. The annoying wind that whistled through the window slit aroused Alley from her sleep. After raising the window, Markie's girlfriend looked through gritty eyes at the scenery whizzing by.

"Where's the fire?" she asked.

"I have to get to work, so I'm trying to make some time."

"Is that a reason to get us killed?"

"Go back to sleep," he replied without turning to look at her. He found her to be a distraction.

Alley closed her eyes and faced the window. Life with the sergeant had taught her that there wasn't any room for idle conversation once he became focused on work. His job was a force she couldn't compete with; it always came first. As the miles traveled accumulated, she grew increasingly annoyed by his lack of communication. Her efforts at initiating a dialogue were met with abbreviated responses. By the time they reached Brooklyn, the tension was running high. When Markie braked abruptly in front of Alley's building, the car came to a jerking stop, causing Alley's head to spring forward.

"HEY!" she shouted. "What are you trying to do, snap my neck?"

"Sorry about that," he answered.

Markie hurried to gather Alley's luggage from the trunk. Standing on the sidewalk with her belongings in tow, it irked him to see that she was still sitting in the car. He found her lack of expediency stressful enough to say something.

"C'mon, shake a leg, will ya?" he said impatiently.

Markie opened the car door in an effort to move her along. Taking the hint, Alley hastened her departure from the vehicle. As they proceeded to her building, Markie began to gently bump the suitcase he was carrying against Alley's backside to keep her in motion.

"Stop pushing me!" she said nastily.

"I'm trying to get you moving!"

In answer to Markie's rude behavior, she began moving slower. Frustrated, Markie briskly stepped ahead of her. Now several feet in front of Alley, he turned around to look back. "If you want to lag, lag!"

"Who's lagging? I'm coming!"

"I'll leave the luggage upstairs by your door."

Alley was two flights behind him when Markie reached her apartment door. He put the luggage down and hustled down the stairs. "I gotta run. I'll call you," he said without stopping.

Detective Oliver Von Hess was parked outside Markie's residence, waiting patiently for his boss. He was doing the crossword puzzle in the newspaper when the sergeant arrived home.

"What do you say, Ollie?" greeted Markie from the sidewalk. "Do you want to come in?"

"That's alright, boss. I'll wait here. I was surprised to get your call. You made good time."

"Yeah, I gunned it coming home. I won't be long. I just have to clean up and get dressed."

"Want coffee, boss?"

"That would be great."

By the time Von Hess got back from the store, Markie was outside waiting.

"How was Myrtle Beach, Sarge?"

"We had a good time. So what's the deal with this caper?"

"The grease monkeys made a pinch. They're holding a guy in a Brownsville car lot. Supposedly he has information on the Cornell Mathis missing person case. Do you know about that case, Sarge?"

"I do, it's another Judge Crater caper," said Markie, referring to the New York Supreme Court judge who was reported missing many decades prior to Mathis.

"Correct."

"Who is the snitch, Ollie?"

"I have no idea. All I know is that he was arrested by auto crime for stolen cars and a gun arsenal."

"Is there big interest in this missing person case?"

"You know Chief McCoy, he'll pull out all the stops for good press."

"Does anyone suspect foul play?"

"Nobody really has a clue one way or the other, boss. Everybody seems to think that Mathis just took off to get away from his old lady."

"Did he empty out his bank accounts?"

"I've got no idea. You know as much as I do."

When the investigators arrived at the Brownsville car lot, they met with the auto crime lieutenant who apprised them accordingly.

"What kind of guy is he?" asked Markie.

"He's actually not such a bad guy, at least from what I can tell."

"What's he doing with the guns, then?"

"You'll have to figure that out when you talk to him."

"Where is he?" asked Von Hess.

"He's inside the office watching television with one of my men. I'll take you to him."

Markie noted that the prisoner was neatly groomed and had hands that were callus free. The sport jacket and pipe on the office desk gave Lemon something of an intellectual image. After the introductions were made, Markie and Von Hess were left alone with the prisoner.

Before taking a seat to talk, Markie glanced at the television. "That's an old one," he commented, referring to the screen adaptation of W. Somerset Maugham's novel *Of Human Bondage*. "Just take a look at this next scene," he said, digressing from the business at hand.

The three men watched as the actress Bette Davis cruelly raged against the clubfooted medical student she had been taking advantage of. With great animation, she wiped her mouth with the back of her hand, declaring that this was what she did after kissing him..

"She was sensational in this movie," said Markie.

"Right *now* I got other things on my mind," said the prisoner, wondering what was wrong with Markie.

Lemon's comment embarrassed the sergeant enough for him to shut off the television. Markie opened the interview by trying to show that he and Detective Von Hess were not judgmental.

"You don't seem like someone who's spent much time in handcuffs," said Markie.

Lemon shrugged his shoulders. "What more can I say other than I'm a victim of circumstance?"

Markie offered no rebuttal. "I hear you. Shit happens sometimes."

"You're not the first guy who got caught up," injected Von Hess.

"Yeah, I suppose not," agreed Lemon.

The prisoner evaluated the two investigators as they engaged him in conversation. Lemon was sophisticated enough to know that he was being played but respected the palatable way in which the detectives fashioned their talk. Having been around the criminal element, Lemon trusted his own judgment when it came to reading people. Since the detectives looked him straight in the eye, he concluded that Markie and Von Hess didn't seem the sort who would perpetrate a double cross.

"Look, I'd be willing to work with you guys," said Lemon. "But before I commit, we need to come to some kind of an understanding. I need to know what's in it for *me*."

"I'm not going to give you any false assurances," conveyed the sergeant honestly. "All I *can* promise to do is talk to the district attorney's office on your behalf. I can ask the DA to be lenient with you. But to be clear, for that to happen, you have to have something that tickles his interest."

"I get that."

"They'll loosen the screws, but only if *we* can dangle a carrot that they want. That's the way things work." Markie was being clever with his choice of words. He intentionally used the word "we" to subtly convey that theirs was a collective effort.

"I got the key to unlock the Cornell Mathis National Guard case for you. How is that for a carrot?"

"Sufficient," replied Markie.

"I'll fill you in, but you have to give me the right return on my investment," stated Lemon.

"What do you think the information is worth?" asked the sergeant.

"Enough for me walk away with no jail time," replied the prisoner.

Markie reacted as if unaffected by the prisoner's expectation. He casually turned to look at Von Hess, waiting for the detective to weigh in.

"Look, let's not get ahead of ourselves," injected Von Hess. "How about you give us a general idea of the particulars?"

Lemon remained mute as he pondered how to respond. Finally, it was Markie who broke the impasse, putting Lemon on the defensive.

"Let's put this in its proper perspective," he said. "First of all, what are you doing with all the guns?"

Lemon swallowed hard at the question. "Sometimes when I get cars, I find them inside the vehicles."

"So that justifies you having them?"

"What am I supposed to do with them?"

"Guns translate into a serious rap," noted Von Hess.

"I know. That's why I'm looking for a deal."

"Alright, then, what choices have you got? How about you give it to us in small pieces?" said the sergeant. "We'll evaluate the worth of what you tell us bite by bite as we receive it. If we're on the same page, we'll continue on. If not, you can clam up at any point with no hard feelings."

"Look, Sergeant . . . I'm not trying to be unreasonable. I'm just not looking to screw myself."

"C'mon, man. We understand that it's your neck in the noose," assured Markie. "Nobody here is out to burn you. Look at us. Career wise we're an inch away from feeding the pigeons in some park."

"The sergeant's being honest with you," added Von Hess. "We got no illusion of going up some ladder. We're in the late innings. Why would we look to con you?"

After some thought, Lemon relented. "Okay, I'll take a chance," declared Lemon.

"Is the soldier alive or dead?" asked Von Hess.

"He's gone."

"That's a start," said the detective. "What were the circumstances? Do you know?"

"What if I was to tell you he was murdered by mob guys?" asked Lemon.

The detectives noted how easily the prisoner's words flowed. His fluidness suggested truthfulness.

"Murdered by the mob?" Impressed, Markie bit down on his lower lip. "I think it's safe to say we're in business."

"Are we?" Lemon asked, now seeking to find out how he would benefit from an arrangement.

Markie spoke as honestly as possible. "I can't make you any promises. *But* I'd be untruthful if I didn't say that I'm optimistic that we can do business with the DA if we can unravel this murder."

"No jail?"

"Just give us the story," encouraged Markie. "Once we know more, we'll know exactly how to present it to the DA so that it's in your best interest."

"That's right," injected Von Hess. "Once we get all the facts, we can advise you on what to hold out for . . . and that's square business."

Seeing no alternatives, Lemon agreed. "Alright, I'm in your hands. Continue with the questions."

"How do you know the sergeant was murdered?" Von Hess asked. "Did you actually see it?"

"No, I didn't see the murder . . . but I know it definitely happened."

"Someone told you about it? Somebody admitted it to you?"

"No, it was nothing like that."

"Then how do you know?"

"On the day before it came out that the soldier was missing, these two young guys came into my lot to drop off a car. They practically put a gun to my head to make it disappear."

"You knew them?"

"Yeah, I knew them. I had a business relationship with them."

"What kind of business relationship?"

"They would bring me hot cars."

"And . . . ?"

"The car they dropped off that day was the car that was later reported in the papers. It was the missing solder's car."

"How are you so sure of this?"

"The license plate reported in the paper matched the plate I took off the car."

"Who are these guys?" asked Markie.

"They're the James Brothers."

"And who exactly are the James Brothers?"

"At that time they were young buck bandits who stole cars," answered Lemon. "I was the one who tagged them with the nickname Frank and Jesse James."

"So what's their real name?"

"I never knew their last name. They're brothers, so I always called them the James Brothers."

"Do you know their first names?"

"Yeah, of course I do. They're Chris and Jasper."

"How did you come to know them?"

"I forget exactly. Anyway, I always paid well, so whenever they had a car to unload, they'd come to me."

"You ordered the soldier's car stolen?" asked Von Hess.

"No, no, no! They caught me by surprise with that. They just showed up at the lot with the car. I was pissed off that they didn't call me first. I never like surprises."

"Did they tell you that they'd committed a murder when you took the car from them?" asked Markie.

"They never mentioned a word about murder or the soldier. All they said was that they were in a spot and that I had to get rid of the car. I pieced it together later."

"How did you do that?"

"Tell you the truth, at first I figured it for just some kind of a rip-off."

"What made you think it was a rip-off?" asked Markie.

"Jesse was wearing this ring on his pinkie. It was a wolf head ring, a very unusual piece because the wolf had emerald eyes and one ear. It was very unique. Anyway, Frank flipped when he saw that Jessie had the ring on. He made him take it right off. That's why I figured somebody got ripped off."

"Which one is Jesse again?" asked Von Hess.

"Jasper is Jesse. Chris is Frank."

"So when did you find out it was murder?" asked Markie.

"When the story hit the papers that the soldier was missing, I put it together. They must've killed him."

"That made you assume *they* killed him?" asked Markie.

"No, Sergeant, you didn't get the whole story yet. Let me finish."

"Enlighten me."

"The James Brothers showed up in army uniforms," advised Lemon. "They came to the lot in fatigues. The newspaper reported that there were two soldiers with the missing sergeant at the armory that day. I figured right off that they must have gotten into a beef with him. If you read the old news accounts, the details will all be there."

"I do remember some of that, Sarge," said Von Hess.

"What did you do with the car?"

"I called my brother-in-law in Bayonne to come get it. He had some guys in a truck come to take it to his junkyard, where he got rid of it. His place did that kind of work in those days."

"Why didn't you just tell them to take the car to your brother-in-law directly?" asked Von Hess.

"It didn't work like that. Their history was with me. Besides, they trusted me."

"Is your brother-in-law around?" asked Markie.

"No, he's been dead awhile."

"Are the James Brothers still alive?" asked Markie.

"Jesse is definitely alive. Frank . . . that's Chris . . . got sick and died sometime back."

"Do you know what this Jesse has been up to lately?"

"He's got businesses. Those boys ended up making a ton of money. They own a string of Laundromats as well as other legitimate businesses. I heard Jesse bought a bar on Third Avenue in Bay Ridge."

"You know the name of the bar?"

"It's called the James Brothers Saloon. You want to know something else?"

"Shoot."

"When they came around as kids, I taught them the ins and outs about running a business. How about that? I should have been smarter . . . and maybe gone in with them."

"Are you saying they went legit?"

"I can't say that 100 percent. From what I heard, they may be dabbling in dope."

"You know that for a fact?"

"No, that's only what I heard. The kids who come around here with cars keep me up on what's happening. They all smoke pot and snort coke. They hear everything that goes on in the street."

"Do you still see Jesse?" asked Von Hess.

"Last time I saw him was at a friend's Christmas party."

"Whose party was that?"

Lemon paused before answering. "Does that really make a difference?"

Von Hess frowned. "Whose party?" he repeated.

Lemon could see that Von Hess wasn't giving him an inch. "Silky Seggio," he finally answered.

The investigators looked at each other and then back at Lemon. They recognized the name as that of a major organized crime figure.

"Do you have anything to back up your story in terms of proof? This is not for us. We believe you. I'm thinking ahead just in case there is pushback from the DA."

"It's good that you think ahead, Sarge. I do the same thing. After I read about the soldier, I figured that knowing what I knew might be valuable someday. So I took steps to have a bargaining chip just in case I ever needed one, if you get my drift."

"What steps were those?"

"I kept the license plates of that car they brought to me. That's my proof."

"You still have the plates?"

"The plates are in my basement at home on Staten Island."

"Beautiful," said Markie. "Sit tight a minute."

The sergeant reached out to a friendly bureau chief over at the office of the Brooklyn district attorney. He received assurance that Lemon's case would be adjourned for as long as necessary.

"We're in luck. You'll be out after your arraignment," Markie advised.

"My charges are going to be dropped?" asked Lemon hopefully.

" The case will be adjourned until we finish the work we have to do."

"What do you need from me, Sergeant?"

"First we sign you up as a confidential informant. Then we go get those plates. After that, we get you arraigned. When you get released you just go back to your car lot and operate legitimately. If anybody asks, you tell them that your case got adjourned and you're going straight until it's cleared up.

"That's it?"

"All you have to do is sit tight until you hear from us. We'll be in touch."

11

The James Brothers Saloon

BUSTER ROMAN HAD BEEN A BORDERLINE YOUNG HOOD when he came to the attention of Silky Seggio. He became big news in the neighborhood after boldly interrupting a middle-of-the-night home invasion of the house he shared with his parents. A light sleeper, he heard intruders tampering with the front door. Buster's subsequent investigation resulted in his firing multiple shots at the burglars as he chased them down a Brooklyn street in his underwear. Impressed by this, Silky sent men to bring Buster to his club. Aware of the gangster's prominence, Buster welcomed the opportunity to meet with someone he considered to be a criminal icon. Soon after, he signed on as member of Silky's crew. Now, many years later, Silky was faced with the need for someone capable of managing the new bar he had purchased with Jasper. The silent partner thought of Buster as being a good fit. Silky arranged a meeting between Jasper and Buster in his social club office.

"Jasper, I know that you're in need of a manager at *your* bar. I think it's a good idea that you and Buster get together," said Silky, who never let on that he held a half interest in the business.

"Yeah, Silky, I've been looking for someone," said Jasper, playing along.

"You can depend on Buster to keep the peace. He's also got the brains to run the day-to-day bar operation and whatever else you plan on doing over there."

Jasper nodded agreeably. "Great," he said. He knew Silky was referring to the gambling that was going to be taking place in the cellar of the bar.

"Is this something you have an interest in, Buster?" asked Silky.

"If you say so, I do," replied Buster.

"See, Jasper? You're getting a loyal man. Work out the numbers., okay?" Both men acquiesced.

Designated as the owner of record for the James Brothers Saloon was an old-school Seggio loyalist named Johnny Blondell. For a stipend of five hundred dollars a week, Johnny gladly signed on to look after Silky's interests at the bar. Blondell was a killer who had once been acquitted of murder. Thanks to an astute attorney, this arrest had been sealed by the court, basically leaving him with a clean record. A binge drinker, Blondell's erratic behavior was what stood in the way of advancement in the mob. Having murdered together as young men, Silky considered him to be his most loyal friend. Blondell was the only crew member with knowledge of *all* of Silky's interests, including the drug initiative with Jasper.

#########

IT WAS AT THE WEDDING OF A mutual friend that Buster first got friendly with Spanky. Even though they both worked for Jasper, they rarely interacted. Fueled by alcohol, both men talked openly.

"I have to ask, are you getting a fair shake over there at the James Brothers Saloon?" asked Spanky.

"I'm working for what I'm getting, that's for sure. Why?"

"I've been getting screwed by Jasper from the beginning," lamented Spanky, the first to convey that he was disgruntled.

"What's your business with him?"

"Cocaine," whispered Spanky. "Major deals."

"I didn't know Jasper was in the drug business," said Buster. "That could be dangerous."

"We're careful," replied Spanky. "You got a problem with the drug business?"

"Personally, I don't care what a man does to make money. The only thing I'll say is that if Silky ever finds out, it just might be too bad. Pushing drugs is against the rules."

"I don't know anything about Silky or any rules," admitted Spanky. "All I know is that I'm the whole freaking business and I'm getting peanuts," advised Spanky. "I've running back and forth between here and Vegas, where Jasper's got me holding hands with some bitch."

"You may not know the rules, but Jasper does." Buster went on to shed some light on Jasper's association with Silky and the Palsy-Walsy Social Club.

"See, that's another thing! I ain't privy to any of that," said Spanky.

"Don't feel so bad, I'm getting a shafting at the bar," admitted Buster. "I manage the joint. I handle the gambling. I loan out money *and* even go out and collect from the deadbeats. For what I do for this guy, he's paying me peanuts! I even mentioned this to Silky; he's the one who put me in with Jasper in the first place. He tells me I gotta work it out with Jasper. I feel like a chump."

"We just may have to start looking out for ourselves," said Spanky, planting a seed. It took.

By the end of the night Spanky and Buster agreed to partake in a joint venture designed to better their financial situation. The double-crossing drug dealer put forth a partnership proposition in which he would provide the cocaine and Buster would sell it in small quantities to recreational users. Spanky neglected to inform Buster that it was Jasper's cocaine that they would be cutting and drawing from. Neither man was aware of Silky's actual financial interest in the drug enterprise.

"We just have to be careful that Jasper doesn't find out," warned Spanky.

"Jasper doesn't worry me; Silky does. The old man will have my head if he finds out I'm selling drugs.Remember that technically, I'm with Silky."

##########

WHEN MONEY STARTED COMING IN FROM THE DRUG TRANSACTIONS, Las Vegas Lucy felt better about her decision to align herself with Jasper. Among her business leads was a former motorcycle gang member she had always gotten along well with. She had heard that he was now making an honest living as a self-employed mechanic. After tracking him down, she contacted him telephonically.

"Hey, handsome . . . guess who this is?" she asked when he picked up the phone.

"I haven't got a clue. . . ."

"It's Lucy, the love of your life," she flirted.

"Lucy! How the hell are you?"

"I'm good. I hear you've been behaving yourself."

"You heard right. I settled down and got married. I even have a couple of kids, the whole bit."

"Good for you!"

"What about you? What have you been doing?"

"Well, that's what I wanted to talk to you about. I have a proposition that may interest you."

"I've been a good boy, Lucy. Everything has been above board with me these days."

"Don't get nervous. You'll still be a good boy. There's no risk in this." As expected, he accepted her invitation to meet for a drink.

When they met, Lucy was surprised to see that her old friend's appearance had greatly improved since she had last seen him. He was neatly groomed, had a new set of teeth, and had lost some of his bulk.

"You haven't changed a bit, Lucy. You're as beautiful as ever."

Lucy was hoping to hear that. His noticing would make things easier. "I try," she replied.

"Incarceration takes a toll on a lot of people," he said, "but not you."

"I did my time and came out of it alright. I see that you survived jail pretty well."

"Yeah, one stretch was all it took to straighten me out. Now it's all about work and home for me."

When Lucy got around to conveying that she was now in the cocaine business, the mechanic took it calmly without any reaction. "Just be careful, Lucy," was all he had to say about it.

"Since you fix bikes, you must still see a lot of people, right?"

"That's true."

"Can you think of anybody who'd be interested in doing kilo business? All I'm looking for is a referral. I'll cut you in for something, of course."

"I might. There is this one guy who may have an interest."

"You know someone?" she asked anxiously.

"Maybe I do. A few weeks ago I overheard a customer bitching to another guy. They were having their bikes fixed. He was saying how things were drying up for him. They were talking about drugs."

"Do I know him?"

"Not likely. He comes in to see me from Baker, California."

"Can I meet him?"

"Look, Lucy, I'm not looking to get too involved in this," he advised. "The guy is bringing his bike in next Monday. If you drop in to say hello, I can introduce you to him as a friend. You take it from there."

"Thanks. That's all I want." Lucy then gave him a peck on the cheek and said, "I'll see you Monday."

The introduction proved to be a very profitable one for Lucy. She boarded the airplane bound for New York quite happy. She was on her way to turn in money and collect her commission. Once seated, she closed her eyes and rested her head back in her seat contemplating future riches.

"Did you say something?" asked Lucy, hearing a voice that seemed to be directed at her.

"I said that it's a great day for flying," said the woman seated next to her. Lucy smiled politely without answering. "That's an interesting piece you have," commented the woman, admiring the miniature police shield Lucy wore on a silver neck chain. "Are you with the police?"

"No, but my brother is," Lucy lied.

Lucy took to wearing the piece regularly. She did so to give the impression that she had a connection to law enforcement. She feared running into a suspicious cop somewhere along the line. Her hope was that the miniature shield would work to curtail police suspicion. Lucy noticed that the woman wore no wedding band. The cut of her hair, stylish outfit, and fashionable sunglasses all suggested that the passenger put effort into looking good. The tautness of the skin on her face was an indication of her having undergone some cosmetic surgery. Lucy was impressed enough to wonder who the doctor was that had performed the work. The drug dealer considered such maintenance at a certain point in life to be money well spent. The drug dealer thought that the woman alongside her had the look of someone who might favor cocaine. She sent out a feeler to find out. "New York is a real *party town. Do you party?*" asked Lucy.

By the time the plane was making the descent at Kennedy Airport, Lucy knew all about the much older married plastic surgeon her new acquaintance was going to see. Lucy also gathered that the surgeon furnished her fellow passenger with all the recreational feel-good drugs she would ever need.

"What about his wife?"

"She knows all about our arrangement. As long as her little world doesn't topple, she's okay with it. I honestly think she sees it like I'm doing her a favor . . . you know, less wear and tear on her."

"Clearly you can get lots of men," complimented Lucy, "But what do you really get out of it?"

Lucy's new friend laughed aloud. "Use your imagination, honey," she said as she stroked the gold watch she wore.

Lucy stared at her own watch. The contrast caused her to start thinking. Soon she would be meeting with Jasper, in whom she now saw further opportunities.

########

BREAKING OUT OF SYRIA'S TADMOR PRISON wasn't easily accomplished. However, torture, executions, and human rights violations were great incentives for the three political dissidents to take risks. It took striking a man over the head with a pipe and great trickery to enable the escape of the trio. The youngest escapee was an eighteen-year-old who felt he could travel faster on his own once on the outside. After committing a series of thefts, he eventually acquired the capital necessary to arrange travel to the United States. The harsh realities connected to pursuing political ideals convinced the teenager to abandon his quest for change. Once arriving on American soil, Mustafa Derki found it necessary to sleep at the airport terminal for several days. A break came when he met a compassionate countryman who pitied him. Through the intervention of the stranger, he secured work off the books at a car wash in Coney Island. Mustafa slept nights in a sleeping bag in the car wash storage room. A fateful chance meeting turned things around for him. Jasper, who was having his car cleaned, took notice of how Mustafa jumped to attention whenever his name was called by the car wash manager. Mustafa's movements reminded Jasper of a scared mouse. Jasper, who possessed compassion for boys coming from disadvantaged circumstances, felt the need to do something for the teenager.

"Hey, kid. How would you like to get out of this dump?" asked Jasper.

Jasper's intervention was similar to how Silky had taken him under his questionable wing decades prior. One of the first things Jasper did was to give Mustafa a nickname. The illegal alien was dubbed Mousey. Like many nicknames, it stuck. Jasper put Mousey to work in one of his Laundromats, where there was a spare room large enough for the teenager to call home. As Jasper's protégé, Mousey felt blessed. In return for Jasper's largesse, Mousey exhibited extreme devotion to his employer. His fealty was comparable to the loyalty of a large canine rescued from a small cage in a kennel by a kind master. Mousey went on to be Jasper's troubleshooting mole who bounced from Laundromat to Laundromat. Eventually Mousey graduated to being the person in charge of every Laundromat. He was so effective in his duties that when Jasper opened the James Brothers Saloon, Mousey was reassigned to "learn the ropes of the bar business." A major part of this transfer had to do with keeping an eye out for any in-house thievery.

Jasper visited the bar specifically to see how Mousey was doing. With him was Spanky. Jasper signaled to Buster to join him in the back of the bar for a private word.

"Who are those two guys sitting at the bar? They look like cops."

Buster looked at the two men. "I know them. They're regulars who work in the neighborhood."

"Where do they work?"

"They work for Zelhoyt Movers."

"Good," said Jasper, now satisfied. "You've been looking out for the Mouse, right?"

"Definitely, I'm showing him the ropes just like you want. The kid is doing great."

"Good. I want he should know everything in case we ever open another place. Where is he now?"

"I sent him out to buy a few decks of cards for the game tonight," replied Buster.

When Jasper finished talking to Buster, he rejoined Spanky, who had been waiting for him at the front of the bar. Seeing Jasper and Buster speaking privately put Spanky on edge. He feared that the bar owner might be getting wise to his sneak partnership with Buster.

"Everything alright, Jasper?" asked Spanky.

"Yeah, it's all good. Don't forget, you have to go pick up Lucy at the airport."

"I know."

"Bring her right to the hotel after you get her. I'll be there waiting."

"I figured as much. She must really be worth it."

"She'll do," replied Jasper. Jasper, who had never gotten over his suspicions of Spanky, noticed how well his underling was dressed. "So how do you like the new wheels you bought?"

Spanky perked up. "This Corvette is the best car I've ever owned."

"What made you get yellow?"

"My wife has a black Jeep, so I wanted to get something sporty looking."

"But yellow? That'll be a tough car to unload when you go to sell it. How many people are gonna want a canary yellow Corvette?"

Spanky shrugged. "I'm not worried about it. I love the color."

"Pretty expensive car," noted Jasper.

"Yeah, but you only live once."

Beneath the surface of what seemed like a casual conversation, Jasper harbored concerns over Spanky's purchase of the Corvette. Adding to his worry was some talk about Spanky's having an eye on a larger house. These were red flags. Where was the money coming from all of a sudden? Sure, Spanky was making nice money . . . but enough to float these extras? Spanky's sole income was supposedly coming from his commissions in the drug business, and Jasper *knew* what that came to. Jasper had plenty of money from his diversified interests so he could afford to live large, but how could Spanky? This was a question that Jasper felt needed answering.

"Here comes Mousey. Let me have a word with him privately before we go," said Jasper. Determined to find out if Spanky was up to something, he decided to put Mousey on the case.

"Look, Mousey, I need you to keep an eye on Spanky for me whenever he comes around."

"No problem, Jasper."

"Matter of fact, keep an eye on all these bastards."

"I got it covered."

After Jasper left with Spanky, Buster walked over to the two men who were drinking at the bar.

"How are you boys doing?" asked the bar manager. "Need anything special?"

"Things are good," answered one of the men. Then, rising from his chair, he whispered, "Could you fix us up with some blow for the weekend?"

"No problem," replied Buster, foolishly doing business inside the James Brothers Saloon under the curious eye of Mousey.

##########

ALLEY CAT ARRIVED AT THE HAIR SALON EARLY to get her hair cut. She sat in a chair reading a fashion magazine while waiting her turn. Her attention was distracted by the boasting of a customer who was getting her hair done. Speaking loud enough for others to hear, the content of the customer's conversation had to do with her husband, their children and the vacations they took. Alley recognized the security that came with the symbolic gold band the woman wore on her finger. The sight of the ring caused her to reflect on her relationship with Markie. While Alley was a self-reliant woman, there were nevertheless times she lapsed into moments of insecurity. She certainly didn't *need* Markie. She had long proven that she was resilient enough to stand up to any hardship thrown her way. Her solo migration from London with limited funds proved that. Yet there was no denying that the institution of marriage afforded certain reassurances. As far as Markie himself went as a man, she loved him, warts and all. The fact that he had no money to speak of and plenty of baggage, including kids and an ex-wife, didn't diminish that affection. Absorbed in such thoughts, she was surprised when the haircutter called out her name to take a seat in the chair.

When finished at the hair salon, Alley proceeded to her bartending job at Fitzie's. Fitzie was behind the stick pouring beers for several of his regular patrons when she arrived. After placing fresh refills in front of a crowd of men living their lives decades behind the times, the former fighter resumed holding court. This time he recreated Floyd Patterson's controversial loss to Joey Maxim at the Eastern Parkway Arena in 1954. Fitzie had all the particulars down pat as he recounted the bout, round by round, to his audience. Alley Cat, careful not to break the flow of Fitzie's narrative, simply waved hello as she passed him on her way to the back of the bar. Seeing the old-time pug crouched down with his fists up around his eyes, imitating Patterson's peek-a-boo boxing style, caused her to smile. As was her custom, she was almost an hour early for work. She used the free time to reach out to Markie.

"It's me. What are you doing?"

"I'm working," answered Markie. "When are you leaving for work?"

"I'm at the bar now waiting to hear how the Patterson–Maxim bout turns out."

"I think that was won by Maxim."

"Don't ruin it for me!"

"Are you over your snit?"

"My snit?" she asked with great surprise at the question.

Markie chucked. "You know how I get. I'll come by tonight when I'm done, okay?"

"Are you staying over?" she asked.

"*Certainly*, I'm staying over. I'm off tomorrow," he answered.

Alley was glad he was coming by after work to pick her up because she had something to talk to him about. The couple went directly to Alley's apartment after she finished work. They weren't there more than five minutes before Alley set upon him as if she were a striking panther. Markie hadn't seen such passion on her end since the beginning of their relationship. When they rose the next morning, Alley prepared a breakfast for him consisting of coffee, toast, and scrambled eggs with ham.

"What kind of vitamins have you been taking?" he asked.

"Are you complaining, luv?" she asked coyly.

"No ma'am. No argument on this end."

Alley watched him as he ate. She sipped her tea, wondering if the time was right. The sergeant noticed the funny way Alley was looking at him. "What's up?" he asked.

"Nothing's up."

"C'mon, I know that look. What's on your mind?"

Alley Cat decided that she would go for it. "I was thinking we should get married."

Markie's mouth dropped open. Marriage was a topic he hadn't expected to hear about. The sergeant immediately started to back away. "Married?" he asked, gulping. "What brings this on all of a sudden?"

"Is it such a terrible idea?" she asked. "What's the big deal? You do love me, don't you?"

"Well, of course I do . . . but for God's sake, I haven't been divorced all that long."

"It's been plenty long. What are you talking about? You spend half the time here anyway. We go away together and everything, don't we?"

Markie didn't like being pushed into a corner. "Look, Alley, forget it. I'm not ever getting married again . . . TO ANYBODY!"

The emphatic rejection tore at Alley. She felt the crumbling sensation in her eyeballs that always preceded tears. She tried desperately to control her emotions, but the effort fell short. The pained look on her face made her state of mind obvious. Seeing her eyes fill up caused Markie to feel his own eyes give way to emotion. He promptly stood from the table and turned away to avoid Alley seeing this sensitive side of him. Emotions weren't a sufficient enough force to alter his position on marrying a second time.

"Is it because you don't think I'm good enough to marry?" asked Alley, now revealing her insecurity. It was the first time Markie had ever seen her so vulnerable.

"What are you, crazy? I'm lucky you ever even talked to me," he replied.

His words made her feel a little bit better. "Then what is it?" she asked.

Markie had no answer for her, at least not one he was willing to share. When he thought of marriage, regardless of their differences, he thought of only one woman . . . Florence. Divorced or not, *she* was his wife, the mother of his children. This was one area in which Markie exhibited tremendous inflexibility.

"Look, Alley, let's talk about this another time. I have to go home and get ready for work. I'll call you," he said, knowing that it would be awhile before he actually would.

Alley Cat watched him leave without saying another word. She knew he was running away. She also knew that this was his day off.

12

A Tangled Web

SINCE JASPER HAD NEVER VISITED MOUSEY'S APARTMENT, he was looking forward to the opportunity to do so. With this in mind, he telephoned his eyes and ears for an update regarding Spanky. It was Sunday, Mousey's regular day off. Jasper's protégé was relaxing at home rolling a joint as he listened to music. He stopped what he was doing to answer the telephone.

"It's me," said Jasper into the phone. "You got anything to tell me?"

"I think so," replied Mousey.

"I'll come by then."

As he awaited the arrival of his boss, Mousey took pains to erase any traces of his marijuana use. He turned on his air conditioners at full strength in the hope that that would suffice in ridding his apartment of the telltale odor caused by the weed. Jasper had made it clear to Mousey early on that he frowned upon his use of the substance, often warning that the use of ganja came with a price. "Anybody I know who smoked too much of that shit got dopey in the head," were Jasper's exact words. Mousey had begun using marijuana as a mechanism to help suppress his tendency to jump at the call of his name. When the bell rang, Mousey was true to form. He leaped from his chair as if he had just sat on a tack.

"Is it you, Jasper?" he asked, before buzzing in his visitor.

"Yeah, it's me, Mouse. . . . Open up."

"What a stink in this place!" Jasper declared. "What did I tell you about that frigging weed?"

"I wasn't smoking. It was the girl I had over. She's the one who likes to smoke."

"Do me a favor; turn down the air conditioner," requested Jasper. "You got me freezing over here." Mousey immediately did as instructed. "These are pretty nice digs. It's a one-bedroom?"

"Yeah. I got a new bathroom too."

"Nice. So what's the verdict?"

Somewhere along the line, Mousey had learned the wisdom of sandwiching bad news with positivity. "So far, everything is cool at the bar regarding money. The estimated number I've been reporting to you is in line with what Buster is turning in, right?"

"Yeah, Mouse, the numbers are good. Now tell me what isn't good. . . ."

"Spanky and Buster got something going." The revelation got the bar owner's full attention.

"Are you saying that Spanky's in cahoots with Buster?" While he had always had his doubts about Spanky, collusion with Buster had never entered Jasper's mind. "What are they up to?" he asked.

"Spanky shows up at the bar late at night a few times a week, usually on a Friday and Saturday."

"He goes inside the bar?"

"No, Buster goes outside to see him when he pulls up in his Corvette."

"Then what happens?"

"Buster gets in the car, and they drive off. Five minutes later, Buster comes back into the bar alone."

"What happened to Spanky?"

"He ain't around. The last I see of him is when he drives off with Buster in the car."

"What does Buster do when he returns to the bar?"

Mousey cleared his voice before speaking. "That's when he starts chatting up the customers."

"Does he look around to see if anyone is watching him?"

Mousey nodded in the affirmative. "Buster always looks around when he talks to customers."

"Has Buster ever noticed you scoping him out?"

"No. I'm careful about that," advised Mousey. "I make sure never to be in his line of vision. Matter of fact, just in case, I wear tinted glasses so it's hard for anyone to tell where I'm looking."

Jasper nodded approvingly. "Does he go back and shake hands with customers *after* he sees Spanky? You know, like he giving them something or taking something from them."

"Now that you mention it, yeah, I think so."

"These mothers!" thundered Jasper angrily. "Good job, kid. Let me ask you one more thing. Did you ever actually see Buster take money off a customer?"

"Not exactly . . ."

"What does 'not exactly' mean?"

"I've seen money exchange hands. I thought he was making change."

"It's time you got clued in, kid. They're pushing coke. And let me tell you another thing: these two ain't getting away with robbing from me! Buster caught me by surprise," he admitted, "but I never trusted that little weasel Spanky from day one. My brother liked him, not me."

"I didn't know—"

"They're partnering at *my* expense."

"What are you going to do about it?"

Jasper ignored Mousey's question. He was too peeved to discuss it further. "Do you think you know enough to run the bar on your own? I'm talking the works, upstairs and down."

"Yeah, I think so. But I'd need *some* help. . . ."

"I'll get you somebody with muscle to handle collections and any other bullshit that comes up."

"Then I definitely could do it."

"Even the gambling?"

"Yeah, even the gambling."

Jasper was pleased to hear that. "How are my bartenders?"

"No problems with them from what I can see."

"What about Johnny Blondell? Does it look like he might be in with Spanky and Buster?"

"Oh no, Johnny is solid. Everybody respects him. Matter of fact, Spanky and Buster don't do anything when he's around."

"Okay, good. For now, you sit tight and just keep your eyes open. I got plans for you, kid . . . big plans."

"Thanks, Jasper."

After Jasper left, Mousey felt puffed up with pride. He saw himself as someone with a future. Maybe he'd be driving his own Corvette one day . . . only his would be black. Mousey lit up a joint while having these good thoughts. He closed his eyes and began relaxing after his first toke.

13

Saddle Up

VON HESS CONTACTED THE MISSING PERSON SQUAD in an attempt to gather information on the Mathis disappearance. As expected there was no one with firsthand knowledge of the case.

"We'll have to go to the records room, Sarge. They have nothing for us at missing persons."

After getting set up at headquarters with the microfilm, Von Hess reviewed the reports on the Mathis case from a desktop reader. The documents primarily consisted of the interviews conducted. There were no notes or personal insights by those who worked the case. Contained in the reports were the identities of the two privates who were assigned to work with Sergeant Mathis at the armory on the day he disappeared. The names Gaspare Stanlee and Cristofaro Stanlee were of significance because they lent credibility to the information confided to them by Lemon.

Von Hess conducted background checks on both men. Neither brother was found to have a criminal record, which meant that there was no arrest photo on file. Aware that the brothers were in business, Von Hess checked with the department's pistol license section. He ascertained that the siblings had applied for a rifle/shotgun permit. He further learned that photos of the men were on file at that office.

"No criminal record, Sarge, on either man. But both guys have a shotgun permit. They got photos of them on file over in the license section. They're digging them out for us as we speak."

"Great. Now see if you can get a line on the wife of Cornell Mathis. Let's see if she's still around."

Von Hess wasted no time in picking up the phone. He reported back to Markie within minutes.

"I just spoke to her, Sarge. She's still living on Staten Island but at a different address. She kept the same telephone number. She's okay with seeing us anytime," advised Von Hess.

"How did she sound to you over the phone?"

"Other than being surprised to hear from the police after all these years, she was fine."

"That's good. Maybe she can shed some light on this."

"Guess what? About a mile away from where she lives is the rehab place where they've got Fishnet Milligan on ice. I heard through the grapevine that Fishnet's condition has greatly improved."

"Get the hell outta here," said Markie. "How is that possible?"

"I don't know, but according to the union rep he'll be walking around soon. Can you imagine?"

"Go figure that," said Markie. "If one of us took a bullet in the melon, we'd be long planted."

"It really is amazing."

"Come on, Ollie; we might as well go pick up the photos and head out to Staten Island."

Once on Staten Island, a thought came to Von Hess. "Say, since we're going to be out on the Island anyway, how about we swing by the rehab place and see Fishnet?"

Markie expressed no enthusiasm for the suggestion. He still held ill will toward the corrupt detective who had miraculously survived a shoot-out with Red Harris in *The Case of Two in the Trunk*.

##########

THE INVESTIGATORS PULLED UP IN FRONT of a nicely maintained house on Staten Island that sat on a hill. They both took notice that a late-model Mercedes-Benz was parked in the driveway. A smartly dressed woman in her early sixties answered the door. Standing perfectly erect, she smiled politely. She wore white slacks, an olive-colored long-sleeve shirt, and white running shoes. Her short silver hair was spiked. The fused strands scattered across her head appeared soldier-like as they stood frozen stiffly in place. A pair of reading glasses could be seen hanging from her neck.

"Mrs. Mathis?" asked Von Hess.

"I'm Mrs. Mathis-Johnson now," she corrected.

"I'm Detective Von Hess. We spoke earlier."

"Yes, of course," she acknowledged. "Please come in." She spoke with a grammatical correctness, carrying herself in a way that suggested she was a woman of breeding and education.

Upon entering, Markie visually scanned the interior of the house. Based upon his observations, it was clear to him that the home belonged to people of means. It was also evident that their host had stepped up in status since the disappearance of her husband. A lanky man with a neat white mustache and bald head met them in the living room. His slim physique was similar to that of a marathon runner. He wore a white button-down shirt, light gray slacks, and brown loafers that looked pricey.

"This is my husband . . . *Mr. Johnson*," said Johnson's wife. "These are the detectives, dear."

"Sorry to bother you Mr. Johnson," said Markie. "We won't take up too much of your time."

"No problem, Sergeant," said the septuagenarian, a retired actuary. "Can we get you anything?"

"Nothing for me, sir," said Von Hess.

"I'm good, thanks," replied Markie.

The detectives took seats in the parlor. The couple listened attentively as Von Hess explained the purpose of their visit. When he was finished, Mrs. Mathis-Johnson readily answered questions, informing both detectives of the little she knew about what had happened to her first husband.

"In the beginning, I really didn't know what to think. I was very conflicted. Frankly, I was quite puzzled by his disappearance," she confessed.

"Why were you conflicted, ma'am?"

"I was influenced by all the speculation. Everyone thought Cornell left just to get away from *me*. However, that simply made no sense. Cornell had all the freedom—"

"They don't want to hear about any of that, dear," interrupted her second husband.

"Please, Mr. Johnson, let your wife continue," said Markie. "Please go on, ma'am."

Mr. Johnson cleared his voice and nodded. "Sorry," he said, backing off.

"Cornell had all the freedom in the world to do what he wanted. There was no reason for him to find it necessary to get away from me. Even though our relationship had been on the decline for a long time, Cornell was oblivious to my unhappiness. His disappearance was hardly the end of the world for me."

The detectives entered an area that they were finding awkward. Nevertheless, Markie forged on. "You don't have any independent suspicions concerning Cornell's disappearance?"

"No I don't. Way back, one of the detectives said that bad news travels fast. He said that if anything bad had happened to Cornell, we'd soon find out. When there was no news forthcoming, people began to assume that he'd left of his own volition to escape his domestic responsibilities."

"Well, if Cornell was in an accident, arrested, hospitalized, or found to be the victim of foul play, the police would have notified you," advised Von Hess. "But that doesn't always have to be the case."

"Since no one found his body or car, I suppose it seemed plausible that he ran away on his own."

"Do you think there might have had another woman he was interested in?" asked Von Hess.

"Cornell with another woman?" she asked, seemingly astonished at the suggestion. "I hardly think so."

Markie harbored thoughts that didn't subscribe to the theory that Cornell left home willingly. Aside from the information Lemon provided, he based this opinion on the framed photo of the young woman that sat atop the living room mantelpiece. Cornell's wife had been a stunning, model-thin beauty whom a man would take a lot from before leaving. Had it not been for Lemon's account, Markie would have considered the possibility of foul play orchestrated by Cornell's widow and her second husband.

"Is that you, Mrs. Mathis-Johnson?" asked the sergeant, pointing to the photo.

"Yes, that's me a long time ago," she replied.

"You've hardly changed at all," Markie complimented her.

"Thank you. I've been in a good place for a very long time now," she said. "Would you gentlemen like to hear something about Cornell that no one knows?"

"Of course . . ." replied Von Hess, who was very interested.

"I've never shared this with anyone before, and perhaps I shouldn't now. But I will. My first husband had serious psychological problems."

Von Hess glanced at Markie, who sat emotionless. "What kind of psychological problems?" he asked.

The detectives came to learn of the sexual abuse Cornell Mathis had sustained at the hands of Billy Weaver, his late stepfather. They were informed that as a child, Mathis had been repeatedly victimized.

"That's a terrible thing to happen," said Von Hess, showing compassion. "Those wounds never heal."

"While it's no justification, of course, as his wife I came to appreciate Cornell's hostility when it came to people who reminded him of Billy Weaver."

"Hostility?" questioned Markie.

"If you reminded Cornell of his stepfather, you were guaranteed to be in for a hard time."

Her remark was informative. "Do you know what Billy Weaver looked like?" asked the sergeant.

"Yes, of course," she replied, providing a description.

"Ollie, show her the pictures we got from the pistol license section."

Mrs. Mathis-Johnson was taken aback when she saw the photos of Jasper and Chris Stanlee. "Why, these men look very much like Billy Weaver, especially this one," she declared, indicating Jasper. "Who are they?" she asked, not having any idea as to their identity.

"Just people of interest," answered Von Hess.

"Did Cornell ever act out on his negative feelings toward his stepfather?" Markie asked.

Mrs. Mathis-Johnson looked down to the ground. When she looked up, she answered candidly. "To be honest, he did at every opportunity. There were times his actions were terribly embarrassing."

"How so?" asked Von Hess.

"Cornell could be a very vindictive man. Anyone who reminded him of Billy Weaver paid the price."

"Is Billy Weaver dead or alive?"

"He's been dead for years now."

"How did he die?"

"Bone cancer. . . . He suffered terribly. Cornell celebrated the news by taking me to dinner."

"Was Cornell apt to get into physical confrontations?" asked Markie.

"He was always ready to do battle with anyone who looked like his stepfather."

"I see. Can you give us an example of how he acted out in public?"

"He'd do stupid little things such as sending food back if a waiter happened to *look* like Billy. He'd say something was wrong with the meal and then leave without tipping. There were times he pulled this after practically cleaning his plate. That generally would cause a stir."

"What else would he do?"

"One time he took a pair of old shoes he removed from the trash to a shoemaker for repair. He asked to have them fixed and then never went back to pick them up, all just because the shoemaker *spoke* similarly to Billy Weaver. Things like that," she advised.

"There were no actual *physical* altercations that you know of?" asked Markie.

"None that I was ever aware of," she answered.

"Excuse me for interrupting, but I have a question," said Mr. Johnson. "What exactly brings you here today after all this time? Don't tell me you've found Cornell?"

"No, I'm afraid not. Like we said earlier, we're just following up on a lead we recently received," advised Markie. "We'll post you folks, of course, if anything comes of it."

" We'll never know what happened to Cornell," stated Mr. Johnson pessimistically.

"Mrs. Mathis-Johnson, do you have a picture of Cornell that we can borrow?" asked Von Hess.

"I do." Leaving the room for a few minutes, she returned with an eight-by-ten color photo.

"Take this. I had copies made up when everybody was out looking for him."

Von Hess took the color photo that depicted Cornell Mathis as a young man. Mathis was smiling broadly, revealing a slight separation between his two front teeth. The photo reflected Cornell posing for the camera, with his right fist to his chin. The one-eared wolf head ring with emerald eyes was clearly visible on his pinkie.

"He appears to be very happy in this photo," observed Von Hess.

"He was. That photo was taken shortly after Billy Weaver was diagnosed with bone cancer."

"What kind of ring is that he's wearing?" commented Markie. "It's very unusual looking."

"Cornell adored that ring. It was specially made by his cousin in Mobile, who gave it to him as a gift."

"Really?" said Von Hess. "Was he a jeweler?"

"Still is," she answered. "Arthur is eighty-two years old, still in business."

"Do you happen to have a contact number for Arthur?" asked Von Hess.

"I do. But don't wait another thirty years. . . . He probably won't be around then!" she said.

##########

VON HESS MADE IT A POINT TO SWING by the rehab facility on their way back to Brooklyn. He pulled over so that he and Markie could get a good look at the exterior of the facility that housed Fishnet.

"What do you want to do, boss?"

"What do you mean?"

"You want to go in and see how Fishnet's doing?"

"Why? I know all I need to know about that hump."

"I feel the same way about him, but what the hell. He did take a bullet in the line of duty."

Markie thought about it for a minute. "Ollie, I really don't want to see this son of a bitch. If you do, go right ahead. I'll wait here for you," the sergeant said.

Von Hess wasn't going in alone. He slowly pulled away from the curb. "Where to?" he asked.

"Let's go take a good look at that armory in Park Slope, Ollie. If Lemon is right, then there is a good chance that the body might have been dumped somewhere in the vicinity of the armory."

"Righto," agreed von Hess. His not contributing to further their conversation sent Markie a message.

"Alright, you win," conceded Markie. "We'll stop in and see Fishnet next time we come out here."

########

INSIDE THE STATEN ISLAND REHAB CENTER, Fishnet Milligan sat quietly in his wheelchair in deep thought. He held no doubt about achieving a full recovery. In fact, he was thinking of his future. He was of the opinion that if a bullet to the head couldn't stop him, nothing could. The former detective's health had first turned the corner when he regained the ability to move his fingers. This milestone was followed by the gradual use of his limbs. Feeling stronger each day, Fishnet eventually began taking steps. These strides, along with a changing sensation in his throat, convinced him that one day he'd regain the ability to speak. Part of Fishnet's advancement probably had something to do with his being obstinate. The former detective was determined to receive what he considered his due. From Fishnet's perspective, all ceremonial recognitions, awards, and media attention afforded to a surviving hero were entitlements he was deserving of. Mentally, Fishnet's scheming mind was up to par. As would an inmate in a prison, all he thought of was life on the outside.

Watching television one Sunday, a thought came to Fishnet as he stumbled upon a religious show while channel surfing. He viewed the audience as do-gooders who were prime candidates for bilking.

As Fishnet was considering his options, the woman he'd come to dread interrupted his train of thought. She neared him, humming the tune "No Woman, No Cry." It was Hope Gilmore, a certified nursing assistant. Particularly disturbing was the CNA's tendency to shout her words when speaking.

"You ready to go outside, *Mr. Fish-Hook*?" she asked, in her choppy way. The CNA was sucking on a sweet candy that caused her to emit an accidental saliva spray as she spoke.

Jeez, will ya save a little for yourself? You're freaking drowning me! said Fishnet internally. Although no words could be heard, the message conveyed by his glaring was understood by the attendant.

"Now, be nice, Mr. Fish-Hook. . . . Don't you be cross with me," she said. Her tone was condescending, as if she were speaking to a child. "I noticed that your skin is very dry, so I brought you a powerful cure that I made special for you. It's a restorative. You drink it every other day and you'll never have to worry about dry skin again," she said.

Fishnet closed his eyes. *Now, isn't this just dandy,* he thought. *Granny Clampett over here wants to feed me a horse sweat and possum piss tonic that'll cure everything from dandruff to skin tags!*

"Now, remember, you must never let anyone know about this. I could get in big trouble," she said after giving Fishnet a spoonful of her homemade remedy.

Hope wheeled Fishnet outside into the facility yard. An expansive area with grass, trees, benches, and bushes, it was designed to create a park-like setting. Once outside, the former detective focused his attention on an attractive twenty-something female CNA. Fishnet found the pretty young woman much more to his liking than Hope.

Fishnet watched with interest as the young assistant helped adjust the position of a patient, a very old man who sat quietly in a wheelchair. His envy skyrocketed as he watched her ever so gently massage the man's frail shoulders. The former detective could only imagine what her touch would feel like on his own shoulders. In his current situation, Fishnet viewed such feminine pampering as a gift.

What a waste of talent, thought the former detective. He coined the name *Old Buzzard* for the elderly patient. His mind traveled far off into his private world of fantasy. Fishnet possessed devilish thoughts as he pictured himself strutting like a peacock along the deck of an ocean liner in the cool evening breeze of a summer night at sea. The young CNA held his arm tightly as they strolled. The blissful fantasy he conjured progressed as they stopped by the ship's lounge to treat themselves to a sweet cocktail. Old Buzzard now had all his teeth and was out of his wheelchair. He stood erect in his immaculate white jacket behind the bar, mixing their beverage.

"Thank you, my good man," said Fishnet, taking the two tropical drinks from Old Buzzard.

In his mental illusion, the former detective saw his object of desire remove the plastic straw from her glass and place it to her lips. Fishnet reacted to this figment of his imagination by slowly raising his fingers toward her cheek. . . . Then, out of the blue, an immense verbal tidal wave rocked his imaginary love boat.

"*MR. FISH-HOOK!* I'm talking to you!"

"What do you want?" he spat out, furious at being disturbed by Hope. His words came with great clarity.

"Mr. Fish-Hook," declared the astonished Hope, "you spoke!" The CNA was elated over Fishnet's unexpected vocal advancement.

Realizing that he had made a major breakthrough, Fishnet sought further confirmation. "Am . . . I . . . really . . . talking?" he asked, measuring each word when he spoke.

"You are talking *wonderfully*!" she answered. "You could be on the radio giving the weather! God has blessed you, Mr. Fish-Hook! This is indeed a glorious miracle!" she shouted gleefully.

"Yeah . . ." he said. It was all he could say as he wondered if the tonic had anything to do with his gain.

"This was God's work!" said Hope with great enthusiasm. "I'm going to get the doctor! Now, don't you go anyplace!" she instructed.

Fishnet watched Hope, a large woman, dart off. He had never seen her move with such alacrity before.

"Don't go anyplace?" he asked aloud, taking joy in hearing himself. "Where the hell does she think I'm going?"

14

The Deep Six

VON HESS PULLED UP TO THE FRONT of the Park Slope armory. From their car, he and Markie paused for a moment to admire the massive bronze sculpture that stood atop a granite pedestal in front of the main entrance. The piece depicted a World War I doughboy advancing with his rifle. After parking, the detectives stopped in front of the sculpture to read the stone inscription:

"Dedicated to the men of the 12th Infantry who were engaged in World War 1917–1918," recited Von Hess, who read the words aloud.

"And now it's a homeless shelter," commented Markie, shaking his head. "C'mon, let's go inside."

The detectives were met with cooperation by the staff working at the armory. Accompanied by a designated escort, they proceeded to examine all areas of the massive structure. After a while, it became evident to the guide how time-consuming the effort was going to be. Excusing himself, the guide left the detectives to explore the facility on their own. Soldiering on, Markie and Von Hess eventually found themselves below ground. The two subterranean levels were rarely visited areas.

"Ollie, we need more lighting down here. Let's go get the flashlights."

After securing flashlights from their vehicle, they resumed their visual inspection. The investigators soon began making surprise discoveries. They came upon a long-retired gun range, horse stables, and even a bowling alley. They surmised that the area had probably been used for both official and recreational purposes by the soldiers attached to the armory. While shining his supplemental illumination along the walls, Markie noticed something that struck him as interesting.

"Take a look over here, Ollie."

Von Hess stepped in closer to the brick wall where Markie stood. "What am I looking for?"

"Look at the top of this rounded archway," directed the sergeant, shining his light upward at the bricked enclosure. "This was likely a passageway that was sealed up. Now look at these bricks," he said, bringing his light inches away from the area pointed out.

"What about them?" .

"They all have the same coloring, grouting, and degree of decay. Everything aged pretty much alike," Markie noted. "Now look below, do you see the difference?"

Von Hess shined his own light up close to where the sergeant was indicating. "Yeah, I do. The consistency is broken. The pointing of the cement seems different. It looks like two different jobs."

"Get a load of this one brick, Ollie. It's a totally different color altogether from the rest of them."

Von Hess zeroed in on the brick in question. "Are you thinking what I'm thinking, Sarge?"

"I'm thinking these bricks might have been removed and later put back in and re-grouted," speculated Markie. "This one brick is totally out of whack. It could have originally faced the other way."

"That just might account for the coloring being different," observed Von Hess. "I'll go back upstairs and see if they have any old work orders concerning down here," said Von Hess.

The detectives established that there was no record of work having been performed down below. Furthermore, it seemed that no one in recent memory had ventured into the area long known as The Deep Six, a term coined by soldiers. Those currently working at the armory believed the area to be haunted, as did the soldiers who were once stationed there. No one knew exactly what this belief was based on, yet the legend nevertheless lived on. Staffers ventured below only when absolutely necessary.

"It looks like we might have to satisfy our own curiosity, Ollie."

Markie contacted Lieutenant Wright over at headquarters. After being briefed, the lieutenant wasn't sure of what Markie had in mind. "So what are you looking to do over there?" asked Wright.

"I think we need to see what's behind this wall," replied Markie.

"You mean you want to break it open?"

"I know we may or may not be bending a rule here, but Mathis had to end up someplace."

"Yeah, I know . . . but Jesus."

"This Sergeant Mathis hated anyone who reminded him of his chicken hawk stepfather."

"Did you say 'chicken hawk'?" asked Lieutenant Wright.

"That's right, boss. Mathis was sexually abused as a kid."

"So what's that got to do with anything?"

"Mathis was alone in the armory with the twin brothers Lemon told us about. We showed the Mathis widow a picture of the Stanlee brothers, and bingo, she said the brothers are a lookalike for the pervert stepfather. Based on what she told us, we figure that this resemblance could have triggered a beef."

"So you figure there was a squabble in the armory and Mathis got clipped there?"

"I see that as a real possibility. Remember, the armory was vacated that weekend. Everyone was in the field except the sergeant and the two privates. There was ample opportunity."

After a few seconds of thought, Wright conceded the point. "Alright, sit tight. Let me go run this by the chief. I'll call you right back." After ten minutes had elapsed, Markie's cell phone rang.

"Al, you got Chief McCoy's okay to go ahead. I gotta tell you, McCoy has steel balls. He's not worried about any heat. He said to call in emergency service to go through the wall. You want me over there?"

"Nah, I got it covered."

"Okay, keep me posted. Call me if you need me to smooth out any bumps."

Emergency Service responded with the proper tools and the best portable lighting available. After breaking through the wall, the ESU officers entered the tunnel. At their heels followed Markie and Von Hess. It was an emergency service officer who first spotted the remains of Cornell Mathis.

"Here we go!" exclaimed the officer as he stood over what was left of the body inside the green fatigues. His mouth and nose covered with his hand, Von Hess crouched down for a closer look. He pointed his flashlight on the breast area of the green fatigue shirt. Focusing on the black lettering, he was able to read the name tag sewn onto the garment.

"It's our boy," alerted Von Hess. "The name on the shirt is Mathis."

"Can you make out anything else, Ollie?"

Von Hess scanned the body with his flashlight. "Something ain't right with his hand, Sarge."

"Like what?"

"He's missing a pinkie. Hold it a second. I think maybe his little finger is on the ground here."

"Well, what do you know about that?" stated Markie. "You got anything else?"

"His wallet is here next to the body."

"Does it look like a robbery?"

"It could be. I don't see any jewelry, and there is no money in the wallet."

"I'd love to know where that ring ended up," declared Markie.

"I was thinking the same thing, Sarge," chimed in Von Hess.

"Leave everything for the local squad to find. C'mon, Ollie, let's get the hell out of here."

Once they were outside in the fresh air, Markie notified the Crime Scene Unit. He had Von Hess notify the local precinct and Lieutenant Pearlie Darkenlove, the precinct squad commander.

"Ollie, let's grab something quick to eat before this turns into a circus."

On their way to the car, Markie abruptly stopped walking. Standing flat-footed with his mouth agape, he stared toward the opposite side of the street. A scowl soon formed on his face.

"What's the matter, Sarge?" asked Von Hess, noticing the sudden transformation.

"Nothing," the sergeant answered curtly. "Just find us a place where we can get a drink."

"Whatever you say, Sarge," replied the perplexed Von Hess. Realizing that something was amiss, he wondered what had occurred. Von Hess found a suitable bar restaurant just a few blocks from the armory. "Do you want to sit in the back, boss?" he asked.

"No, let's sit at the bar," said the sergeant. After assuming a seat on a stool, Markie ordered a scotch straight up and a beer chaser from the young woman tending bar.

"A ball and a beer coming up," acknowledged the bartender. "You want a boilermaker too?" she asked, addressing Von Hess.

"No, let me have a ginger ale."

The bartender returned shortly with the drinks. Seconds after placing the refreshments down, Markie drained his shot glass. He then poured his beer. After taking a sip of the beer, he ordered another shot.

"Do you have a menu?" asked Von Hess, wanting to eat right away. He was concerned that Markie might be entering into a drink-fest.

When the bartender returned, the men ordered burgers. By the time the food arrived, Markie had already consumed three shots.

Markie was staring at the bartender as she worked. The sergeant estimated her age to be in the late twenties. The sleeves on the black Guinness Stout shirt she wore were hiked up toward her elbows. A tiny blue-ink tattoo of a lock adorned her left inner wrist, while a key decorated her right inner wrist. Markie briefly contemplated saying something about the decorations. Instead, he turned to confide in Von Hess as to what was troubling him.

"I saw my ex-wife, Flo, with that dentist boss of hers."

"Where was that?"

"They were holding hands and going into a building across from the armory. It was a matinee for sure."

"You can't be sure of that, Sarge. Maybe they were just visiting someone."

"Nice try, Ollie . . . but it is what it is. She's fooling around with that married tooth puller.

"Look, Sarge, if you can't patch it up with Flo, you have to let it go. It's been a long time now."

"I know, but what the hell could be going on in that head of hers?"

Von Hess let out a deep sigh. "I know this may be difficult to swallow, Sarge, but I'm talking to you like a friend. Florence is a free agent now. She can do what she wants with who she wants."

"I know that, but I can't help how I feel. For the first time it's like . . . like I feel I really lost something."

"I suppose you really did."

"How crazy is that? The woman drove me nuts enough to welcome divorce, and now listen to me."

"It's not crazy, boss. You two were married for a lot of years. You've got kids together."

"Yeah, I guess that's it."

"Hey, cheer up. At least you're not without a port to go to."

"Yeah, I got Alley . . . for now."

##########

BY THE TIME MARKIE AND VON HESS RETURNED TO THE armory, crime scene had already begun their work. Lieutenant Pearlie Darkenlove of the local squad was present at the scene with one of her people.

"So you found Mathis," voiced Lieutenant Darkenlove. "Nice job."

"Thanks, boss," said Markie. Darkenlove did a double after smelling the alcohol on Markie's breath.

The sergeant wasn't concerned because he knew Darkenlove wouldn't cause a problem. Protection was one of the advantages of working directly for the chief of detectives.

"We can notify the widow if you like, boss," offered Markie. "We already met with her once."

Darkenlove thought for a moment before answering. "Okay, you do that. Just document it on paper that you made the notification and send us the report."

"No problem. What number is this for you?" asked the sergeant, referring to the number of homicides in the precinct for the current year.

"This is number five for us."

"Maybe we can get lucky and help solve it for you."

"Yeah, maybe," replied Darkenlove, not sure if the sergeant was getting smart with her.

Markie reached out to a friendly bureau chief at the Brooklyn district attorney's office. He sought an opinion on the Mathis investigation based on the facts to date. He was informed that more evidence was desired before they'd consider prosecuting Jasper Stanlee.

"There is never enough evidence to satisfy these lawyers," complained Von Hess

"I'll get more evidence," said Markie.

"How?" asked Lieutenant Darkenlove.

"I haven't figured it out yet, boss."

Lieutenant Darkenlove didn't appreciate Markie's independence in working on what was technically her squad's case. There was little she could do other than watch him walk off.

Markie, Wright and Darkenlove met with the chief of detectives the following morning. The chief was amenable to Markie's suggestion of initiating an undercover operation. Darkenlove was appalled at Markie's ease in taking the lead. Feeling upstaged, she posed a question. "I assume that I'll be overseeing everything?"

"Wright's people will be in charge of the undercover investigation," said McCoy."Once they gather the evidence required, the case will fall back to you to make the pinch."

"The body was found in *my* precinct," Darkenlove reminded. "That makes it *my* responsibility, chief."

Chief McCoy wasn't one to sit still for a pushback. "Hey Pearlie, just chill out," he said in a harsh tone.

Markie left the office certain of one thing: Darkenlove wanted to hand him his ass.

15

Busting Up Buster

JASPER WAS THE SORT OF MAN WHO wouldn't let a betrayal go unaddressed. In the case of Spanky, he was compelled to curb his urge to retaliate until he found a replacement for his disloyal underling. Identifying the right fit to introduce into his drug operation was going to take time. Jasper chastised himself for allowing Spanky to become so vital. This was a mistake that he had no intention of repeating. He made a decision to cross train his people. He began to incorporate some of his James Brothers Saloon crew into his drug enterprise.

While searching for someone to replace Spanky, Jasper found a way to temporarily appease his appetite for revenge. Satisfaction came in the form of tormenting Spanky psychologically. Jasper embarked on a pattern of behavior that made Spanky suspect that his payback could come at any time.

Since there was nothing insulating Buster from being held accountable for his role in the collusion, he was to immediately be made an example of. Jasper intended to ratchet up the pressure by saying nothing to Spanky after Buster received his comeuppance. He relished the moment he'd be able to watch Spanky wilt as he pondered the uncertainty of his future. The thought of creating a knot in his underling's stomach was delightful in terms of temporary relief.

Jasper took a morning drive to Silky Seggio's Long Island home. When he arrived he was greeted at the front door by the gangster's wife, a sturdy, traditional woman with neatly coifed gray hair. Her nails were colored a subdued light tan. Her olive skin seemed to exercise control over the aging of her face. The glasses she wore projected an air of intelligence, which she possessed.

"Are you here to see Settimo?" she asked, offering a modest smile.

"Yes, Mrs. Seggio."

"Come in. He's expecting you," she said in a somewhat subdued way. "He's outside in the yard."

Jasper followed her through the house and into the yard. The caller found Silky sitting on a large cushioned seat within an octagon gazebo with a bell-shaped roof. The gangster was drinking a chilled Manhattan Special while reading one of the several newspapers he had delivered to his home each morning. Jasper wasn't used to seeing Silky in such a tranquil setting. Outside the home, his public face was one that rested somewhere between a frown and a sneer. However, when among the grapes hanging from the arbor in his yard, there was no edginess evident. Silky was so relaxed that he sat contentedly with the top button of his pants undone. The zipper on the black slacks he wore was fully lowered for added breathing room.

The racketeer was wearing oversized black glasses that were too big for his face. Although old age had steadily altered his appearance, the one thing that remained immune to change was his confidence. His self-assurance was bolstered by an unrestrained ruthlessness that kept him competitive in his world. The Mafioso looked up from his reading when Jasper reached the gazebo entryway.

"Thanks for letting me come out to see you, skipper."

The gangster nodded his hello. "I was just reading about this *astro-nut*." Silky's lips were taut and hardly moved as he spoke out of the side of his mouth.

"You mean the guy going back up in space?"

"Yeah. If I ever do anything like that, lock me up in a room with a coloring book and crayons," said the gangster. "Talk about pressing your luck . . ."

"I guess he sees money and glory in it," conjectured Jasper.

Silky acted out his disapproval by throwing his open hand forward and down in Jasper's direction.

"C'mon, will ya?" he said dismissively. "Talking about money . . . you got something for me?"

"Yeah, here you go, Silky," said Jasper, handing his silent partner an envelope containing cash.

Silky opened the envelope and began thumbing through the large bills. He reacted by slightly tilting his head, raising his eyebrows, and curling his mouth downward. It was clear that he was impressed.

"My friends up north are very pleased," advised Seggio, referring to his drug connection.

"So far everything is running great," said Jasper.

"If things are going great, what urgency brings you to my home?"

"It's nothing *that* urgent, Silky. We got an itch, and I just want to be respectful and touch base with you before I scratch it."

Silky didn't like what he was hearing. "Let's cut to the chase, kid. Where's the problem?"

"It's Spanky and Buster."

"Don't tell me those two are making waves. . . ."

"Yeah, they crossed us big time."

Silky's eyes narrowed as his voice took on a sinister tone. "What are they up to?"

"They went in business for themselves. They're selling our coke in the bar, and I'm pretty sure—"

Silky slammed his right fist into the palm of his open left hand, shutting Jasper up. "Enough!" Seggio said harshly, his temper getting the best of him. "What kind of proof do you have?"

"I got them cold. The kid Mousey saw them doing it with customers from the bar."

"Who is Mousey again?"

"You know him. He's the kid from the car wash who I took under my wing."

"What's Johnny Blondell been doing over there, sleeping? He didn't know this was going on?"

"Johnny is aces. I think they were smart enough to work around him."

Silky scratched his chin as he pondered the situation. "Do we need these two bastards?"

"Yes and no."

"Stop with the riddles," said Silky impatiently. "Are they needed or not?"

"Buster is expendable. Spanky I need until I can come up with a replacement. I'll take care of business with these two; don't worry about that."

"*You'll* take care of business?"

"What? I'm capable."

"It's not a question of you being capable."

"So what do you want me to do?"

"Leave Buster to me, he'll be made to regret the error of his ways. You got a replacement for him?"

"Yeah, I got Mousey."

"He's kind of young, ain't he?"

"I'll back him up with somebody who has a strong reputation and who can maintain order."

"Good. As far as Spanky goes, you should have never let him get that powerful in the first place," lectured the gangster. "For now, you focus on finding a replacement for Spanky. We'll square his account after you do."

##########

SILKY WAS PLAYING SOLITAIRE IN HIS OFFICE at the Palsy-Walsy Social Club. The booming voice of Jimmy Roselli singing his version of "Mala Femmina" could be heard throughout the club. When the cousins Primo and Nino arrived at the office, Silky held up a finger to silence them.

"*Aspetta*," he said, telling them to wait. The men stood quietly as they listened along with Silky to Roselli's warbling.

"Jimmy really knows how to put over that song," said Silky at the conclusion of the tune. "Who is your favorite singer, Primo?"

"I like Frank," replied Primo, the older of the two cousins.

"Who Frank?"

"Old Blue Eyes....the Chairman of the Board. Who else is there?"

A pained look came over Silky's face. "And you?" asked the gangster, directing his question to Nino.

"I have to go with that," answered Nino, figuring he couldn't go wrong with Sinatra.

"What's the matter with Frankie Laine?" asked Silky aggressively. "You got something against the paisan from Chicago? You know, his name ain't really Laine; it's LoVecchio. The guy's got gold records under his belt and *you* don't know who the hell he is?"

The two cousins were taken aback. Both were at a loss for words. Finally Primo spoke up. "Jeez, I forgot all about him! He's gotta be number one," he said, trying to make amends for his wrong answer.

"Yeah," agreed Nino quickly. "What was I thinking? He's tops in my book too!"

"You gotta buy his records, and you'll hear some real singing. Give me Frankie Laine *any*time over Sinatra," emphasized Silky.

"We'll definitely do that," said Primo.

"Alright, listen . . . enough with this bullshit," said Silky. "I have a job for you. You know Buster, right?"

"Yeah, of course we know him," answered Primo.

"He got out of line, and he needs an education at three o'clock," said Silky, referring to a time when classmates settled their differences after school.

"You want his schooling to land him in the hospital?" asked Nino.

"Yeah, send him in for a stay."

"No problem, Silky," said Primo. "You want him in for the whole semester?"

Silky shrugged. "Just hurt him good, but don't kill him. Be sure to bust up his hand while you're at it."

"You sure you don't want us to put him away permanent?" asked Nino with a wry smile. Both cousins were chomping at the bit to commit a murder. They saw homicide as a career path to getting made a soldier in the family. Silky didn't entertain the suggestion. He just pointed to the door,

While walking on the street Buster was blindsided late one night by Silky's goon squad. Nino snuck up on him and cracked his skull with a jumbo-sized blackjack. The cousins quickly scooped up their dazed victim off the sidewalk and stowed him in the trunk of Primo's Cadillac Fleetwood. They transported Buster to a desolate location on Staten Island, where they deposited the still-dazed Buster on the ground in a heap. Primo removed an aluminum bat from the back seat and went to work on his victim.

"Remember, don't kill him," warned Nino.

Nino winced as he watched Primo's final swing strike the assault victim between his legs. The blow resulted in Buster letting out a bloodcurdling yelp.

"That should do it," declared Primo as he stood straight, catching his breath.

"Oooo, you forgot something. Give his hand a whack," said Nino.

Primo viciously came down with the bat on Buster's left hand. Nino lifted Buster's head by his hair and spoke directly into his ear. The message came out clearly, leaving no room for misunderstanding.

"Don't *ever* steal from the James Brothers again."

"C'mon, give him a kiss goodbye and let's go," said Primo, who was anxious to get going.

Nino unleashed a smash across Buster's face with his blackjack. The blow landed low, breaking Buster's jaw. The cousins left their unconscious victim in a commercial area lying atop the few blades of grass that were growing between the cracks in the cement. Buster was discovered a few hours later by a factory worker, who immediately called the police. He was subsequently removed to the nearest hospital, where he was admitted for a multitude of injuries that included a concussion, a broken jaw, a severely damaged hand, and a testicular trauma so serious that it left him sterile.

By the time the local precinct detectives were able to interview him, Buster was lying in his hospital bed being fed juice through a straw. They found the crime victim uncooperative. After being the recipient of such a battering, there was no way Buster would ever agree to talk to the law. Once the doctors made it clear that Buster was going to survive, the detectives didn't waste any more time on the matter. They returned to their precinct, closed their felony assault case, and moved on to more worthwhile crime victims.

########

AFTER A RELATIVELY LENGTHY HOSPITAL STAY, BUSTER RETURNED TO THE HOME of his parents. Under their care the healing process began. In time he attained the mobility necessary to venture outdoors.

Looking for answers, his first stop was Spanky's bachelor apartment.

"Jesus, Buster . . . you look terrible," said the surprised Spanky after opening the door.

Buster nodded. "I know," he uttered weakly.

"I heard about what happened. How are you doing, man?"

"I don't think I'll ever be a hundred percent," he said bitterly.

"I meant to go see you, but you know how it is."

"Sure, I know."

"Maybe you shouldn't be walking around so soon," said Spanky. "Did the doctor say okay?"

"It's okay. Is there anybody else here?" Buster asked after hearing noise coming from the bedroom.

"I got a girl here, no one else."

"Get rid of her. We need to talk."

Spanky called the young woman into the living room. "Do me a favor, baby. Go out for a walk. I need a few minutes with my friend." After she left the apartment, the two men resumed their conversation.

"What do you hear about what happened to me?" asked Buster, looking very serious.

"Nobody told me a damn thing."

"There's been no talk?"

"If there is, I'm not privy to it," advised Spanky. "You have to understand something. . . . I can't appear to be too interested."

"Do you want to know what they said before leaving me to die?'"

"What?"

"They said I shouldn't steal from the James Brothers!"

"So it did come from Jasper. . . ."

"Who else?" asked Buster, his bitterness evident in the tone he used. "He must've run to Silky. It was a couple of Silky's leg-breakers who worked me over."

"Yeah, it seems like something Jasper would do."

"But what was I stealing? I never robbed from Jasper!" protested Buster. "I turned in every nickel to him. He got everything that was due him from the bar business, the gambling, *and* the shylock money. Why wouldn't he talk to me before running to Silky?"

Spanky struggled to find the right words. "He must have gotten wind about you dealing his coke."

"*HIS* coke?" asked a wide-eyed Buster. "I thought it was your personal stash! You never told me it was Jasper's coke! I figured that there would be no problem with Jasper as long as I wasn't obvious. I mean, he was in the same business. Now you tell me it was his shit? No wonder I caught a beating."

"Well, technically it was Jasper's coke that I was cutting. I stepped on it to give you some product to sell so you could make a few extra bucks."

"You did it for *me* to make a few bucks? Let me ask you something, asshole" said Buster, his tone morphing from pure outrage to homicidal. "How is it you ain't busted up like me?"

"I don't know the answer to that," answered Spanky honestly. "Maybe he ain't sure that I was in with you. One thing I do know, he can't afford to lose me.

Remember something: without me making things happen, he's left with no customers."

"So I get to take the rap for both of us?"

"I'm afraid that's about the size of it, Buster. Maybe what happened to you was done as a message to me . . . and to tell you the truth, I'm still not convinced I'm off the hook. Jasper is treacherous."

"So what do we do about this situation?" asked Buster, who now had a direction to go in.

"*We* aren't doing anything, my friend. I'm not committing suicide by going up against Jasper. As if he ain't trouble enough on his own, his play is backed by Silky Seggio . . . so we got no choice but to forget about this and chalk it up to experience," advised Spanky.

"I know all about him and Silky. Remember where I came from?"

"Look, Buster, I don't think it's a good idea for us being seen together. Our business relationship has to come to a close. My advice to you is to just stay away . . . especially from me. Maybe you can talk to Silky to square things after some time passes."

"So tell me, smart guy; what am I supposed to do for money until then?"

Spanky shrugged. "I guess you'll just have to take a hit. I mean, I can throw you a few bucks. . . ."

"No, no, no, my friend, you got that wrong. *You're* the one taking the hit."

"What do you want from me, Buster? I have to stay away from you. Our business has to be over."

"How did Jasper find out?" asked Buster. "He never saw me do anything. Did you tell him?"

"Me?" asked Spanky, astonished at the very suggestion. "You think I'm nuts? How could I admit to Jasper that I was stepping on his product to sell it with you?"

"Then who told him?"

"It had to be that little shit Mousey. He's Jasper's fair-haired boy. He must have seen you."

"But we were careful. You never even came in the bar. . . ."

"Mousey probably saw something and then reported it to Jasper. Jasper is no fool. He knows how to put two and two together."

"So it was the Mouse that squealed on me?"

"Had to be," answered Spanky. "You underestimated the little bastard. You weren't careful." "WHAT? *I wasn't careful enough?* You were the one coming by in the friggin' yellow Corvette! Real discreet, weren't you?" shouted Buster.

"Hey, take it easy. You can't blame this mess all on me, Buster. We both took our chances, and you happened to come up short. That's the whole story. Now I have to be on the lookout for my own ass."

Seeing that he was getting nowhere, Buster withdrew a revolver from under his shirt. "I need money, Spanky, and you're gonna give it to me."

"C'mon, man, put that away," said Spanky dismissively. "I have no money for you. . . ."

"You got one minute to come up with the cash . . . or I swear on my mother, I'll put one in you right here and now," threatened Buster.

Spanky could see that Buster was serious. He backed up a couple of steps, convinced that Buster would shoot. Facing the barrel of a gun left Spanky without many alternatives.

"Alright, don't get excited. You win. I'll cough up the money," he said. Followed by Buster, Spanky retreated to his bedroom. He removed ten thousand dollars in cash from a tin box and a quantity of cocaine in a small plastic bag. "Here, take this. It'll get you back on your feet again."

Buster took it . . . and more. He reached into the tin box and helped himself to all the money. He then tossed the ounce of coke back to Spanky. "You keep Jasper's coke." The tin box contained more than he'd expected to get out of Spanky. "I'll be back for more when I need it, *partner*."

"You can't get away with this. . . ." protested Spanky.

"Who you gonna cry to, Spanky . . . Jasper? See you next time."

"Hey, wait a minute. We just parted ways. . . . This is over now, right, Buster?"

Buster stopped to look over his shoulder when he was halfway out the door. "I can't have any kids because of a squealing Mouse," Buster said bitterly. "Think about that before you talk to me about it being over."

16

Useless Eustice

WHEN LEMON ARRIVED HOME AFTER WORK, he wasn't surprised to see his neighbor waiting out front for him. The retired man, like Lemon, was a widower. The two men had grown close, to the extent of checking on each other daily. It was their way of making sure the other was not in need. To help ease their loneliness, they played rummy several times a week in the evening. When the weather permitted, they'd go for evening walks.

"How was work today, Sheldon? Did you sell any cars?" asked the neighbor.

"I sold one, a Toyota."

"Those are reliable cars."

"Yeah, they are."

"You know, I had 1953 Mercury many years ago. It was red and black. Let me tell you, was that car ever a lemon!" Lemon winced upon hearing the word used to describe the car. The friend was unaware that most people called the business owner by that name. "You feel like going for a walk later?"

"No, I can't tonight. I have some people coming by. You know how it is, business first," replied Lemon.

"Sure, I understand. How about we do it tomorrow?"

"Yeah, that could probably work. I have to go inside now."

"I'll call you later, Sheldon. I'm gonna sweep the front of the house now. I'll do yours too."

"Okay, I'll talk to you tomorrow."

As the neighbor swept, two men arrived at Lemon's door. Curious as to their identity, the neighbor initiated a conversation with them.

"Who are you looking for?"

"It's alright. Our friend is expecting us," advised Von Hess.

131

Lemon looked out the window when he heard the voices coming from the front of his house. Seeing it was Markie and Von Hess, he immediately went to let them in the house.

"Your company is here, Sheldon," said the neighbor as soon as the door opened.

"Come on in," said Lemon. Once inside the house, Lemon voiced his concern. "I really don't like meeting here. That nosy son of a bitch won't rest until he finds out who you are."

"You worry too much," said Markie. "We're gonna partner you up with an undercover detective. All you have to do is hang out with him at the James Brothers Saloon."

"The James Brothers Saloon?" exclaimed Lemon. "People might know me there. . . ."

"Yeah, that's the idea. Show him the pictures, Ollie."

"Are these the two who brought you the car?" asked Von Hess, producing the photos.

"Yeah, it's them. This one is Frank James," he said, pointing to the photo of Chris. "This other is Jesse. So what am I supposed to do?"

"Relax. You'll have drinks at the bar with our man, a little chitchat with each other, and that's it. The objective is for our guy to be seen having a drink with someone who is known."

"But I've never even been in that place before. . . ."

"We're figuring that somebody will probably know you."

"What do I do if Jesse is there?"

"We're hoping he *is* there."

"What exactly am I supposed to say to him?" Lemon was growing squeamish as the reality of his obligation became real. He began to seriously wonder if jail might have been a better option after all.

"Do what you would normally do if you ran into him. You say hello. If he comes over to talk, introduce the undercover as a friend who worked for your dead brother-in-law, Monte," instructed Markie.

Lemon recoiled at the idea. "I don't know if I can pull this off. . . ."

"Back up, Lemon," said the sergeant sternly. "You'll have to pull it off or go to the can."

The reminder of incarceration caused Lemon to silence himself. He knew he had no choice but to go along. Von Hess sensed Lemon's discomfort.

"Take it easy, Lemon," said the older detective. "Trust us. We do this regularly. You'll be in no danger."

"I wish I had your confidence," commented the informant in a low voice to no one in particular.

"Someone will be in touch," said Markie, ending the conversation as he stood to leave. He had little patience for such nervousness.

A few minutes after the detectives left the house, Lemon's doorbell rang. It was Lemon's neighbor.

"Is everything alright, Sheldon?"

"Yeah, everything is fine."

"What did the cops want?"

Lemon was stunned by the question. "How did you know they were cops?" he asked in amazement.

"I don't know; cops just look like cops."

Lemon nodded knowingly. "Maybe you better come on in."

Once the neighbor was seated, Lemon went to a closet and removed a bottle of Rémy Martin. He gave one of the two stiff drinks he poured to his perceptive neighbor. He then collapsed in his favorite chair. He needed to share his burden with someone or go crazy.

"What are we celebrating?"

"It's a long story," replied Lemon. "I need a sympathetic ear."

The neighbor leaned forward in his chair. With drink in hand, he listened to his friend's narrative. When Lemon concluded his account, he swore his neighbor to secrecy.

"Don't worry about me, Sheldon. I won't say a word," assured the neighbor. "I had no idea you were involved in that kind of stuff."

"I know you didn't," said Lemon, who was feeling better after getting the heaviness of his secret off his chest. "Let's play some rummy."

##########

THE DETECTIVES WERE DRIVING ALONG THE STREETS of Staten Island when traffic came to a crawl.

The cause of the slowdown was motorist rubbernecking due to a vehicular accident.

"Everybody has to see what happened," commented Von Hess.

"Things will open up once we pass by the accident."

"So what are we doing about an undercover, boss?" asked Von Hess.

"I originally thought Detective DeCesare over in the West Village would be perfect. But then I realized that he isn't old enough to have worked for Lemon's brother-in-law years ago. So he's out."

"You want the undercover to be a guy, right?"

"Definitely," replied Markie. "I'm saving the females for later on when I need to tickle the interest of the people in the bar. Can you think of anybody about fifty who might make a good undercover?"

"What about the English guy from the senior citizens' squad?"

"No, he looks too imposing," replied Markie. "I prefer someone who looks a little dopey but isn't. You know the type, somebody who could fit in without worrying people."

"You don't want anybody *too* soft."

"I definitely don't want anybody too soft. I want an average looking street guy, one not too smart and not too dopey. The ideal would be a conniver . . . a chameleon who can adapt to any situation."

Von Hess began thinking about potential candidates. Soon he had one. "How about Eustice Costello from night watch?" he proposed. "He lives right here on Staten Island."

"Now, there's a guy who can fit the bill," agreed Markie. "What do they call him over there again?"

"They call him Useless Eustice."

Markie laughed aloud at being reminded of Costello's nickname. "He's definitely our man. No one would take him for a cop, *and* he can scheme with the best of them. They'll never make him."

"The question is, do you think he'll want to do it?" asked Von Hess.

"We'll convince him if he doesn't. Call up the borough and get his number and home address."

After securing the detective's home number, Von Hess contacted Costello. Arrangements were made to see the detective at his house.

As they got closer to the accident, Markie noticed that an elderly woman was involved. She reminded the sergeant of an incident long past. "That woman looks like Tessie Fingers."

"Who is that, Sarge?"

"When I was a rookie cop on the Lower East Side, this little old woman Tessie Fingers used to walk her dog along Second Avenue. The first time I met her was when she tapped on the window of the radio car. We were parked by Slugger Ann's joint. Before I could roll down the window, the guy I was working with told me to get out of the car and see what the old lady wants. When I did, he locked the car doors. The next thing I know the old lady makes a grab for my pecker. I'm on Second Avenue circling the radio car to get away from her while she's chasing me with the dog. She's got the dog leash in one hand and reaching for me with the other while wiggling her fingers."

"What about your partner?"

"My partner?" asked Markie. "He sat inside the car busting a gut. Talk about sexual harassment!"

"Your partner knew she would do that?"

"Sure he knew. The whole precinct knew about that old lady but me. She was harmless, but you know how it was in those days, everybody got baptized by fire."

"That's a pretty funny story, Sarge."

"It *was* pretty funny. C'mon, step on it. Traffic finally opened up.

When the investigators arrived at Detective Costello's family home, a woman in work clothes came to the door. Looking beyond her, the investigators could see a paint tarp on the dining room floor, a ladder, and an open can of paint with a wet brush atop it. It was clear that Mrs. Costello had been working.

"Can I help you?" she asked.

"I'm Sergeant Markie, and this is Detective Von Hess," answered the sergeant. "We're here to see Eustice. We spoke to him a little while ago, so he's expecting us."

"And where are you from?"

"We're from headquarters."

"Is Eustice in trouble?" she asked with concern in her voice. "I'm his wife."

"No, of course not. . . . We just need his help on a case we're working on."

"You must be desperate," she said snidely. "Come in. He's upstairs. I'll go get him."

When Mrs. Costello got to the second floor, she found her husband sitting at a desk in front of his computer. The faint wheezes she heard indicated to her that her husband was sound asleep. The detective's head was thrown back over the chair, and his left index finger rested on the keyboard's letter *X*. The computer screen reflected an *X* rapidly traveling from left to right and continuing downward to create page after page of the letter.

"EUSTICE!" she called out crisply. Her voice caused the detective to jump up in his seat. "JESUS CHRIST! Is that supposed to be funny?" Eustice asked with agitation. "Don't ever wake me up like that. . . . You can give me a heart attack."

"Don't be so dramatic," said the detective's wife. "You have company downstairs."

"Oh shit. I forgot about that," he said, rising from his chair.

Eustice was a stocky man in his late forties who was sensitive about his thinning hair. What attracted him to the overnight squad was that it was an assignment that came with little responsibility. Simply put, the function of the unit was to hold down the borough until the precinct squad detectives reported for duty at 8:00 a.m. At that point, whatever happened overnight was handed off. What sweetened the overnight shift were those peaceful nights that enabled the squad to avail themselves of sleep. The assignment was a perfect fit for someone looking to avoid working hard.

Yawning, the night watch detective scratched his head and made his way down the steps, where he convened with Markie and Von Hess. "What's up, Sarge?"

"We have a proposition for you," said Markie.

The detective immediately became wary. "What might that be?"

"We have a need to fill an undercover assignment."

"You want *me* for an undercover assignment?" asked Eustice with surprise. "I'm no longer any good for that stuff, Sarge. I couldn't get over in an old age home if I had to figure out who wore Depends."

"Look, this is a good deal." Markie proceeded to explain the assignment in detail to the detective.

"I don't know, Sarge. Honestly, I kind of got used to working in night watch."

"This is only a temporary assignment, Eustice. You'll go back to night watch when it's over."

"I know it looks that way now, but those gigs can wind up going on and on forever."

Markie gave a look to Von Hess. He was seeking support in putting his pitch over.

"You know, Eustice, this job isn't *all* work," pointed out the senior detective.

"What do you mean?"

"What do you think comes along with an assignment like this? Use your imagination."

Eustice began thinking about the latitude he'd have. He soon became interested in hearing more.

"I suppose if there is a lot of hanging out in bars and so on, I could probably do that," said Eustice.

"Some days you may work just a few hours, with the rest of your time at home doing reports or whatever you need to do," advised Markie.

"Do I get an expense account?"

"Yeah, you'll get to spend some of the city's money."

The wheels were turning in the mind of Eustice as he began to think in terms of advantages. "Do you see any gambling connected to this case?"

"There's bound to be gambling."

"To get close to the target, I'd have to hang out, do some gambling, or whatever it takes, right?"

"That's correct," answered Markie, knowing where Eustice was coming from.

Eustice, if given the department's money to gamble with, recognized the opportunity to make a few bucks. Since he'd never admit to winning, he'd never have to turn any money back in to the department.

"Talk to him about the job, Ollie, while I use the little boys' room. Is that okay, Eustice?"

"Help yourself, boss. It's off the kitchen."

"You know, Eustice, if you succeed in this assignment, the sergeant can put you in for a promotion to second-grade. We're Chief McCoy's pet unit. This is a job that could potentially pay off plenty for you."

The idea of a promotion *and* a good time sold Eustice. A word from Chief McCoy meant he would be pretty much a shoo-in for a grade promotion.

"Alright, count me in. Where do I sign?"

Markie was delighted to hear this. "I'll reach out to the chief and get you assigned to our office," he said. "Oh, and one other thing, Eustice . . . we'll fix you up with a rented car with dummy plates, new identification, and a new name."

"What's my name going to be, boss?'

"Robert Jerome. You'll be called Bayonne Bob. We'll be in touch. In the meantime, learn all you can about Bayonne and the auto crime business."

After leaving the Costello residence Von Hess made another attempt to get Markie to agree to stop at the rehab center to visit Fishnet Milligan. Being friendly with a union delegate positioned Von Hess to receive updates concerning Fishnet's progress. Von Hess was encouraged by the delegate to evaluate Fishnet's condition for himself.

"Before we head back to Brooklyn, do you want me to swing by the rehab center?" asked Von Hess.

"Again with the rehab center. . . . What for?" asked Markie.

"To go and see the miracle man."

"Do you really care, Ollie? We both know the guy is no good. I don't know how he got on the job in the first place. He should be doing his recovering in a cell."

"I hear you, Sarge. I'm no fan of his either. . . . You know that. I'm just curious. You said—"

"I know, I know. Maybe next time we're out this way, Ollie."

"No problem."

##########

THROUGH THE OPEN DOOR OF HIS ROOM Fishnet Milligan watched the attractive CNA from his chair. He always looked forward to seeing the young woman. She activated the carnal desires of the recuperating former detective. His lust led him to inquire about her. Fishnet ascertained that the CNA's name was Wayna Garcia, a single woman who lived with an aunt in the Sunset Park section of Brooklyn. Fishnet slipped onto his bed before calling out to her.

"Excuse me, miss . . . could you please help adjust my position a little?" he asked politely.

"I'll be there in a minute," she replied.

When she approached the bed, the retired detective, who possessed far more mobility than he let on, inhaled deeply in order to suck in the sweet smell of the perfume she wore. His mind traveled further with each intake of the jasmine-like fragrance. With closed eyes, he relished the pleasurable sensation connected to the innocent feel of her hands on his body. As she tried to turn him, she lifted him upward. Finding Fishnet to be extraordinarily heavy, the assistant moved in closer, grabbing his upper clothing tightly. Now with a firmer grip, she made a greater effort to turn him. This time, instead of working his weight against her pull, Fishnet went with the flow. He briefly considered propelling himself upward as if shot out of a cannon and coming down face-first into the CNA's ample chest. He wisely decided against doing this. Instead, Fishnet attempted to charm her.

"You must be taking the Charles Atlas course," he said, referring to the famed bodybuilder. The CNA just smiled. "I've been cooped up in here for so long that I'm going stir-crazy," explained the former detective. "What's your name?"

"I'm Ms. Garcia," she replied.

Fishnet nodded approvingly. "Now, that's a really nice name . . . a professional-sounding name. How about you sit and talk with me, Ms. Garcia?"

"I don't think I can right now," she replied.

"I'd love to *see-ya, Ms. Gar-ci-a*," he said in a singsong voice.

"Oh, please!" she replied, unable to conceal what was possibly a trace of amusement.

Fishnet reminded the CNA of someone whom she couldn't quite put her finger on. His resemblance to Clark Gable, the king of Hollywood in his day, was so striking that many people recognized the physical similarity. As their discourse continued, the assistant found herself becoming drawn to Fishnet.

"You know, you inspire me to get well," said Fishnet.

"Oh boy . . . here it comes," she said. "How do I do that?"

"How do you think?"

The assistant blushed. "You are too much!" she said, wondering what he'd say next.

After Wayna left, a lingering question stayed with her. She wondered what Fishnet was going to be like once he was all cleaned up and at full strength. It was a thought that held her interest.

17

Q-Ball Otto

JASPER ARRIVED AT SILKY'S SOCIAL CLUB WITH a bald-headed neighborhood tough known as Q-Ball Otto. Otto was used to provide protection for Spanky during drug transactions. Jasper was now seeking to secure Silky's concurrence in employing Otto at the James Brothers Saloon. Otto was felt to be an imposing resource capable of supporting Mousey's efforts as bar manager. There was little doubt that Otto could maintain order at the saloon and also be effective in collecting money from those reneging on their loan obligation. Otto's only drawback was his limited intelligence. It was a deficiency that the thirty-nine-year-old offset with his Herculean power. While many could outthink Otto, few could stand up to his Popeye-like forearms and big hands when called to action.

While Jasper was engaged in Silky's office, Otto waited patiently at the club's counter/bar. A small time forger who was acquainted with Otto decided to have some fun at the dullard's expense. He began inflating Otto's ego by praising him for his awful impression of the actor James Cagney.

"You do a great Cagney impression," said the forger. "How about giving the boys a treat?"

"Yeah, c'mon and do Cagney," encouraged someone else.

"Go ahead and do him," urged yet another.

"Now?" asked Otto.

"No, do it a week from Tuesday," replied the forger sarcastically. "Of course we want to see it now."

Complying with the request, Q-Ball Otto squared his shoulders and tightened his facial muscles. Believing that he now actually looked like the psychopathic Cody Jarrett as portrayed by Cagney in the movie *White Heat*, he went into his impression. He reenacted the jail scene in which Jarrett goes berserk after learning that his elderly mother had been shot in the back by Big Ed, a disgruntled member of the Jarrett gang. Otto became so engrossed in his portrayal that he forgot where he was. As he thundered the words *"MA'S DEAD!"* he began bouncing barstools off the floor.

"Ooooooo, what are you doing?" yelled one of the seated card players, not appreciating the ruckus.

Otto, embarrassed by the reaction, realized he might have overstepped his bounds. Walking lightly, the sometime gravedigger immediately began picking the stools up off the floor.

"I knew this dumb moron would go nuts!" commented the forger to another club patron.

The comment was heard by Otto, who was exceedingly self-conscious over his meager allotment of gray matter. Aware that he was being made fun of, Otto set after the snickering forger.

"I'LL BUST YOU UP!" roared Otto as he took a step toward the man who had belittled him.

"WHAT'S ALL THE RACKET ABOUT?" shouted the unmistakable voice of Silky from the back of the club. These few words silenced the room. Recognizing the presence of the mob boss, Otto froze in his tracks.

"This halfwit is out of his mind," said the forger, fingering Otto. "He came in and started throwing stools all over the place . . . and now he's looking to fight."

"He's with me, Silky," whispered Jasper.

"*YOU* . . . get in my office," the gangster ordered, addressing Otto. "You too, Jasper," he added.

"Let's go inside, Otto," instructed Jasper, who failed to immediately comply with Silky's order.

"Where do you get off coming in here and disrespecting *MY* club?" asked Silky, once they were alone.

"I meant no disrespect," said Otto, looking at Jasper for relief.

"You ain't welcome here. Don't ever let me see you set foot in my club again. The only reason you're walking out of here in on piece is because Jasper is under some illusion that he has a need for you."

As Otto was leaving the office, he was told by Jasper to wait outside on the street for him.

"What's wrong with him?" asked Silky.

"I know he was way out of line, Silky . . . but I could still use him at the bar."

"I just bounced him out of here. What good is he gonna be at the bar?"

"You just got an idea of how he could take care of himself. He could be useful."

"But he's a dope," pointed out Silky.

"You don't need to be too smart for what we need him for. Besides, we got Johnny Blondell at the bar.

Silky thought about it for a moment before responding. "I forgot about Johnny being there," said Silky, remembering the man he'd committed murders with. "Ahh, go ahead. We'll give the dumb bastard a try. I'll tell Johnny to keep him in line."

After leaving the club Jasper and Otto went to the bar. Jasper was sure that he'd made the right decision by appointing Mousey the new manager of the James Brothers Saloon. He saw little risk because Mousey had proven to be fiercely loyal to him. The added presence of mobster Johnny Blondell practically guaranteed that things would run smoothly.

Jasper called Mousey down to the basement of the bar so that they could talk privately. "Remember this, Mousey. . . . *You* are my man in charge over here," advised Jasper. "That means your word is law."

"I got it, Jasper."

"Any bumps pop up and I'm not around, go right to Johnny. He'll guide you on what to do."

"I will," agreed Mousey.

"Keep this in mind: y*ou* control the money the others make upstairs. Whatever they go home with in their pocket, they can thank you for. You assign the days, shifts, and hours that they work," lectured Jasper. "Never let them forget that whatever you give, you can take away." Mousey nodded respectfully. "Anybody looking to come in here to do business, drink or gamble downstairs is gonna need to kiss your ass. Understand?"

"I got it, Jasper."

"If somebody goes bust and needs a transfusion of funds, the approval has to come from *you*."

"Can't Johnny okay a loan on his own?"

"No, *you're* the man who controls the bank. Johnny can recommend a loan he wants to make, but you approve it. Johnny's job is to counsel you when you ain't sure on how to handle something."

"What about collecting from deadbeats who don't come up with the money on time?"

"When that happens, you give them a little breathing room. We're not vultures looking to pick people's bones. You give them a little more time to make their juice payment."

"And if they still don't pay after I give them a break?"

"Then you send in Q-Ball Otto."

"Who is he?" asked Mousey.

"He's your new collector, bouncer, and bodyguard," advised Jasper. "Otto is going to be the protection in this joint. With him, all you got to remember to do is to give him exact instructions. He's no big thinker, so don't strain his brain. He'll also be helping out Spanky from time to time."

"When do I get to meet him?"

"He's upstairs." A short time later, Jasper introduced Otto to Mousey.

"What do you think, Mousey?" asked Jasper. "Could he scare a lot of people or what?"

"He sure could," said Mousey, nodding approvingly.

"Now look, Otto; I want you to remember that this job doesn't require you to be no rocket scientist. All you gotta do is what Mousey tells you to do."

"I got it, Jasper."

"You're here to protect him, throw out any assholes, and walk Mousey to his car with my money at closing time."

"No problem; I got it. You said you wanted me to do collections, right?"

"That's right, that too."

"What about going out with Spanky?"

"That won't change. It'll still be like a part-time job for you. You'll get paid after each run."

"I get paid different in here?"

"Here you get paid in cash every Monday. You're happy with the number we discussed, right?"

"Yeah, it's good. When do you want me to start?"

"Right away," replied Jasper, extending his hand to shake. He smiled as he felt the power in Otto's grip. "Yeah, you'll scare a lot of people," commented Jasper.

With Q-Ball Otto and Johnny having his back, Mousey felt invincible. It wasn't long before he began walking with a swagger. When bar patrons who had been copping cocaine from Buster saw that Mousey was now in charge, they began feeling him out to determine if he was to be their new source for cocaine. Careful not to overstep his bounds, the newly appointed manager consulted Johnny Blondell.

"Go leash for now. I'm gonna have to find out about that," advised Blondell.

The next time Jasper arrived at the bar, he went straight to Mousey to see how things were going.

"We had a really good game going the other night . . . lots of action," answered Mousey.

"Nice. How are you doing with collections?"

"So far we've collected everything we had coming to us. Otto is really good at collecting. I send him out, and it's like withdrawing money from the bank."

"I figured that. There ain't gonna be too many people willing to try and fluff him off."

"Jasper, did you talk to Johnny?"

"Yeah, I did."

"So what do you want me to do with the customers looking to cop some shit?"

"That ain't happening," he replied. "Just tell them we aren't in that business. Remember, we don't get involved in chicken shit. That's how you get pinched. Kilos of coke are our meat and potatoes."

"So what do I do if somebody is looking for a kilo?"

"You call Spanky. Just remember, anybody you refer to Spanky I want to know about."

"No problem, Jasper."

##########

LAS VEGAS LUCY'S MOTHER BEGAN ASKING for money ever since the death of her husband. Financially weakened, she was compelled to rely on the contributions of Lucy to see her through. The mother and daughter were sitting at the kitchen table going through their expenses. Once-welcomed celebratory family occasions were now being viewed as burdens. Every other week seemed to introduce a new cost that further bled Lucy's savings. First there was the new bathroom, then the new kitchen appliances. After that came the need for a new roof. Two weeks after that, her mother had broken a front tooth. While the money being earned from the drug business made it possible for Lucy to absorb these expenses, it was derailing her long-term plan of amassing enough capital to retire on. Frustrated over these financial challenges, Lucy was more determined than ever to get her hands on more money.

"Lucy, we just received an invitation to your cousin's wedding in Los Angeles," said Lucy's mother.

"Another wedding?" asked Lucy, clearly annoyed. "And it's in Los Angeles? That means even more money!" protested Lucy.

"We have to go. She's your first cousin," the older woman stated.

"My having to truck out to Los Angeles every time she gets married is beginning to get a little old."

"What can you do? Your cousin made some bad choices. But she's cleaned up now. She's been working steady for two years now."

"I forgot that," said Lucy, brightening. "She works on Skid Row . . . right?"

"Yes. It's very bad there."

Seeing a possible opening to push product on a small scale directly to users, Lucy ceased voicing her resistance concerning the wedding. "I suppose it would be a good idea for us to go," she finally said.

Lucy now viewed her cousin, who was no stranger to drugs, as a potential lifeline who could further her goal to accumulate enough money to retire with her mother and daughter to a far off destination where they could live well. After settling the financial affairs with her mother, Lucy retired to the privacy of her room. Without even talking to her cousin, she called up Jasper in New York. In the comfort of her bed, she lit a cigarette as she listened to the phone ring.

"Hi, it's me," she said after Jasper answered his cell phone.

"Who is me?" he asked curtly, not immediately recognizing the voice.

"Lucy," she said.

"What's wrong?" he asked, not happy that she was disturbing him at home.

"Nothing is wrong. I'm just calling to talk to you."

"Hang on a minute." Jasper stepped outside of the house to continue with the call. "If this is a social call, you caught me at a bad time."

"I want to talk to you about business. I know how we can make big things happen in Los Angeles."

"Not on the phone," he cautioned.

145

"When are you coming out West?"

Jasper hesitated before answering. Since a physical attraction did exist, he thought about it. "Let me get back to you on that tomorrow. I have to go."

After sleeping on it, Jasper decided to go to Vegas. He called Spanky to apprise him of his decision.

"We're taking a trip to Vegas."

"We are?" Spanky was leery of the offer. The beating of Buster was still fresh in his mind.

"I was thinking of going later in the week."

"Is there something special happening out there?"

"I want to see Lucy. She has a possible business opportunity for me."

Jasper's motive for inviting Spanky was twofold. Firstly, he wanted Spanky to worry over whether or not he'd be coming back in one piece. Secondly, Jasper wanted Spanky to spend time with Dotty, Lucy's girlfriend. Jasper intended for Lucy to probe Dotty about her pillow talk with Spanky. It was Jasper's way of staying one move ahead on the checkerboard of deceit.

"What kind of business opportunity?" Spanky asked.

"I'll be able to tell you after our date with the girls. I'll know more then."

"What girls?"

"I'm talking about Lucy and her friend Dotty."

"You can't do business with Dotty. Trust me, she's not the type," warned Spanky.

"I didn't say that we were doing business with *her*. Don't worry so much. She's just there to frolic with you while I spend time hearing out Lucy. *She's* the one with some big idea."

Although Spanky wasn't against hanging out in Las Vegas, he swore to himself he wasn't venturing far from the strip. Spanky didn't put it past Jasper to have notions of burying him in the desert sand.

Jasper got back to Lucy to inform her when they would be arriving in Vegas. Lucy was surprised to learn that Spanky would be tagging along. At first she resisted Jasper's request that she invite Dotty to make it a foursome.

"Why do we need them?" she asked.

"I got my reasons. Just line her up."

Lucy didn't argue. She didn't want to sour her opportunity to advance her plan. If she could convince Jasper to entrust her with expanding his drug

146

operation into Los Angeles without the assistance of Spanky, she'd have it made. With the help of a cousin who worked on Skid Row, she'd be able set up an independent operation of her own without Jasper's knowledge.

Lucy and Dotty arrived at around 4:00 p.m. They walked with their heads held high as they entered the lobby wheeling their luggage. Dressed fashionably, they carried themselves as if they were people of great importance. Lucy dialed Jasper's number.

"We're in the lobby," advised Lucy.

"I'm up in the room. I'll be right down." Jasper, who had taken two adjoining rooms, headed downstairs to meet the women. "You both look sensational," he said, sounding unusually chipper.

"Lucy insisted we look our best for you guys," said Dotty, her hand swinging toward Lucy.

"Smart girl," replied Jasper. "C'mon, let's go upstairs and get rid of those bags. I got us rooms next to each other. Dotty, you can drop your bag and freshen up in Spanky's room."

"Where is he?"

"He's in the casino someplace trying his luck." Jasper checked the time on his Rolex. "I'll call him and let him know to come upstairs," he advised. "Let's figure on the four of us meeting up at the lobby bar for drinks at 6:00 p.m. That gives *you* some time to gamble, take a nap, or do whatever. After drinks we'll have dinner and maybe catch a show. Here's the room key."

Dotty looked at Lucy knowingly. "Very good. Don't do anything I wouldn't do," she said cutely, taking the spare key card to Spanky's room.

Once alone with Lucy, Jasper locked the interior door that separated the two rooms.

"Do they have soda in there?" Lucy asked, pointing to where the beverages were stored.

Jasper checked the small cooler. "What kind do you want?"

"Give me whatever is coldest."

Jasper felt the cans. "They're all about the same," he said, taking a can randomly. Before pouring the soda, he washed out a glass. "Here you go," he said, handing her the drink.

Lucy looked at Jasper as she sipped her drink. "So do you want to hear about my idea?"

"That's why I'm here."

"And I thought you came just to see me," she said coyly.

"Let's talk about what you're proposing."

Lucy turned serious. "I can do for *us* in Los Angeles what we have going here in Vegas," she said. "All I need is the money and product. In time, we'll probably match what you're taking in back home."

"And how do you know what I take in?"

"Do you really think Spanky can keep his motor mouth zipped? I got the whole lowdown from him."

"When was that?"

"I got the story in New York the first time he picked me up at the airport."

Lucy was shrewder than what Jasper originally thought. He proceeded warily. "Let me ask you something, Lucy. What's your endgame in all this?"

"My goal is the same as yours, to make lots of money," she answered. "I want enough of it to walk away without ever having to worry again."

"You have a number?"

"I think so."

"I have to respect that. Talk to me about how you intend to kick-start this big idea of yours?"

"I see us as equal partners in Los Angeles," she said without hesitation.

Jasper smiled. Her announcing that she wanted to be his full partner immediately disqualified her from serious consideration. It was a reality that he didn't share with her.

"Go on . . ." he said, feigning interest.

"I have friends in Los Angeles, and I know others willing to relocate there."

"And . . ."

"We can use my people to open up a private gentleman's club that caters to the right crowd. We'll steer clients from Vegas and New York to our new club. They'll have a place to go to when in town."

"This sounds like a stretch," said Jasper in all honesty.

"Let me finish. I know lots of women willing to turn tricks under the right circumstances."

"So now you got me opening up a whorehouse?"

"Will you please let me finish?" said Lucy, exasperated.

Jasper backed off. "Go on. Continue."

148

"Once we get the right clientele to go once, the girls will take it from there. They'll know just how to pluck the chicken. All I'll need is financing and product."

"Just who are these girls?"

"They're women who know men."

"Tell me something; where do you get this crazy shit from?"

"There is nothing crazy here," Lucy replied, sounding insulted. "The working girls will get us up and running on the coke end once they get the customers on the mattress."

"Did you forget that I only deal in weight?"

"That won't change," she advised, not sharing her intentions to use some of his product in launching her own independent enterprise with her cousin.

Jasper wrestled with the idea, trying to understand if it made any sense. "What happens when you get to that magic number?"

"When I reach my number, I'll be done. I'll walk away, and you can have it all. I'll be someplace where I can live life in comfort without ever having to worry about money."

"I know you said you went away once. What was that story again?"

"That's my yesterday story, Jasper. When I ask you about yours, you can ask me about mine," she replied. "So what do you say? Do we have a deal?"

"Let me think this over," said Jasper.

"Remember, it'll be partners . . . you and me. We—"

"Alright already, let me just think about it," he said, cutting her off. "Stop breaking my balls!"

"So think about it," she answered, backing off.

"One thing . . . if we were to move on this, are you still going to be able to handle Vegas? We *are* making money here, you know."

"No problem, Jasper. I've got it covered."

Lucy decided it was time to pull out all the stops. She drew the room curtains and turned on some music. She stripped to her panties and began to sensually dance as she approached the sitting Jasper. He closed his eyes as she proceeded to give him a lap dance. This consideration was extended to further her second objective. Whether Jasper knew it or not, he was going to buy her a gold watch.

##########

ALLEY SAT AT HOME ALONE, OVERTHINKING her relationship with Markie. She turned to the usual avenues of relief to ease her troubles, but television, radio, and reading were just temporary solutions. Feeling isolated, she began binge eating Godiva chocolates to comfort herself. Her sullenness had everything to do with not hearing from the sergeant after reaching out to him several times. She had felt certain that Markie would eventually show up at Fitzie's for a drink at some point. His failure to appear there was an omen that something was definitely wrong. His whereabouts became a question that gnawed at her. It was followed by a multitude of speculative thoughts. *Was he hurt? Could he have gone back with his wife? Did he meet someone new? Has he moved on?* The more she dwelled on these things, the less rational she became. Bordering on obsession, she began blowing up Markie's phone.

Markie was sitting behind the wheel of his car when his cell phone rang. His concentration elsewhere, he answered the phone without checking to see who called.

"Hello?" he asked impatiently, not happy at being disturbed while conducting surveillance.

"Al?"

The sergeant immediately recognized Alley's voice. Regretting that he'd answered the call, he hesitated for a second before speaking. "Alley?"

"What's going on? Are you alright? I haven't heard from you," she asked.

"I've been very busy. Look, I can't talk now. I'll have to call you back later."

"Oh, okay," she answered glumly.

Not knowing what else to say, Alley hung up, struggling to find a bright side to their brief conversation. Eventually she found the silver lining she sought. *At least he's alive and picked up the phone! If he didn't want to talk, he would have never picked up*, she told herself. With this tidbit to cling to, she prepared herself a cup of coffee as she waited for his callback.

Markie resumed watching the office building after cutting short his conversation with Alley. He sat alone in his personal car off duty. The sergeant frequently glanced at his watch to check the time. He could only put in about another hour of surveillance before he would have to report for duty. After thirty minutes had elapsed, he finally saw what he had been waiting to see.

"Son of a bitch," Markie said under his breath as watched his ex-wife, Florence, exit the office building with her boss. "SON OF A BITCH!" he repeated more loudly as Florence and the dentist got into his Mercedes-Benz convertible. "At least the bastard has the decency to keep the top up," he thought. He was worried what people would think of his ex-wife cavorting with a married man.

Markie followed the black Benz to the apartment house near the armory. When they emerged from the car, he saw the dentist place his arm over Flo's shoulder. It pained him to see Florence reciprocate by placing her arm around the dentist's waist. When the dentist slipped his hand down to Flo's buttocks as they entered the door to the building, the scene turned much too graphic for Markie to endure. He felt himself weakening emotionally. The sergeant's desire for satisfaction took over, blunting all rational feelings. Having turned on a dime, he thought of greeting the dentist with the tire iron he kept under the front seat. Markie's rational side ultimately prevailed but only after venting his anger. His release came from violently punching the dashboard of his car. With the pain came the realization that his divorce from Flo was the final word. He knew that he had no right to think that Flo had been taken away from him. Now, thinking sensibly, he could see Flo going for a professional man with money. Why not? There was value in such a liaison. Besides, maybe the dentist was divorced or even a widower. Whatever the case, it was over with Florence. The department had sufficiently hardened Markie to where he could face facts once the emotions were set aside.

The sergeant closed the door that should have already been closed. The area behind that door was now floorless. Markie was relegated to just one nest to return to. He dialed up Alley Cat. After the usual apologies, his request for forgiveness was welcomed with an invitation to fly into her receiving arms that night after work.

18

Bayonne Bob Jerome

CHIEF MCCOY WAS A MAN WHO INSISTED ON PUTTING a face to a name. Before signing off on the temporary transfer of Eustice Costello, he ordered Lieutenant Wright to arrange a meeting in his office. Aside from wanting to evaluate Costello, it was a way for him to remind everyone who was in charge. He subscribed to the belief that there was no benefit to being the boss unless subordinates knew it.

"Al, the chief wants to meet Eustice before he signs off on the transfer," advised Lieutenant Wright.

"Doesn't he trust our judgment?" asked Markie.

"What do I know?" replied the lieutenant. "Have Costello in the office tomorrow at 10:00 a.m."

Prior to producing the detective, Markie and Von Hess made it a point to prep their candidate for the meeting. Wanting Costello to project authenticity in the role he was to play, they told him to dress the part of Bayonne Bob Jerome for his meeting with the chief. Markie emphasized to Eustice that while it would be best to show enthusiasm for his new assignment, his responses to questions should nevertheless remain brief.

Detective Costello, Lieutenant Wright, and Markie sat at the long table that touched against the center of the chief's desk. The chief liked the T-shape setup, feeling that it accentuated his authority. McCoy visually scrutinized Eustice, who wore a royal blue velour blazer, charcoal slacks, black loafers, and a white open-collar shirt. Completing the picture before the chief was a black onyx ring and a thick gold chain Eustice had around his neck.

"Is that your own personal jewelry?" asked the chief.

"No, it's on loan from the department's property clerk," advised Markie, answering for Eustice.

Chief McCoy noticed that Eustice parted his hair low on one side of his head. The chief, whose own hair was struggling for survival, favored a close-cropped military cut for men with thinning hair. McCoy commenced to ask the proposed undercover a few questions, which Eustice fielded well. After granting his blessing, the chief had Wright outline the rules pertaining to drug use and criminal behavior when working in an undercover capacity. Wright also emphasized the importance of ethics. As these parameters were being explained, the egocentric Eustice was only half listening. His thoughts centered on whether or not he'd have the discipline to face the temptations that would inevitably come his way. Apart from the danger, he knew only too well that engaging in criminal misbehavior, if he were caught, could result in his arrest and the loss of his job.

"Here is your new identification," said Wright, handing a driver's license to the undercover. "You are now Robert Jerome of Bayonne, New Jersey."

"What was the nickname you want him to go under, Sarge?" asked McCoy.

"Bayonne Bob Jerome, Chief,." Markie answered. "The cover story is that he lives in Bayonne and had worked in the car business with Lemon's brother-in-law, Monte."

"Have you met the informant yet?" McCoy asked Eustice.

"Yes, I did, Chief. I just met him a little while ago."

"Do you think you can work with him?"

"No problem, Chief," assured the undercover. "I can work with anyone."

Chief McCoy nodded his head, again confirming that Eustice was acceptable. The chief then pointed to the lieutenant, indicating for him to continue. McCoy broke into the conversation from time to time when something interested him.

"We got you a car, Eustice," said Wright, handing the detective the key. It's a black 1998 Lincoln Continental. You'll find it in the garage downstairs." The car affirmed Eustice's belief that the undercover opportunity was worthwhile.

"What about an address for me?" asked Eustice.

"We have an apartment building in Bayonne at our disposal. The owner is a retired cop. He keeps one apartment vacant for himself for when he wants privacy, so we'll have his place accessible to us if need be," advised Lieutenant Wright. "I don't really see that happening, though; do you, Sarge?"

"Not likely," advised Markie. "But it's good for Eustice to have access just in case."

"Do you think I should stay there a couple of nights a week?" asked Eustice.

"No, that won't be necessary," answered Wright.

The question didn't go unnoticed by Markie. *Fat chance*, he thought to himself. He could see that Eustice was going to need watching.

"Remember, the goal is to get in the pocket of this fellow Jasper so that he talks about offing Mathis."

Everyone nodded in agreement at Chief McCoy's reminder. "Alright, then, if there is nothing else, we are done here."

Lemon and Von Hess sat in the conference room a few feet from Chief McCoy's office. As they waited for the meeting to conclude, Lemon began thinking in terms of self-protection. He convinced himself that he should have a say in how things were going to go down.

"I think that this is how things should go. . . ." began the informant.

"Save your breath," said Von Hess, taking exception. Lemon's attempt to control the action was nothing new to him. He had experienced this type of behavior with other informants in the past. "You got no say in how anything is going to go, Lemon."

"Yeah, that's fine for you to say. It's not your ass on the line out there. . . ."

Markie and Eustice entered the office as Lemon was protesting. "What's the problem?" asked Markie.

"I think I should have a say in what concerns me," stated Lemon adamantly. "Detective Von Hess over here doesn't seem to think so. What do you say, Sergeant?"

"I say forget it," replied Markie, clipping the informant's wings abruptly.

"But I'm an agent for you. . . ."

"Let's put the cards on the table, my friend. You can call yourself an agent, a confidential informant, a government witness, a resource, or whatever the hell floats your boat. At the end of the day, no matter how you slice the cake, you're still a rat. You're caught in a trap and looking to get out from under," reminded Markie callously.

The informer stiffened at the rebuke. "But I'm doing this to help you guys!" declared Lemon, trying to retain a degree of dignity.

"Spare me the bullshit. Don't pass yourself off as some kind of patriot. Look, if you've got a problem playing ball, say the word. Keep in mind, though, that if you bow out the next dump you take will be in a prison toilet."

Lemon remained silent as Markie's words resonated. Once the message sunk in, Lemon succumbed to the authority of those who held the key to the handcuffs.

"Whatever you say," said Lemon meekly.

"There is nothing personal in this, Lemon," reminded Markie, switching to a softer tone. The sergeant then turned to address Von Hess. "Ollie, what did you find out about this guy Jasper?"

"Jasper owns lots of businesses. He's shady, but the money he spreads around does a good job in cloaking his dark side for those who don't want to see it. I'm told that it'll be hit or miss as to when to catch him at the bar," said Von Hess.

"You want Lemon to ask for Jasper when we go in the bar, Sarge?" asked Eustice.

"No. Just go in and mind your own business. Have a couple of drinks and keep to yourselves. Don't talk to anyone unless they begin talking to you first."

"What about the bartenders? Don't you want us to engage them?"

"Wait for them to make the first overture," replied Markie. "I want to avoid any appearance of pushiness. I want them wondering about you."

"You don't want me to just shut them out altogether, right?" asked Eustice.

"What the sergeant is saying is that if they start asking anything, stay tight-lipped without being rude," answered Von Hess. "Don't forget, you aren't supposed to be a legitimate guy."

"That's right. After you have a drink or two, you leave a big tip and go," instructed Markie. "That'll be remembered. We'll be outside in the surveillance van."

"Got it," said Eustice. Lemon sat quietly, taking everything in.

"After the first visit to the bar, plan on going back a couple of days later to do the same exact thing. After that, depending on what happens, I'll decide the next step. Can you think of anything else for them, Ollie?"

"Yeah, try to sit by the big front window where we can see you from the street," said Von Hess. "If you encounter a problem inside, and I'm talking an emergency where you need us to come running, just face the front glass and start waving us in. We'll come to the rescue."

"Are you going to give me spending money up front, Sarge?"

"No. You lay out the money, and we'll reimburse you when you submit an expense report."

155

"Very good," said Eustice, wondering how much he could pad his expenses without drawing attention.

"Look Lemon, never call Eustice anything other than Bob or Bayonne Bob. That's his name from now on: Bayonne Bob Jerome. Remember . . . Bayonne Bob Jerome."

"I got it," answered the informant soberly.

"Oh, and Eustice, take the wood grips off your gun and wrap the handle in black tape. If anybody sees it on you, I don't want it to look like a cop's gun," ordered Markie.

"Will do, boss."

"And don't use a holster. Just stick the gun your pocket or waistband."

Markie's plan was set to commence with Eustice and Lemon visiting the James Brothers Saloon midweek at 3:00 p.m. Before they were dismissed, the sergeant had Von Hess take a photo of them.

"What's the picture for?" asked Lemon.

Markie smiled. "It's for my scrapbook."

As they left the building, Lemon looked to Eustice for an answer to his question. Eustice hunched his shoulders. "Search me. . . . That Markie dances to his own tune," was the answer given.

On the day of the visit to the bar Detective Von Hess parked the surveillance van next to the fire hydrant located opposite the James Brothers Saloon. After he shut off the engine, he and Markie relocated to the back of the van. They sat on wooden folding chairs facing the smoky side window of the van. Taped to the window glass was a green plastic trash bag. Von Hess cut away two small pieces of the plastic so that they could see the front of the bar. The detective was confident that he and Markie couldn't be seen from the street. Unless someone decided to walk right up to the van's window, they'd go undetected. Von Hess raised his binoculars to his eyes, zeroing in on the front glass of the James Brothers Saloon.

"What kind of eyeball have you got, Ollie?" asked Markie.

"Good, boss. I can see a little beyond the front of the bar. I can even make out the bartender."

Eustice drove past the front of the bar in his Lincoln. He parked at the end of the block at a meter.

"The UC [undercover] and the CI [confidential informant] just drove by the joint," announced Von Hess, putting down his binoculars to wipe his eyes.

"Where did they go?"

"Hang on a second, boss. . . . I think he's parking," said Von Hess, bringing the binoculars back up to his eyes. "Yeah, he's parking."

"Too bad he couldn't get a spot right in front of the place. I'd like people to see his car."

##########

LEMON GOT OUT OF THE PASSENGER SIDE of the Lincoln. He walked around to the driver's side, where he waited for the undercover detective.

"What happened? Having a hard time getting out?" asked Lemon.

"I was just checking something. You got any change for the meter?"

"I've got no change," said Lemon, shaking his head in the negative.

The undercover detective frowned. Forget it, let's go to the bar."

##########

VON HESS GAVE A QUICK LOOK OUT THE front window of the van. Seeing that the car parked in front of them was pulling out of the metered parking space, he moved to the front of the vehicle to pull away from the fire hydrant. After advancing the car to the legal spot, he returned to the back of the van.

"Eustice just parked by a meter," said Von Hess.

"Did he feed the meter?"

"Not that I saw, Sarge."

"Then he's sharper than he looks," commented Markie.

"Why's that?"

"He knew that bad guys don't usually go around feeding parking meters."

"Just get a load of these two," said Von Hess. "They really *look* like they belong together."

"They *do* look like two peas in a pod, don't they?" said Markie as he watched them enter the bar.

##########

157

EUSTICE POINTED TO THE UNOCCUPIED BARSTOOLS situated off to the right of the entrance. The seats enabled the two men to assume desirable positions at the front of the bar.

"We got us a good spot here by the window," said the undercover.

"Yeah, that's nice," replied Lemon, his lack of enthusiasm for being at the James Brothers Saloon coming through.

The profiles of both men were visible to the surveillance team positioned on the street. The jukebox, which was silent, was located a couple of feet from where Eustice sat. The undercover noted that several men were seated mid bar. They were drinking bottled beer that was kept cold in ice-filled tin buckets that rested atop the bar.

The man behind the bar had a weathered look to him. His craggy face was comprised of deep lines that made him appear much older than his actual years. Decades of smoking had transformed his voice into a rasp. When he noticed the new arrivals, he walked over to see what they wanted to drink.

"What'll it be?" he asked.

"Let me have Jack on the rocks," said Eustice, putting a C-note on the bar. Fronting the one-hundred-dollar denomination was intentional. He *wanted* to be remembered by the bartender.

"And you?"

"Make mine the same," answered Lemon grimly, welcoming the fortification.

Through the corner of his eye, the bartender watched them as he fetched the drinks. He was trying to figure out the two strangers. Eustice and Lemon conversed in low voices. It seemed to the bartender that they were plotting something. The bartender's attention was diverted when he heard his name called by a man who had just entered the bar. The newest visitor was wearing a hard hat, jeans, and a utility belt.

"Hey, Scratchy," he called out, addressing the bartender. "Is Mousey around?"

Based upon the bartender's voice, Scratchy was an apt name for him, thought Eustice. Scratchy nodded at the man who was asking for Mousey. It was obvious to Eustice that the two knew each other. The bartender dialed a number on his cell phone.

"The telephone man is here," advised Scratchy.

Within minutes, Mousey emerged from behind a door located at the back of the bar. Eustice continued to watch as the two men got together. Lemon purposely looked down at his drink. He was trying to limit his involvement. Eustice observed the telephone man hand Mousey money.

"You staying for a drink?" asked Mousey, loud enough to be heard.

"No, I gotta get back on the job, thanks."

"Okay. See you next week if not before."

After the telephone man left, Mousey took a tiny notebook out of his rear pants pocket. He then stepped behind the bar, secured a pen, and made a notation in the small book. Based upon these observations, Eustice was able to reasonably suspect that there was a loan-sharking operation taking place. After having a second drink, Eustice left an above-average tip and departed the bar with Lemon. Once safely distanced from the bar, Eustice called Markie.

"It all went well, boss," advised the undercover. "We're heading back to Staten Island. I'll drop off Lemon and then head home."

"Did we get any results?"

"Some. We identified the daytime bartender. They call him Scratchy. He looks like an old junkie."

"Did you identify anybody else in there?"

"Yeah, somebody named Mousey. He's a young kid, but I think he's in charge of running the place."

"What makes you think that?"

"The bartender called him on his cell phone to meet with a guy who came in to give this kid Mousey money. It seemed like he was the boss."

"What was it, a shy payment?"

"I'd say so, Sarge. This Mousey made a notation in a small book he had on him after taking the money. I heard him say that he'd see him next week," advised Eustice.

"What about drugs? Lemon heard that they were in that business."

"I didn't see any drug activity."

"Anybody named Johnny in the place?" asked Von Hess.

"No. Who is he?"

"Supposedly he's the owner. His name is on the books," advised Markie. "Put it all in your report. Describe Scratchy, Mousey, and the guy making the payment. Spell out exactly what they did and said. Be sure to include the approximate times."

"Okay, boss," said Eustice. "So I'll go off duty from the field; is that alright?"

Markie looked at his watch. "Yeah, do that. Keep track of what you spent. I'll talk to you later."

Lemon was impressed at how the detectives worked. "You noticed quite a bit in there," said the informant after Eustice concluded his phone call.

"How do you think I got where I am, by sleeping?" asked Eustice, not taking into account how that statement would sound to those who really knew him.

"Well, it's *your* business to notice things, I suppose."

"You mean to tell me that you didn't catch what was going down in there?"

Lemon shrugged. "I make it my business *never* to have big eyes," he answered. "It's healthier that way. Besides, whatever goes on is your worry." The informant never mentioned to the detective that he had neglected to see the big bald-headed man who stood at the back of the bar watching Mousey. He couldn't understand how anyone could miss noticing Q-Ball Otto.

After Eustice dropped Lemon off at home, he placed a second call into Markie. "I just dropped off Lemon."

"How did he do?"

"He was fine. What's the next step, Sarge?"

"In a few days we do it again. This time you guys go there later in the afternoon. Sit in the same place if possible," said Markie. "Next time stay a little longer, say . . . for three drinks or whatever."

"What's keeping me in there so long?"

"Let the other side wonder about that. I want you creating an air of mystery," explained Markie. "As long as you're in there with Lemon, all is good. Once someone recognizes him, people will assume that you're okay. For now, the mission is just to be seen together."

"Okay, I get it."

One other thing: next time there might be someone who comes in after you get there. That person will say hello to you. Remember this. Whoever it is, is an old friend. So buy drinks and just shoot the shit as you normally would with any old friend."

"How will I know this person?"

160

"You won't; whoever it is will know you. Now you know why I took the pictures of you guys at headquarters."

"I'll let Lemon know to be ready. What do I do tomorrow?"

"Do your reports from home and rest up. What did your expenses come to?"

"I have to check what I have on me," said Eustice, who hadn't yet figured out much he intended to up what he'd actually spent.

"Okay."

Markie expected Eustice to inflate his expenses. He was okay with it because he wanted to keep his grass-eating undercover happy. He'd only worry if Eustice evolved into a meat-eater. There was no way the sergeant was going to allow the undercover detective to get the taste of pocketing big bucks.

"One last thing: that was sharp of you not feeding the meter. I was impressed that you knew that wise guys don't go around putting money in meters," said Markie, complimenting the undercover.

"Hey, I figure everyone knows that," answered Eustice, smiling. "I'll be home if you need me, Sarge."

##########

THE FOLLOWING DAY, MARKIE AND VON HESS visited the offices of the Drug Enforcement Administration Joint Task Force (DEAJTF). They were visiting Markie's former boss to ask for a favor. As they waited for the elevator, Von Hess looked about the lobby of the high end office building.

"Pretty nice real estate," commented Von Hess.

"Yeah, it is. I worked here for a year as a detective."

"This is supposed to be one of the best places to work."

"Yeah, they got it pretty good over here," acknowledged Markie. "But it wasn't for me, so I asked out."

"Was there a corruption problem?"

"No, it was nothing like that. I just always wanted to work in a precinct detective squad."

"I'll bet they found that hard to believe."

"They thought I was nuts to ask out."

Supervisory Agent Dominick Leardi was in charge of a DEA cocaine group. Each task force group was comprised of federal agents, city detectives, and state investigators who worked collectively on major cases. What made the unit especially desirable, in addition to having weekends off, was that every investigator was given a car to take home. Furthermore, there were few restrictions. Members of the task force were permitted to initiate cases anywhere and against anyone they suspected of selling drugs. Another benefit was that prisoners could be taken to either state or federal court for prosecution. This, along with deep pockets, access to high-priced informants, a group secretary and the amenities that came with a plush work environment, made it one of the choicest of assignments.

The Bronx-born Leardi had a gruff, no-nonsense style that tended to undermine his high intelligence. Markie was well aware that his fifty-year-old former supervisor ruled his group with an iron fist. Once Markie and Von Hess were alone with the cigar-chomping Leardi in his office, they filled him in on the case they were working.

"So how can I be of help, Al?" asked the agent.

"I'm hoping you have access to a snitch, somebody known around Bay Ridge."

"I thought you said that you already had a snitch. . . ."

"I'm looking for someone known in the Ridge to show up at the James Brothers Saloon. I want to give further legitimacy to our people."

"You want someone to firm up their bad guy reputation."

"That's right."

"What's the story with the target in the case?"

"Our target is a guy named Gaspare Stanlee. They call him Jasper. We have reason to believe that he's the hidden owner of the James Brothers Saloon."

"How do you spell that?"

"S-T-A-N-L-E-E."

"That's Gasber Stanlee?"

"No, the first name is Gas-pare, G-A-S-P-A-R-E. They call him Jasper."

"Is he connected?"

"I think so."

"Is there a drug connection here?"

"We believe that to be a strong possibility."

Leardi nodded. "Give me a minute. Let me see if there is anything in NADDIS," said the agent

"He may even be referenced in the NADDIS computer as Jesse James," advised Markie. "Do me a favor and also throw in the names Chris Stanlee and John Blondell.

"What's NADDIS?" asked Von Hess, who was unfamiliar with the term.

"It's a data index. NADDIS stands for the Narcotics and Dangerous Drugs Information System. The database contains information gathered by agents during investigations conducted throughout the country, Ollie," advised Markie. "It's a great investigative tool."

Leardi returned to his office twenty minutes later. "We don't have anything in our database concerning the gin mill or the Stanlee brothers," said the agent. "But we didn't come up totally dry. John Blondell is actually Giovanni Blondellini. Our agents put him and Settimo Seggio at the wake of a major narcotics trafficker up around the border. Seggio is a member of the Cosmo Guarini crime family. That's what now makes your investigation interesting. I'm sure that we have a confidential informant who lives in Bay Ridge. Let me get back to you on this."

"Thanks," said Markie, handing Leardi the photographs taken of Eustice and Lemon. "These are my people."

"Give me a day or two, Al."

Leardi jumped right on it. After identifying a suitable Bay Ridge informant, he had his agents bring her to his office the following day. He also ordered a copy of a surveillance photo of Silky Seggio and Johnny Blondell that had been taken at the wake of the narcotics trafficker ten years prior.

########

SANDY WAS A LONGTIME DEA INFORMANT. The former heroin addict had deep roots in Bay Ridge. She had done time in prison for her role in a haphazardly executed liquor store robbery. After serving her sentence, Sandy emerged from prison free of her addiction. Now a born-again Christian, she supported herself from two sources. She worked as an office cleaner in Manhattan and as a DEA confidential informant. Sandy, who was in her thirties, was considered a highly reliable source by the feds.

"Sandy, what do you know about the James Brothers Saloon?" asked Leardi after sitting her down in his office. Also present in the room was a female DEA agent.

"I know the place. It hasn't been open all that long," answered the federal informant.

"You've been in there?"

"Sometimes I go there to see my friend."

"Who is that?"

"Brenda. She's a girlfriend of mine who works as a bartender there, so I go and see her."

"How come you never mentioned this place before?" asked the female agent, her suspicions aroused.

"Because there are no drugs in there," answered Sandy defensively. "My friend has been clean for years. She even gave up smoking pot. If there was anything big going down, she wouldn't be there."

"So you are telling us that there is *no* illegal activity going on in there at all?" asked Leardi.

"My girlfriend said they gamble there at night, loan out money . . . you know, stuff like that."

"Did you ever ask her about drugs?"

"Not really."

"So how can you be so sure that there are no drugs being dealt out of there?" asked Leardi, raising his voice.

Sandy backed up. "Well, of course there *might* be . . . but if there is, I don't know anything about it."

The agents now suspected that there *was* drug activity going on at the James Brothers Saloon. "Why didn't you let me know about this place, Sandy?" asked the female agent.

"Because the last time we spoke, I didn't know there was drug activity going on there," Sandy replied, tripping herself up.

"But now you do *know* there is. . . ."

"Alright, look . . . I didn't want to get my friend in trouble," confessed Sandy. "Besides, I didn't know you wanted to know about every line being snorted in Brooklyn."

164

"Let us decide that in the future," said Leardi. "Who owns the James Brothers Saloon, Sandy?"

"Jesse James is the owner."

"Do you know him good?"

"Not really. I just met him once or twice. My girlfriend introduced me to him."

Leardi's eyes studied Sandy as she spoke. "Who is your girlfriend again?" he asked.

"Brenda."

"Does Brenda have a last name?"

"Brenda Helmicki," answered Sandy.

"Give me the names of the other people you know who work in the bar."

"I know that Scratchy is the day bartender," she advised. "The old manager was a guy named Buster, but now it's a young kid called Mousey. I don't know their real names."

"Are these guys pushing coke or heroin?" asked Leardi. He received no response. "Are they?"

"I heard that Buster used to sell a little blow," she answered.

"I have a small job for you next week, Sandy. We'll get back to you with the details."

"Same pay like last time?"

"Yes, same pay."

After Sandy left, Leardi reached out to Markie to advise him of what he'd learned.

"How about we do this?" suggested Leardi. "I'll let you have the snitch and a female agent so that you can get established. Once your people settle in, you bring us into the operation. We'll do a thorough narcotics investigation and wipe out the whole filthy nest of them. I'd love to get my teeth into Seggio and the Guarini family. Do we have a deal?"

"You got a deal."

Markie now had to sell the idea to his bosses. Following the chain of command, Markie apprised Lieutenant Wright as to what had transpired with the DEA. When Wright posted Chief McCoy, the chief reacted bitterly. He was miffed at not being consulted prior to Markie's meeting with the feds. McCoy finally settled down after getting the venom out of his system by vilifying

Wright, the messenger. He concluded his tirade by warning, "Now you know how I work."

"It won't happen again," replied Wright.

"Consider this matter closed," said Chief McCoy, abruptly ending the meeting.

"Thank you, Chief," replied the lieutenant, rising from his seat. "So we have your blessing to proceed with the DEA?"

"Now that you've committed us, go ahead with it," answered the chief.

19

Agendas

WHILE THE WOMEN EXPLORED THE VEGAS shops, Jasper relaxed by the hotel pool with Spanky. To amuse himself he subtly brought up Buster's condition in conversation. He knew it would upset Spanky. Listening to his underling's voice quaver was worth the price of the trip to him.

"I heard that Buster has to wear a bag," said Jasper, adding a fictionalized ailment.

"I . . . uh, didn't know that," replied Spanky. "I was never close to Buster," he added, looking away.

"He must have pissed off someone real good, wouldn't you say so?"

Spanky rose to his feet. "I'm gonna go for a swim," he announced, ducking further conversation.

After taking a dip, Spanky returned to the lounge chair alongside Jasper. As he dried off Jasper resumed tormenting him. "The time always comes to pay the piper. Nobody can escape that."

"I suppose," said Spanky, covering his head with the towel as he dried his hair. He used the cloth as a partition to separate himself from further talk.

"You know, Lucy is after me to finance her in a gentleman's club in Los Angeles. She feels she'll be able to develop a clientele that would have an interest in doing business."

"You believe that?" asked Spanky, perking up enough to remove the covering.

"She's confident that she can put it over. She's a tough negotiator."

Spanky did a double take after hearing Jasper's second comment. The notion that Lucy might be in the midst of striking a deal that might be superior to his was disturbing.

"She's dreaming," said Spanky. His negativity made his jealousy evident.

"I don't know about that," voiced Jasper, making it seem as if he were genuinely interested.

"Are you saying that she could move kilos?"

"She knows a lot of people."

"Maybe a lot of the wrong people," warned Spanky. "She'll be totally unsupervised in Los Angeles."

"I've had no problem with her yet," reminded Jasper. "But you make a good point."

"Which point is that?"

People do need supervising, don't they?" asked Jasper, launching a zinger. He shot Spanky a knowing look as he added, "You can't *trust* anyone, can you?"

The word *trust* jolted Spanky, who was reminded of his own disloyalty. Their exchange lost its edge when the subject of the prior evening arose. The tone shifted when they began speaking of Dotty.

"So how did it go last night, Spanky?"

"Let me tell you, that Dotty's something else. She wants me to take her for a three-way . . . *twice*."

"Why twice?"

"Because she's horny," answered Spanky. "First she wants it to be me, her, and another woman. Then . . . she wants to go an inning with me and another guy!"

"Did you agree to this?"

"I'm only springing for one triple at the ranch . . . me, her, and another woman."

Not wanting to see Spanky so happy, Jasper decided to throw a wet blanket on his gleefulness. "Oh, I forgot to tell you," he said. "Lucy's looking for a 50-percent partnership if we make a move in LA."

The news bulletin twisted Spanky. It was the reaction Jasper sought.

While Jasper and Spanky were at the pool, Lucy and Dotty happily went from store to store. They chatted away with the usual amicableness that exists between friends. Lucy made it a point to look at expensive watches.

"What do you think of that one?" asked Lucy.

"That'll cost an arm and a leg," commented Dotty, who had less of an interest in a fancy watch.

"I know."

"So how was your night, Lucy?" asked Dotty, touching a topic that she found to be more enjoyable. Lucy's friend was actually dying for the opportunity to talk about her own experience.

Lucy shrugged her shoulders. "It was nothing special. Jasper's pretty tame when you get him off his feet," advised Lucy. "How did things go with you?"

"Spanky is an animal! He has a real wild side, that one."

"Really?" asked Lucy, somewhat interested in hearing the details.

"He wants us to go back to one of those places where anything goes . . . you know, the ranch."

"You went to the ranch with him?"

"I had to go," answered Dotty in an innocent way. "You don't know the man. He won't be denied."

"C'mon, you could have told him no," said Lucy stiffly.

"Well, I did tell him no at first, but that's one boy who can be pretty persuasive," explained Dotty.

"Jasper is nothing like that at all. With him, all he cares to do is finish up and talk about business."

"How boring is that?"

"What does Spanky talk about during the breaks?" Lucy began to pump her friend for information that she could later pass on to Jasper, who was expecting to receive a full report.

Dotty thought for a second before responding. "Oh, I don't know if I can believe half of what he says."

"So tell me, like . . . what does he say?" pressed Lucy.

"He told me he once did it five times in four hours," answered Dotty. "Is that possible?"

Lucy shrugged her shoulders after receiving information she wasn't looking for. "I suppose it can be done," replied Lucy. "Doesn't he ever talk about business, his goals or his ambitions?"

"Oh, sometimes he does. You wouldn't think it, but he's got big ideas," said Dotty.

"What kind of ideas?"

"He was bragging to me how he was the whole business. He said that he didn't expect to be with Jasper forever . . . you know, stuff like that. I still don't know what the hell they do. Do you?"

"I'm not exactly sure," fibbed Lucy, "but I know Jasper owns a lot of businesses."

"How is your new job going? It must be great working from home."

"Yeah, it is," replied Lucy. "Spanky plans on leaving Jasper?"

"It sounded that way," said Dotty. "He said he's been looking for partners to branch out with."

"He did? What else did he say?"

"He really didn't elaborate."

"Did he say he's going out on his own without Jasper?"

"That's the impression I got."

"Did he say when?"

"He didn't exactly say. Besides, we were kind of busy most of the night," noted Dotty.

"He must have said something else."

"Well, he did say that he was tired of doing all the heavy lifting. You know, stuff like Jasper was getting too old, it was time for Jasper to retire, things like that. Just between us, Spanky did mention that a showdown was inevitable."

"He did? Did he say what he had in mind?"

"No, and I didn't ask. That's between the men."

"It sounds like Spanky has big plans."

"Yeah, especially for tonight!" said Dotty, reverting back to something that appealed more to her.

Later that evening, when alone with Jasper, Lucy filled him in on her conversation with Dotty.

"Be careful, Jasper," warned Lucy. "There may be plans underway to make a move against you."

"Dotty said that?"

"I don't think Spanky makes for a very good *long-term* association."

"Did Dotty say that Spanky planned on doing something?"

"She said that a showdown down the line was inevitable."

"The little louse!" said Jasper, reacting angrily. "He'd never have the nerve."

"Aren't you concerned, Jasper?"

"Nothing concerns me," he replied with cockiness. 'He ain't got the backing to make a move."

"What are you going to do?" she asked.

"I'll tell you what I'm going to do. Later we're gonna clean up and go downstairs to buy that watch you like so much. What do you say to that?"

A big smile came over Lucy's face. "Giddyap!"

########

IN AN EFFORT TO REGAIN HIS PRIOR PHYSICAL FORM, Buster partook in a fitness program in the family basement. Loud grunts emanating from the lower level could be heard throughout the house as he bench-pressed weights. Buster's father, a retired private sanitation worker, became alarmed after hearing an exceptionally loud guttural bellow. The concerned parent immediately went downstairs to investigate. He found his son on the workout bench lying flat on his back and staring blankly up at the ceiling.

"Buster, are you okay?" asked the worried father.

"I'm fine, Pop."

"You're doing too much own here! What are you looking to do, kill yourself?"

"I'm okay, Pop. I just need to stretch out and rest for a few minutes."

"Buster, you better pull it in a notch," the older man lectured. "You gotta *gradually* build yourself up."

Buster, who was wearing black shorts and a white wife beater undershirt, sat up. "I have to keep pushing, or I'll never get back to where I was."

"I know, Buster . . . but you've had enough for today. Go wash up and then come and eat something. We'll watch a movie. I'll put on *The Godfather*."

"Alright, Pop, you can get the movie ready. I'll be with you in a few minutes. I just want to smoke a cigarette and then run under the shower."

Buster kept a small combination safe on top of his bedroom dresser. He opened the safe door to inventory the contents. As always, everything was undisturbed. The loaded Colt handgun was resting on its side next to the spare bullets. Everything was in the same position as he had left it. He then examined the cherry bombs he stored in the safe, making sure all eight were accounted for. Satisfied that his tools of destruction were readily available, he closed the door to the safe. After dressing, Buster went to watch the movie. By the time Clemenza said to leave the gun and take the cannoli, Buster was famished.

"You got anything to eat?" Buster yelled out to the kitchen.

"You want a nice pepper sandwich on Italian bread?" his mother shouted out.

"Yeah," he shouted back. He then felt the jab of his father's elbow. "Make it two, Ma."

########

EUSTICE'S WIFE WAS CLEANING THE WINDOWS of their modest home. An American flag was prominently displayed next to the front entrance. Mrs. Costello, who had served in the Navy, was especially proud of the flag she put on display because it had once hung atop the White House in Washington. Seeing a car stop in front of the house, she ceased cleaning.

"Hello, Mrs. Costello," said Markie. "Is Eustice around?"

"Oh, hi," she greeted. "He's inside. Come in. Our son is coming over with one of his college friends, so we're just tidying up."

When the detectives entered the house, they found Eustice with his feet up, dozing in a brown leather recliner in the living room. The undercover detective's arms dangled lazily off the side of the cushioned chair. Von Hess pointed to a feather duster on the floor just beneath the slumbering detective's extended fingertips. Von Hess picked up the duster and used it to ever so gently tickle underneath the napping detective's nose. Feeling the faint contact, Eustice began wiggling his nose, finally pinching away the itch with his fingers.

"It's no use," said Von Hess. "He's dead to the world."

Markie gently shook the detective's arm to wake him.

"I'm coming, honey," said Eustice groggily, not yet fully awakened.

When the detective's eyes finally opened, he reacted by quickly shaking his head clear. It took a second for the detective to get his bearings.

"Oh, hello, Sarge," he said. "I didn't hear you come in. The old lady has me working like a dog."

"I can see that," answered Markie.

The sergeant spent several minutes advising Eustice on what he was expected to do at the James Brothers Saloon. Once his mission became clear, Eustice voiced just one question.

"So you want me to take Lemon along on this outing, right?"

"That's right; he'll be waiting for you to pick him up. Remember something: once you're inside the bar, stay close to him. He's still a snitch," the sergeant reminded. "Figure on arriving at 7:00 p.m."

After leaving Eustice, the detectives had some free time on their hands. "What do you say, Sarge? We've got plenty of time right now. You want to swing by and see Fishnet?" asked Von Hess.

Markie was thinking more along the lines of stopping off someplace for a burger and a beer.

"Jeez . . . Ollie, will ya quit harping on that? When you get your teeth into something, you don't let go."

"Okay, forget it."

"I have to ask you . . . what is this big obsession with seeing a crooked bastard like Fishnet?"

"To be honest, I'm getting a little pressure, Sarge."

"Who is giving you pressure?"

"My friend is a union delegate. He's in the same VFW post as me," answered Von Hess. "Every time I stop in for a pop I run into him. He's got no clue about the real Fishnet, so he goes to see him. He keeps telling me that Fishnet keeps asking for me."

"So you're embarrassed?"

"I suppose that's it. The trustee stays awhile to shoot the shit with him. He's the one who told me that it's a miracle how well Fishnet is doing. He said Fishnet wanted to know if I retired."

"So?"

"So now I even feel kind of guilty, his having sent his regards and all. What else can I tell you, Sarge?"

"I understand, Ollie. But you *know* what that bastard was all about just as I do."

"I know, but I'd still feel a little better if I took a minute to see him."

Markie softened. "If it's that important to you, we'll find the time and do it . . . just not today."

########

FISHNET MILLIGAN OPENED THE CALENDER he kept at his bedside. It seemed as if he had been marking off days forever. His habit was to place a pen line across the box that reflected the past day. Each new stroke penetrated the paper a little deeper than the day prior. These impressions were inspirational gestures that proved to the former detective that he was growing stronger.

Fishnet began thinking about the black Mercedes-Benz he always wanted. It was going to be his present to himself once he was released. To finance this longing, Fishnet intended to perfect his scheme to defraud people. This illicit revenue stream would supplement his tax-free disability pension and Social Security disability check. He had gotten into the habit of watching musical television shows with a religious theme. He was taken by how into it the audience was.

"I can turn this into the perfect racket, and I won't need any band either," said the wayward detective.

Fishnet watched closely as the television camera scanned those seated in the audience. Instead of seeing halos above the heads of people, he saw Benjamin Franklin gracing a one-hundred dollar bill.

"Will you look at these people?" he said, considering them a naïve crowd. "I'll get them to swallow my swill and pay big for the privilege!"

Fishnet entered into deep thought as he pondered ways to implement his con. He knew a forger who could provide him with appropriate credentials, but perhaps he didn't have to go that far. Since Fishnet always enjoyed writing little rhymes, he considered using catchy words as a way to help get the attention of those slated for victimization. He even evaluated the feasibility of employing a cleverly placed shill. Whatever the path, Fishnet knew that his being shot would do much to advance his nefarious intentions. After all, wasn't his recovery a miracle come true? Being spared the final curtain would serve as his reason to devote himself to virtuous work. Death's door was the perfect cover story for his having had face time with the man upstairs. Now thoroughly motivated, Fishnet was anxious to get going. To amuse himself, he picked up a pen and began to jot down verses to poems on a piece of paper. The words came easily, randomly popping into his head. His contemplation of acquiring future riches put him in a whimsical frame of mind as he penned, "Giving," the title of his first rhyme.

To give neighbors, is the thing to do.
Allow those in need, to accrue.
Spread the wealth, sisters and brothers.
Fill the pockets of impoverished others.

After penning several short poems, Fishnet wandered off into one of his daydreams. As master of his own domain, the conniving former detective pictured himself speaking before congregants of an entity he had formed called Fishnet's Give. He majestically climbed white marble steps to take a lofty position behind a circular pulpit. Attired in an appropriate white suit and tie, he addressed those seated before him in pews. They were listening attentively.

A live one, thought Fishnet, zeroing in on the sparkling necklace worn by a woman seated up front.

Once Fishnet got her waterworks flowing with his depressing tales of impoverishment in far-off lands, he made his pitch for donations. The charlatan licked his lips as he watched the woman he was focusing on reach for her checkbook. Just as she took out her pen, Fishnet heard the bellowing voice of Hope, who was once again interrupting his fantasy.

"MR. FISH-HOOK! It's time for you to exercise."

The CNA's intrusion destroyed the moment. Abruptly returned to reality, the former detective responded sourly, "I've still got some time before I have to go in the ring."

"We only have five minutes."

"Okay."

"The doctor said that you'll soon be going home," Hope said with a smile. "Are you going to miss me?"

"Like a case of the crabs," the patient said under his breath.

"Hope has some nice Juicy Fruit gum. Do you want some?"

"No," he answered, shaking his head. Fishnet watched her rifle her purse for the gum. *Her poor husband*, he thought, pitying a man he'd never met.

"Okay, time for us to go for your therapy. Let's go. We don't want to be late."

Fishnet, in responding to her call to move, inadvertently let the paper he had been writing on fall to the floor. When he went to pick it up, Hope beat him to it.

"Don't you worry, *Mr.* Fish-Hook. I'll get it for you." Hope picked up the piece of paper and noticed the writing on it. "What are these . . . little poems?" she asked. Before Fishnet could reply, she began to read the one entitled "Exercise Therapy."

I huff, I puff, and sweat my butt . . . as I watch the clock.
I work out hard to the music of therapeutic rock.
And when my muscles begin to ache, like that of any jock,
I'll drop my drawers and wave to doctor . . . as I shake my massive cock.

"Ohhhhh . . . nooooo!" exclaimed Hope. "MR. FISH-HOOK! This is *so NASTY!*" The attendant was genuinely appalled at such bawdiness. "You are *sooo, sooo* bad! Shame on you! What causes you to write such things? Back home they would say you are the devil!"

"You are right, Hope," he said, feigning shame. He kept his head bowed down as he continued speaking. "It *was* the devil that took hold of me. Help me, Hope. . . . I want to change, and I need a God-fearing, righteous woman like you to help me find the way."

Nothing could have been more rewarding for Hope than to hear Fishnet express repentance. She found his cry for help touching.

"Of course I'll help you, Mr. Fish-Hook," Hope replied in a nurturing voice. She then escorted him to where he needed to be for his physical therapy. "We can beat back this devil together!" she declared confidently. "We've been touched by the hand of God. It was the Lord's will that united us."

"Are there many sad cases back home, Hope?" asked Fishnet, looking to see if she had access to unfortunates to exploit.

"Oh yes, indeed there are."

"When I get out of here, I'm going to devote myself to helping such people."

"It is so wonderful to hear you talk like this," enthused Hope.

The former detective covered his eyes with his hand. "Praise the Lord, I have a calling!" he declared emotionally, peeking through his fingers. He was checking to see how effective his words were with Hope. Satisfied, he removed his hand after he thumbed at his eye in order to generate a tear.

20

Eustice Eases In

VON HESS ONLY HAD TO CIRCLE THE BLOCK a couple of times before the space by the fire hydrant became available. When the delivery truck pulled away he took the spot opposite the bar.

"I'm going inside the joint to get a visual," advised Markie.

"Want me to go, boss?"

"No, I'll go. I have to tap a kidney anyway."

Markie walked into the bar as if he belonged. He found the familiar odor of whiskey and beer to be tempting. "Let me have a Johnny Walker Black neat," he announced to the bartender, putting his money on the bar. "Where's the restroom?"

"In the back," the bartender answered, pointing to a door at the rear of the bar.

When Markie returned, he found his drink waiting. He made a mental note of the bartender's appearance as he drank up. Right away he noticed that he was drinking a cheaper scotch than what he ordered. The next time the bartender was at the register with her back facing him, he departed the bar without leaving a tip.

"What does it look like inside, boss?" asked Von Hess.

"It's dead, just a couple of people at the bar drinking. The bartender is a female about thirty-five, average height. She's got thick, pushed-back dark hair and a hairy mole on the left side of her chin."

Von Hess recorded the time, date, and description of the bartender. "What name should we give her?"

"Call her Female Bartender until we figure out who she is."

"Is it nice inside?" asked Von Hess.

"Actually it is. But they play games with the booze."

"That's not surprising," said Von Hess as he raised the high-powered glasses to his eyes. He wanted to get a glimpse of the bartender. "The bathrooms are in the back, boss?"

"There are two back there. There is a third door on the opposite side of the room back there."

"Where does that lead to?"

"I don't know."

After about twenty minutes, the surveillance team spotted Eustice and Lemon walking toward the bar.

"They must have parked around the corner," commented Von Hess.

"That's too bad. We can't seem to catch a break. I want people to see the car he drives."

Eustice and Lemon once again took seats in the front of the bar where they would be visible to the detectives in the van. As instructed, the undercover took out a one-hundred-dollar bill to pay for drinks. Markie had been right about fronting a large denomination. The century note drew the bartender's immediate attention.

"Hi. What will it be?" asked the woman behind the stick. She addressed Eustice, who was clearly the younger of the two men.

"Old Grand-Dad on the rocks," ordered Eustice.

"I'll have a rum and Coke," said Lemon.

As the drinks were being prepared, Eustice noticed two men emerge from the back. The undercover recognized Mousey, who was wearing crisp jeans, brown boots, and a long-sleeve white shirt. The small notebook was once again visible sticking out of the rear pocket of Mousey's pants. Eustice was unfamiliar with Q-Ball Otto, the second man. The bald-headed Otto took a seat at a small table against the wall opposite the bar. It was obvious to the undercover that the unidentified man's undivided attention was on Mousey. Things soon began to fall into place for the detective.

"You want something, Otto?" asked the bartender, addressing the man sitting alone at the table.

"I'm good, Brenda," replied Otto.

The ability to link a name to a face made things easier for Eustice. After a couple of drinks, Eustice became chatty. It began to dawn on Lemon that the undercover was having fun.

As customers began arriving, the room livened to where a buzz could be heard. A trim man of seeming importance entered the bar alone. The blue blazer, red polo shirt buttoned to the top, tan pants, and black tasseled loafers he wore made him seem overdressed for the James Brothers Saloon. He was of interest to Eustice because he looked like a wise guy. From afar he could have been mistaken for a younger man. He was tanned and freshly shaved, and his hair had been recently cut. An up-close view would reveal crow's feet at the corners of his eyes, a furrowed brow, and deep lines coming down both sides of his nose. These were telltale signs of his true age. It became obvious that the man was known.

"Otto, can you do me a favor and go to the store?" asked the bartender.

"I can't do it, Brenda. I have to stick with Mousey." Brenda frowned after being denied her request.

"What do you need?" asked the well-dressed man. He spoke in a husky and direct way.

"I need two packs of cigarettes. You don't mind going for me?"

"Why would I mind? I'm only supposed to be the boss around here. What kind do you want?"

"Get me a couple of packs of Marlboro Lights," said the bartender, holding out the money.

"No problem, Brenda," he answered, taking the cash. "Do you want anything from outside, Otto?"

"Nah, I'm good, Johnny."

Lemon looked away as the man walked past him on his way out. He elbowed Eustice discreetly. "That's Johnny Blondell. He's one guy who would recognize me. He's Silky's right hand man."

"Have another drink," said Eustice, "and stay calm."

Everything became clearer to Eustice. Brenda was the bartender. Otto served as the gatekeeper and Johnny Blondell likely represented Silky Seggio.

"Do you have any singles, Brenda?" asked Eustice after getting her attention.

The bartender took his ten-dollar bill, made change, and returned. "Here you go," she said, counting out ten singles in front of the detective.

"Give us another round. We're going to play a little liar's poker," advised Eustice. "Want to play?"

"No thanks, but good luck," replied Brenda, leaving to refill their drinks. After a few minutes, the barmaid returned to the front of the bar with their beverages.

"Who's winning?" she asked.

"This guy is a ringer," declared Lemon, after taking a large gulp of his drink. "Nobody can whip Bayonne Bob at any kind of poker," he added.

Eustice was astonished by Lemon's taking the initiative. The informant he released showed creativity in getting the word out that Bayonne Bob was a gambling man. Why he extended himself was puzzling.

The investigators in the van recognized Johnny Blondell from the surveillance photos provided by Agent Leardi of the DEA. Markie got out of the van and followed Blondell on foot to a grocery store located a half block away on the avenue.

"He went into the grocery store, Ollie," said the sergeant when he returned to the van. "He'll be back."

"Hold up a second, boss. Look at this Mercedes that just double-parked in front of the bar."

"See if you can grab the plate, Ollie."

"I can't get it from this angle," replied Von Hess. "This guy could be Jasper. . . . He's getting out. Male, white, average height, mid- to late forties, gray suit," reported Von Hess. "He's going in the bar."

"Got it," said Markie. "I'll go out and get the plate."

After mentally recording the plate, the sergeant kept walking. He later doubled back to the van. Once back inside the surveillance vehicle, the sergeant called in the plate. In minutes he received his results.

"That's our boy, Ollie," announced Markie. "The plate comes back to Jasper."

Jasper spotted Lemon immediately after entering his bar. Happy to see the older man, he approached Lemon to extend a cordial greeting. "Hey . . . look who it is!" said the bar owner, smiling broadly. "How's it going, Lemon?" Lemon rose from his stool so that they could embrace. "What brings you here to this neck of Brooklyn?"

"We're slumming," replied Lemon. "You look good, Jesse. You never change."

"Hey, a man has to take care of himself," answered the bar owner cockily. "When did I last see you?"

"I think it was at the Christmas party at the club a couple of years back," said Lemon, sitting back down in his seat. "I heard that you've been packing the coin on the edges with this joint."

"I do alright," answered Jasper, feeling proud. "You know something? You look the same as you did thirty years ago . . . old!" said the former car thief jokingly.

"Time catches up with all of us. You know what they say: the strongest oak must fall," stated Lemon.

"I say to hell with that. I make the most of things while I can." Jasper then turned his attention to Eustice. "Who is your friend?" he asked.

"Say hello to Bob."

Jasper put out his hand to shake. "I'm Jasper. Where are you from, Bob?"

"Bayonne," answered Eustice.

"Bayonne Bob used to work with my brother-in-law, Monte," said Lemon. "You remember Monte, don't you?"

"Of course I remember Monte. How could I ever forget *that* guy? He got me and my brother in the National Guard back in the day. He's dead, right?"

"Yeah, Monte died awhile back."

"What from?"

"Poor Monte died from Parkinson's. He had it for years."

"That's a tough way to go," noted Jasper. "My brother used to joke that Monte would cash in his chips by breaking his neck after falling off his wallet."

"Yeah, Monte did well for himself."

"You still got the car lot in Brownsville, right?"

"Yeah, I'm still in business."

"That'll keep you young. If you ever want to cash out and sell that business, call me." Jasper called over to Brenda, "Hey, give my friends over here a roof," he said, instructing Brenda to give the two men drinks on the house.

When Johnny returned from his errand, he was stopped by Jasper.

"Hey, Johnny, look who it is. . . . It's Lemon."

"How's it going?" asked Blondell. His greeting was modest because he didn't know the person sitting alongside Lemon.

Von Hess could see the goings-on inside the bar. As far as he could tell, things were under control.

"They're both talking to Lemon," advised Von Hess. "It seems like they're pretty chummy, boss. Jasper and Lemon even embraced."

"Beautiful," said Markie.

"Where do we go from here?"

"It'll depend on how this ends up."

"People are starting to pour in. They must be giving the booze away," said Von Hess after a group of four men entered the saloon. "I hope they don't stay much longer. I need to use the head."

"We got plastic trash bags in the glove compartment."

"That's reassuring," said the older detective.

Inside the bar Eustice's attention was drawn to a man who engaged Mousey in conversation. When they relocated to the rear of the room, the undercover detective rose from his stool.

"I'll be right back," he announced to Lemon, proceeding to the men's room.

Eustice was hoping to overhear something or make an observation that could prove to be fruitful. By the time Eustice got to the restroom, he was close enough to see money being passed to Mousey.

"This is for two weeks," Eustice overheard the man with black eye say.

"Good. Just try not to make it a habit of falling behind," said Mousey as he reached for his book.

When Eustice exited the men's room, he caught sight of Mousey, Jasper, and Johnny walking through the mysterious back door. Before they disappeared from view, Mousey called over his shoulder to Otto. "I'll be in the cellar if you need me," he said.

"So that's where that door leads to," thought Eustice, rejoining Lemon. "Let's have us another drink," said the undercover after reaching his station.

"I'm done," expressed Lemon. "If we're staying, I'm switching to club soda."

"Come on, loosen up," said Eustice as he waved to Brenda. "You're doing great in here."

After a while, the cumulative effect of the hard alcohol consumed by Eustice enfeebled his judgment. Lacking inhibition, he became flirtatious with Brenda. The now-loquacious undercover directed a multitude of compliments her way. She seemed to be receptive. Out to impress the bartender, the undercover began expanding upon his fictional history.

By this time, Lemon could see that the detective was a cowboy. His being concerned as to where things might be heading had a sobering effect. As Lemon was evaluating the situation, Sandy, the federal informant, along with a female DEA agent, entered the bar.

"Where the hell were you the other day, Sandy?" asked Brenda loudly, as she mixed cocktails.

"I didn't feel good," replied Sandy. "This is my friend," she said, introducing the agent.

The federal agent, who was cordially received by Brenda, was asked what she wanted to drink.

"I'll have a screwdriver," answered the agent.

"A Diet Coke for you, Sandy?"

"Yeah, give me the usual."

Two male customers who were drinking at the bar struck up a conversation with the undercover federal agent and the informer. The women were polite but not encouraging. Midway into their discourse, Sandy received a subtle nudge from the agent. The poke was an intended reminder for her to acknowledge Eustice. Sandy responded accordingly.

"Hey, it's Bayonne Bob!" Sandy said, loud enough to be heard. "Let's go say hello."

The two women relocated to the front of the bar to join Eustice and Lemon. The animated conversation that followed was orchestrated to give the impression that they knew each other for years.

"Brenda, back the girls up," ordered Eustice, who welcomed playing the role of a big sport.

With a party now underway, Brenda delivered a round of drinks for all. The continued flow of alcohol intensified Eustice's efforts to charm Brenda. His flattering overtures were successful enough for Brenda to overlook his referring to her hairy mole as a chin puff. Sandy picked up on the amorous vibes existing between the two. Torn between loyalties, Sandy's commitment to the feds remained firm. How could she ever communicate to Brenda that she was a federal informer? As things grew more festive, Eustice began to get increasingly careless. Jasper's emergence from the door in the back went completely unnoticed. Eustice was so into being Bayonne Bob that he seemed to forget that he was a cop.

Von Hess stared intently through the binoculars at the front window of the James Brothers Saloon.

"It looks like Jasper is making his goodbyes, Sarge. Do you want me to follow him?"

"Not in the van. I don't want to blow it out."

"This Eustice is a pisser," commented Von Hess.

"What's he doing?"

"He's by the jukebox with one arm around the agent and another around the female snitch. . . . They're boogying to the music."

"I guess he's into the role he's playing."

"I'd say so," agreed Von Hess. "Take a look," he said, passing the binoculars to the sergeant.

"He's got his paw on the informant's ass!" said the amazed Markie.

"That's all?"

"What else do you want?"

"He was working his way down the agent's back when I was looking."

As the events unfolded Mousey signaled for Brenda to join him at the other end of the bar.

"Who are those two guys up front?"

"Jasper's known the old guy a long time," answered the bartender.

"What about the guy with arm around the girl?" asked Mousey, referring to Eustice.

"He's alright. Sandy knows him."

"If Jasper knows the old man and Sandy knows the other guy, it's all good."

"Bob likes to gamble," advised Brenda. "I think he likes me."

"How do you know that?"

"A woman just knows."

"I mean how do you know he likes to gamble?"

"Because they play liar's poker," replied Brenda.

"See if they'd be interested in getting in the game downstairs sometime," instructed Mousey.

"Okay. I'll feel them out."

"Make sure they get a buyback. Let's make them feel welcome."

##########

MARKIE AND VON HESS RECONNECTED WITH EUSTICE and Lemon near the waterfront at the foot of Atlantic Avenue. The undercover detective exhibited superior recuperative ability, successfully concealing the effects of the intoxicants he had consumed at the expense of the city. The detective filled the sergeant in on what had transpired inside the bar.

"There's definitely a loan-sharking operation going on inside the bar, boss," said Eustice.

"What about drugs?"

"Not that I saw."

Markie turned to Lemon. "Did Jasper remember you?"

"Oh, sure he did."

"Did you recognize anyone else in there?"

"I recognized one guy, Johnny Blondell."

"Where do you know him from?"

"He drives Silky Seggio, or at least he used to. He's Silky's main man."

"Alright, Lemon, you did a good job," Markie complimented him. "Detective Costello will drive you home. We'll reach out if we need you again."

"That's it?"

"Yeah, that's it for now."

"What's the next move, Sarge?" asked Eustice.

"Tomorrow I want you to go out and pick up extra-large black Champion sweatshirts."

"What am I supposed to do with sweatshirts?"

"In a couple of days, you're going into the bar alone with them. It'll be an in-and-out thing. You go in, order a beer, and make a phone call to me. Then you'll wait five or ten minutes for my call back. We shoot the shit for a minute, and then you leave the bar like you're on a mission. I want them to see you as a guy conducting some kind of business."

"What do I tell them if they ask me what kind of business I'm in?"

"I doubt they will. But if they do, you just tell them you do *things,*" answered the sergeant.

"But what do I do with the sweatshirts?" asked the undercover, repeating his original question.

"Just have them with you when you go to the bar. Make sure they see them. I want them thinking that it's swag. Don't say where they came from. Let their imagination take over."

"No problem, Sarge. Should I try to sell them?"

"Don't look to peddle them. If they ask to buy one, then sell them one. If they don't ask, maybe you just give one away to draw their attention."

21

Baiting the Hook

WHEN THE CHIEF OF DETECTIVES RECEIVED NOTICE that financial concerns in the department existed, it was his cue to monitor overtime and expenses. Long accustomed to tightening the belt from time to time, Chief McCoy called for a citywide overtime cap for his detectives. Markie's squad was no exception. Before addressing the cost restrictions with Lieutenant Wright, McCoy listened attentively as Wright briefed him on the progress of the Mathis investigation.

"So at the end of the day, how much more is this going to cost?" asked McCoy.

"That's hard to say, Chief. We've been very careful with the overtime and expenses right along. Do you want to see what we spent broken down . . . or can I give you a total number?"

"All I want is a total number for now."

"I'll be right back, Chief," said Wright, excusing himself.

The lieutenant returned to the chief's office with a piece of paper in his hand a few minutes later. Wright passed the paper to the chief without saying anything. McCoy looked at the figure without flinching. It was better than he'd anticipated. The chief reached into his pocket for a Life Saver.

"You want one?" he asked, holding out the roll.

"No thanks, Chief," replied the lieutenant, politely declining the offer.

"For this quarter, see if you can get people to take whatever overtime they've got coming in time instead of cash. You can't insist, of course, but try and use your influence."

"I'll do what I can, Chief. But to be honest, there has been very little overtime involved in this case."

"So what's the next move on the case?"

"We're laying groundwork to show that the undercover makes money. We want Jasper interested in the undercover and not vice versa. We want him to think he's missing out on something."

"I see, you figure that will make them get friendly," said the chief. "

"Correct. Markie is looking to introduce a couple of female detectives at the bar."

"What does he plan to do with them in the bar?"

"He wants them to make a cameo appearance. They'll go into the bar, say hello, hand Eustice some money, and leave. It should only be a one-shot appearance for both of them."

"What is the sergeant trying to do, pass them off as hookers?" "Yes and no. Markie wants the people in the bar to draw their own conclusions. He's convinced that the people in the bar will fall for this charade and go running to Jasper."

"Okay, keep me posted," said the chief.

#########

EUSTICE MADE IT A POINT TO WEAR ONE OF the dozen black Champion sweatshirts he'd purchased. Along with white sneakers, a Yankees cap, and dark jeans, he achieved the look he was after for his visit to the James Brothers Saloon. He put five of the remaining eleven sweatshirts, all extra large, in a travel bag before leaving his Staten Island home.

"Where did all these sweatshirts come from?" asked Mrs. Costello.

"The six left in the box are ours."

"You paid for them?"

"Yeah, but don't get excited. I'm getting reimbursed."

"The job is letting you keep them?"

"Stop with the inquisition already," snapped Eustice, who didn't want to answer questions.

Mrs. Costello curbed her inquisitiveness, preferring to focus on who would probably like a sweatshirt.

"Are you going to be late?" she asked as her husband headed for the front door.

"It'll depend on how things go," replied Eustice. "I'll give you a call if I get stuck."

Once outside, the undercover detective noticed that a bird had soiled the roof of the new car that the department had leased for him. After cleansing the defiled area, he stepped back to admire the vehicle he had grown quite fond of. Sitting behind the wheel of the Lincoln made him feel special. It gave him the opportunity to present himself to the neighbors as someone important. He felt the same way about carrying his gun. Since he carried the weapon legally, he was someone to be envied. Eustice proceeded to the James Brothers Saloon with a mindset of a big shot. He found a parking spot on the avenue close to the bar. After exiting the car, he went directly to the rear of the vehicle. For the benefit of anyone who happened to be looking, he made an elaborate gesture of looking in all directions prior to opening the trunk. After he made it obvious that he was checking to see if any police were in the area, Eustice removed the travel bag containing the sweatshirts.

Markie held the binoculars as he maintained an eyeball on the James Brothers Saloon. Von Hess sat at his side with a pen and paper at the ready.

"We're in business, Ollie," said Markie. "Eustice is on the set. He's wearing one of the sweatshirts."

"You didn't think he was going to miss out on a freebie, did you?"

"Not a chance, Ollie."

The undercover detective made his way to the center of the room, where he found suitable space to stand. Once bellied up to the rail, he nodded to Johnny Blondell, who sat alone at the far end of the bar drinking coffee. Tending bar was Scratchy, who remembered the generous tip he'd received from Eustice the last time he saw him. The bartender went to see what his generous customer was having.

"Hey, how is it going?" asked Scratchy. "It's Bob, right?"

"Right," replied Eustice, pleased that the bartender remembered his name. The undercover detective placed his travel bag atop the bar. "Let me have a cold beer."

"Bud?"

"That's fine," agreed Eustice as he unzipped his bag and began thumbing through the contents. He was pretending to be counting the number of sweatshirts.

"A bucket?" asked Scratchy.

"No, I won't be staying that long."

Eustice watched Scratchy as he walked away. He couldn't help but notice that the bartender was a little bowlegged. When he completed his count, Eustice walked over to the jukebox by the front glass to play music. He did so to provide the opportunity for the others to look at the contents of the travel bag he'd left open. As Eustice surveyed the music selections, the bartender returned with the beer. Scratchy, as expected, seized the opportunity to check out what was in the bag. When the undercover detective returned to his place, he put some money on top of the bar.

"Hi, Bob," greeted the voice coming from Eustice's rear. Turning, he saw it was the evening bartender, Brenda, who had just arrived to work her shift.

Eustice smiled crookedly. "How's it going, gorgeous?" he asked.

"Good. I'm just coming on. Where's your partner?"

"What partner?"

"The old guy you play liar's poker with."

"Lemon's not my partner; he's just my friend. He's in Brownsville at his lot."

"I'll be back in a minute," Brenda advised, not really caring where Lemon's was.

Within minutes, Brenda was behind the bar relieving Scratchy. Eustice made it his business to tip the exiting bartender. "See you next time," he said, slipping money to Scratchy.

"That's a nice sweatshirt you got on," Scratchy commented.

"All I got left is extra large. You want one?"

"How much are they?"

"For you, I'll let one go for fifteen bucks."

After paying his money, Scratchy took a sweatshirt and left. Eustice was sipping on his beer with satisfaction after pocketing the money that he had no intention of turning in.

"So how have you been?" asked Brenda from behind the bar. Her smile revealed her interest.

"I've been good, but I'm doing even better now."

"Are you ready for another?"

"Let me have a bottle of Bass Ale this time," said Eustice, switching brews.

The undercover studied Brenda as she walked off to fetch the drink. At this stage of his life, the long-married detective was vulnerable to the attention afforded by any woman. With his high-octane libido activated, Eustice watched

Brenda place the long neck of the Bass bottle into the six-ounce beer glass. As the liquid slowly bled from the bottle into the glass, he began to have thoughts.

"Some people like to mix the Bass in with the regular beer," Brenda advised. "Want to try it?"

"Yeah . . . I like *mergers*," answered Eustice invitingly. His suggestive look expressed exactly what was on his mind. It didn't go unnoticed.

With a puckish smile, Brenda capped off the half glass of regular beer with the remaining Bass Ale. As she did this, she noticed the sweatshirts on the bar. Eustice picked up on her interest.

"What size are you, Brenda?"

"It depends. What have you got there?"

"Champion sweatshirts, just like the one I have on. All I have are extra large."

"It'll be alright even if it's a little big. I like to wear oversized sweatshirts," she said, hoping he would give her one. "How much are they?"

Eustice didn't disappoint her. "For you there is no charge. Here, take one . . . my gift to you."

Eustice didn't have to say it twice. Brenda scooped up the shirt and put it up against herself. "This will fit fine," she said. "Thank you, Santa."

"Remember, you have to be good if you want to please Santa."

The bartender was impressed by her customer's largesse. Generosity wasn't a common attribute among those frequenting the James Brothers Saloon. She tapped her knuckle on top of the bar to indicate that there was no charge for the Bass. Johnny Blondell, who saw that Brenda was given a sweatshirt for free, inched his way over toward Eustice. Just as Johnny got close to him, Eustice received the call he was expecting from Markie. The undercover detective stepped a few feet from the bar to talk into his phone. Cognizant that Brenda and Johnny were within earshot, his volume was just audible enough for them to overhear his end of the conversation.

"Never mind that," Eustice could be heard saying. "I want you to get yourself over there and make him happy," said Eustice authoritatively. He then abruptly hung up.

"Is everything alright?" asked Brenda, falling victim to her curiosity.

Eustice looked at the bartender in a puzzled way, as if she were nosing into his business. "Don't start writing books, Brenda." he said sharply, intentionally wanting to show her a dark side.

The sudden behavioral reversal exhibited by Eustice caught Brenda off guard. Not sure how she should react, she stepped back out of striking range before answering.

"You were gonna be chapter one," she replied, smiling with just the slightest trace of defiance. She was feeling her way along with the man she knew as Bayonne Bob.

Before he could respond, Eustice's cell phone went off again. As planned, it was Markie. This time Eustice remained in place while taking the call. After listening a moment, he responded with the same level of audibility as previously used.

"Two?" he asked. His tone was less serious than before. Eustice nodded, making it appear as if he'd received an answer to his question. "Okay, give me a few days." He then hung up and began to pick his money up off the bar.

"Are you leaving already?" asked Brenda.

Eustice peeled off tip money from the wad of cash he held. "For you," he said, dropping the money on the bar. "I'll see you later."

"Are you coming back?" she asked hopefully.

Eustice smiled. "Opportunity knocks," he said, not letting on what his plans were.

The mystery surrounding Eustice stimulated Brenda's interest. It also tickled Johnny's curiosity.

"What did he give you?" Blondell asked.

"What? He gave me a tip . . ." replied Brenda.

"No, not the tip. . . . What is that, a shirt you got?"

"Oh, this . . ." she said, holding up the Champion sweatshirt.

"How much did it cost?"

"He gave it to me for free."

"Why? Scratchy had to pay for his."

"He likes me," she said proudly, her ego soaring with feel-good vibes.

"It must've fallen off the back of a truck," conjectured Johnny as he rubbed his chin.

"That wouldn't surprise me," answered Brenda. "What's the difference?"

Johnny left the bar area without responding. He headed to the basement, where he sought out Mousey, who was downstairs with Q-Ball Otto. Johnny apprised the two men of Bayonne Bob's actions.

"You can't allow people to earn like that without them paying rent. Know what I mean?" asked Johnny.

Mousey understood the point being made. The bar manager turned to Otto. "From now on, nobody sells *anything* in here without getting taxed," declared Mousey, laying down the law.

Otto nodded in the affirmative. "Nobody will get away with that on my watch," assured Otto.

They all went upstairs to take a look at Brenda's gift, with Mousey leading the way. "What did that guy try to sell you?" he asked.

"Nothing," she answered, sounding innocent. "Bayonne Bob just gave it to me."

Mousey was taken aback. He turned to Johnny for an explanation. "I thought he was selling shirts."

"He was," insisted Johnny. "He sold a shirt to Scratchy."

Mousey turned to Brenda. "Let me see that sweatshirt," he said.

Brenda handed the sweatshirt over for his inspection. "He had a few of them, so he gave me one. He was just being nice," she explained.

"He gave you one for nothing?" asked Q-Ball Otto, sounding skeptical of Eustice's benevolence.

"Yeah, dull skull . . . for nothing," she answered curtly, annoyed at his interfering. "Bob's a nice guy."

Otto let out a deep breath, controlling his temper. He didn't want to risk losing his job by getting into a confrontation with a coworker.

"They were all like this, the same color?" inquired Mousey, feeling the material of the sweatshirt.

"Yeah, the same color, but I think the only size he had was extra large."

"These are pretty nice," commented Mousey. "Who is this guy again, Brenda?"

"He was the guy who was in here with the old man who Jasper knew. You remember . . . Bayonne Bob? I told you about them. They were playing liar's poker," related Brenda.

"Oh yeah, I remember. Otto, next time he comes in, make sure you wise him up . . . but do it nice. Tell him that he needs a permit to sell anything in here. Remind me to tell him about the game downstairs."

##########

JOHNNY BLONDELL STEPPED OUTSIDE THE JAMES BROTHERS SALOON to have a smoke. As the saloon's owner of record, he harbored some resentment. He felt that ranking behind a young kid like Mousey in authority was demeaning. Due to his long history with the mob, he couldn't help but feel minimized. Had it not been for a few drinking binges, he'd have received his button alongside Silky long ago. He was engaged with another man in casual conversation about baseball when the late-model Lincoln parked at a meter in front of the bar. Johnny's eyes widened when he saw it was Bayonne Bob behind the wheel.

"I'll catch ya later, pal," said Johnny, dismissing the man he was talking to.

Eustice was dressed sharply in a dark sport jacket, black shirt, tan slacks, red socks, and black loafers. The undercover detective shot Johnny a quick glance when he stepped out of the car. He acknowledged Johnny by raising his chin as he proceeded toward the bar entrance.

"Nice wheels you got there," said Johnny.

Eustice paused to respond. "Thanks," he said.

"Brand-new, ain't it?"

"Certainly it's new. You like it?"

"What's not to like?"

Eustice saw an opportunity presenting itself. "Come on inside. Have a drink with me."

"Hello, handsome. What'll it be?" asked Brenda. Smiling broadly, she was glad to see Eustice.

"Let me have that concoction you made me last time," ordered the undercover detective.

"You want the Bass mixed with regular beer, right?"

"Yeah, that's it," confirmed Eustice. "And give Johnny whatever he wants, baby."

Johnny stood quietly by, evaluating Eustice. He envied the undercover for being younger.

"Gimme a double Jack Daniel's," said Johnny, stepping up. "Make it neat."

Blondell looked at Eustice through the corner of his eye for a reaction. His order was an exhibition of macho drinking designed to show his vitality.

"Oooo . . . Johnny!" said a surprised Eustice. "You're the man!"

"I am all man, my friend. When I drink, I drink like one."

194

After checking his watch a second time, Eustice stepped away from the bar. He took out his phone and dialed Markie's number. After closing his flip phone, he returned to sip his beer as he awaited the arrival of the first female undercover.

An avenue away from the bar a blond haired female detective sat in her car. After receiving telephonic notification from Markie that it was time for her to go into the bar, she checked her face in the rearview mirror before heading out. When she stepped onto the sidewalk, people took notice. A tall, shapely woman, she stood out in the tight white slacks and the red heels she wore. Her low-cut top revealed an ample bosom that completed the attention-gathering image she sought to project. Ten minutes later, she was in view of the detectives in the surveillance van. Von Hess was the first to comment.

"Here she comes now, Sarge," said the detective. "Let me tell you, she looks absolutely perfect."

"Let me see those binoculars," said Markie. The sergeant took a long, hard look. The low whistle he let out signified his approval. "She'll go over big in that outfit, Ollie."

"She'd go over wearing a burlap bag," commented the detective..

Johnny Blondell might have been getting long in the tooth, but he was far from dead. He looked with interest at the blond-haired undercover as she entered the James Brothers Saloon. His mouth dropped open when she approached Eustice at the bar and gave him a gentle kiss on the cheek. Johnny leaned in closer to better hear their conversation. He got close enough to whiff the liberally applied perfume worn by the female undercover. The potency of the fragrance caused Johnny to rub his nose in order to alleviate the tickle.

The female operative also captured the attention of Brenda, who began to vigorously wipe down the bar. Brenda's strokes intensified after Eustice placed his arm around the waist of the female undercover. She found his gesture of familiarity disturbing because by now, she had her own designs on Eustice.

Eustice took the blond-haired detective by the hand and guided her a few steps away from the bar. Once isolated, they engaged in a whispered conversation. When Johnny saw Eustice take money off the female detective, Bayonne Bob graduated in status in his eyes. After pocketing the cash, Eustice escorted the female detective out.

"I'll see you later, baby" were Eustice's parting words as he tapped her on the butt with his open palm.

What a lowlife, thought the blond undercover, who didn't appreciate Eustice's unnecessary touch of familiarity. She let his taking liberties go unanswered rather than potentially open up a can of worms.

"Let me have a scotch on the rocks, and set up Johnny with another," said Eustice, behaving as if he were the main attraction at the circus.

"No more for me," said Johnny, finishing his drink.

By this time, Brenda had sore hands from sanding down the mahogany with her bar rag. She couldn't contain her feelings. "Did your friend go back to her corner?" asked Brenda sarcastically.

Eustice was amused to see that the bartender was being catty. "Ouch!" he laughingly said. "She's just a work associate of mine."

"It's none of my business who she is," commented Brenda, pretending not to care.

Eustice loved the fact that Brenda was jealous. Many years had passed since he had incurred such emotions from a woman. The drama made him feel great.

When the blond female detective left the bar, the investigators in the surveillance van looked for her signal. When she paused to put on sunglasses, she was communicating to them that all went well.

"She gave the signal, boss," said Von Hess. "It looks like all is good; she put on her glasses." Von Hess detected something peculiar in the way the female detective walked. It prompted him to focus on her face through the binoculars.

"Is something happening, Ollie?"

"She's stomping. Here, take a look," Von Hess said, passing the binoculars.

"She does seems pissed off," commented Markie.

"You think something went on inside?"

"I don't know, but if she has a beef, we'll hear about it soon enough." Markie returned the binoculars to Von Hess. "Look at this. A sanitation sweeper just double-parked and killed our view."

The driver exited the truck and went into the bar.

"He's a white male in his thirties, blue bandana, black mustache, black hair, about five feet, eight inches and stocky," advised Von Hess. "You want the truck number?"

"Nah. Why get the guy in trouble with his job?" answered Markie.

Eustice continued to drink at the bar while chatting up Brenda. He barely paid attention to the visiting sanitation worker, who was there to make a payment on the loan he had taken.

"Another one?" asked the bartender.

"Sure, why not? What time do you finish up here, Brenda?"

"It depends. Usually I'm through anywhere between three and five in the morning. Why?"

"I was thinking that maybe we could get together after you finish up one of these nights."

"Come by," she stated, receptive to his proposition.

Eustice slowly nodded his head once, acknowledging her suggestion. "I'll see you later," he said. He then finished his drink, said goodbye, and left a substantial tip.

Eustice wasn't gone five minutes before Johnny hustled downstairs to fill in Mousey and Q-Ball Otto about how a *"blond bombshell"* had come around to turn in money to Bayonne Bob.

"Who was she?" asked Mousey.

"She looked like a hooker to me. She came in, gives him a hug and a kiss, then kicks in with the money, and takes off," advised Johnny.

"How much money did she give him?"

"I couldn't tell," said Johnny. "He's driving a big-ass Lincoln, so he must be earning."

"You been drinking, Johnny?" asked Mousey, noticing that he was more animated than usual.

Johnny took exception to being questioned. "Back up, kid," he said. "There are parameters."

Two days later, the scene at the bar was replicated. This time an attractive Latino female detective was dispatched to hug, kiss, and pass money to Eustice. She also took exception to the way Eustice touched her backside as she walked off. However, her reaction was slightly different from that of her blond counterpart. When she abruptly turned to face him, Eustice attempted to pull her close. Eustice's gesture was met with a quick backhand jab below the belt. This exchange also went unreported.

"She' a firecracker," was all Eustice could think of saying to Johnny, who witnessed the encounter.

After hearing from Johnny about the second visitor, Mousey made it his business to get to know Bayonne Bob, whose reputation as a swag-pushing pimp was now establish. His opportunity came days later. Mousey sauntered over to the man he wanted to know just minutes after he entered the bar.

"Hey, how is it going?" asked Mousey.

Eustice was careful not to be overly receptive. He engaged Mousey cautiously, pretending to be leery at being singled out. "I'm alright."

"I noticed that you're in here a lot. I manage this place."

"You do?" asked Eustice, feigning surprise.

"You're from Bayonne, right?"

"Yeah. How do you know that?" asked Eustice.

Q-Ball Otto, who was standing a few feet away, stepped up to stand beside Mousey. "It's our business to know," announced Otto, entering the conversation. Otto's presence added a menacing element to the conversation. It was made vividly clear to Eustice that Mousey was not without substantial protection. "And just so you know, nobody sells shit in here without getting taxed," added Otto.

"Ease up, Otto," said Mousey. "Bob is new around here. He doesn't know the rules yet. He's good friends with one of Jasper's pals. Ain't that right, Bob?"

"Yeah, that's right. What's your name again?"

"Everybody calls me Mousey," answered the manager. "I want you to know that you're welcome here, Bob," said Mousey. "Everybody says you're good people, bro."

"Thanks. That's good to know," replied Eustice, happy to be engaging amicably.

"If you're ever up for a little action, just let me know. We run games downstairs."

"What kind of games?"

"Mostly cards. Sometimes dice."

"Thanks. That sounds good. I like a little action once in a while."

The following weeks saw the undercover detective take full advantage of the access he had been granted to the cellar. In addition to partaking in the illegal gambling, Eustice borrowed money when he underwent a particularly bad run of luck. When making payments at usurious rates of interest, he made sure to involve each member of the triad that consisted of Mousey, Otto, and Johnny.

As the criminal trio grew more accustomed to seeing Eustice, they became exceedingly careless. A new breakthrough came the day Eustice was making a juice payment to Mousey at the bar. The exchange was interrupted by Otto, who began speaking in a way that he thought was clever.

"Alfalfa's friend called," Otto said, referring to Spanky. "He wants me to take a ride with him to drop off a record that plays a song in the key of C." He was communicating cryptically that Spanky wanted him to accompany him on a kilo cocaine transaction.

"When?" asked Mousey.

"He wants to go right now."

"Bring a kazoo with you in case you want to play along," replied Mousey, advising Otto to take a gun.

The coded conversation wasn't inventive enough to prevent Eustice from deciphering. After making his payment, the undercover detective ordered a drink for himself. After a few minutes, he casually went to the men's room, where he reached out telephonically to the surveillance team in the van.

"Sarge, something is about to go down right now. Keep an eye on Otto when he leaves. I think they're about to make a kilo delivery of coke."

"You saw the package?"

"No, boss . . . I heard them talking about it."

"Got it," said Markie. After hanging up the phone he relayed the information to Von Hess.

"Are you looking to take anybody down, Sarge?" asked Von Hess.

"No. Eustice didn't actually see any cocaine. We're going to wait and see what this guy Otto does."

Their wait wasn't a long one. The yellow Corvette that pulled up to the bar was met by Otto, who found it a struggle to get down into the passenger side of the sports car. After a minute, the vehicle drove off. Von Hess read off the plate number of the Corvette.

"What do you want to do, Sarge?" he asked, looking for direction from his boss.

"I hate to chance burning out this van, but it looks like we've got no choice. Follow him."

Von Hess loosely tailed the sports car to a nearby playground. The detectives observed Spanky park the Corvette and then exit with Q-Ball Otto. Side by side, the two entered the playground. The detectives maintained a visual from their vehicle until the two men were out of sight.

"It looks like the driver of the Corvette is carrying a large FedEx envelope in his hand," said Von Hess. "Do you want me to walk into the park, Sarge?"

"No. Let's just keep an eye on their car. They have to come back. In the meantime, I'll call in the plate and identify the registered owner." After a few minutes, Markie received the results he had requested. "Does the name Ritzland ring a bell with you, Ollie?"

"No. Hey, look. . . . They're coming out of the park." When Spanky and Otto returned to the Corvette, there was no longer any sign of a FedEx envelope. Instead, Spanky was carrying a large red cloth pouch. "Looks like they made some kind of a switch," noted Von Hess.

"Yeah, it certainly does, Ollie. Let's stick with them." The detectives followed the Corvette back to the James Brothers Saloon.

Spanky pulled over to let Otto off. "Later," he said.

"What about the money?"

"What about it?"

"Didn't you get the memo?" asked Otto.

"What memo?"

"Jasper said that from now on, all money goes direct to Mousey."

The news of this new arrangement stunned Spanky. He immediately got Jasper on the phone for verification. After hanging up, he unhappily handed the money-filled pouch to Otto for delivery to Mousey. Spanky interpreted this operational alteration to mean that he was a step closer to getting aced out of the organization . . . and possibly his life. The stress to Spanky that was generated by this belief was exactly what Jasper had set out to achieve. It temporarily pacified his appetite for the ultimate revenge.

22

Playing Nice in the Sandbox

AGENT LEARDI STOOD OUTSIDE Volare's Restaurant with a cigar dangling from his mouth. The black haired federal agent presented a broad shouldered and rugged appearance. His hairline ran in a straight line a couple of inches above his eyebrows, giving him a caveman appearance. Leardi's choice of apparel suggested a different sort of person. He was dressed old school collegiate in a gold-buttoned blue sport jacket, a light blue three-button Oxford shirt, jeans, and burgundy loafers that he wore without socks. A large college ring was visible on his ring finger. It would seem there were strong influences in Leardi's life that were a far cry from the rough and tumble Bronx neighborhood he grew up in. Leardi's oratorical skills, while proficient, came with an unmistakable urban gruffness.

When Markie and Von Hess arrived at the front of restaurant they engaged Leardi in the customary pleasantries, after which they walked down the few steps that led to the eatery. The law enforcement officers settled into one of the restaurant's quaint wooden booths. They immediately ordered cocktails.

"I love this place," said the agent, looking around the room. "It's like we're back in time."

Once the drinks were served, they bypassed further small talk and got around to the purpose of the meeting.

"So, what's the story, Al?" asked Leardi. "I'm guessing that you got work for me in Brooklyn, right?"

"Yeah, we do. It looks like they are pushing kilos of cocaine out of the James Brothers Saloon."

"Your boy is comfortable introducing one of our agents?"

"Our guy can definitely bring your people into the game," answered Markie. "They're running a gambling operation in the cellar, and our undercover plays in the card game they operate. He even took a shylock loan. You still got that snitch that knows people over there?"

"Yeah," said the agent. "Have you done any drug deals?"

"No, we stayed away from that. I figured you could handle that end of it," advised Markie

"Tell me how you know they're selling cocaine."

"Our undercover overheard a cryptic conversation between this kid Mousey, who manages the bar, and the bouncer, a guy they call Q-Ball Otto. Their talk was about selling weight. The undercover got word to us, and we followed this Otto and a guy named Spanky Ritzland to a nearby park, where we believe they did a hand-to-hand."

"You didn't see the transaction?"

"Not exactly," replied Markie. "We saw Ritzland, with Otto, go into the park carrying a big FedEx envelope and come out with just a red cloth pouch."

"You saw that?" asked Leardi.

"Through binoculars," clarified Von Hess.

"They left the bar with the FedEx envelope, Al?"

"No, the envelope came with this guy Ritzland, who showed up at the bar to pick up Otto in a Corvette. It seemed like Otto just went along as protection. When they were done, Ritzland dropped him off at the bar with the red cloth pouch and went on his way."

Leardi nodded his head, indicating that he understood. "What color is the Corvette?"

"Yellow."

"Kind of loud, but that's okay."

Markie knew what Leardi was thinking. If the federal agent could orchestrate a drug deal in the Corvette, he'd get to confiscate it and later claim it as his own to use at the conclusion of the case.

"So no one actually saw the product or witnessed the actual transaction, correct?"

"Correct."

"Are the players positively identified?"

"Yeah, we got Ritzland's name off the plate of the Corvette. Mousey's real name is Mustafa Derki. It seems that they all report to Jasper Stanlee," explained the sergeant. "Jasper is our target in the soldier homicide. You already checked him out for us, remember?"

"What, do you think I'm going senile?" asked Leardi. "Of course I remember. Talk to me about this guy in the Corvette."

"The guy with the Corvette is positively identified as Edward Ritzland," advised Markie. "He has a few collars under his belt for grand larceny, criminal mischief, and a couple of other things. We pulled his picture so our identification is solid. They call him Spanky on the street."

"Is it a new Corvette?"

"Yes."

"Great. So what's with this Q-Ball Otto?"

"He's a bouncer and muscle at the bar."

"Why is he called Q-Ball?"

"He's got a bald head," answered Markie. "We haven't identified him yet. He drives a white Audi."

"So what are you looking to do, turn this case over to us?"

"Here's the rub on that. I'm under orders to lock up Jasper for homicide as soon as I can."

"What's the rush?"

"The powers that be are pinching pennies," advised Markie. "So I'm thinking that if we can pass our man off as a big-shot drug dealer—"

"—then Jasper will want to know *him*," said Leardi, finishing the sentence.

"Correct. If the undercover can get chummy with Jasper, info on the homicide will leak out."

"Jasper just might see him as competition," pointed out Leardi.

"He might and he might not," countered the sergeant.

"You know how we work, Al. We'd want Jasper out there to lead us to the source of the drugs."

"I know that," answered Markie. "We'll bust Jasper, flip him, and have you sign him up as your snitch. We can both go talk to the DA and make sure he gets bail on the homicide charge. That'll keep him available to work for you on the street."

"What if he decides not to roll over and cooperate? Then what, Al? Where does it leave me?"

"At the very least...driving a brand new Corvette," answered Markie without missing a beat.

It took about three seconds for Leardi to respond. "Alright, Al, we've got a deal," agreed Leardi. "So what do you need from me to move this thing along?"

"How about we start by you making up two dummy kilos of cocaine for me?"

"Why?"

"I want Eustice to be seen doing a bogus kilo sale to one of your undercover people. It's a win-win. Eustice will get put over in the street as a drug dealer, and it'll be the first step in introducing your people. What do you say?"

"I say let's get another round of drinks."

########

MARKIE AND VON HESS HAD TO squeeze into their uniforms. It had been years since they'd last donned their police blues. After borrowing a radio car from the local precinct, they scoured the vicinity of the James Brothers Saloon in search of Q-Ball Otto's white Audi. After coming up dry, they decided to wait near the bar for Otto to come by. When they observed a white Audi looking for parking, Von Hess pulled alongside it. Recognizing Otto, the detective sounded the siren. Reacting to the yelp, Otto immediately pulled into a bus stop.

"What do these guys want?" Otto asked under his breath.

Parking behind Otto, the investigators exited the patrol car. Von Hess approached the driver's side of the Otto's vehicle while Markie covered the passenger side.

"Turn off your engine," ordered the detective.

"Did I do something wrong?" asked Otto politely.

Von Hess ignored the question. "Shut the engine off," repeated the detective. After Otto complied, Von Hess asked to see his license and registration.

"You ain't gonna tell me what I did?"

"Are you gonna give me your papers, or are you looking for an argument?"

Otto noticed Von Hess slip his thumb in the leather loop of the blackjack that hung from the small rear pocket of his uniform pants. This precautionary step was not lost on Otto, who sized up Von Hess as a man who just might put a knot on his head if he gave him a hard time. Having a .25 caliber automatic in his pocket influenced Otto's decision to comply.

"Here," said Otto, producing the documents requested.

"Sit tight," said the detective after taking the paperwork.

Von Hess returned to the radio car to examine the documents. Markie remained vigilant in the street, concentrating on the driver. Von Hess recorded Otto's information onto a legal pad. He then called the central dispatcher. After establishing that Otto had a number of suspensions on his license, he went to confer with Markie.

"The car is registered to him, Sarge. We could take him in. He's got five suspensions."

"No, give him his stuff back," directed the sergeant.

"Do you want me to give him a toss?"

"No, we're not looking to pinch him."

Von Hess returned to the driver's side of the vehicle.

"Here you go," said Von Hess, returning Otto's driver's license and registration. "You caught a break with all those suspensions. We just got a priority job, so we got no time for you now. Consider this to be your lucky day."

"No problem, boss," replied Q-Ball Otto, greatly relieved. He let out a deep sigh as he touched the gun in his pants pocket. "Cocksucker," he muttered as Von Hess walked off.

When the investigators later checked Otto's criminal record, they found that he had numerous past arrests for assault.

#########

SINCE MARKIE'S NEXT MOVE WAS SURE TO RAISE eyebrows at the James Brothers Saloon, it was critical that Lemon be prepared in the event he was later questioned. The sergeant and Von Hess met with their informant in a small public haven known as Cobble Hill Park.

"If anyone should ask you about how Bayonne Bob makes his money, remember to say that all you know is that he has something going with people from Harlem," instructed Markie.

"How am I supposed to know that?" asked Lemon.

"Just say he comes around the lot from time to time with uptown people looking to buy a car."

"What if I'm asked how I got hooked up with him?"

"Stick to the original story. He worked for Monte."

"But that was supposed to be years ago."

"Just say you reconnected when he came around looking for a car to buy."

When he was finished with Lemon, Markie telephoned Agent Leardi. He wanted to make sure that Sandy, the DEA informant, was armed with an appropriate explanation as to how she knew Bayonne Bob. Sandy was instructed to say that she had bought drugs off Bayonne Bob when she was addicted. The last person to be brought up to speed was Eustice.

##########

IT WAS AROUND THE TIME MOST people have supper when Eustice arrived at the James Brothers Saloon. He sauntered up to the bar with the confidence of a regular patron who belonged. Thanks to the deep pockets of the federal government, Agent Leardi had afforded the undercover detective the opportunity to expand his wardrobe. Eustice felt like a million dollars wearing the newly purchased black velour jogging suit and gray sneakers.

"Hello, stranger," greeted Brenda, who found the casual look Eustice projected to be to her liking.

"I've been busy," he replied, looking about the bar to see who was around. "It's kind of quiet around here. Where is everybody?"

"People will be in later. Do you need to see anyone in particular?"

"I only need to see you, baby."

"You already saw enough of me. . . ."

"There ain't ever enough of you. Let me ask you something; who has the apartment on the first floor in the building where you live?"

"The super lives on the first floor. . . . Why?"

"I thought I saw somebody come to the window when I left last week."

"It was probably him. He's a snoop. You want a Bass and beer?"

"Let me have a brandy."

Just as Brenda went to fetch the drink, Johnny Blondell came into the bar. Eustace signaled him, indicating that he should join him for a drink. When Johnny got there, Eustice put his arm around his shoulder affectionately. Taking offense at the undercover detective's familiarity, Blondell reacted by taking a step back to free himself. Blondell shrewdly recognized that such an overture was purely a showboating gesture aimed at impressing others.

"Sorry, Johnny," said Eustice, realizing that he might have overstepped.

"Don't puff yourself up at my expense," said Johnny coldly. "I've been around too long to be used as a stooge by somebody looking to build a reputation."

Surprised at how quickly Blondell had turned on him, Eustice quickly backed off. "C'mon, Johnny, I meant no disrespect," said the detective, raising his hands in a defensive manner. "I'm sorry if I offended you. Let me buy you a drink?" asked the undercover detective.

"Forget it," said Blondell curtly. He was satisfied that he'd made his point. "Brenda, bring me a drink."

"Neat, Johnny?" she asked.

"Yeah, you know what I like."

After a couple of drinks, Eustice could see that Blondell was softening. He took advantage of the opportunity to put his plan into action.

"Hey, Johnny, what do you say about you and me taking a ride in my new car?"

"Why?"

"Because I remember that you said you liked it. C'mon, you can drive."

Blondell, who was a car aficionado, agreed. "Alright, let's go for a spin."

"Hold those drinks, Brenda. We'll have them when we come back," said the undercover.

Johnny drove around the neighborhood slowly. He took his time because being seen behind the wheel of such a nice car made him feel important. In this regard, both he and Eustice were alike.

"This car does ride real nice," acknowledged Johnny, pulling over to the curb. "Here, you take the wheel. I drove enough."

"Hey, Johnny, I gotta make a stop for a minute," said Eustice after assuming control of the vehicle. "It'll only take a couple of minutes. You don't mind, right?"

"Go on. I got no place to be," replied Blondell. Eustice proceeded to a prearranged location where Von Hess and Markie were waiting. "Where are we going anyway?"

"I gotta run an errand."

"What is this, some kind of business thing?"

"Yeah," replied Eustice, not elaborating. The remark put to an end to their chitchat. While curious, Blondell was conditioned not to ask lots of questions.

Eustice pulled into a vast outdoor parking lot. Seeing the Cadillac he was looking for, he proceeded to the far corner of the lot. where several unattended trailers were parked. He stopped about twenty yards from the Cadillac.

"I gotta get something out of the trunk, Johnny," said Eustice.

Eustice returned to his vehicle with a bag containing bogus kilos of cocaine. He looked into the bag, making sure that Johnny got a glimpse of what was inside. Eustice then reached over into the glove compartment to remove his black revolver with a taped grip. The undercover placed the revolver between his legs.

"What's all this?" asked Johnny, clearly agitated.

"There is nothing to worry about. I got it under control," replied Eustice.

The undercover pulled up alongside the Cadillac, where two DEA undercover agents of color were sitting in the front seat. At a distance of a few feet, Eustice exchanged nods with the men in the Cadillac. Alarmed, Blondell cursed Bayonne Bob for not forewarning him of what they were to encounter. Had he known of the nature of the meeting, he wouldn't have gone along, or, if he had, he would've been armed. Eustice slipped his gun in his waistband and covered it with his shirt before exiting his car. Eustice turned to look at Johnny. "Sit tight," he instructed. "I know these guys."

Johnny responded with a feeble nod. He wasn't comfortable being so ill prepared. The transaction of the bogus kilos in exchange for cash went off as planned. Completing the trade, Eustice returned to his car to rejoin Johnny. The drive back to the James Brothers Saloon was taken without discussion. The silence was broken by Eustice once he double-parked in front of the bar to let out Johnny.

"Here you go, bro," said Eustice, slipping his travel mate five one-hundred-dollar bills .

Filling his hand with cash went far in appeasing Johnny. He tucked the five C-notes in his pants.

"Thanks, Bob," he said, his anger now gone. "Next time, just let me know what I'm walking into."

"I should have done that," acknowledged Bob. "But if I did, you might not have come," he added.

"Listen, you don't worry about me being there. Anytime you need me, let me know in advance. I'll come heavy; that way I can back you up. The only thing is this has to stay between us."

"Okay, Johnny, we're on the same page. . . . Loose lips sink ships."

Johnny winked at Eustice before getting out of the car. He felt invigorated as he stood on the sidewalk watching the undercover detective drive off. He entered the bar having serious thoughts of murdering Eustice after their next outing and pocketing all the money. After some consideration he decided against going that route. Instead he reached out to Jasper telephonically.

"Are you sure about this?" asked Jasper.

"I'm telling ya, I saw the deal go down with my own eyes," stated Johnny emphatically. "He gave me five C-notes for tagging along. I bullshitted him into thinking that I'm with him all the way."

"Why did he need you?"

Jasper wasn't happy to learn of what he felt to be an encroachment on his territory and staff. He came to the James Brothers Saloon in a huff.

"Let's talk downstairs," directed Jasper.

"So you went off the reservation with an outlaw?" questioned Jasper.

"Back the hell up, Jasper. There was no intent involved in this thing. I had no idea what he was up to. The guy just asked me to go for a ride with him," explained Johnny. "He never told me what the mission was. I thought I was just doing him a favor. He could have been going to pick up a birthday cake and needed someone to sit in the car for all I knew."

"Didn't you ask where you were going?"

"I did ask him, but he never gave me a straight answer. All he said was that it would just take a few minutes, so what was I supposed to do, get out and walk? I had no idea he was the competition."

"Alright, Johnny," said Jasper, having heard enough. Let's go leash until I get a line on this freaking Bayonne Bob."

########

JASPER'S UNEXPECTED APPEARANCE AT THE BROWNSVILLE car lot sent shock waves throughout Lemon's body. The informant's uneasiness resulted in a physical reaction.

"Hello, Lemon," greeted Jasper upon entering the trailer office.

"Hi, Jesse," greeted Lemon in a low, controlled voice. The dancing tremble coming from Lemon's lower lip was beyond his control. "What," he gulped, "what brings you to Brownsville?"

"I need to talk to you," announced Jasper. "What's with the lip?" he asked, noticing the tremble.

Lemon came up with a fast explanation. "It's a damn medical condition," the owner of the lot replied.

"What medical condition?"

"I've had a neurological disorder for years. I left the house this morning forgetting to take my medicine." Jasper, not versed on exactly what a neurological disorder was, took Lemon's word for it.

"Well, you gotta remember to take your medicine. Tie a friggin' string around your finger."

"I may have to start doing that."

Jasper returned to the purpose of his visit. "Talk to me about Bayonne Bob. What's his game?"

"All I can really tell you is that he worked with my brother-in-law, Monte, for years."

"Yeah, but Monte is croaked. So what does Jasper do *now*?"

"All I know is that whatever it is, it has something to do with Harlem."

"How do you come to know that?"

"He came to see me with a Harlem friend who wanted a car."

"Do you think they're in the junk business?"

"I can't be 100 percent sure of that, Jesse, but it wouldn't surprise me."

Now more relaxed, Lemon was forced to intentionally quiver his lip in order to keep up his pretense.

"I want you to set up a meeting for me to talk to this Bayonne Bob. I'll get back to you."

#########

MARKIE PAID ALLEY A SURPRISE VISIT at her home. He arrived with a shopping bag filled with the things she loved. He brought her the latest issues of her favorite magazines, several five-dollar lotto scratch-off tickets, two boxes of the mint Oreo cookies she loved and tickets to see Tony Bennett in concert.

"What's all this for?" she asked while opening the plastic that contained the cookies.

"I miss you," he replied.

"Yeah, I get that. It's been awhile. But why did you bring all this?"

"I've been thinking. . . ." he said .

"Thinking about what?"

"Us. . . ."

23

Shepherd Fish

FROM THE WINDOW OF HIS HOME, LEMON WATCHED for the arrival of the detectives. The meeting had to do with Jasper's recent visit to Lemon's place of business. Eustice was the first to arrive. They sat in the living room watching television as they waited for Markie and Von Hess.

"You know, I don't why they want to have these meetings here at my house," complained Lemon.

"They think they're doing us a favor because we both live on Staten Island."

"What happens if someone recognizes you guys as cops?"

"Just say you reported lost property and needed a police report for the insurance company."

"But suppose—" His sentence was interrupted by the bell. It was Markie and Von Hess at the door.

"You didn't park out front, did you?" asked Lemon.

"No, we parked on the next block," advised Von Hess.

"So Lemon, tell me, what exactly did Jasper want?" asked Markie, taking a seat in the living room.

"He wanted to know about Bayonne Bob. I told him everything you guys told me to say."

"He swallowed it?" asked Von Hess.

"I think so. He said he might want me to set up a meeting with him and Bayonne Bob."

Markie calculated the risks for a moment. After doing so, he made a decision. "Alright, if a meeting is what he wants, that's what we'll give him. We'll make the meeting in a public place," said Markie.

"Shouldn't we let Jesse pick the location?" asked Lemon.

"No, we need to control the venue," said Markie.

"A restaurant with outdoor seating would work," suggested Von Hess.

"What do I tell him if he has a specific place in mind?" asked Lemon.

"No good," advised Markie. "He could ask to meet in some basement."

"So what am I supposed to tell him if he insists?"

"Tell him Bayonne Bob feels more comfortable in an outdoor location." If he balks at that, set the meet wherever he wants. We'll come up with an excuse to cancel at the last minute and reschedule."

The following morning Lemon retrieved a message on his office answering machine. It was Jasper asking him to set up the meeting. Within the hour Markie and Von Hess were at the car lot with equipment to record the return call.

"Make sure he tells you who he wants to meet," instructed Markie. Lemon nodded before dialing.

"Hello. It's me, Lemon."

"I need you to set up that meeting for me," said Jasper.

"What meeting?"

"What do you mean what meeting?" asked Jasper, sounding surprised. "What are you trying to be, funny?" Lemon held the phone away from his ear so the detectives could hear Jasper sound off.

"Honest, Jasper . . . my short-term memory isn't worth a shit anymore," explained Lemon. The law enforcement officers were impressed with how fast Lemon came up with an answer.

"Alright, alright, forget it. Just set up a meeting with your friend from Jersey."

"You mean Bayonne Bob, right?"

"Yeah, Bayonne Bob."

"I'll call him now," advised Lemon, "but he's gonna ask me why. What should I tell him?"

"Just tell him I got a business proposition for him."

Lemon waited fifteen minutes before getting back to Jasper. "It's a go," he advised. "Where and when do you want to meet up?"

Lemon scribbled something in the air indicating to Von Hess that he needed a pen. He jotted down the time, day, and location of the meeting proposed by Jasper on a pad. He showed the pad to the detectives as he continued speaking on the phone.

"This should be good, Jasper," advised Lemon after receiving Markie's nod of approval.

"Should be?" asked Jasper. "What is he, a prima donna?"

"No, he's not that way. He's just a cautious guy."

"I suppose careful ain't such a bad thing," commented Jasper. "Look, it makes no difference to me where we meet. Let him pick the place"

Lemon raised his hand, gesturing to the detectives with his thumb up. "Okay, let's do that. I'll talk to him again and get right back to you." Ten minutes later, after conferring with the detectives, Lemon again telephoned Jasper.

"What's the verdict?"

"He wants to meet overlooking the water on Shore Road. Okay?" Lemon read off the pad exactly where the meet was going to be.

"That's fine," agreed Jasper.

"You don't need me there, do you?"

"No. I'll take care of you after I see him."

"Thanks, Jasper." After ending the call Lemon turned to Markie. "No problem with me keeping the money Jasper intends to give me for putting the meeting together, is there?"

"You earned it, didn't you?" replied the sergeant.

##########

FISHNET WAS RESTING ON HIS BED, attempting to identify a proper alias to use. In reinventing himself, he was searching for something not easily forgettable. He briefly considered passing himself off as *Brother Enlightenment*, a man put on this earth to help others. Eventually realizing that the name would be a bit over the top, he settled on the honorific of Shepherd Fish. Whenever Fishnet's imagination was allowed to wander off to his other world, there was no limit to his creativity. His most outrageous fantasy saw him marketing his very own *Purity Seed*, at a premium price, to those in need of reproductive assistance. He was still working on this pipe dream when Hope once again returned him to the real world.

"You have mail," said Hope, interrupting his thinking. "It's a package."

"Huh?" he said, startled by the CNA's appearance. "Oh, it's you."

"Yes, it's only me Mr. Fish-hook."

Doubting that Hope would ever get his name straight, Fishnet long ceased correcting her. He glimpsed down at Hope's feet. A cruel smile crossed his face after noticing the flip-flops she wore. Her exposed toes always posed as an irresistible temptation for him.

"Could you open up the package for me?"

Hope opened the cardboard box. To her delight, she found that the box contained a king-size Bible.

"Ohhhhh . . . my goodness, look at this," she said with great enthusiasm. Impressed, Hope began to caress the white cover of the good book as if it were a child. "It's the most beautiful bible I've ever seen! But it's very heavy. You expected this?"

"The union asked what they could get me so I told them to get me a nice Bible."

"What a wonderful a gift! The Lord is the best medicine of all," she assured him. "I have to go now, but I'll be back."

"Let me have the book before you go. I'd like to do a little reading."

"Here you go. Be careful now. It's *very* heavy."

Fishnet took the Bible from Hope. Pretending the Bible was too challenging for him, he purposely dropped the book on Hope's exposed toes. He fought to maintain a straight face as she let out a howl.

"Oh, I'm so sorry, Hope. It was heavier than I thought," he said as she continued to yowl.

"Oooooo . . . I think my toes are broken," she said, squinting as she sat to massage her injury.

"You'd better go see one of the doctors about it," recommended Fishnet. "But before you do, could you pick up the good book and put it on my lap?"

After placing the book on Fishnet's lap, Hope limped off to find a doctor. "I'll say a prayer for you," he shouted after her.

During Hope's absence, Fishnet resumed scheming. He was convinced that a well-packaged cover story that tugged at heartstrings would, in many cases, loosen purse strings. He counted on Hope being an unwitting resource who could identify indigent youngsters from her home country. Fishnet planned to build his larcenous pitches around their sad stories, using genuine photos from overseas to support his bilking efforts.

"I'm back," announced Hope.

Seeing that her toes were taped, Fishnet feigned concern. "How are the toes?" he asked.

"Not so good, so I'm going home now," advised Hope.

"That sounds like a good idea. Feel better."

After Hope left the room, Fishnet began to vigorously leaf through the pages of the Bible. "Jeez, I hope I live long enough to get through all these pages," he said in a low voice to himself. As he thumbed through the book, he became so absorbed that he never heard the footsteps coming toward his bed. His lips parted in amazement when he saw Von Hess.

"So how are they treating you, Fish?" asked Von Hess.

"Hello, Ollie! Jeez, I never expected to see you here."

"I heard you were getting well again, but I never expected you to look this great. God bless!" said Von Hess sincerely. "What have you got there? Don't tell me a warhorse like you is into reading the Bible."

"Yeah, getting shot was an awakening," he answered. "I'm pitching for His team now."

"Good for you," said Von Hess, who secretly questioned the former detective's sincerity.

"They say it won't be too much longer before I'll be out and about."

"Do you have any plans once you are released?"

"Right here," said Fishnet, jabbing his finger onto the Bible. "I've seen the light, Ollie. No joke," Fishnet stated with great passion. "I got so close to the other side that I've had a sit-down with the commanding officer," he declared, feigning emotion. "From now on, it'll be nothing but good deeds."

"Well, you're on track now," said Von Hess, not knowing what else to say.

"I want to thank you and the sergeant for cleaning up after me that day, brother," said Fishnet bluntly.

Von Hess cleared his throat, not wanting to go there. As far as he was concerned, Fishnet had gotten shot up and was a hero, not a corrupt cop who committed a multitude of crimes.

"You need anything from the outside, Fish?" asked Von Hess, who was now looking to leave.

"Nah, I'm all set. I've got a lot of catching up to do with my new partner, the good book here. How is Sergeant Markie doing?"

"He's alright. He said to say hello to you," fibbed Von Hess.

Fishnet just nodded. "Tell him I said hello . . . and thanks. What have you got there in the bag?"

"I almost forgot. Here's a salami and provolone hero. We weren't sure if it's allowed, but we figured that it's been a long time since you had one of these, so I smuggled one in for you."

"That's dynamite! You've got no idea how I'm gonna enjoy this." Fishnet was appreciative of the consideration exhibited by Von Hess. As his reward, he placed the detective high up there in his private world. Von Hess was bestowed the title of Prince Von Hess, part of the royal family in the magical kingdom of Fishnet's imagination.

When Von Hess departed the facility, he couldn't help but feel a little better about himself for having made the visit. When he reached the waiting unmarked vehicle, he found Markie reading a newspaper.

"Well, that's done," said Von Hess.

"So what's the verdict in there?" asked the curious sergeant.

"It's pretty unbelievable, boss. The guy looks like he can get up and go fifteen rounds."

"No shit."

"I'm telling you, whatever the hell work they did on him, those doctors deserve an award."

"Well, they say only the good die young," commented Markie.

"Get this, Sarge. . . . Fishnet found religion. He had a Bible on his lap and everything."

Markie raised his eyebrows. "Get the hell out of here," he said with great pessimism. "I don't buy it for one second. He's bullshitting you. A leopard doesn't change his spots. He's just running scared right now maybe. Wait and see; he'll revert back to his old ways . . . sure as I'm sitting here."

Von Hess shrugged, not committing one way or the other. "By the way, Fishnet sent you his regards."

"Now, isn't that nice of him?" stated Markie sarcastically. "Did the bum like the hero he got?"

"He loved it, Sarge. He really did. I only wish you'd have let me tell him that it was your idea and that you paid for it."

"C'mon, forget it. I only did it hoping that the son of a bitch might choke on the skin of the salami."

24

Old Bones and an Old Photo

WITHOUT THE CONTRIBUTION OF HIS BROTHER, CHRIS, navigating the complexities of multiple businesses was not without challenges for Jasper. While the asphalt corporation remained consistently profitable thanks to lucrative city contracts, some of his other interests had begun to show signs of distress. Once aware of the drop-off in returns, he ordered his accountant to start conducting audits. Jasper soon learned that his Laundromats had taken a downward turn after reassigning Mousey to the James Brothers Saloon. The accountant informed Jasper that he suspected employee theft. Jasper had the accountant move on to another business while he personally looked into the theft problem.

The Laundromats employed part-time employees who were assigned to designated stores on a regular basis. The only person with access to all of the Laundromats was the manager who had taken Mousey's place. He was a sixty-five-year-old retired employee of the parks department, whose duties included collecting the coins from the machines. Jasper drove to each location until he spotted the manager's blue van. While Jasper waited for his manager to return to his vehicle, he sat in his car monitoring the customers who entered and left the location. It was clear to him that business was brisker than what the proceeds being turned in reflected. When the manager finally emerged from the Laundromat, he was carrying the large canvas bag he used to put the collected money in. Surprisingly to Jasper, he was also toting a brown leather gym bag.

"Two bags!" said Jasper in an astonished tone. "What is this, one for me and one for him?"

Jasper controlled his outrage as watched as the gray-haired man in the tinted glasses walk to his van. Top-heavy and on the short side, the manager appeared o be seemingly carefree. When he got behind the wheel and drove off, Jasper followed him. The van came to a stop at an off-track betting parlor. The manager parked, got out of his vehicle, and entered the gambling den. He exited with what appeared to be a stack of betting tickets sticking up from the breast pocket of his shirt.

"So that's where my money has been going," said Jasper bitterly.

The manager was tailed to another laundry location, where he engaged in the same two-bag behavior.

"Look at this!" said the infuriated Jasper. "This guy made himself a partner!"

The next stop was at a hospital not far from the Laundry. Double-parking, the manager waited until a tall woman in her early sixties climbed into the front seat. Her thick reddish hair was worn up in a bun. Based on the uniform she wore, Jasper could see that she was part of the cleaning staff at the hospital. He followed the couple to a nearby hotel that was well known for their short-stay room offerings.

"Unbelievable!" said Jasper aloud as he watched the manager enter the lobby alone. After a few minutes, he emerged from the building and signaled to the woman in the van by pointing to a side door to the building. She promptly exited and met her paramour there. Just as they were entering the building, Jasper pulled up, tooting his horn. The manager's mouth dropped at being discovered by his boss. He passed the access card to the room to his lady friend.

"Go to the room, number 247. I'll be there in a few minutes," instructed the manager. Annoyed by the intrusion into her lunch hour, she took the card and complied without question. The wayward employee then walked to Jasper's car to face the music.

"Have you gone totally insane?" asked Jasper icily.

"What can I say, Jasper? My wife ain't well and can't give me what I need, and this one is clean."

"I don't give a shit if she just came out of one of the washing machines!" scolded Jasper. "You steal from me? You leave my money in a van unattended while you frolic with some geriatric trollop?"

"The money is safe here in the lot. . . ."

"Don't give me that. . . . And what are you doing with two bags? You ain't just taking a few bucks over here for a pack of cigarettes. Did you really think you can get away this shit?"

The accused swallowed hard. "I know I screwed up, Jasper. What are you gonna do?"

"I'm not sure what I'm going to do," answered Jasper, letting out a deep breath. "The only thing preventing me from breaking your neck right now is the effort involved in finding a replacement."

"Jasper, please don't over react..."

"Over react...you better shut up and go get those money bags and put them in the trunk of my car." Since he was soon scheduled for an appointment elsewhere, Jasper couldn't devote any more time to this problem. Once he had the money, he advised, "We'll straighten this out tomorrow."

"I'll pay you back every penny, Jasper. . . ."

"Q-Ball Otto is gonna have a conversation with you about that. He'll call on you tomorrow, and I better not hear that you were hard to find," warned Jasper.

"Alright, Jasper, whatever you say." The manager's face was ashen. As he watched Jasper drive off, he could only wonder how bad a beating he was in for.

Jasper began to slowly shake his head. While rightly irked, he couldn't prevent himself from also being rather amused at the thought of his manager's assignation with a grandmotherly cleaner. Jasper already knew that he wasn't going to be as harsh as he would be on others for a similar offense. But since he had a reputation to maintain, he had to do something. The retired parks department worker was destined to receive a cuffing around at the hands of Otto. Jasper was thinking of having Otto bust a few of his fingers and put him on a payment plan to repay what he had stolen. He hadn't fully decided. With this situation basically under control, Jasper headed for his meeting with Bayonne Bob.

###########

EUSTICE SAT ALONE ON A BENCH facing the bay. The whizzing noise of the speeding highway traffic on the Belt Parkway was at his back. While waiting for Jasper, the undercover detective took several rapid puffs on his cigar as he watched the boats pass in the distance. Eustice gazed over at his backup team to see what they were doing. Markie and Von Hess were positioned approximately one hundred yards away. Posing as fishermen, they were leaning over the guardrail with their lines in the water. Eustice wasn't used to seeing them out of their usual jacket and tie. Markie wore a lightweight newsboy cap that gave him a thuggish look. The fedora worn by Von Hess with the brim turned up had the same effect.

Jasper walked by the bogus fishermen without giving them a second look. He moved with the swagger of someone who was an ardent believer in his own self-importance. His shoulders were thrown back, and his raised chin left little doubt that he considered himself the dominant player. He nodded his acknowledgment to Eustice, receiving the same gesture. Jasper's confidence stemmed from having Silky's backing. Eustice's power emanated from having the law on his side.

"Why were you worried about meeting me?" said Jasper.

"I'm here, ain't I?" replied the undercover detective. "What do you want to see me about?"

"We got a couple of things to discuss."

Eustice took on a serious look, as one would if anticipating trouble. "Yeah, like what?"

Jasper raised his index finger to his nose and began tapping the opening. The gesture signified the snorting of cocaine. "Your business is no secret, my friend," he declared.

Eustice didn't confirm or deny Jasper's insinuation. "Your point?" he asked.

The question riled Jasper. "My *point* fuck-o is that nobody turns a buck in *my* joint without *my* okay and without paying a tax."

Eustice feigned ignorance. "So what am I supposed to have done other than lose money gambling in your joint?" asked the undercover detective innocently.

"How about selling swag, hustling hookers, and using my people to bodyguard drug runs?"

Eustice feigned umbrage at Jasper's accusation. "Who's filling your head with all this?"

"Forget about who tells me what. If it weren't for you knowing Lemon, you'd have a real problem, my friend. Let's get down to basics so we know where we stand with each other. Are you with anyone?"

"I'm with me."

"You got no one behind you?"

"I work independent. Who are you with?"

221

"I'm with lions, my friend," declared Jasper. "I make one phone call and you become a memory."

"Look, man . . . I'm not looking for problems."

"Good," said Jasper, satisfied that Eustice was backing down. "This doesn't have to be a hostile meeting. I called for you because I think you might have value to me. I want us to be *friends*."

"How can I be valuable to you?"

"I'm looking for someone with your experience. I'm talking about getting together."

"You want me in the bar business with you?" asked the undercover, pretending to be naïve.

"You don't have to play it cute with me. By now you know that we're in the same business," said Jasper flatly. "I want you with me, pitching *my* product."

"With all due respect, I'm doing okay on my own," answered Eustice, not wanting to appear anxious.

"That could change fast," warned Jasper. "Besides, how well are you really doing if you need to use *my people* to take rides with you?" Jasper was clearly flexing his muscles.

Eustice took out a hankie and blew his nose before responding. In doing so, he alerted his backup team that there might be trouble coming. Markie nudged Von Hess before placing his gun in his jacket pocket.

"Look, Johnny was there, so I used him," explained Eustice. "He could've said no. Anyway, how was I supposed to know that he was with you and what you got going?"

Jasper acknowledged Eustice's point. "I'll give you that. But you know the score *now*."

Eustice began to use flattery to work his way into Jasper's pocket. "I have to hand it to you; you've got your people trained well. I would have never figured Johnny to go running back to you."

"There are consequences associated with a lack of loyalty," noted Jasper.

"Look, Jasper, if I got my wires crossed with yours, it was an innocent mistake. It's not my thing to go around pushing my nose in where it ain't wanted."

Jasper nodded approvingly. The undercover was showing him respect, and that was reassuring.

"Do you have a family, Bob?"

"I have a wife in Bayonne but no kids. My wife can't have any," replied Eustice.

"I'm sorry to hear that. Adopting ain't the worst thing. You know, I saved Mousey from a shit life."

"I didn't know that."

"Does your wife work?"

"Yeah, she works for Social Security as a clerk. She thinks I'm a liquor salesman."

"So she's a fed," said Jasper, not being serious. For the first time he smiled.

Eustice laughed. "Yeah, she's Eliot Ness," he answered, referring to the legendary FBI agent.

"Keep her in the dark. They can never use her to hurt you if she doesn't know anything."

As far as Jasper was concerned, Bayonne Bob was a logical choice to replace Spanky. All he needed to do now was sell the opportunity. "Come in with me, Bob?" he said. "It'll be in your interest."

"How so?" asked the undercover.

"To begin with, you'd be protected. I can't emphasize enough what it means not to walk alone." Jasper was indirectly emphasizing that he was mobbed up. Getting the message, Eustice nodded.

"Maybe I'd be interested if my end was right. But I'm not looking to take any crazy risks."

"Relax, my friend. You're coming into an organization that believes in minimizing risk. I've been looking for someone like you to handle strictly weight transactions."

"Why me?" asked Eustice.

"You know the business, and you're known by people I know. Plus, you've been able to operate under the radar without bunking heads with anyone up to now. *That* says something for you."

"I see. . . ."

"We operate in New York *and* Las Vegas. Somebody even wants me to plant a flag in Los Angeles."

"I didn't realize how big you are. Can I ask who would be behind us?"

"You could ask, but I'll never tell. Try taking a guess. . . ."

Eustice decided to risk gambling. "You're with the Guarini family."

Jasper raised his eyebrows. "Who told you that?"

"You could ask, but I'll never tell," replied Eustice, echoing what Jasper said previously.

Jasper nodded. "Bob, I think *now* you might *have* to come on board."

"I'm in. What's my end?"

"We'll merge your operation into mine. Bob, you'll make plenty throwing in with me. I'm continually expanding into different businesses, and I'll always need a guy with a brain. You play ball with me and you'll end up richer than you ever thought possible." After some haggling, they came to terms.

"I just got one thing I have to tell you, Jasper. . . . All my customers come out of Harlem."

"No problem. The money is green up there, ain't it?"

"That it is."

"That's all that matters. Where does your connection come from?"

"I get my shit from Philadelphia," answered Eustice, making up a source location.

"Don't worry about keeping your customers happy. Our product is the best around. Oh, there is one other thing you'll be happy to know."

"What's that?"

"Consider yourself like Superman . . . invulnerable! Nobody can touch you." Jasper put his hand out to shake. "We're in business, Bob. You'll be on record with me now that we've worked things out. I was afraid that I might need to launch a rocket up your divider. I'm glad it didn't come to that."

"I'm glad too."

Their understanding meant a lot to Jasper because it put him closer to Spanky's execution day.

While Jasper and Eustice were hammering out a deal Spanky was amusing himself by watching a squirrel go up a tree in John Paul Jones Park in Bay Ridge. He was waiting for Jasper. He turned his attention to a fifty-eight-ton cannon that had helped establish the three-mile limit for territorial waters that rested nearby. As he stared at the huge weapon, the image of Jasper toting a gun crept into his mind. Spanky nervously began picking at his fingers. Unsure of why Jasper had called for the spur-of-the-moment meeting only enhanced his perturbation. Strongly suspecting that Jasper was aware of his cocaine arrangement with Buster, he felt a perpetual danger looming over his head. The irony of the situation escaped Spanky. Here he sat a coward in a venue dedicated to an American Revolution patriot who once declared, "I have not yet begun to fight."

"I just left this guy Bayonne Bob," announced Jasper, taking a seat next to Spanky on the bench. Jasper's plan called for luring Spanky into a sense of false security

"What's up?" asked Spanky.

"Bob's into selling coke. I'm taking over his business and merging it into my operation. We're gonna show him how we operate here and then send him out to Vegas to keep an eye on things out there."

"Does Lucy know about this?"

"No, I didn't tell her yet.. The big picture is eventually to have Bob run everything."

Spanky was now baffled. "What do you mean by everything?" he asked, feeling threatened.

"I'm talking the works, both New York and Vegas."

"What about me?"

"Relax, kid, you're figured in. I'm setting this chump up for the big deal I've been working on."

"What big deal?"

A grave look came over Jasper's face. "I've got an exit strategy for *us*, Spanky."

"Did you say *us?*"

"Yeah, so don't worry about a thing. I'm selling out to these Russians I know. With the money I give you from that deal, there will be enough for you to go into a couple of legit businesses if you want."

Spanky was skeptical. "There will?"

"Don't you understand? I'm walking away with all the marbles and cutting you in. We can't go on forever walking between the raindrops in this drug game."

"So you want to sell out? Take the money and run?"

"Yeah, now you get the idea. We're getting out before there is any chance of the roof falling in on us. Maybe we'll open up a restaurant together."

Spanky couldn't believe what he was hearing. He began to wonder if he could have been wrong all along about how much Jasper knew about him and Buster. "Are you talking full partners?" he asked.

"As long as we both put up the same amount of money, we'll be equal partners."

"What about Lucy and Bayonne Bob?"

"What about them?"

"Where do they fit in once you sell?"

"The Russians will have to keep them around long enough to get their arms around the operation. Once that happens, their run is over."

Spanky looked at Jasper as if he were seeing him for the first time. "You mean . . . ?"

"They'll get rid of them," said Jasper, taking on a somber tone. "Those two represent the only road that can lead back to us. It's in our interest that they go bye-bye."

"What about your connection to the product?"

"It's transferred to the Russians."

"But what about all the time we spent in Vegas with the girls?"

"What about it? We banged a couple of girls we picked up . . . period."

The realization of just how ruthless Jasper could be awed Spanky. "What's the time frame for pulling the pin on this?"

"I'm shooting for the first of the year."

"And then we get to do something else . . . together as even partners, right?"

"That's the plan. It'll be just you and me, kid. Don't worry; we'll do big things," assured Jasper, leading Spanky on. "What do you think of our owning a nightclub?"

"I like that better than a restaurant!" Spanky enthused. Spanky was so enamored by the idea of having a piece of his own playpen that it blinded him to the obvious risks involved when embracing Jasper at his word. "So what's the next step, Jasper?"

"You gotta educate Bayonne Bob. You know, show him the ropes over here. Then go out West with him to meet Lucy and get him comfortable with the operation out there."

"I can do that," said Spanky, whose fears evaporated due to the fortune he envisioned coming his way.

##########

AS THE SON OF A RETIRED NYPD detective, Agent Leardi took pride sitting in the office of the chief of detectives. After years of hearing police stories growing up, the federal agent came to envy those who held a birds-eye view of what his dad referred to as the big show.

"I had our organized crime analysts do some homework," advised the agent. "They came up with something I thought you people might find interesting. Take a look at this surveillance picture."

Leardi produced an enlarged black-and-white surveillance photo of three men. He put the photograph on the table for the others in attendance to see.

"Where did this come from?" asked Markie while looking at the photo.

"It was taken by an investigator from the Brooklyn district attorney's office years ago."

Markie looked at the back of the photo. It reflected the names Settimo "Silky" Seggio, Cristofaro Stanlee, and Gaspare Stanlee. Also visible on the rear of the photo was the date and time the surveillance photo had been taken. It was recorded as 1400 hours (2:00 p.m.), July 2, 1973. A small notation below this line identified the Stanlee twins as *Seggio runners.* A second notation indicated that Silky Seggio was a soldier in the Cosmo Guarini crime family.

"Where was this photo taken?" asked Markie.

"It was taken as they came out of Silky Seggio's social club," advised Leardi. "The DA's squad was looking into Seggio's gambling operation. They must have been trying to build a case against Seggio, but for some reason it never came to fruition. It was so long ago that no one is around anymore who remembers what happened."

Markie stared at Jasper's photo. The sergeant removed a magnifying glass from the top of the chief's desk and placed it against the photo, after which he sent Von Hess for their case folder.

"Ollie, look at this picture," said Markie once Von Hess returned with the folder. "That's Jasper adjusting his shades. Zero in on his hand."

Using the magnifying glass, Von Hess examined the photo. "THE RING!" blurted out the detective.

"What ring?" asked Chief McCoy.

"Show the chief, Ollie." Von Hess reached into his case folder and removed the photo of Cornell Mathis that the missing man's widow had given him. When put alongside the surveillance photo, it was apparent to all that the ring in each photo seemed to be a match.

"All we need now is just a little icing on the cake," said Markie. "I'm starting to feel good about meeting your timetable, chief," he added confidently.

"Blow up the ring in both pictures and then compare them," ordered the chief. "I want you to be certain that those rings are a definite match."

The conversation next switched to the drug aspect of the investigation. Most of the questions were addressed to Eustice.

"So Jasper wants Spanky to educate you regarding the drug operation, right?" asked Agent Leardi.

"Correct," replied Eustice. " Spanky is an unbelievable talker. He's been telling me all kinds of things, including who they sleep with." Chief McCoy and Lieutenant Wright shot glances at each other.

"Did he tell you who their source was for the coke, Eustice?" inquired the agent.

"That's something even Spanky doesn't know. The only one who has the answer to that is Jasper."

"They are definitely doing weight?"

"That's it. It's strictly kilos of cocaine being sold. According to Spanky, he developed a nice client base."

"What's the setup in Vegas?"

"I think that it's the same as in New York."

"Why all of a sudden are these guys letting you in on all this, Eustice?" asked Leardi, who found what he was hearing difficult to digest. "They don't even know you."

Eustice felt insulted by the skepticism expressed. "What can I say? They recognize my talent," answered the detective, sounding egotistical. "I've been playing them like a violin."

Markie wasn't one to encourage braggadocio. "There is no love affair here with these people," said Markie. "Let's not kid ourselves; this Jasper has something up his sleeve. He's courting you for a reason."

"You read my mind, Al," said Leardi in agreement.

For the first time, Eustice felt that he might be exposed to some type of danger that he hadn't foreseen. "You think they might suspect me?"

"I wouldn't worry about that, Eustice. But you must be pretty important to Jasper," conjectured the agent. "He's probably got a plan of some sort."

"You should be safe . . . for now anyway," injected Von Hess. The senior detective couldn't resist tossing Eustice a panic pill. His words caused the undercover detective's mouth to drop open.

"Relax, Eustice," said Lieutenant Wright, entering the conversation. "All we're saying is that Jasper has to have a purpose for taking such an interest in you."

"Maybe he's looking to clean house and needs Eustice to carry on," suggested Chief McCoy. He was thinking as a manager. "Are there any internal shake-ups underway?"

"I don't really know," answered Markie. "But you make an excellent point, Chief."

"Eustice, are you comfortable introducing one of our agents to these people?" asked Leardi.

"They expect me to keep doing business with *my clients,* so I can introduce a lot of agents as people looking to buy drugs," replied Eustice, welcoming the presence of more good guys into the mix.

"Could you swing that kind of an introduction out in Vegas too?" asked Leardi.

"Probably, but I'll know better once I get a lay of the land out there. Whatever people I introduce into the picture out there should probably originate from New York," advised Eustice.

The federal agent nodded in agreement. "Do you see any weaknesses with this crew?"

"Spanky is nuts for women, so I suppose we could work that angle at some point," suggested Eustice.

"Keep something in mind," stated Chief McCoy. "I haven't got a bottomless pit for a budget. Let's not lose sight of the fact that *our* interest in this is the homicide of the National Guardsman. We need to concentrate on advancing that front in a timely and cost-effective fashion."

Leardi became a bit alarmed. "You're not going to take Eustice from us, are you?"

Chief McCoy assured the agent that the feds could keep Eustice for as long as they needed him, provided that Jasper is arrested in a timely fashion. He made it clear that the presence of Markie and Von Hess had a shelf life. The terms were amenable enough to appease all concerned.

25

The Wolf Quartet

EUSTICE KNEW IT WAS GOING to be one of those days. Having overslept, he began his morning behind schedule. In his haste, he cut himself shaving. It was an annoying nick just below his nostril that stubbornly refused to stop bleeding. To stem the tide of blood, he placed a tiny piece of toilet paper against the cut. By the time he boarded the plane to Vegas, the wound morphed into a bloody crust.

"What happened?" asked Spanky, noticing the protective crust.

"I cut myself shaving," replied the vain detective curtly.

"What did you use, an axe?" Spanky's comment further agitated the already self-conscious detective.

The men were going to meet with Las Vegas Lucy. Eustice, who detested flying, was assigned to a window seat on the airplane. He was acutely aware that once airborne, the view of the clouds would enhance his discomfort. The particles of condensed vapor would be a constant reminder of how far above the ground he was. To help alleviate his dismay, he asked Spanky to switch seats. After moving to the window seat, Spanky agreed to pull down the shade in order to shut out the sky.

Spanky reached into his pocket and removed a small pill. "Here, take this. It'll make things easier."

Realizing that the pill was a controlled substance, Eustice's initial inclination was to decline the valium being offering. "Nah, I'll have a shooter when they come around with the cart later."

"Whatever floats your boat," said Spanky, popping a pill. "This could make things a lot easier for you."

Eustice suddenly had a change of heart. "Okay, on second thought, let me have one."

After taking the pill, Eustice rested his head back. A man in his late fifties stood alongside him in the aisle. He was a tall, distinguished-looking gentleman with a neatly trimmed white mustache. He squinted as he struggled to read the boarding ticket he held in his hand.

"I think I'm assigned the center seat," he announced. "The stewardess said we should expect some turbulence due to the rain," advised the stranger, trying to make conversation.

Spanky turned his face away from the voice, shutting out the man assigned to the center seat. The man held his tan attaché case between his legs as he began unbuttoning the off-white raincoat he wore. He proceeded to rearrange items in the overhead in order to create an appropriate space for his things. Eustice remained oblivious to the activity above his head. Just as the stranger was placing his attaché case in the overhead, a stout passenger brushed against him while en route to his seat. The surprise contact made him fumble his attaché case, causing it to land squarely on top of Eustice's head.

"OWWW! . . . WHAT IN THE . . . ?!" blurted the detective, reacting to the pain he felt.

"Oh, I'm so sorry! Excuse me, sir," the man immediately said. Sensing hostility by the expression on Eustice's face, he curtailed his apologies, quickly placing the attaché case in the overhead.

As Eustice earnestly massaged the lump on his head with his fingers, the stranger hastily took off his raincoat to place in the overhead. The garment, which was extended to full length, subsequently enveloped Eustice's head. Realizing that he had swaddled Eustice's skull with his coat, the man again expressed remorse at his clumsiness. The disturbance of the undercover detective's hair caused him to detonate. After being the recipient of a heated volley of expletives, the oafish passenger sheepishly slipped into his center seat. Eventually all was forgiven thanks to the little pill Eustice took. When the detective stepped off the plane, he looked to see if he could spot the DEA surveillance team that was waiting for him to land. The agents on the ground proved themselves adept at being invisible. The federal agents recognized Eustice by his photo and the clothing that he had promised to be wearing.

Scheduled to be introduced to Lucy the following morning, Eustice had time to relax. After checking into his room at the casino hotel, he decided to go to the pool. He put on the yellow bathing suit he hadn't worn in years. Since he had added poundage since last wearing the suit, Eustice found looking at himself in the full-length mirror to be depressing. He could clearly see that he'd become too much man in the wrong places. Scratching off the scab under his nose didn't help matters. Now bleeding again, he went to the bathroom to put more tissue against the reopened cut. As he waited for the blood to stop flowing, he placed a white washcloth down the front of his swim suit. While still too much man, the supplement at least made him feel a little better.

With his arms folded, Eustice waded in the low end of the pool where the water reached no higher than his thighs. When through cooling off, he returned to his room to freshen up. He reunited with Spanky at the hotel bar.

"What about your connection?" asked Spanky.

"My connection isn't fast, but he puts out some good stuff," advised Eustice.

"Where is it coming from?"

"It comes out of Philly. My only beef with Philly is that my guy isn't always around when I need him," answered Eustice. "Do you ever run into a supply problem?"

"Never," answered Spanky, "and Jasper's stuff ain't exactly coming from around the corner. It comes from up north someplace, in Buffalo, I think, or maybe even Canada. We never have to wait long. They must be shittin' out the stuff up there."

"You go pick it up?"

"Nope, the product is delivered to me direct at my apartment."

"You pay them when they deliver? What about a possible rip off?"

"Not a chance of that happening," said Spanky with confidence. "Jasper worked out a consignment deal. They front the stuff, and we send them money later, after we get paid."

"*You* send the money up north?"

"No, I don't do anything. I just give Jasper the money; he takes it from there. To tell you the truth, I don't know how things work on his end."

"This setup takes a lot of trust," observed Eustice. "I would have never thought that Jasper had it in him to arrange something like this."

"Jasper ain't got the brains for it. His dead brother did all the thinking. I even think that there is somebody else in with him."

"You think so?"

"Jasper thinks I'm asleep at the wheel. I might not know all the details," he confided, "but I do know that he's not the only one pulling the strings. Like I said, I don't know exactly what the arrangement is, but Jasper doesn't take a leak without talking to certain people."

"Now I'm confused, Spanky. Who the hell are you talking about?" The undercover was trying to get Spanky to open up further.

"That shit has got nothing to do with us. So let's just do each other a favor and forget it."

Eustice tried another avenue to gain information. He zeroed in on Spanky's ego, hoping to spur him into talking. "C'mon, you're just speculating."

"Speculating?" replied Spanky, taking his being doubted to heart. "You consider Jasper's coziness with Silky Seggio to be speculation?" asked Spanky pointedly.

"Silky is Jasper's connection?"

"Hey, back up, man. I never said *that*. This kind of talk can get us both hurt," warned Spanky.

"This is some heavy shit," said Eustice, genuinely impressed.

"Look, Bob, all you got to know is to keep your nose out of Jasper's business. It's all very simple. When we need more shit, we tell Jasper. After a couple of days, the product gets dropped off at my apartment . . . end of story."

"What if the need is out here in Vegas?"

"It's our responsibility to move the shit to Vegas."

"You take it out here?"

"Sometimes I do. Sometimes Lucy comes to New York and then goes back with whatever she needs."

"What's happening with LA?"

"I think it's a dead issue. Lucy was the one pushing that idea."

"She's got juice with Jasper?"

"As long as she keeps bending over for him she does. She wants to run girls out of a club she wants to set up. You'll meet her," advised Spanky. "Hey, talk about that, you ever been to the Ride-Em Ranch?

"No, never," advised Eustice.

"You don't know what you're missing, Bob. We'll go one night."

Eustice hesitated before answering. Aware that he was under federal surveillance, he didn't know how far he wanted to push the envelope. "I gotta think about it," replied the undercover.

Spanky's tone suddenly changed to one of suspicion. "What's to think about?"

Thinking fast, Eustice came up with an answer. "I don't know if I want one girl or two."

"I have the same problem. I got a local down here who I take along sometimes."

"I have to stop at a bank," said Eustice. The statement caused Spanky to laugh out loud.

"Stop at a bank? Are you kidding me, Bob?"

Eustice knew he was going to have to start taking chances in order to maintain his credibility. "Yeah, I gotta go to the bank. Where do you keep your money, up your ass?"

Spanky backed up. "No. I'm just surprised that you come to Vegas and need to go to a bank."

"I want to save my cash for gambling. I didn't figure on this."

"They take credit cards."

"I can't do that. My wife sees the credit card charges."

"It won't show up as Ride-Em Ranch. It'll show up as the Getsum Corporation."

"I'm going with cash," declared Eustice, ending their conversation.

Spanky indicated that he wanted to do some coke in his room before heading out. Since the drug dealer wasn't paying too much attention, Eustice was able to successfully fake a blow. When they arrived at the brothel, Eustice had to make a decision. He could actively partake or just engage one of the girls, pay for her time, tip well, and have the prostitute later say that they had a wonderful time. The undercover still hadn't made up his mind after entering the private room with the girl he'd selected.

########

ARTHUR JEFFERSON MATHIS JR. WAS the first cousin of National Guard Sergeant Cornell Mathis. For over fifty years the octogenarian operated a successful jewelry store in Mobile, Alabama. He agreed to meet the NYC investigators at his home, a midcentury two-story. They were greeted warmly.

"Come on in. Let's take seats in the library," said the jeweler. He led the investigators into a quaint room, where mahogany bookshelves lined the walls. Markie noticed that there was a portable bar in the corner of the room. Several cushioned chairs were situated around a nearby small circular cocktail table.

"Can I offer you gentlemen a libation?"

Markie and Von Hess looked at each other. "I'll take the Jack Daniel's," said the sergeant.

"An excellent selection," voiced the host.

"That works for me too," echoed Von Hess.

"I'll make it three of the same," said the jeweler. The business owner, round shouldered and slightly stooped, would have been considered tall for his generation. The white hairs coming out of the top of his head were few and far between. The tan slacks he wore made his lower abdomen seem swelled. Mr. Mathis wore a burgundy cardigan sweater over a white shirt. His orthopedic shoes were black.

"What's your preference? Neat, on the rocks, or with water?" asked the host.

"Straight up," replied Markie. His preference was echoed by Von Hess.

"That's the only way," said the jeweler as he began to fill the three Waterford Crystal whiskey tumblers with bourbon. "So how was your flight?"

"Very smooth," answered Markie.

"Did they sit you at the back of the plane because you're armed?"

"Yeah, but it was fine back there," lied the sergeant. He and Von Hess had been upgraded to first class. The courtesy extended by the airline was the type of consideration that the detectives didn't talk about.

"This is quite an album of stamps you have on display, sir," said Von Hess, changing the subject.

"Yes, some in my collection go way back," said Mathis. "I suppose I'm really a philatelist at heart."

Markie stared at his host blankly, unsure of what the word meant. He sought a clarification.

"That isn't a term we often hear in New York. What exactly is a philatelist?"

The elderly jeweler let out a hardy laugh. "Not too many people around here use it either," he said.

"It's a person who collects and studies stamps." The investigators nodded, indicating that they got it.

"Well, to your health, gentlemen . . . and to old Cornell," toasted the jeweler.

After taking a sip of the drink, Markie began his inquiry. "Do you remember the one-eared wolf ring you made for your cousin Cornell?" he asked.

"Certainly I do. Lots of people wanted me to make up a ring like that for them. I declined every offer."

"Why is that?"

"There are only four like it in the world. I made them special for the four Mathis men in the family."

"What's the story with the one ear?"

"Everyone asks me that. My grandfather fought off a wolf during the Civil War. After he killed it, he sliced off an ear and kept it as a token reminder of the incident. The rings are a tribute to him."

"That's pretty interesting."

"I gave my dad the first ring I made. Another went to my uncle, Roosevelt Cromwell Mathis, Cornell's dad. Those two were buried wearing their rings. Number three I gave to Cornell, my only male first cousin. The fourth, of course, I kept."

"You still have your ring?" asked Von Hess.

"I most certainly do," answered Mathis.

"They're all identical?" inquired Markie.

"Yes, they are."

"Can we see it?"

"Alright, let me fetch it. It's upstairs on my dresser." The old man left the room to retrieve the ring. He returned a few minutes later. "Here you go," he said, handing the ring to the sergeant.

"This is a beauty. Here, take a look," said Markie, passing the ring to Von Hess.

Von Hess examined the ring closely. "I see you have the number four engraved on the inside. Why?"

"I numbered the rings. Remember, there are only four rings like that in the world. Cornell's has the number three engraved inside his ring."

"Mr. Mathis, can I ask you to do us a big favor?"

"What is it, Sergeant?"

"We think we know what happened to Cornell. We just need a little more evidence to make our case."

"So it *was* foul play, then?"

"I'm afraid it looks that way."

"Tell me what I can do to help."

"I'd like to borrow your ring for a little while."

The jeweler was taken aback by the request. Parting with his ring was something unexpected. "If I give you the ring, it'll only be for a short time, right?" he asked. "I don't want it tied up in court forever as some kind of evidence. I want to be buried wearing that ring; it's in my will."

"You'll get it back; that's a promise," assured Markie.

"Well, alright then, take it. I have one question, sir. What did happen to old Cornell?"

"I'm not at liberty to speak on that, Mr. Mathis," Markie advised, staring into his empty glass. Then, looking up at the jeweler, he added, "But I promise you, when we return the ring, we'll fill you in on everything, soup to nuts." He held out his empty glass while making this statement.

"That's a deal. Let's have another for the road," suggested the jeweler. After taking Markie's glass, he reached for the bottle of Jack Daniel's. "Sit back. I'll tell you how my grandfather came to kill that wolf."

When Markie and Von Hess ended their meeting with the jeweler, they were in good spirits. With only four rings in existence and three accounted for, Jasper had to have Cornell's ring.

##########

MARKIE AND LEARDI WERE OF THE OPINION that once Spanky was in handcuffs, he could be convinced to cooperate. From Markie's vantage point, there was a chance that Spanky might be able to provide insights into Mathis homicide. For the DEA, a cooperative Spanky would be a direct conduit to Jasper.

Eustice was called upon to facilitate a hand-to-hand kilo drug transaction between Spanky and a DEA agent. Leardi recruited Yardstick, the federal agent who had partaken in the previously staged bogus cocaine transaction that was staged for the benefit of Johnny Blondell. The cover story was that Yardstick, posing as a Harlem drug dealer, was in dire need of a kilo of cocaine within twenty-four hours.

Eustice made his pitch to Spanky. "We've got a good opportunity with my Harlem people, Spanky."

"What is it?"

"Yardstick needs a key of coke by tomorrow."

"He needs it by tomorrow?"

"It's a rush job. I can intro you as the guy responsible for delivering on such short notice."

"Who is this guy again?" asked Spanky.

"Yardstick is one of the guys from Harlem who I do business with," answered Eustice. "Johnny knows him; he saw us do business."

"What's his big rush?" asked Spanky.

"I don't ask questions," said Eustice. "All I can tell you is that the man uptown wants he wants. We either meet the demand or I tell him he's got to look someplace else. I'm not even reaching out to my regular connection because he'd never be able to make the deadline."

"Relax. We can accommodate your uptown boyfriend," advised Spanky. "Due to the short notice, I'm gonna have to up the price."

"We could probably get away with that," said Eustice. "But I don't recommend it."

"Why is that?"

"If we deliver on this order, I can make it seem like *you* made the magic happen. That'll impress Yardstick. Trust me, I know these guys uptown."

"Look, if we jack up the price we could pocket the extra money ourselves," said Spanky.

"I hear ya," said Eustice, "but if we deliver without taking advantage, I know Yardstick will appreciate it. I've got a good relationship up there. Besides, I am not looking to cross Jasper."

"Alright, alright, forget it. Pick me up tomorrow at my apartment. I'll have the product ready to go."

"How about 7:00 p.m.?"

"Why so late? I thought there was supposed to be some big rush."

"There is, but I don't want them to think it was easy for us to deliver," replied Eustice.

"Just make sure you bring a roscoe," instructed Spanky. "I'll be packing myself."

"I've had no problems, so I don't expect one this time."

"You're more trusting than I am," said Spanky, who wasn't one to take risks.

##########

EUSTICE WORE A CONCEALED RECORDING DEVICE to memorialize the drug transaction between Spanky and Yardstick. In heading the tape, he recited his rank, name, time, date, and destination. He also indicated whom he was meeting with. His final sentence before shutting off the device was, "The next voices on this tape will be the undercover in conversation with the subject, Spanky Ritzland."

"Are you good to go, Eustice?" asked Markie.

"Yeah, I'm ready."

"How about you Yardstick, ready?

"All set."

Did you copy the buy money?" asked Leardi. "Are all the serial numbers legible?"

"It's all taken care of," replied Yardstick..

Dressed in all black, Yardstick fit the part he was to play. At thirty-five years of age, he was a physically trim man who stood about six feet. When his lips tightened, his face turned into a cruel, intimidating one. The three-inch scar just under his right eye contributed to an aura of danger. Leardi turned to his second undercover agent, Tonto Montgomery.

"Tonto, I want you at the bar inside the Western View Hotel ten minutes before Yardstick gets there."

"No problem," replied Tonto.

Leardi then turned to Markie. "Let's rock and roll."

##########

SPANKY WAS IN HIS APARTMENT WAITING to be picked up by Eustice. He was glancing out of his bedroom window when he saw the undercover detective's Lincoln double-park in front of his building. The drug dealer gathered his things and headed downstairs without procrastination. He looked to both sides of the street before walking off his stoop. Contained within the bag he carried was a

239

kilo of cocaine. Spanky quickly scooted to the waiting car and entered the passenger side. The loose-fitting shirt he wore outside of his pants effectively concealed the gun he carried in his waistband.

"Drive carefully, Bob," said Spanky as he adjusted the front seat to meet his comfort. "We don't want to get pulled over by the cops with shit in the car."

"Don't worry; I'll get us there," assured Eustice.

"Are you sure you don't want to up the price?"

"I'm sure."

"I don't know why this guy couldn't come to us in Brooklyn," complained Spanky. "I don't like the idea of going uptown one bit."

"I already told you why I couldn't ask him to make the meet in Brooklyn. We always switch it up, and it's my turn to go to him. It just won't look right if I change things up now, especially with you along. Besides, he's probably just as concerned about a rip-off as you."

"He knows I'm coming?"

"Yeah, he knows your coming. The idea is to get him comfortable with Jasper's people, right?"

Spanky nodded in the affirmative. "You're packing, right, Bob?"

"Yeah, for the hundredth time, I'm packing. I always got a gun when I do a deal."

"Good," said Spanky, lifting up his shirt to reveal the butt of the .380 automatic he carried.

Seeing the automatic gave Eustice pause. "Look, Spanky . . . I've had no problems uptown, and I don't expect any now," Eustice reminded him. The undercover detective feared that Spanky might overreact.

"Don't be so trustful, my friend. There is always a first time."

Eustice remembered to scratch the right side of his face with long, slow strokes. "I got this damn itch," he stated, feigning annoyance. He wanted Spanky to notice the pinkie ring he wore. His pretext worked.

"Say, what kind of ring is that, Bob?" asked Spanky, taking notice of the wolf's emerald eyes.

Eustice held out his hand. "It's a wolf head ring. . . . Check out the eyes, man. Those are real emeralds."

"This is nice . . . but the friggin' wolf has only one ear," observed Spanky. "Why is that?"

"I got no idea. Anyway, that's what makes it different."

"I never saw a wolf with one ear like that before. It's sort of like a lone wolf. Where can I get one?"

"You got me. This is the only one I've ever seen like it."

"Well, where did you get it?"

"The tooth fairy left it for me," answered Eustice, lacking a better response.

Spanky was persistent in trying to find out the origin of the ring. "No, seriously . . . where'd you get it?"

"No comment," replied Eustice, adding to the mystery surrounding the ring.

"C'mon, man . . ."

"Maybe one day down the road I'll tell you . . . when I know you better."

##########

AGENT TONTO MONTGOMERY, A TEN-YEAR veteran agent of the DEA, was the first of the undercover operatives to arrive at the Western View Hotel. He parked his vehicle on the street where it was in clear view of the surveillance teams. The Western View was an ideal venue for a drug deal because it was located in a uniquely isolated area. It also had a bar that few people frequented.

The agent exited his vehicle and headed to the hotel's Lazy Lounge Bar. Expanding his substantial chest, the agent swaggered as he walked. He carried himself in a way that made it clear to anyone looking that he was one bad dude. Tonto Montgomery took a seat at the end of the L-shaped bar. Other than the bartender, there was no one else there. The agent sported a thick Fu Manchu mustache and small Afro. Dressed in a black suit, a black long-sleeve shirt, and dark sunglasses, he was credible in his portrayal of a bodyguard for a drug dealer.

"Give me a cognac," ordered the federal agent.

"Hennessy good?" asked the bald-headed, potbellied bartender with the thin mustache. Montgomery nodded his head, indicating yes. He wasn't one to talk much when play acting.

A short while later Eustice showed up with Spanky. Leading the way, Eustice entered the hotel with the drug dealer following behind cautiously. Once inside, Spanky scanned his surroundings suspiciously.

"We're supposed to meet him inside the bar," said Eustice. "Follow me."

"Is that him?" asked Spanky, raising his chin to where Agent Montgomery sat at the bar.

"Nah. He's not here yet. Let's get a drink."

"I'm not waiting here all night," warned Spanky. His edginess was becoming more apparent.

"Relax. He'll be here," assured the undercover detective.

Agent Montgomery looked up from his drink. His glance lasted no more than a second or two. In that brief span of time, the agent noticed that Spanky wore his shirt outside of his pants. It was an indication that he was likely armed.

"Where the hell is he?" Spanky asked impatiently. He stood approximately a foot away from the bar. Looking around the room, he focused on Montgomery. Spinning around to position his back to the agent, he faced Eustice. "Check out this dude behind me," he whispered. It was clear to Eustice that Spanky was a nervous wreck.

Eustice took a quick glance at the undercover agent. "What about him?"

"Keep an eye on him. I'll bet my ass that he's with this prick we're supposed to meet," said Spanky.

"I think you may be right. He does look a little familiar. I think he drives Yardstick sometimes."

"You think?" asked Spanky, sounding shocked. "This is the last time, man. I don't like being up here one damn bit. I just hope we don't have to back our way out of this joint."

"Chill, will ya?" said Eustice. He then turned to the bartender to order two beers.

When Yardstick finally arrived, he was carrying a blue nylon bag containing the buy money. He walked directly up to Eustice.

"Hey, man," greeted Eustice, extending his hand to shake.

"What's happening?" said Yardstick, taking his hand.

"Say hello to Spanky. He's the guy I was telling you about."

Yardstick reacted with a cool nod. "We ready to do business?" he asked.

"You got the money?" asked Spanky.

Yardstick opened the nylon bag to flash the money. "You want to count it?" he asked.

"C'mon, Yardstick," injected Eustice, "you know we go back too long for that shit."

"Let's get it done then," said the federal agent. "I got places to be."

Leaving money for a tip, Eustice picked up his remaining cash off the bar. "Let's do it," he said.

The men headed toward the door. Spanky did a double take when he noticed that Tonto Montgomery rose from his seat to follow them out. The drug dealer stopped dead in his tracks.

"Tonto's *my* man," said Yardstick, taking notice.

Spanky gave Eustice a look that communicated, *What did I tell you?*

The hand-to-hand drug transaction between Spanky and Yardstick went off without incident. On their way back to Brooklyn, Eustice asked Spanky where he wanted to go.

"My place so we can count up the money," replied the much-relieved drug dealer.

"I thought Jasper said that we have to turn this over to Mousey."

"We do . . . *after* I count it," advised Spanky, adding, "You know these guys; I don't."

"Very good," said Eustice.

"What kind of freaking name is Yardstick anyway?" asked Spanky.

"I think it's a nickname," advised Eustice.

"What kind of nickname is that for somebody?"

"Who knows? Maybe he's big down below," conjectured Eustice. It seemed like a logical explanation.

26

Heading for Home

CHIEF MCCOY GREW TIRED of waiting. He began to pressure his detectives for results in the Mathis investigation. Now dragooned to fast-forward things, Markie summoned Eustice to headquarters. The undercover detective reported to the puzzle palace not knowing what to expect.

"You're going to have to make something happen pronto, Eustice," advised the sergeant.

"What do you mean, Sarge? I just got us on the sheet with a hand-to-hand buy with Spanky."

"I know; I was there," reminded Markie. "Remember, our objective is to put the Mathis case to bed."

"That'll come. . . ."

"Look, Eustice, all I'm saying is that we need to ramp this thing up."

"I'm trying. . . ."

"I know that. But by hook or by crook, you have to make Jasper see that wolf ring."

"I'm almost there, Sarge," answered Eustice. "Spanky saw the ring already, and he absolutely loved it."

"Did it mean anything special to him?" asked Markie, perking up.

"Nah, he just admired it. He wanted one for himself."

"If we got some rings made up, Eustice could ask Jasper if he wants one," suggested the Von Hess.

"That's a little obvious," said Markie."I'm thinking swag. These guys can't resist something hot."

"How about a laptop?" suggested Eustice, who was thinking he'd be able to get a free one himself.

"We don't need to go crazy spending money," said Markie. "I'm thinking clothes."

"A leather jacket might do the trick."

"Done," decided Markie. "Tell Jasper you got a black leather jacket for him."

"He might say to leave some jackets at the bar for him," cautioned Von Hess..

"Eustice could tell him that he only has a couple and the sizes run funny, so he's gotta try it on."

"That can work, boss," agreed the undercover. "If he sees me wearing a nice jacket, he'll want one."

##########

BUSTER PULLED INTO THE GAS STATION after noticing Q-Ball Otto sitting behind the wheel of his car. Otto was lighting up a cigarette as his tank was being filled. Otto's arm was hanging out of the driver's side window between puffs.

This bozo's perfect, thought Buster, recognizing Otto as someone limited and easy to manipulate.

Having recaptured much of his prior physical form, Buster was anxious to take his revenge. He viewed Otto as a path to Mousey, the man he held responsible for the savage beating he received.

"Hey, Otto, you better put that smoke out," said Buster, "unless you're looking to blow your ass up."

Otto turned to see who had called his name. He was surprised to see it was Buster.

"I guess I should," replied Otto. "I heard about that tune-up you took. Are you okay now, Buster?"

"I'm getting along. Somebody told me you're working with that squealing little rat at the bar."

"Who do you mean, Mousey?"

"Yeah," confirmed Buster. "He was the one who caused my trouble."

"I don't know a thing about that. *I* had *nothing* to do with what went down with you."

"We're good, Otto. I got no problem with you."

"I gotta tell you, a lot of people felt bad about the way you got your ass handed to you," advised Otto.

"*Yeah,*" acknowledged Buster, his bitterness evident. "Tell men Otto. . . . You still paying off that shylock loan you took with me when I was with Jasper?"

"Shit yeah. I'll never get ahead of that loan. I'll be dead before I can clear up that debt."

"I think I know a way to get you relief from that debt."

"You do?"

"Yeah, and all you gotta do is be willing to take a little chance."

The word *chance* was concerning to Otto. Nevertheless, the opportunity to clear his loan made him willing to listen. "How *little* a chance?" he asked.

"It's a very small chance, Otto, very small. All it's gonna take is . . ."

##########

IT HAD BEEN ANOTHER PROFITABLE NIGHT AT the James Brothers Saloon.

"Goodnight," Brenda said, bidding adieu to Mousey and Otto when her ride arrived to take her home.

Now alone with the manager, Otto locked the door. The weekly proceeds of the bar, along with the gambling profits, were contained in the leather satchel Mousey held. Otto, while mounting a stool, pretended to slip. He fell to the ground with a thud, taking the barstool with him as he went down.

"What the hell happened?" asked Mousey. "Are you alright?"

Otto was slow in rising. "I don't know," he answered. "I took a flop when I went to sit down."

Mousey began to laugh at Otto's misfortune. "How did you manage that?"

"I think the floor was wet. I hurt my lower back."

"Let's lock up so you can get out of here." Otto, who was now on his feet, took a few steps that were designed to show that he was in pain. "Oh man, you can't even stand up straight," said Mousey.

It was dark out when they left the James Brothers Saloon. Due to the hour, the streets were desolate.

"How far away did you park?" Otto asked.

"Not far. I'm just around the corner, about halfway down the block."

"If you go easy, I might be able to make it," said Otto, who was supposed to see Mousey to his car.

"Don't worry about it. I'm alright. Go on home, Otto. I don't need you to walk me down the street."

"Thanks, Mousey," said Otto, hobbling off in the opposite direction. He had put in a stellar performance that far surpassed his Cagney as Cody Jarrett impression.

Mousey was a few feet from his vehicle when he heard a voice call out from behind a tree.

"Psst," whispered Buster.

Mousey turned in the direction of the sound and saw Buster with a gun trained on him.

"Turn around," ordered Buster. "We're going back to the bar."

"If you're out for the money, just take it," said Mousey, holding out the satchel.

Buster took the satchel. "Get moving before I let you have it right here on the street!"

"You got the money, what else do you want?"

"We got words."

Mousey, now realizing that this was more than a mere rip-off, complied. Once inside the bar, Buster secured the door from the inside. Buster removed a roll of duct tape from his jacket and taped Mousey's hands behind his back. He then took his captive downstairs.

"Look, are you sure you want to go down this road?" asked Mousey, trying to reason with Buster.

"Shut up!" snapped Buster.

"Listen, I got a—"

Buster placed a piece of duct tape across the younger man's mouth, preventing him from speaking further. Mousey winced as his lips folded uncomfortably beneath the tape. He had wanted to use the coke stash and emergency money secreted under a floorboard as an enticement to barter. They proceeded to where a commercial walk-in cooler stood. Buster removed Spanky's belt and wrapped it around his upper torso just beneath his armpits. He then put his shoulder into Mousey's midsection and lifted his victim by his crotch. Buster hung Mousey by his belt off a ceiling hook inside the cooler, leaving his victim suspended in the air. When Mousey began kicking, Buster viciously punched him in the stomach to neutralize him. Buster then relieved Mousey of his personal money.

"Now . . . for the payoff!" said the sneering Buster. "Somebody should have taught you that every snitch gets stitched. Did you think I was going to take the beating I took without paying you back?"

Having an exceedingly cruel idea, Buster reached to tear the tape from Mousey's lips. Then, having a change of heart, he took his hand away. He decided not to light off a cherry bomb in Mousey's mouth as originally intended. Instead, he ended things quickly by firing one round into the manager's forehead.

##########

FINALLY REALIZING THAT HER BUSINESS PROPOSAL was gaining no traction with Jasper, Lucy abandoned her efforts to do business in Los Angeles. Alternatively, she concentrated on starting a legitimate concern in Vegas. Investing some money, she funded a boutique cleaning service that she staffed with friends and relatives. Lucy came upon the idea after an acquaintance secured a job managing several commercial properties. In return for a kickback, the acquaintance agreed to award Lucy the cleaning contract for the buildings. After proving herself capable of meeting the service demand, she made similar arrangements with other building managers. With her finances now bolstered, Lucy began rewarding herself accordingly. She entered a BMW dealership and leased a Beemer under the name of the cleaning company she established. Lucy departed the dealership without realizing that she was under the surveillance of the DEA.

Lucy proceeded to an appointment with an old friend from her biker days who had reached out to her in desperation. Although distanced by time, Lucy nevertheless felt an obligation to meet with the woman she had been arrested with years prior. Their reunion was held in the parking lot of a supermarket. The former biker girl, who now walked with the assistance of a cane, had exceedingly dark rings around her blue eyes. Poorly maintained teeth contributed to her unflattering appearance. Now in her late thirties, Lucy's friend was standing in the lot with her seven-year-old son when Lucy arrived.

"Jesus, what happened?" asked Lucy once over the shock of the other woman's appearance. "How could you let yourself go like this?"

"It's a long story."

"Alright, get in and let me hear it. Put the kid in the back."

Seated side by side with the woman in the front seat, Lucy listened patiently as her friend conveyed her tale. As the two spoke, they did so under the watchful eyes of a DEA surveillance team. The furthest thought from Lucy's mind was that the woman she had come to help was a federal informant. Agent Leardi had identified Lucy's friend after researching the defendants who had been arrested with her in the biker case. After finding out that Lucy's friend had signed on with the government, Leardi wasted no time in seizing the opportunity to use the Vegas informant in order to get to Lucy.

"I called you because I heard that you were doing really good," advised the informant. "Things haven't been so good for me. I need to get away from that bastard I'm living with."

"Do you have a plan?" asked Lucy.

"I do. I want to go back home to Arizona," she explained. "I just need to raise some money. I heard you were in the coke business. Can I go to work for you? If you give me some shit on consignment, I'll sell it. I'll do whatever it takes to put a deal over. . . You know me; I'll do *anything*. . . ."

Lucy couldn't help but feel pity for her friend. "I can't use you."

"Why?"

"Because you've let yourself sink too far down," Lucy said honestly. "Appearances mean everything."

"With a little help, some makeup, and a few decent clothes, I can get by. . . ."

"Don't even ask."

The friend began begging. "I'm pleading with you. . . . What am I going to do?"

Lucy, for all her toughness, had a weak spot in her heart for the sad story of her friend. "What's in Arizona for you? Your parents disowned you, didn't they?" she asked.

"Yeah, they did. When they found out who I had the baby with, they didn't want to know me."

"Are your grandparents still alive?"

"Yeah, they are. Why?"

"Do you think they'd take you in with the kid?"

"They might. . . ."

"Let me have their number."

The informant didn't figure on this turn of events. "Why do you want their number?"

"Just give me their damn number," demanded Lucy.

"I don't think—" the friend said, beginning an effort to dissuade Lucy.

"Do you want my help or what? Stop the bullshit and give me the number," insisted Lucy.

Lucy got her friend's grandfather on the telephone. After falsely identifying herself as a police officer, Lucy explained that his granddaughter was in dire need. At first the grandfather didn't want to reconcile. It was only after learning that his granddaughter was leaving her husband did he waver.

"Is she really through with him?" asked the grandfather.

"She's in an abusive relationship, sir," said Lucy, trying to sound official. "She wants no part of him."

"Is she cleaned up, Officer?" asked the grandfather.

"Look, she isn't perfect. She's run down and trying to do right here, but she's going to need support from her family," explained Lucy. "She'll be able to turn the corner once in the right surroundings."

"Well, if she's looking for money, then we're not the ones—"

Lucy cut the old man off before he could finish. "Relax," said Lucy assertively. "I'm not talking about financial support."

"No?"

"She has money to hold her over until she gets on her feet."

"She does? Where did she get money?"

"She'll explain it all to you when she gets there," clarified Lucy. "So are you taking her in or what?"

"Hang on a minute," said the grandfather, who needed to consult with his wife. After a minute or two, he came back on the phone. "If you can get her here, we'll take her . . . and she can bring the child."

"Okay, leave the porch light on."

Lucy turned to the shell-shocked informant, advising her that her grandparents would take her in.

"It's all set. C'mon, let's get going."

"I . . . I . . ." stammered the informant, who was dumbfounded by what had transpired.

"I'll pay your way to Arizona," said Lucy, "and I'll loan you a little money."

Although touched at Lucy's kindness, the informant didn't forget her obligation to the feds. "Lucy, let me pay you back. Let me—"

"How are you gonna do that?"

"There is this pimp I know. He's looking for a coke connection. . . ."

Lucy listened with interest. Not one to let an opportunity slip by, she and a federal agent posing as a pimp were soon in telephonic communication. Arrangements were made for the two to meet the following afternoon. After ending the phone call, Lucy addressed her friend.

"Now, c'mon, let's go before I change my mind. We've got to get you two on your way to Arizona."

##########

SUPERVISORY AGENT LEARDI, MARKIE, AND VON HESS met for a drink at Corky's Corner, a Lower Manhattan tavern.

"I still have to get Jasper to see that ring," advised Markie.

"I know that you've been working on that," said Leardi. "Our people in Vegas got great results. We got Lucy on a couple of hand-to-hand transactions with one of our agents who posed as a pimp. They're prepared to drop the hammer on her anytime I give them the word."

"How did you manage all that so fast?" asked Markie.

Leardi smiled. "We do good work," he said, not revealing any particulars.

"Yeah, I'm sure. You must have had a snitch that finagled an introduction."

"Yeah, we did," admitted Leardi. "You know, Eustice is doing an outstanding job," advised Leardi.

"He loves the latitude he has," said Markie.

"What was his nickname again?"

"It *was* Useless Eustice," answered Markie.

"Well, he's not useless to us," said Leardi.

251

27

Bunk Beds

SCRATCHY WAS SITTING AT THE BAR OF THE JAMES BROTHERS SALOON reading the newspaper. He was surprised to see Johnny Blondell arrive unusually early with his coffee and bagel.

"What's new?" asked Blondell.

"I'm reading about the World Trade Center Bank of America robbery," said Scratchy.

"I can't believe that they're still talking about that." Johnny assumed a seat on a stool.

After some chitchat, Scratchy wend downstairs to the cooler bring up some bottled beer. Minutes later Johnny heard a bloodcurdling scream emanating from the cellar. He rushed to the top of the stairs to see what had happened. Scratchy was standing at the foot of the steps when he got there.

"What's wrong?" Johnny called down.

A distraught Spanky wiped his mouth with his forearm. "Give me a minute . . ." he uttered.

Johnny headed down the steps. "What the hell is the matter?"

The bartender took a breath and led Johnny to where Mousey was left hanging. When Blondell saw the murdered bar manager hanging from a hook, a grim look came over him. No stranger to violence, his shock was nevertheless surprisingly minimal.

"C'mon, let's go upstairs. I gotta talk to Otto," said Johnny.

"What about Jasper?" asked Scratchy.

"I have to hear from Otto first."

Before dialing Q-Ball Otto, Johnny felt the need to fortify Scratchy with a stiff drink. Taking a bottle of scotch off the shelf, he poured out a double. "Here, take this," ordered Johnny.

Scratchy downed the drink in one gulp. Feeling Scratchy needed further fortification, Johnny poured another. As he did so, he issued Scratchy a warning that was vividly clear. "A word to the wise: This day is never to be spoken of. It never existed."

Q-Ball Otto was at home waiting for his phone to ring. When the phone finally rang, he delayed answering until the third ring.

"Hello?" he said, faking a weakened condition.

"You need to come to the bar right away. . . . *You* got *a* problem," advised Johnny.

"I got a problem? What did I do?"

"Just hurry up and get in here. You'll see for yourself," replied Johnny curtly, hanging up the phone.

A queasy feeling came over Otto as he tried to figure out what could have gone wrong. Otto rushed to the James Brothers Saloon as ordered. When he arrived, he tapped on the front glass, alerting Scratchy to let him in. Once inside, Otto approached Blondell, who was sitting at a table waiting for him.

"What's wrong?" asked Otto.

"Somebody clipped Mousey and left him hanging off a hook in the basement cooler."

"How is that possible?" asked Otto, addressing himself more than Blondell. He couldn't comprehend how things could have escalated from what was supposed to be only a couple of smacks and a robbery.

"Where were you last night?"

"What do you mean, Johnny? I was with Spanky," declared Otto defensively.

"If you were with him how does he end up on a hook?"

"I don't know anything about that."

"So what happened last night?"

"All I know is that last night I walked him to his car like I always do."

"You're sure about that..."

"Well, last night I watched him walk to his car and drive off."

"You walked him or you watched him, which is it?"

"Well, I....couldn't walk. I hurt my back so I didn't go all the way down the block with him."

"You seem to be walking alright today."

"The Advil helped. Look, I slipped and fell off a stool last night," said Otto, trying to explain.

"Maybe it's better if you wait and tell Jasper the story."

"Are you calling the cops?" The nervousness in Otto's voice was unmistakable.

"Forget about the cops. That ain't happening."

Johnny notified Jasper that he needed to come to the bar right away. Jasper rushed to the James Brothers Saloon to find out what was going on.

"Mousey's gone," said Johnny without mincing words.

"Gone?" asked Jasper in a surprisingly low tone.

"Somebody clipped him and left him hanging off a hook down in the cooler."

Jasper stiffened after hearing the jolting news. "How was he killed?" he asked.

"It looks like a gunshot," answered Johnny. "I sent Scratchy out to find Mousey's car. He found it parked around the corner. The car was locked."

Jasper and Johnny went downstairs to where Mousey was hanging. "The kid is inside the cooler," advised Blondell.

After seeing what had been done to Mousey, Jasper stood quietly staring at the body. It was his way of paying his respects. When he finished reflecting he lifted the body off the hook and placed Mousey on the floor.

"Somebody's gonna pay for this," declared Jasper, vowing revenge. He and Johnny then reconvened with the others upstairs. "Scratchy, was Mousey's car in that same spot when he came to work yesterday?"

"I don't know."

Jasper noticed that Otto was looking at him nervously. Jasper turned his back on him in order to whisper to Johnny without being overheard.

"Did the dimwit have anything to say?"

"He said that he *watched* Mousey drive off."

"Otto told you he saw Mousey drive off?"

"That's what he said."

"Did he say anything about the money?"

"Our conversation didn't get that far."

Jasper returned to the cellar where he removed Mousey's car keys from his pants pocket. He then went with Johnny to where Mousey's car was parked. They searched the interior of the vehicle and around the immediate area for the satchel of money. After coming up dry, Jasper questioned the residents where the vehicle was parked. As a result of that, he learned that Mousey's car had been parked in the same spot since the day prior. The information attained pointed the finger squarely at Q-Ball Otto. Jasper's subsequent conversation with Otto was revealing.

"When you last saw Mousey, he was alright?"

"Yeah, Jasper," replied Otto, "he was fine."

"You walked him to his car as usual?"

"Uhh . . . yeah, I made sure he got in his car like always."

"He got in the car and drove off without a problem?"

"Yeah, just like he does every night."

"Explain to me how his car could be parked in the same spot as when he arrived yesterday for work . . . *if* you saw him drive off?"

Otto stuck tightly to his story. "Uhh, I guess he forgot something and came back."

Jasper didn't bother to ask anything else. He didn't need to.

"I'll be back, Johnny. I'm gonna go see our friend."

"Let me go tell him what happened, said Johnny, who had also heard enough. "He may not want you to be too involved."

Johnny met with Silky at the social club to fill him in on what had occurred. Silky expressed no emotion. His reaction wasn't surprising to Johnny, who knew Silky for the cold-blooded person he was. Truth be told, Silky couldn't care one way or the other about Mousey. What concerned the gangster was Otto's apparent betrayal.

"How do you want to handle this?" asked Johnny.

"No cops," stated Silky. "The body has to disappear."

"I figured as much. You know that Jasper's gonna want to do something about the imbecile."

"Tell him we'll talk about Otto once Mousey's taken care of. You'd better handle it. Go see Bunk-Bed."

"No problem."

"Hey, Johnny . . . one other thing," said Silky, stopping Blondell as he headed for the door. "Hold down the fort at the bar until we find somebody to replace the kid."

As directed, Blondell went to see Bunk-Bed at the Indiviglio Funeral Home. Bunk-Bed was a reliable resource who, for a price, would dispose of a corpse by hiding it underneath the body of a recently deceased citizen set for burial.

"I got a job for you," said Johnny.

"I know. I received a call," replied Bunk-Bed, a dour-looking man with hound-dog eyes. "I've got a top-shelf casket to put your friend in."

"What makes it a top-shelf casket?"

"It's a bronze. Bronze never rots," explained the undertaker. "No worms can get to you."

"That's nice to know," answered Johnny sardonically. "Who are you putting him in with?"

"He'll be beneath a nice young woman who comes from a rich family."

"Alright, stick him in with her. I'll bring the body over around midnight."

##########

SPANKY MOVED INTO THE LIVING ROOM after letting Jasper in. Uncertain as to what the exact problem was, Spanky knew by Jasper's demeanor that something serious must have gone down.

"Do you know anybody who had it in for Mousey?" asked the somber Jasper very directly.

Spanky felt it best to stick as close to the truth as possible. "Just one guy I know of."

"Who is that?"

"Buster, he hates Mousey."

"Why is that?"

"He thinks that Mousey was responsible for that beating he took."

"How do you come to that conclusion?"

"Buster came by to see me. He was looking for money."

"Why did he come to you?"

"Look, Jasper . . . what can I tell you? The guy came around hitting me up for money."

256

"You gave it to him?"

"I had to. . . . He pulled a freaking gun on me."

"When was this?"

"As soon as he could get around on his own after leaving the hospital. Buster held Mousey responsible for—" Spanky paused, wanting to choose his words wisely. "—telling you about whatever it was *he* was doing behind your back."

"I have to hold off on sending Bayonne Bob to Vegas," said Jasper. "I'm gonna need him at the bar."

"What happened anyway?"

"Mousey got clipped."

"What the hell was Q-Ball Otto doing?"

"Yeah, Q-Ball Otto," hissed Jasper, making it clear that he was disgusted with Otto.

##########

MARKIE WAS HAVING AN uneasy night. He turned over in bed to look at Alley, who was resting peacefully. Her face had a contented pleasantness to it, leading him to believe she was dreaming something wonderful. Markie began thinking of the players who comprised the starting lineup of the 1961 Yankees team. When that failed to induce sleep, he rose from bed and made himself a cup of tea. He then moved into the living room, where he sat quietly in an easy chair. He turned on the lamp next to the chair and began reading *The Island of Dr. Moreau*, a book penned by science fiction's H. G. Wells. Markie always kept a book to read at Alley's apartment to help get through those sleepless nights. Dr. Moreau's business of turning animals into people was unfortunately no solution to his insomnia. The tale only served to rejuvenate rather than tire.

When daylight broke, Markie took a shower, shaved, and dressed. Markie's conflicted state of mind was at the center of his inability to sleep. His discomposure was primarily fear based. It wasn't a fear of physical danger or material peril that had thrown off his placidity. Those were conquerable challenges he could easily face. This fear was more of a psychological malady, induced by his committing to enter into a marriage with Alley. Efforts to attribute his proposal of an official union to some alcohol-induced impulsiveness proved fruitless. Markie was too practical a man to deny that he had painted himself into a corner. Markie looked in on his girlfriend, watching in silence as she continued to peacefully sleep. Then, as the dawn light seeped through the bedroom blinds, he wondered if the heavenly ray was some type of message from above. Shaking it off, he fled the apartment for some fresh air.

After she rose, Alley's happiness soon ebbed when she realized that she was alone. At first she was going to telephone the absent Markie, but then decided against it. She began her day by ironing clothes in the living room to take her mind off Markie's strange behavior. Her high spirits returned when the sergeant walked through the door with a brown paper bag containing bagels, lox, and cream cheese.

"I went out to pick up breakfast for us," he said. "What are you doing?"

"I'm ironing."

"How domestic," he commented. He then walked into to the kitchen with the food. Seeing Alley with an iron in her hand sealed his fate. At this point, he knew that he'd never be able to talk his way out.

Markie stayed with Alley until it was time for her to report to work at Fitzie's. When he dropped her off at the Brooklyn bar, he promised to call her the following day. Now alone, Markie made his way to a hole-in-the-wall bar on Canal Street in Lower Manhattan.

It was his second time at Foley's Hideout, a tiny place frequented by an assortment of bohemian types. Markie was on his third shot when the bartender, a rotund man of middle age, approached to have a word with him. The barkeep's ample stomach hung sloppily over his size fifty belt.

"Excuse me, the woman down at the other end is inquiring about you," said the bartender.

"She is?" asked Markie, surprised to hear that someone took an interest in him.

The bartender leaned forward over the bar toward the sergeant and spoke in a low voice. "Look, pal, she sent me over here *specific* to tell you that she'd like to meet you. Get me?"

Markie looked down the rail to where the woman was seated. He didn't recognize her as anyone he'd ever seen before. He then scrutinized the bartender, who sported a tiny mustache that was reminiscent of a misplaced eyebrow. Markie took notice that he wore a wedding band, an adornment he viewed as a sign of stability. The eyeglass case that was sticking halfway out of he breast pocket of his light green shirt was also reassuring in that it suggested that the bartender was a square. These minor observations eased Markie's concerns of possible skullduggery being afoot.

"You know her?" asked Markie.

"Yeah, sure," answered the bartender. "She's a regular who lives in the neighborhood."

"She works?"

"She's a musician, a fiddle player, or maybe it was a harp," answered the bartender. "She's a free spirit, if you know what I mean. So what do I tell her?"

Markie strained his eyes to get a better look at her. "They say the cure for one woman is another."

"What was that?" asked the bartender.

"Ask her if she'd like to join me for a drink."

The thirty-nine-year-old musician readily accepted the invitation. Markie watched her every step as she walked toward him. He was impressed by the smiling woman in the black slacks and red button-down shirt. He thought her attractive with her frizzy hair and fine features. It didn't take long for them to cozy up to each other once she confided that she dated a state trooper and Markie made it known he had his handcuffs with him.

"How about we blow this joint?" asked Markie.

Saying nothing, she rose from her stool, slung her pocketbook over her shoulder, and smiled crookedly without revealing any of her teeth. To Markie, her decisive behavior was a turn-on. The formula of no obligation, expectations, or heavy lifting was for him. Once they were on the street, the musician locked onto Markie's arm. They proceeded on foot to where she lived in a four-story walk-up a short distance away. Inside her studio apartment, she told the sergeant to get comfortable, pointing to a scotch bottle.

"Fix us both a drink," she said. "I'll be with you in a moment."

Markie watched as she retreated to the bathroom. He began to visually examine the apartment. While he had seen worse, it still wasn't one of the neatest of digs. He looked over at the unmade queen-size bed in the corner of the room. On a small nightstand were two four-ounce glasses. Markie examined the glasses. He discovered traces of whiskey still in the glasses. The sergeant then looked at the closed bathroom door. As he listened to the shower running, he began to have second thoughts. Regardless of how well she cleaned up, he didn't like the idea of jumping into her unclean bed.

"What the hell am I doing here?" Markie asked himself as he reflected on the situation.

By the time the musician came out of the bathroom, she was surprised to find that she was alone in her apartment. When she looked out the window, she could see that Markie was talking on the phone as he walked off. He was conversing with Alley.

Vito the Blade

THE PALSY-WALSY SOCIAL CLUB was a hangout frequented by men with dubious reputations. Most neighborhood people, including the police, suspected that everyone who frequented the club was a mobster or at the very least, capable and willing to commit crimes. They weren't wrong.

An obese man wearing a straw hat sat in a beach chair sat outside the club. He was listening to the ballgame on the radio. He puffed on a corncob pipe and aired his feet by resting them atop his black loafers. Sitting alongside him was another unusual type. The second man wore dark sunglasses and an ill-fitting brown toupee that could have been mistaken for a divot had it been green. Every drag he took from his unfiltered cigarette resulted in his spitting out tiny fragments of tobacco. Both men were perfectly content spending the day watching people parade by. Jasper nodded at the two men as he entered the club.

Inside the Palsy-Walsy the tables were occupied by men playing cards. Frequently uttered by the pinochle players was the Italian word *aiuto*, which served as a plea for help when dealt a poor hand. The men were so absorbed in their game that they failed to notice anything else.

"Is Silky in?" he asked one of the men he knew.

"He's in the back," replied the man.

After tapping on the office door, Jasper heard Silky's voice telling him to enter. The gangster was reclining on a brown leather couch, watching the news on television. When he saw Jasper, he pressed the button on the remote to shut off the set. He sat up to greet Jasper.

"We got something to talk about," advised the gangster. "What happened to that kid Mousey at the joint needs addressing. That kind of stupidity puts us at risk. What's going on over there, Jasper?"

Jasper made it clear that it was Buster who had caused the trouble. After doing so, he assured Silky that he intended to remove what he called "the thorn in our side."

"That's something you ain't gonna do," corrected the gangster with definiteness. "To begin with, we don't know for sure if Buster clipped this kid. You *suspect* it, but you got no proof. Am I right?"

"He did it; I'm sure of it."

"Listen up a minute," said Silky. "All you got right now is anger. Besides, you ain't the muscle end."

"I'm capable. I got no qualms about putting somebody to sleep. . . ."

"*Chiudi il becco!*" shouted Silky. Even though Jasper didn't speak Italian, he'd been around the club long enough to know that Silky was telling him to shut his mouth. "Remember something; there's no upside for me if you get knocked out of circulation. I want you out there flourishing."

"So what am I supposed to do . . . nothing?"

"Did I say that we're gonna lay down?"

"No you didn't. Sorry, I'm still upset over what happened. The kid didn't deserve what he got."

"Whether he did or didn't ain't the point," advised the mobster. "What was done will be addressed. If what you suspect is true, this is the second offense for Buster. Leave it for me to investigate."

"Okay, whatever you say."

"I'm supposing that you think that the lamebrain was in on it, right?"

"He had to have been. Otto's job was to walk Mousey to his car with the money after closing up. He claims that he saw Mousey drive off, but I have evidence Mousey never moved his car."

"What about the money?"

"It's gone."

"What else do you have on him?"

"Otto's been into me for money forever. He had to be in on it."

"Could he have masterminded this all by himself?"

"Not a chance."

"Where does this Benedict Arnold hang his hat these days?"

Jasper wrote on a piece of paper the address of the man who had been hired to protect Mousey. He then passed the paper containing Otto's information to Silky.

"I'll get to the truth. You go back and concentrate on business."

"Thanks, Silky."

"I told Johnny to pinch hit for Mousey at the bar until you get someone."

"Thanks, Silky. I got this one guy in mind. I've been bringing him along."

"Anyone I know?"

"You might. He used to work with Monte, Lemon's brother-in-law."

"Where was he shitted out of?"

"Bayonne, New Jersey. Lemon brought him around. They call him Bayonne Bob."

"I've known those Jersey guys a long time. I never heard that name mentioned," said Silky.

"He's alright, Silky."

"Just be sure to do your homework on him. Remember, you're responsible."

After Jasper left Silky called in two of his enforcers. The cousins Primo and Nino were imposing men dedicated to a weight-lifting program that maintained their physical awesomeness. Whenever they entered the office, the room seemed suddenly crowded.

"This is for you," said Silky, handing Primo a written note. Primo took the slip of paper from his boss, read the name and address to himself, and nodded. "I want you to bring him here to me."

When the cousins arrived at Otto's door brandishing a gun, there was no question about Otto's compliance. His own gun was a distance away in a dresser drawer, making resistance a suicidal option.

"C'mon, let's go," ordered Nino, "Silky wants to talk to you."

"What does he want to see me about?"

"He'll tell you all about it," replied Primo.

Within the hour, the disloyal thug found himself sitting on a chair in Silky's social club office. While Otto might not have been an intelligent man, he was smart enough to realize his predicament. Silky took a moment to study the worried Otto. When the mobster finally spoke, his words flowed with a cold confidence that Otto found chilling.

"If you want out of here , you'd better stick to the truth. Was it you that killed that kid Mousey?"

"Me?" asked Otto in an elevated tone. "I never laid a finger on Mousey, Mr. Seggio. . . . I swear it."

"You took a shylock loan from Jasper?"

"Yeah . . . but I intend to pay it off any day now."

"You do? Tell me how."

Otto had to think fast. "My aunt died, so I'll be coming into some money," answered Otto, foolishly thinking he was helping himself. The nervous Otto was now confused as to what he had said to others.

"BULLSHIT!" exploded Silky, smashing Otto across the face with a coffee mug. "Either you ripped that kid off and killed him, or somebody paid you to look the other way. Now, which is it?"

"You got it wrong, Mr. Seggio. . . . I didn't—"

"You keep on insulting my intelligence, you Judas cocksucker, and just see what happens to you!"

"But—"

"But this!" hissed Silky, grabbing his own testicles. "Enough," he said, now returning to a subdued tone. "You know me to be a serious man?" Otto swallowed hard and nodded pathetically. "Then you know I mean what I say." The mobster picked up the hammer that had been left out on the top of his desk. Holding the tool firmly in his hand, Silky raised it to Otto's face. "Look at me," he instructed. "Do you think I bluff?"

Otto's eyes were trained on the hammer. Thinking his doom was at hand, his heart began racing. "No sir," he replied weakly, terrified at the thought of what was coming. "This is all a big mistake. I didn't do anything. . . ."

Silky put his finger to his mouth, indicating that Otto should be silent. Silky placed a thick telephone book on top of his desk. "Put your left hand, palm down, on top of the book, Otto," he ordered.

After Otto complied, Silky removed a large iron nail from his pocket. He held the point of the nail inches away from Otto's hand. "If this nail touches your flesh, I'm not stopping until I drive it all the way through," threatened the gangster. "I'll ask once. Did you do it, or were you paid to help set it up?"

Otto soiled himself. The odor that permeated the office was proof that Silky had achieved his goal in order to get at the truth. The captive Otto was petrified.

"It was Buster who did it!" blurted out Otto. "I swear on my mother, I didn't know what he had in mind. Buster said he was just going to teach Mousey a lesson by ripping off the bar."

"So it was about the money for you?" Otto was unable to offer an immediate answer. "Come on, spit it out. Was it about the money for you?"

"Yeah, I needed the money," Otto finally admitted.

Silky nodded understandingly because committing robbery made sense to him. "So tell me, why did he want to hurt that kid like he did?"

"I had no idea he was gonna do anything like that. No shit, I had no idea."

"So as far as you knew, the plan was to be just a rip-off?"

"Yeah. If I knew he was going to hurt anybody, I would have never signed on," answered Otto.

"No?" asked Silky skeptically. Otto could see that Silky didn't believe him. "Mr. Seggio, I swear it. I wouldn't have gone along with doing anything to hurt Mousey."

Silky held up the hammer and looked at Otto heartlessly. "So when I talk to Buster, he's gonna say that you had *no idea* that there was going to be violence involved?"

Otto felt cornered at this point. Finally he relented and fed more details to the racketeer. "It was just supposed to be a rip-off and just a *light* going-over. You have to believe me. . . ." pleaded Otto.

"Why was a 'light going-over' necessary?"

"All I know is Buster felt that Mousey squealed on him over something."

Silky put down the hammer and took a seat behind his desk. He lit up a cigarette before putting forth his next question. "You received your end of the money?" he asked.

"Not yet. . . but believe what I'm telling you. It was supposed to be nothing serious."

"What's the split?"

"The split is fifty-fifty."

"What made you two think that you could get away with this?"

"Buster said Mousey was a punk and that he could scare him into saying that he was ripped off by a couple of cowboys from out of the neighborhood. If you give me some time, I'll make amends and pay him the money back. I'm sick over this, Mr. Seggio." Otto was pitching hard to get off the hook.

"Good. It's nice to hear that you want to repent," commented Silky without emotion. "Now that you've been truthful, you can have the opportunity to redeem yourself."

"Anything you say. What do I need to do?"

"You're gonna call Buster and tell him it's urgent that he meet you."

"I swear, I'll give him the beating of his life. . . ."

"No, no violence. You just tell him it's urgent that you two meet."

"He'll ask me why."

"You tell him that you were talking to someone who has an uncle who saw things. Let him know that the uncle is looking for a thank-you for keeping his mouth shut."

"Maybe I could even say that the uncle will give the cops a bullshit description. . . ." suggested Otto, desperately trying to ingratiate himself with Silky.

"Just say what I told you to say. Set up a meeting for Buster to meet the *uncle.*"

Silky wrote a number down on a piece of paper and handed it to Primo. "I'll call my friend. He'll he expecting your call. Find out when he's available to meet Buster."

##########

NINO RANG THE ONLY DOORBELL TO THE two-story building on Columbia Street in South Brooklyn. A man in his seventies looked out from the second-floor window above the barbershop.

"We're looking for Vito," Primo shouted up at the man.

"Stay there," answered the old man.

Vito the Blade was Silky's secret weapon. He was a barber who owned the first-floor business and building. He was also Silky's personal assassin who few knew existed. Vito came to the door appearing as someone impoverished. He wore a worn white undershirt, shiny black trousers, and dull black shoes. Several small holes in his shirt were visible under the armpits. In contrast to his distressed garb, Vito was clean shaven and well groomed with a thick head of teel gray hair. A substantial tattoo of a cross draped in rosary beads adorned his right forearm.

"Come on in," invited Vito. His voice was surprisingly pleasant.

"Silky sent us," said Nino.

Nino and Primo followed the older man into the kitchen where they got further acquainted. They began playing rummy as they waited for the others to arrive. Vito was winning steadily.

"So what's on the agenda, Vito?" asked Primo as the older man shuffled the cards between hands.

"Don't worry about it. Concentrate on your cards. I'll take care of everything when the time comes."

When the doorbell finally rang, Vito quickly cleared the table. "You two go and wait in the back bedroom until I call you," directed Vito. "I'll go down and let them in."

The cousins scurried to the back of the apartment as told. Once they were out of sight, Vito went to the window to let his visitors know he'd be right down. Buster entered the apartment first. He thought little of Vito based on his appearance. Judging by the holes in Vito's undershirt, Buster understood why he was being shaken down. With Q-Ball Otto at his side, the impatient Buster got right to the point.

"You think that you've seen me before, pop?" asked Buster, addressing Vito.

"I *think* that maybe yes, maybe no," replied Vito calmly.

"So tell me, where is it that you *think* you seen me?"

"How would you like a cup of coffee?"

Buster was taken aback by the older man's nonchalant attitude. It was something he didn't appreciate.

"Look, old-timer, I'm told that you think you saw something." Otto stood nervously by, not knowing what was going to happen.

"It's a funny thing about that. Who I saw may or may not have been you," answered Vito calmly. "Are you boys sure you don't want something?" the old man asked, walking to the sink.

"I don't want shit," replied Buster, who was in no mood for chitchat. "Where are you going, pop? Get over here if you want to be around to trim your next beard."

"I'm just getting a cold glass of water for myself," answered Vito, letting the water run after washing out his glass. As the water ran, he took a large white towel off the counter. He used both hands to wipe the countertop dry of any wetness. Contained inside the towel was a lead pipe. Turning to face Buster, Vito noticed the unlit cigarette in Buster's hand.

"Let me get you an ashtray," said the barber.

As Buster struck the match to light his smoke, he momentarily took his eye off Vito, who had stepped behind him. The barber came down hard with the pipe on Buster's head. Nearly unconscious, Buster fell to the floor dazed. Vito removed a straight-edge razor from his pocket and slit Buster's throat with the ease of someone slicing a soft melon.

"Okay, everyone, come on out," said Vito in a loud voice. "It's all over."

"We could have done the work," said Nino, looking down at Buster's fallen body.

Vito shook his shoulders. "I'm still capable," he said proudly.

"You can say that again," voiced Primo.

Vito nodded in agreement. "Be sure to tell Silky how good a job I did here."

"Sure, we will."

"Do me a favor and carry him downstairs into the cellar for me."

"No problem," said Primo, who wrapped the towel around Buster's neck to stem the flow of blood. He then turned to Otto. "You . . . give me a hand taking him downstairs into the cellar," he ordered. Otto, who was visibly shaken, complied without question.

They threw Buster's body into a deep hole in the cellar floor that had been dug out earlier by Vito. Two seconds later, a loud groan could be heard coming from Q-Ball Otto. Vito had lodged a Bowie knife deep into Otto's back and dragged the blade in a zigzag fashion before removing it. Vito then shoved Otto's body forward, dropping him into the makeshift grave face down on top of Buster.

"*Finito!*" said Vito in Italian.

"You sure he's dead?" asked the surprised Nino.

Vito was offended by the absurdity of the question. "I just said *finito*," said Vito. "He's finished!"

"Nice job, Vito," said Primo, taking Vito's word that his victim was gone. "How did you do it?"

"There is only one way to do it, my friend. You go in deep with the blade in the right spot, do a little maneuvering, and it's *finito* . . . every time."

"You want us to fill in the hole?" asked Nino.

"Nah, I'll fill in the hole. Then I'll do the cement work after eating something."

"You make your own wine down here?" he asked after noticing the boxes of grapes that were on top of a table in a corner.

"I got the grape arbor in the yard. It gets messy out there after the summer, but there is nothing like having your own grapes and making your own wine. You want to stick around and drink some wine?"

"Nah, next time," answered Primo. .

The cousins left without ever knowing that inside the pockets of the murdered men were some of the proceeds stolen from the bar. Searching the bodies was a detail not overlooked by Vito, who pocketed the money. He viewed the cash he recovered as a gratuity.

##########

AS JASPER ACQUIRED GREATER INSIGHTS into Eustice, he became surer that he had made the right move by bringing him into the fold. They were having a drink at the James Brothers Saloon late one afternoon when Jasper began to delve deeper into the undercover detective's capabilities.

"You ever do any strong-arm work, Bob?"

"No, Jasper, that's not exactly my line of work. I generally like to work out problems cordially."

"What if the situation required muscle? Would you step up?"

"I'd get the job done, but I'd pay somebody to do the actual dirty work."

"My brother, Chris, was a thinker too. He never acted in haste. You got your car here?"

"I'm parked outside."

"Drink up. We're gonna take a ride."

Jasper had Eustice drive him to Silky Seggio's social club. The undercover detective drove slowly so that the surveillance team would have no trouble following behind. Once inside the club, Jasper walked directly to Silky's office.

"That matter has been resolved," said Silky. "You were correct in your assumption."

"Do I need to do anything?"

"There is nothing to do," said Silky. "Both problems have been rectified permanently." Jasper understood this to mean that both Buster and Q-Ball Otto had been eliminated.

Jasper exited the club just as Eustice finished writing down the plates of the cars parked near the club. He did this in order to later try and identify people who might be connected to the social club.

"Let's go back to the bar, where we can sit and talk," said Jasper. 'You want to know something? They should have killed Buster instead of giving him that beating."

"They?" asked Eustice.

"Look, Bob, forget I said that. I'm just thinking out loud. I need you here in New York until I recruit someone to take the place of the Mouse on a permanent basis. Until then, I want you to work double duty. I want you should work with Spanky *and* hold down this bar for me."

"What about Johnny? It looks like he's already handling the bar."

"He'll be around to show you the ropes."

"Where did Mousey go?"

"The kid moved on," answered Jasper, not revealing more.

"Do I get anything extra for double duty?"

Jasper smirked. "Yeah; you'll be well compensated."

Jasper noticed the one-eared wolf head ring on Eustice's pinkie as Eustice steered the car. He commented immediately.

"Let me see that ring," said Jasper. Eustice held out his hand for Jasper to take a closer look.

"No, take it off. I want to try it on."

"Isn't it a beauty?" commented Eustice, elated at having finally drawn Jasper's attention to the ring. Jasper examined the ring before placing it on his only pinkie. After extending his arm out, he lifted his hand in order to check out the ring from afar. "I'll be a son of a bitch! The wolf even has one ear," he said. "It's the same ring." Jasper then took the ring off to see if there was an engraving inside. After seeing the number four inside the ring, he repeated his earlier comment about being a son of a bitch.

"Where did you get this ring, Bob?"

"In a pawn shop down south," he replied.

"I had one exactly like this once."

"Don't tell me this is your ring, Jasper," said Eustice. "Was your ring engraved?"

"Don't worry, Bob. My ring had a different number engraved on the inside. Mine had the number three. This is a different ring."

"What are the numbers supposed to mean?"

"I got no idea," answered Jasper. "Do you want to sell your ring, Bob?"

"I don't know, Jasper. I really like it. Maybe at some point down the road I'll let it go."

"I'll buy it from you at a good price. I always loved that ring."

"Did you buy your ring down south too?"

"I didn't exactly buy the ring. It was sort of bequeathed to me by a guy who croaked unexpectedly."

"He left it to you?"

Jasper snickered. "Let's just say I acquired it on the battlefield. He didn't need it where he was going."

"How did you lose it?" asked the undercover detective, sucking Jasper further into the conversation he was recording.

Jasper held out his hand to show Eustice that he was missing a pinkie. "I had a freak accident years ago and lost my little finger cutting salami. I was in shock at the time, so I was in la-la land. Somebody must have picked the ring up off the floor and glommed it."

"Too bad," said Eustice.

While thrilled at the breakthrough, Eustice was disappointed in one regard: he wasn't going to get the free leather jacket he had been counting on now that Jasper had seen the ring.

29

Las Vegas Lucy Craps Out

EUSTICE AND LEMON TOOK IT UPON THEMSELVES to meet weekly for breakfast. Their carefully chosen venue was a remotely located diner on Staten Island. As long as they were careful, they saw no downside to these unauthorized meetings. Their purpose in getting together was to gauge the temperature on the street in terms of either man having come under suspicion by the people they were building a case against. When they arrived at their regular meeting place, they were disappointed to learn that the establishment was undergoing renovations. Since both men were famished, they settled on an eatery in a more populated section of Staten Island. They soon came to regret their decision.

"So everything has been quiet on your end?" asked Eustice. "No one else has been asking about me?"

Lemon shook his head. "Other than Jasper, no one has asked about you. Has my name come up?"

"Some guy came around the James Brothers Saloon asking for you," stated the undercover detective.

"Really . . . ?"

"I think he was a doctor. He had a doctor's bag with him."

Lemon was perplexed as to who it could have been. "A doctor's bag . . . did he say what he wanted?"

Eustice took a relaxed sip of his coffee. With a serious look, he carefully placed his cup back onto the saucer. "It had something to do with enemas."

"Get the hell out of here!" Lemon emphatically blurted once realizing he was being teased.

The lightness of their conversation was short lived thanks to the appearance of a young man in his early twenties. Frankie Nose was dressed in a short-sleeve green shirt, jeans, and white sneakers. After placing his order, he stood at the counter perusing the room. He grinned broadly after recognizing Lemon sitting in a booth with another man. He walked over to say hello.

"Hey, Lemon, how you been?"

"Hey, how are you doing?" asked the surprised informer, recollecting the visitor by the immense size of his proboscis. "You're Freddy, right?"

"No, I'm Frankie. Ain't this fortunate? I was thinking of calling you. You still got the lot, right?"

"Yeah, I still got the lot. What, are you in the market for a car?"

"Yeah, I'm looking for a convertible. You got anything good?"

"No, I got nothing right now."

"Can you get me one?"

"I'll see what I can do. Give me a call in a couple of weeks. Here, take my number."

"I still got your card. You know, I'm working for Silky full time now," said Frankie proudly.

"Congratulations. You've made the big leagues."

"Thanks. The old man always liked me, ya know," noted Frankie Nose, turning to look at Eustice.

Trying to draw attention away from the detective, Lemon steered the conversation back to himself.

"About the car . . . you looking for any special make?"

"I'd like a Pontiac Firebird or a Ford Mustang," replied Frankie. "Any color is good with me." Frankie again turned to look at Eustice.

Lemon felt compelled at this point to introduce the undercover detective. "Say hello to Bayonne Bob. He used to work with my brother-in-law, Monte. You didn't know Monte, though. You're too young."

"How you doing?" greeted Frankie. After taking a closer look at the man seated at the table, Frankie stiffened. He then cut the conversation short. "I think my food is ready. I'll see you guys around."

"That kid is trouble," said Eustice after Frankie had walked off.

'We got a problem?" asked Lemon, now concerned.

"I'm not sure. I pinched his old man many years ago. He was just a little kid then, but he was there."

"Are you sure it's the same kid?"

"There ain't anyone else New York with a smeller like his. He's half elephant. I just hope he don't have a freaking memory like one. Let's finish eating this slop and get the hell out of here."

When Frankie Nose returned to the car, he passed the bag of food to the fifty year old Muskie, a rotund man who immediately fished out what he intended to eat while driving.

"Guess what I just saw?"

"What am I some kind of mind reader?" Muskie asked between chomps.

"I saw Lemon, the car guy."

"So?"

"So he was having breakfast with a detective."

Muskie stopped chewing, leaving his mouth open. "What was it, a pinch?"

"Nope, the two guys were like asshole buddies."

"Are you sure the guy was a detective?"

"Yeah, I'm sure. When I was a kid, he locked up my old man when we lived in Brooklyn. He came to the house to make the bust the day before Christmas. How's that for being a prick?"

"Did he recognize you?"

"No friggin' way. I was just a little kid then. How could he possibly remember me?"

"You ain't exactly forgettable," said Muskie. The older man thought about it for a second. "Maybe the cop is retired. But either way, you still gotta tell Silky about this."

"I do?"

"Yeah, you do! We don't know the story with those guys. This could mean trouble for people."

"Maybe you're right," agreed the younger man.

"What maybe? Use your head. If Lemon is a rat, what do you think Silky will do if it comes out that we saw him breaking bread with a detective and never mentioned it?"

"I guess I'll have to tell him, then."

"I don't know why the hell you got such big eyes in the first place!" mumbled the older man. "Do me a favor, Frankie. Next time you want to look for a problem, do it when I ain't around, will ya?"

Eustice left the diner feeling as if he were caught between a rock and a hard place. His meeting Frankie Nose at a Staten Island diner was something he couldn't share with Markie for a couple of reasons. Firstly, he'd be reprimanded because his off-duty meetings with Lemon weren't sanctioned affairs. Secondly, apprising the sergeant would likely put an end to his undercover assignment for his own safety. Eustice had become far too spoiled to risk forfeiting the advantages that came with his undercover work. On the other hand, keeping the incident a secret could result in his getting killed. Ultimately, Eustice decided to take his chances. Since Frankie Nose had been very young at the time, he was banking that Frankie mightn't have recognized him. When several days passed without incident, the detective figured he was home free and went back to carrying just one gun.

##########

ONCE CHIEF MCCOY LEARNED THAT MARKIE HAD THE EVIDENCE he needed in the Mathis case, he ordered Jasper's arrest. Now saddled with a definite deadline, the detectives went to see Agent Leardi at his office. The trio put into play a plan to satisfy the needs of all. Las Vegas Lucy was first to fall.

The weather in Vegas was sunny the day the law enforcement officers dropped the hammer on Lucy. She was leaving her house when she was intercepted by several DEA agents who formed a circle around her. The former biker girl was stunned. Speechless, she entered into a state of shock. Lucy was cognizant of what was happening but at the same time felt as if she were elsewhere. She could talk, move, and respond in the present but did so from a far-off place mentally. She allowed her hands to be rear-cuffed without protest. She stood by in an aware but distanced state as she listened to the authoritative voices around her. It was a female agent who asked for the keys to her house and the BMW that was parked in the driveway. Lucy robotically complied. The agents walked her back into her mother's house, where she had continued to live even after her finances improved. Fortunately away, Lucy's mother and daughter were spared the humiliation of watching the agents poke through their personal belongings. The agents confiscated two kilos of cocaine, a scale, and a small red and black journal that contained entries on the transactions and money Lucy had made. They also took charge of her address book that contained client information, as well as coded names and numbers for Jasper and Spanky.

Lucy, who gradually normalized mentally, was placed in the back of an unmarked car for transporting. She stared out the window, wondering how she could have been so foolish to embark on such a reckless return to the world of narcotics. Aware that this was a federal arrest, she knew that going back to jail was inevitable. By the time the feds reached their offices, Lucy had come to a decision. There would be no need for the feds to engage in trickery, convincing, or prodding. She already decided to switch her allegiance to team government. Lucy saw cooperation as the only viable path to limit the years of incarceration she was facing. She hadn't a scintilla of sympathy for those she was prepared to implicate.

After being searched, Lucy was placed in a windowless room, where she sat behind a table opposite the female agent who was assigned to arrest her. Before the questioning commenced, the prisoner was given her Miranda warnings, after which she signed a document confirming that she had received them. Lucy felt cold in the small interview room. She sat quietly with her knees meeting. One hand was cuffed to the chair while her free arm went across her chest and held her shoulder tightly. Lucy watched as the federal agent prepared her questions by writing them down on a legal pad. The pen the agent held in her hand was of a high-quality black felt. Always liking nice things, Lucy was impressed by the writing instrument. Down deep she envied the agent's position. Lucy resented the apparent comfort that came with being on the lawful side of the table. The pension, the respect, and the fear generated by the woman's authority were all things the drug dealer coveted.

What gives this bitch the right to dictate my destiny? Lucy wondered.

Lucy glanced over at the other agent, who sat quietly in the corner of the room. He was a man of about her age. His crossed legs were long, suggesting that he was tall. He possessed a stiff upper lip that conveyed sternness. The prisoner noticed the two agents nodding to each other. It was a sign that the interrogation was to commence. The female agent opened their dialogue employing a very formal tone. This made it clear at the onset that the session was going to be all business.

"If you want something to drink or need anything, let me know now," said the agent. "If you have to use the restroom, now is the time to speak up, not after we get started."

The DEA agent was a thin Latino woman with glasses. She was dressed in all black, and her pants held a sharp crease. Her top was buttoned to the neck. Aside from a trace of lipstick, she was makeup free.

"I'd like some water," said Lucy.

"I'll get it," said the male agent. Well above average height, he wore a black long sleeve shirt, gray slacks and black Nike sneakers. His automatic was lodged in a shoulder holster.

"I'm Agent Carmen Gonzalez," the female fed announced stiffly. Her sitting ramrod straight in her seat hardly put Lucy at ease. "Just so that you are aware, this is not a question of whether or not you're going to jail. It's a question of how long you're willing to go away for."

Agent Gonzalez apprised Lucy of all the charges she faced. After doing this, she provided a narrative of how strong the case was against the defendant. Since the feds had Lucy cold on hand-to-hand sales, there was little need for an oversell of the defendant's predicament.

"Look Gonzalez," said the prisoner, "you can ask me whatever you want. I'll tell you whatever it is you want to know, just as long as I can make a deal."

"Have you no remorse for your actions?" asked the agent out of curiosity.

Lucy was appalled by the question. She wondered what remorse had to with anything. "Look, you got me, so that's that. I'm willing to cooperate."

Gonzalez persisted on her path. "How could you be so callous? Don't you care about the lives you ruin with these drugs? One day you'll stand before a higher authority, one without cooperation agreements."

Lucy rolled her eyes. She then bit down hard on her lip. She didn't appreciate the preaching of someone she now categorized as a religious fanatic. Remaining silent, Lucy took deep breaths, exhaling slowly. Her nostrils could be seen expanding as she tolerated what she was hearing.

"How about we get to the point? The only thing I want to know from you is the kind of deal I can make."

After a strained conversation, a cooperation agreement was finally signed by Lucy. The debriefing continued with Lucy going into detail about how she and her girlfriend Dotty had first met Jasper and Spanky. Lucy went on to reveal the workings of the drug operation as she knew it. She included the little she knew about Eustice.

"What about this Dotty?" asked Agent Gonzalez. "What role did she play in all of this?"

"Dotty had no role in any of this. She's just my friend."

"Are you trying to tell me that she had *nothing* to do with what was going on?"

"She was totally in the dark. Dotty had nothing to do with any of this."

"How can you expect us to believe that?" asked Gonzalez skeptically.

"Why would I hold back concerning Dotty? All I can tell you about Dotty is that she swings both ways."

The female agent tilted her head, projecting a look that conveyed she still was unconvinced. "You said that you entered into a business arrangement with Jasper while being intimate with him. Correct?"

"That's correct."

"So while you were occupied in this *business* session, what was Dotty doing?"

Lucy, noticing the cross affixed to the agent's lapel, couldn't resist sending a zinger. "She was at the ranch having her tank filled from both ends." The edge in her voice was meant to cut deep.

"What?" asked the agent, hardly believing what she heard.

"C'mon now, you know all about *that*," taunted the prisoner.

The insinuation connected to the prisoner's words angered Gonzalez beyond imagination. Furious at the comment, the agent's face reddened. She reacted with venom.

"I don't see you as all *that* valuable to us. I don't think we *need* your cooperation. As far as I'm concerned, you can spend your entire life in a jail cell," declared the agent, abruptly ripping up the cooperation agreement and tossing it into the air in pieces.

Seeing this drastic action was a wake-up call for Lucy. Knowing that she needed to humble herself to get back on track, she wisely did so. In order to make amends the prisoner began apologizing profusely. Eventually she was afforded a second chance. After the preparation of the second cooperation agreement, the questioning resumed.

"Now, once again, what was Dotty's involvement in the drug enterprise?" asked Agent Gonzalez.

"I'm being honest with you. Why wouldn't I be at this point?" began Lucy. "I wear to you, Dotty isn't in the drug business in any way. She just likes three-way sex with men *and* women. That's the truth."

Gonzalez flashed a look at her partner. The male agent shrugged, indicating that he found the prisoner credible. He pulled up a chair close to the desk and began asking his own questions.

"So tell me, regarding Dotty being a switch hitter . . ."

30

Scooping Up Spanky

GREENWOOD CEMETERY IS BORDERED ON ONE SIDE by McDonald Avenue. Students who hiked the incline from Fort Hamilton Parkway to Bishop Ford High School referred to this part of the avenue as "the hill." The darkness of night made the lonely stretch an ideal location for those looking to rob someone walking alongside the cemetery. It was also an excellent venue for the drug transaction that would culminate in the takedown of Spanky.

Markie and Von Hess were positioned opposite the cemetery on a street that fed into McDonald Avenue. Tucked between two parked cars, they slouched down in their seats as they maintained a visual on the undercover detective's vehicle. Von Hess kept the car engine running and the vehicle headlights off as they waited. Agent Leardi and another agent were positioned a distance away at the bottom of the hill. The plan called for Agent Yardstick, backed by Agent Montgomery, to pull in behind Eustice and then do a hand-to-hand three-kilo cocaine transaction with Spanky. Once the sale was consummated, Eustice was to turn on the headlights, giving the signal for the arrest teams to move in. In the event of a problem, the undercover detective was to flash the bright lights once.

"The undercover just parked on the set with the subject," radioed Markie to Leardi, advising that Eustice and Spanky had arrived at the predetermined scene.

"We're ready to roll when the signal is given," transmitted Leardi, winking at his driver.

Eustice doused his car lights and shut off his car engine. Being parked alongside the unlit cemetery provided an eerie touch that contributed to Spanky's unease.

"Where the hell are they?" asked Spanky. The edge in his voice was distinct.

"Take it easy, Spanky. It's early," said Eustice. "We just got here."

"I don't like having to wait. We got a lot of shit with us tonight that we're responsible for. We're sitting outside a graveyard where anybody can come by and rip us off." Spanky placed his gun between his legs for ready access. "You're packing, right, Bob?"

"Yeah, don't worry," answered Eustice. "I'm carrying."

Spanky let out a deep sigh. It was a clear indication that he was stressed.

##########

THE TWO SURVEILLANCE TEAMS sat in silence. Experience had taught them that idle chatter could sometimes result in their missing something they should have noticed. Markie took out his five-shot snub-nosed revolver in order to waste no time once the signal was given. A thought suddenly occurred to him, causing him to holster his weapon.

"I'm going for a short walk, Ollie," advised the sergeant. "I want to take a look at something." He returned to his vehicle a few minutes later. "Leardi's up to his old tricks," he stated to Von Hess.

"What did he do?"

"I saw their car inching up the hill. Leardi must have forgotten that I worked with him."

"Why is he doing that?"

"He moved up because he wants to get in there before we do," advised Markie. "He's worried that we'll be too aggressive when we make the pinch."

"Us?" asked Von Hess. "What about them?"

"That's exactly right! If Spanky makes a wrong move, they'd be the first ones to put one in him, especially since they believe he's packing a gun."

"No problem, Sarge. We'll get in there first."

"You can bank on it, Ollie. I'm getting an early lead on them."

Inside the federal vehicle, Agent Leardi voiced his own amended instructions to his fellow agent.

"Yardstick's gonna take off his hat. That'll be the signal for us to move in," instructed Leardi.

"How come you didn't tell the cops about the signal change?" asked the agent behind the wheel.

"I want to get there first. The cops won't hesitate to crack him one if Spanky doesn't move fast enough for them. The last thing we need is a hospitalized prisoner."

##########

AGENT MONTGOMERY PULLED UP ALONGSIDE Eustice's Lincoln very slowly, stopping when Yardstick and Eustice were face-to-face. After they exchanged nods, Montgomery backed up his car behind Eustice, making sure there was plenty of room between vehicles. Yardstick stepped out of the car and approached Spanky's side of the vehicle alone.

"You got the shit?" asked the undercover DEA agent, forgoing any pleasantries.

"Yeah, we're all set," answered Spanky. "You got the money?"

"It's in my car. Let me see the shit."

"Once you show me the money, man."

Yardstick detected uneasiness in Spanky's voice. It led him to believe that the drug dealer was frightened. Yardstick signaled Montgomery to come forward. The agent got out of the car with a red leather file bag containing the money. Yardstick took the bag and flashed the money for Spanky's inspection. After seeing that the file bag was filled with cash, Spanky produced the kilos of coke. He passed the kilos through the window at the same time he received the money. Yardstick removed his hat, and headed with Montgomery to their vehicle. It was Leardi's signal to move in. The federal agents were in motion, thinking that Markie and Von Hess were waiting for Eustice to turn on his lights. Leardi had underestimated Markie, who advanced alone on foot as soon as he saw Montgomery pull up in his vehicle. Crouched behind a parked car on the opposite side of the street, the sergeant waited for Eustice to turn on the car engine and lights.

Once the undercover agents left Spanky, Eustice turned on the car engine. After putting on his headlights, he engaged Spanky in conversation in order to delay their departure. He was affording his backup teams the time necessary to reach them.

"So what are you waiting for, Christmas?" asked Spanky. "Let's get out of here."

"Let me light up a smoke, for Christ's sake," commented Eustice, stalling. "Roll down that window so we can get some fresh air in here."

After complying with the request to open the window, Spanky waited for Eustice to light his cigarette. This procrastination gave Markie enough time to creep up on the Lincoln. Gun drawn, the sergeant snuck up on Spanky's blind side. Markie entered the barrel of his revolver into the hollow of Spanky's ear. The drug dealer froze as he felt the intrusive cold steel. The federal agents pulled up to the scene seconds after Markie took action. Von Hess got there a couple of seconds later.

"POLICE! DON'T MOVE!" shouted Markie. Taken totally unaware, Spanky froze. "Put your hands on top of your head," ordered the sergeant. "Do anything different and you're a memory."

Spanky's mind began to race frantically. While trying to think, he somehow failed to notice that Eustice had a gun pointed at his midsection. Undecided whether or not he had it in him to make a fight of it, Spanky's trembling hand slowly moved toward the gun he had secreted between his legs.

"Don't try it, pal," said Eustice, quickly reaching over to pin down the hand that was going for the gun. Spanky now finally noticed that Eustice's gun was pointed at him.

Markie ordered Spanky out of the car. When Spanky hesitated, the sergeant holstered his gun and reached into the car to take hold of the drug dealer by the top of his shirt collar. Markie pulled the drug dealer through the open window in one sweeping motion. From the cement sidewalk, Spanky looked up at the sergeant. Angry at being pulled through the window, he made the mistake of resisting arrest. When Spanky sprung to his feet, he kicked at the sergeant, brushing him below the belt. Markie responded with rapid a one-two fist/gun combination that resulted in blood leaking from Spanky's eyebrow. With the fight now taken out of him, the drug dealer allowed himself to be rear-cuffed. With his head now clearing, the handcuffed Spanky began to look around. He dropped his head in anguish when it finally became apparent that everyone on the scene, including Bayonne Bob, was on the side of the law.

"Thanks a lot, Bob!" yelled Spanky bitterly. "You screwed me real good."

"Hey, don't blame me for your mistakes," Eustice shouted through the car window. "He had this gun between his legs, Sarge," added the undercover detective as he held up the weapon for Markie to see.

Markie and Leardi faced each other without speaking. Both wore crooked smiles. Markie's was wider.

########

AFTER RECEIVING A COUPLE OF STITCHES AT THE HOSPITAL, Spanky was transported to the DEA offices for arrest processing. He was photographed, fingerprinted, and read his Miranda warnings. Spanky was seething over his predicament. His anger was no longer directed at law enforcement but rather at Jasper for introducing him to an undercover detective. His ire was magnified after learning that it was the DEA busting him. Things only grew bleaker when the drug dealer was informed that the Las Vegas operation had been beheaded. When the feds offered him the opportunity to serve up Jasper in return for leniency, as expected, the prisoner didn't dither. After signing on, Spanky detailed his history with the James Brothers and agreed to wear a wire. He only held back when queried about Silky Seggio.

"Look, Spanky, don't be afraid to open up," said the sergeant. "Whether you talk about Seggio or not, if they catch up to you, the payback won't change. Either way, you're facing bullets."

"If you can help deliver Seggio, then maybe a place like Arizona will be in your future sooner than you think," encouraged Leardi. "Maybe even a nice little house and business . . ."

Hearing this convinced Spanky to be forthright. "Jasper has some kind of an in with Silky Seggio."

"Go on," said Markie.

"Silky is a made guy," advised Spanky.

"Is Jasper a part of his crew?"

"I think so," answered the prisoner. "Silky is one person Jasper never ever talks about."

"What do you think their relationship is?"

"All I know for sure is that Silky and Jasper have some kind of understanding."

"What kind?"

"Silky makes Jasper bulletproof," explained Spanky. "Jasper pays Silky for that privilege.

"Silky's got a piece of the drug business?" asked Leardi.

"I don't know about that, but whenever a problem exists, Silky is the remedy."

"Have you ever met Silky?"

"No, never . . . and I don't want to."

"Do you know if Silky has a piece of *any* of Jasper's businesses?" questioned Markie. "Or maybe Jasper fronts for Silky?"

Spanky thought about the question before answering. "I don't know, but any of that could be."

"Do you know if Jasper ever killed anyone?" Markie asked.

"Not as far I know."

"Do you think he's capable of killing anyone?"

"Is Jasper capable? Definitely," replied Spanky. "He'd kill you and not lose an hour's sleep over it."

"What makes you so sure of that?"

"I know the man. This guy Buster used to manage Jasper's bar. He got caught stealing from Jasper," advised Spanky, neglecting to implicate himself in his account. "He ended up getting beat bad."

"But he wasn't killed?"

"No, that time it was just a beating."

"There was another time?"

"Buster must have done something else because he ain't been seen no more."

"Are you saying that Jasper killed Buster?"

"I don't know for sure. Like I said, Jasper's hooked up with Silky Seggio. Everybody knows it was Silky's boys who did that first number on Buster. They almost killed him *that* time, left him for dead in the street. I overheard Jasper say that he regretted not doing the job himself. So you tell me if he's capable."

"Silky beat him?"

"Nah, Silky's an old man. He has a couple of goons that do his dirty work."

"What are their names?"

"That's something I'm glad I don't know."

"Where did Buster get the coke from?" asked Leardi.

Spanky did a double take at hearing the question. "I don't know."

"C'mon, cut the bullshit and tell us the truth," demanded the agent.

"Were you and Buster in cahoots, stealing Jasper's coke?" chimed in Markie.

"I think you know more than you let on," Spanky complimented them. "I guess it *was* partly my fault."

"C'mon, open up."

"Alright, I cut Jasper's coke and provided it to Buster to sell on the side," confessed Spanky.

"You stepped on Jasper's coke?" asked Leardi. "Pretty risky thing to do . . ."

"Yeah, I know. I guess it makes little difference now."

"Didn't you think Jasper would come after you if he got wind of it?"

"He wasn't supposed to find out."

"He didn't miss the product?"

"Nah. Jasper never deals with the powder once I get it. He had no way of knowing. I'm not sure that he even knows all that much about coke."

"I'm curious about something. Was there any particular reason why you took this chance?" asked Von Hess. "Cutting Jasper's coke *was* taking a chance, wasn't it?"

"Yeah, it was taking a chance, and there was a reason," replied Spanky. "The twins denied me my due. I should've been a partner from day one."

"So technically you were as guilty as Buster."

"Yeah," acknowledged Spanky, "that's one way of looking at it."

"How did Jasper get wise?"

"Jasper found out about it because his snitch ratted out Buster. Do you guys know his snitch?""

"No, tell us."

"It was Mousey, the kid who replaced Buster as the manager of the bar. Buster took his beating because of Mousey."

"But not you," said Markie. "How did you manage to slip through the net?"

"I figure that I walked away from a beating because Jasper needs me. I'm the guy who sells the product. Without me, Jasper's up shit creek and he has no drug business.

"Did Jasper ever confront you?"

"He knew I'd get the message after seeing the beating Buster took . . . and the bastard uses that to torment me!"

"Torment you?"

"He keeps me guessing if and when I'll be getting mine."

"Who is Jasper's drug source?" asked Leardi.

"All I know is that the shit is coming from somebody way upstate or from Canada. I'm kept in the dark. They kept the formula simple. I would tell Jasper what I needed and then stay away from my apartment. When I returned a couple of days later, I'd find the kilos I asked for in my apartment."

"Where are you when this happens?" asked Leardi.

"I go home to my wife. I split my time between the apartment and home. Whoever makes the delivery has a key to the door so I don't have to be there. That's the arrangement."

"And the money . . ."

"Whatever I collected went to Jasper. He pays me a percentage."

"Do you maintain a stash in the apartment?" asked Leardi.

"I usually keep four or five keys on hand. One of those kilos is the one I cut when I was working with Buster. Now you got it all."

"So what's the story with Mousey?" asked Von Hess.

"Jasper told me that Mousey's gone. If I had to bet, I'd say Buster killed him."

"Did Buster take off?"

"I don't know. Either that or Jasper already took his revenge. Buster ain't been seen around."

"So you think Buster's dead?"

"All I know is that Jasper loved that little asshole. If Buster did something to Mousey, Jasper would definitely look to get even."

"Let me ask you about something else," said Markie. "Did Jasper ever talk about a National Guard soldier he had a problem with?"

"I know that the James Brothers were in the National Guard."

"Did they never talk about having a beef with anyone in the National Guard?"

"They never mentioned anything like that to me."

"I got a question for *you*," said Spanky, addressing Markie directly.

"What is it?"

"Why did you hit me with the gun?"

"What did you expect me to do, give you another chance to kick me in the nuts?"

Not having a counterargument, Spanky just nodded. He understood.

287

31

Silky Sweeps Up

MUSKIE RETURNED FROM FLORIDA sporting a tan. He was happy to return to his Brooklyn routine. His mood soon changed after his conversation with Frankie Nose at the Palsy-Walsy.

"How was the wedding?" asked Frankie.

"Good," replied Muskie. "What did Silky say about you spotting Lemon eating with the detective?"

"Oh, I didn't get to tell him yet. Maybe it's better to forget about it and not get him all riled up."

"What did I tell you?" asked Muskie, who was incredulous at Frankie's lack of responsibility. "Are you crazy or what? You should've told him the day it happened. You better go tell him now or I will."

"You don't have to do that. I'll go tell him."

Frankie Nose journeyed to the rear of the Palsy-Walsy Social Club with trepidation. He proceeded as if he were a blindfolded mutineer walking the plank of the *Queen Anne's Revenge* on the order of Blackbeard the pirate. Even though the numbers runner visited the club daily, the private office of Silky was foreign territory for him. Frankie placed his ear at the door before knocking. Hearing voices coming from within, he gently tapped on the office door.

"Come on in," came Silky's voice from within the room. After opening the door, Frankie stood in the doorway, hesitant to enter. "What do you need, kid?"

"Can I have a minute in private, boss?"

The mobster's eyes were concentrated on Frankie's nose. "Yeah, just do me a favor and let me know if you gotta sneeze. I'll take cover," said Silky, making light of Frankie's oversized proboscis. Accustomed to crude remarks concerning he size of his nose, Frankie took the affront in stride. "So what's on your mind, kid?" ask Silky once the office was cleared.

"I saw something that I think you should know about," said Frankie. "I saw Lemon, the car guy, in a Staten Island diner having breakfast with an NYPD detective."

Silky displayed no overt reaction to the news. Instead he asked, "Male or female?"

"Male."

"How do you know the guy was a bull?"

"I know him. . . . I even spoke to him when I went over to say hello to Lemon."

"Lemon introduced him as a detective?"

"No, he didn't have to. I already knew who he was."

"How do *you* come to know this cop?"

"He pinched my old man. I'd never forget his face because he upset the hell out of my mother. I was just a kid then, but I remember him coming into the house."

"How much of a kid were you?"

"I was about five or six."

"Did he remember you?"

"I doubt it."

Silky exhaled deeply. "This is of concern," said the mobster. "Do you remember the detective's name?"

"Yeah, his name is Costello. He worked in the precinct where we lived."

"What was the charge against your father?"

"It was a bullshit charge. He passed a bum check."

"You are certain about this?"

"Not the slightest doubt. It was definitely him. I remember how pissed my old man got when my mother offered him a cup of coffee. The guy took it too!"

"That's something you'd remember," noted Silky. "I don't blame your father for getting pissed off. Did Lemon say who he was?"

"He just said his name was Bob. He was bullshitting me. Lemon said the guy worked with his brother-in-law in Bayonne."

"That mother . . . !" blurted the gangster, showing his first sign of anger. "You did right, kid. Coming to me with this shows you got more upstairs than just a big sniffer. I won't forget this, Frankie."

Frankie was puffed up after hearing these words. "Thank you, Mr. Seggio."

"Does anyone else know about this?"

"Only Muskie knows. He was waiting in the car when I went in the diner to get breakfast for us."

"Didn't he see the potential for harm?" asked Silky. "Where has he been anyway?"

"He's been in Florida. Things got clearer to him once I explained it," said Frankie, altering history.

"Say, when was it that you saw Lemon with that bull?"

"It was last week sometime."

"LAST WEEK!" raged Silky, slamming his hand on his desk. He began to shake his head in disgust. "I'll take this up with you guys later. Now, get the hell out!" shouted the mobster. Silky knew he needed to act fast. His first step was to call one of his enforcers. "Primo, get your cousin and get over to the office. Come heavy."

Silky was not a man to dither when it came to his own well-being. Frankie had brought a problem to the forefront that required immediate action. From Silky's perspective, the presence of a detective was akin to having a cancer invade his body. Since killing a cop would draw too much heat, he had no choice other than to opt for the alternative. While Lemon was small potatoes, Jasper's elimination would be costly. Unfortunately for Jasper, his being a direct link to the elderly gangster was his Waterloo. Silky attributed the fate of Jasper to being just one of those unavoidable things.

When Silky's enforcers arrived at the club, they found their boss waiting outside and ready to travel.

"Stay put," Silky said to Nino, who was in the front passenger seat of the car. "I'll get in the back."

"Where are we going, Silky?" asked Primo, who was driving.

"Go to Lemon's car lot," ordered Silky. "You boys are getting your chance to make your bones."

The cousins were delighted because they saw murder as a career path to getting made a soldier.

"No problem," said Primo.

"Brownsville really changed from when I was a kid!" said Silky after entering his old neighborhood.

"Was it always this lousy around here?" asked Primo.

"Eastern Parkway was beautiful years ago," said Silky.

"Was it really?" Nino asked, sounding surprised.

"Are you kidding? Some of the players on the Brooklyn Dodgers lived on Eastern Parkway."

"So you know this end of Brooklyn then," said Nino.

"I should. I did my first work on Pitkin and Saratoga."

"Murder Incorporated?" asked Nino.

Silky just laughed without responding to the question. "Make a right turn on the next block. The car lot is around the corner on the left. Pull in and go all the way into the back out of sight," directed the gangster when they arrived at their destination.

Lemon was finalizing a car sale with a customer when the three men entered his trailer office. His face turned pale when he saw Silky enter with his two bruisers. He was so discombobulated by Silky's unannounced visit that he forgot all about his customer.

"Hey," he said, "what brings you here?"

"Finish up with the young lady," said Silky in a gentlemanly manner. "We have time."

Lemon hurriedly blew through the paperwork. He turned the car keys of a white Honda over to the purchaser of the car. "Good luck with the car," he said as he escorted his customer outside. He couldn't help but notice that Nino was trailing behind him. Lemon waved goodbye as the woman drove off. He then turned to look at Nino and smiled nervously.

"It's her first car," the seller commented meekly, not knowing what else to say.

"Good for her," replied the enforcer, adding curtly, "Now, back inside."

Lemon gulped as he scanned the hard faces of the three men who were visiting him. It was evident to him that he was on the spot. .

"It's my understanding that you acquired *new* friends," stated Silky evenly.

"I don't understand. . . . What new friends?"

"Explain to me how it can happen that you break bread with a bull," demanded the gangster.

"A bull?" asked Lemon, feigning ignorance. "I don't know any detectives. The only cops I see are the precinct guys who come in to buy a car once in a while."

"A little bird with a big beak told me that he saw you. You got two minutes to convince me otherwise."

"Oh . . . no, no, no!" said Lemon, his false smile quivering. "I got no idea what you're talking about."

"Frankie Nose pinned you in a diner eating with a bull; that's what I'm talking about."

"Ohh, I understand. I was with Bayonne Bob when that asshole came over to us in the diner that day. He asked me to get him a car," explained Lemon, thinking as fast as he could. "What the hell made him think Bob was a cop?" After a second, he added, "Bob worked with Monte in Bayonne for years."

"Who are you bullshitting?" asked Silky through tight lips.

Lemon began scrambling. "That kid Frankie is making a mistake, Silky."

Silky's face was now devoid of emotion. "Tell me who this bull is and how much he knows."

"I'm telling you, Bob's no bull. He's a guy who worked with my brother-in-law," replied Lemon.

"Then fucking Monte must have been in the police academy with him because the guy you ate with was a detective named Costello! Now, either you knew that or you've been suckered. Either way, you're responsible for bringing around the law."

"But Silky, you got me wrong. . . . Everybody knows Bayonne Bob," pleaded Lemon.

"And the kid with the big honker would remember a guy who pinched his old man on Christmas Eve."

Lemon knew the charade was over. "Silky, they had me by the short hairs. . . ."

"*How* much does this detective know?"

"They were sending me up to do a stretch. At my age, I can't survive jail. I had to give them something to get out from under . . . but I swear it, I *never* once mentioned you. All they wanted to do was take down Jesse James."

"Why are they gunning for Jasper? What does he have going that makes him so important?" asked the racketeer, fishing to see how much was known about the drug operation.

"They want to nail him for something that happened years ago."

"What happened years ago?"

"He killed that National Guard sergeant who went missing. You must remember that. . . ."

Silky recalled the incident. " I thought the story was that he took off with a girlfriend."

"The James Brothers killed that guy. They came to me to get rid of his car."

Silky found this information fascinating. "Why did they do it?"

"I got no idea why. They came to the lot out of the blue in their army uniforms with the guy's wheels. They begged me to help them out by disposing of the car. So I did them the favor."

"So you turned rat the first time the cops come scratching at your door," accused Silky.

"Yeah, I got scared . . . but I swear it, I never spoke about you. I snitched to stay out of the can. You think I'd ever deal with the cops and the DEA if they didn't have me cornered?" asked Lemon.

"THE DEA!" shouted Silky. The situation had now taken on a new and much more serious turn. Now the mobster knew he had a real problem.

"I just didn't want to die in jail, Silky," Lemon declared sorrowfully.

"Don't worry about that. You won't," declared Silky chillingly.

Lemon now knew for sure that he was facing a death sentence. "Silky, have a heart."

"Nino, go outside and close the gate to the lot. Put up a sign saying the joint's closed for lunch," directed the mobster. Looking every inch the cold-blooded killer he was, he turned to face Lemon. "Life is about making choices," said the mobster coldly. "You made yours, so goodbye Lemon."

"Silky, show me some mercy," pleaded Lemon, his voice cracking.

"Primo, put him out of his misery," ordered Silky. "I'll be in the car."

"Silky, nooooo. . . ." cried out Lemon. The eyes of the doomed man bulged with fright as he faced the knife in Primo's hand.

Silky could tell that Primo and Nino were quite proud of themselves. After lighting up cigarettes, they began to blow smoke rings. Silky related to their feeling of accomplishment. He recollected experiencing the same euphoria after committing his own first murder.

"Don't make plans for Friday. I got more work for you that night."

##########

CHIEF MCCOY IMPATIENTLY TAPPED HIS PENCIL AGAINST the telephone on his desk as Lieutenant Wright spoke. He often did this when he was growing tired of waiting for results. He was irked that Jasper hadn't been arrested for the homicide of Cornell Mathis yet.

"The feds want to know if Eustice could be transferred permanently into their C-9 group."

"Tell them that can have him," said McCoy. "All I'm interested in is getting the Mathis case wrapped up. If that don't happen soon I'm flopping everybody . . . including you!" threatened the chief.

"No problem, Chief. That's happening Friday."

After Wright left his office, Chief McCoy remained at his desk. He tried to think of the pleasure he'd get in announcing that his detectives, after so many years, had cracked the Cornell Mathis case. Even this thought couldn't put him in a better mood. He turned to his standby to accomplish that. He opened the door to his locker and removed a bottle of Irish whiskey. Holding the bottle to the light, he could see he was beginning to run low. He picked up the phone to call his go-to man, Detective Silverlake. The detective, who was stationed at a desk just outside the chief's office, picked up on the first ring.

"Detective Silverlake speaking. How may I help you?"

"I'm running low on courage. It's time to replenish."

"No problem, boss. I'll go now."

"No rush. I still have enough left for a session," advised the chief. "Come on in and bring a couple of Dixie cups."

########

THE OIL DRIPPED FROM THE PIZZA, SOILING Markie's sport jacket. He decided that it was time to buy another one.

"It looks like it'll be an early night, Ollie," said Markie on the drive downtown.

"Yeah. I have to call the wife and let her know I'll be home. She's cooking up roast beef hash for me."

"That's with the egg and potatoes, right?"

"Yeah. That's one of my favorite dishes," noted Von Hess. "I'm figuring that she probably wants something from me."

Markie had to laugh. "Nah. Your wife is great. You know something, Ollie? When I was married to Florence, she always used to cook what I liked."

"I think those days may be long over for guys."

"It's probably better that people learn how to cook for themselves anyway."

"I'm just glad that I'm long past any of that," said Von Hess.

"You know, whenever I fought with Florence, she'd use the kitchen as a weapon. When she got mad at me, whatever I liked to eat was never available. If I said I wanted to eat veal cutlet, I'd never see one. It was the same thing with Sunkist oranges. After every spat, all of Brooklyn seemed to run out of veal cutlet and Sunkist oranges."

"What can you do?" said Von Hess. He chuckled and continued to drive.

"Do me a favor; I want to make a stop downtown."

"Where to . . . ?"

"Take me to Crappy Erwin's. It's time for a new sport jacket."

Von Hess drove to Erwin's Secondhand Wear in Lower Manhattan. Everyone, with the exception of Erwin and Markie, considered most of the previously owned clothes being sold at Erwin's to be of an inferior quality . . . or, to put it more plainly, crap. Erwin was also a tailor who willingly threw in free alterations for law enforcement. Markie liked Erwin because he was usually able to wrangle a good deal that fit his budget. At four feet, eleven inches, the wispy-haired Erwin was built along the lines of a bowling pin. He could usually be seen toiling with a tape measure around his neck and pins in his mouth.

"What do you say, Erwin?" greeted Markie after entering the store.

"Mmmmm," replied Erwin, careful not to swallow the pins. Smiling tightly, he nodded his head.

"Erwin, take the pins out your mouth. You could choke on them," warned the sergeant.

Erwin picked away the pins that were between his lips before speaking. "What are you worried about? I've had pins in my mouth for fifty years and never swallowed a one," he said with a trace of pride.

"Okay, whatever you say, Erwin," said Markie. "I'm looking for a sport jacket."

"I'm afraid I have to disappoint. Right now I've got nothing in your size."

"Are you expecting some in?"

"Of course, something will come in at some point. Do you want me to call you when I get something?" "Yeah, do that. Do you need my size?"

"No, I already know it. Depending on the cut, you're a forty-four or forty-six regular, right?"

"This man is good, isn't he?" said Markie, turning to Von Hess. The detective was no longer there. He had wandered off to the back of the store.

Von Hess was preoccupied, staring at a large portrait of Theodore Roosevelt that was partially hidden behind a rack of clothes. He returned to where Markie was.

"Say, Erwin . . . I was just looking at the Roosevelt you got back there. Is he available?"

"Come," said Erwin as he moved from the behind his counter. "Let's go look."

"Ollie loves history, Erwin," advised Markie.

When they got close to the picture, Erwin took a small piece of cloth from his rear pocket and wiped the wooden frame that was covered with dust. It was a huge frame that had probably once hung in a library or private club. Whatever the origin, Von Hess envisioned having the picture of the former president and New York City police commissioner hanging over the bar in his finished basement. He saw it as a good conversation piece.

"What do you want for the Rough Rider?"

Erwin could see that the detective had a legitimate interest. "You want to buy *my* Teddy Roosevelt? He's been with me since I opened the business."

"So what do you want for him?"

"*That picture?* It's a work of art. Ohhh, let me tell you the history it has."

Von Hess looked at Erwin and smiled. "Skip it, Erwin. I like it but not enough to get stuck up for it."

"What do you mean? That's a valuable item. . . . Make me an offer."

"Sorry, Erwin, no soap," said Von Hess, ending the discussion. "I'll be out in the car, Sarge."

Markie shrugged his shoulders. "Put aside a jacket for me when one comes in, Erwin," said Markie.

"Sure, Sergeant," replied Erwin. "I don't know what's wrong with your partner. I was just negotiating."

"You may have overplayed your hand on that one, Erwin. Don't worry about it."

"Well, do me a favor. See what he wants to spend, then, will you? I can't give things away for nothing."

"Don't worry about it, Erwin. I'll thaw him out."

32

And Justice for All

SILKY LOOKED CLOSELY INTO THE LARGE glass in front of the barber's chair he sat in. Vito the Blade moved a handheld mirror from left to right behind his head. Silky nodded his head, indicating his approval of the haircut he had received. Feeling the smoothness of his face, he again nodded satisfaction, this time for the shave he'd received.

"Good job, paisan. I'll see you next week," said the gangster to his countryman, confirming his regular grooming appointment. After Silky left the barbershop, he returned to his social club. The first thing he did when he entered his office was call his wife. This had long been a ritual with him. Every Friday he'd advise her that he wouldn't be coming home that night.

"It's me, Settimo. I'm staying in Brooklyn tonight."

"So I won't bother to cook, then," said Silky's spouse of forty-eight years.

Long accustomed to her husband's Friday routine, she didn't bother to ask if everything was alright. As far as she knew, Friday was his poker night. He occasionally added to his deceit by fabricating an additional reason for being away from home. This particular Friday he told his wife that there was an issue at the apartment house he owned.

"I have to straighten out a problem at the apartment house. The tenants are beefing."

"Can't you find someone reliable to handle things for you?"

"What can I do? They want to see me because I'm the owner."

"You mustn't spoil the tenants by being so available."

"Alright, stop with the sermon," said the gangster, cutting her off. "I'll see you tomorrow."

"Be sure that you eat something. Do you know what you're having for dinner?"

"I don't know yet."

"Are you going to sit down someplace?"

"Nah, I'll probably have something delivered to the club. I'll play cards, watch some television, and sleep over on the couch in my office."

"Alright, you might as well. It's supposed to be raining all night tonight anyway."

"It's gonna rain tonight?"

"That's what the prediction is. Do you have all your medicine?"

"Yeah, don't worry. I got all my pills."

"What about the dynamite pills?"

"Yeah, I just said I got all my pills."

"Alright, then, I'll see you tomorrow."

"Alright," he said. Before hanging up, he added, "If you feel like cooking later, make some sausage and peppers. You can give it to me tomorrow for breakfast in an omelet with a couple of eggs."

"Alright, that's what I'll do, then."

Silky sent several smacking kisses to his wife before hanging up. Once off the phone, the gangster concentrated on what he really had planned for the evening. After lighting up a cigarette, he picked up the telephone to finalize his nocturnal arrangements.

"Hello?" answered the thirty-seven-year-old Eva from her bed.

"I'll come by later. What are you cooking?"

Eva squinted, wondering if she'd heard right. Silky's mistress knew that the role she played in his life exempted her from such chores. "Cooking?" she asked, feigning indignation. "Since when did I grow a mustache? You're taking me out to dinner, *old* man."

"Oh yeah?" asked the amused Silky. Her brashness was a tonic for him.

"You rather me cook?"

"What, you're above cooking now?"

"Alright, I'll cook for you. What would you like, big shot?" she asked, taking liberties with the racketeer that no one else dared try.

"The big shot wants you should make something special for him."

"How about pigeon stew?" she asked without missing a step. "It'll be nice and fresh. I'll scrape it off the window ledge now."

The seventy-one-year-old gangster found the sharp-tongued dialogue with his irreverent girlfriend to be to his liking. Her disrespectful verbal jousting prepared him for when the lights went dim. He'd answer her irreverence with a jackhammer-like performance that always culminated with a spent Silky flopping back onto the mattress alongside her. Looking up at the ceiling, he'd struggle to catch his breath while reaching for a cigarette. While these were dangerously taxing sessions for a man with a heart condition, he embraced the risk he felt to be worthwhile.

"I'll pick you up at 6:00 p.m. sharp. We'll go for drinks at Pino's and then grab dinner."

"Again you want to eat there? We always go to Pino's. I'm starting to feel like a pasta pig."

"That's okay, as long as you're not built like one, sweetheart."

"That's something you'll never have to worry about, pops," she assured.

"Alright, forget Pino's. How about we go to Steinborn's Steak House?"

"Yeah, let's go there."

"Alright, I'll see you later."

"Wait a minute. Before you hang up, when do you plan on having the workers come in and start the renovations? Did you forget about the overhead mirror?"

At first Silky rolled his eyes at the thought of the expense. Yes, the mirror was his idea . . . but not the new kitchen, bathroom, and floor. Those were her idea. Silky accepted the fact that he was being taken advantage of. At his advanced age, he considered the return on his investment worth it. For the sake of appearances, he lodged a modest protest prior to consenting.

"What do you want from me?" he asked, shaking his hand in the air while pressing his thumb against his index finger for emphasis. "You haven't paid me rent in years, *and* you want me to renovate the joint too!" he shouted into the phone.

"This apartment is old-fashioned. I want it modernized," she countered. "Besides, if you follow through on your promise to renovate, I *might* just be willing to do what you've been asking me to do," she said suggestively. "You know how you always want you want. Well, this is your chance."

The kept woman knew just what to say to rev up the aging mobster's motor. "Ahhh, maybe the place could use an overhaul." When Primo and Nino appeared at his office door, he cut the call short. "I gotta go. I'll make arrangements for the apartment tomorrow. I'll see you later."

"Are we all set?" asked Silky, quickly switching to his role as a mob boss.

"All set," replied Primo. "Jasper will be waiting for us at his bar tonight to pick him up."

"What did you tell him?"

"Just what you told me to say, Silky. He thinks he's going to Red Hook to meet somebody about a business deal. I told him we'd pick him up at half past seven."

"He went for it?"

"Yeah, he did, hook, line, and sinker."

"Good," said Silky. "Remember, I don't want his face marked up. He was a good kid. It's a shame that he has to be put down," he lamented. "I want you to make it quick and painless. Leave him someplace down there in the Hook where the cops can find him before the rats get at him."

"No problem," said Nino.

"Rip out his pockets, take his wallet, ring, watch. . . . You know, make it look like a robbery."

##########

SPANKY WAS USED AS THE BAIT to draw out Jasper. Markie and Leardi had Spanky dial up Jasper from the DEA offices.

"Jasper, it's me. I need to talk to you about something."

"What?"

"I got a personal problem. I need some advice."

Relieved that the meeting wasn't money related, Jasper agreed to set time aside for Spanky. "I'll be at my bar later. See me there."

"What time?"

"I'll be there early, say at 7:00 p.m."

"I'll see you there."

"No, wait. Come later," advised Jasper. "I have to run out to a meeting, but I'll be back at the bar after my meet. Figure on 9:00 p.m. I might be a few minutes late, but I'll be there, so wait for me."

"No problem."

Spanky hung up the phone and turned to Markie and Leardi. "He wants me at the James Brothers Saloon at 9:00 p.m. He'll be there at 7:00 p.m. but has to run out to a meeting."

"That works fine," said Markie.

"We'll wire you up," added Leardi.

"How about we get to the bar early?" suggested Von Hess. "Maybe we can tail Jasper and see where he goes and who he meets."

Markie was amenable to the suggestion. "We'll take him down once he returns to the bar," said the sergeant. "We'll have Eustice give us the heads-up He'll step outside and light a cigar when it looks like Jasper's getting ready to go to his meeting,"

"Sarge, I got one question," said Von Hess. "What about Lieutenant Darkenlove? Jasper's ultimately going to be her squad's homicide collar."

"We'll notify her squad once we have Jasper in a cell."

##########

PRIMO CAME TO AN EASY STOP AS he reached the traffic light. When he turned to look at his cousin, he could see that something was troubling him. They were on their way to pick up Jasper at the bar.

"What's the matter with you tonight, Nino?"

"Nothing's the matter."

"Be happy; this job is gonna get us big recognition."

"How many of these hits is it gonna take before we get to graduation day?"

"This is what it takes," Primo reminded him.

"After tonight, I'm flat out asking the old man about proposing us for membership. We've made our bones now, so I think we've earned the right to a button."

"That ain't how things work. They'll let *us* know when it's time. It'll come one of these days. I got my suit and tie all ready for the call."

"And in the meantime . . . ?"

"In the meantime we do what we're told," said Primo. "I want to juggle that burning saint in my hand too," he added, referring to the Mafia ceremony taken by those being inducted into a crime family.

"I just want to hear Silky say he'll propose us when the books open up."

"Speaking of Silky, did you smell the aftershave he had on?"

"That surprises you, Primo? It's his date night. Every Friday he stinks up and wears his ruby cuff links . . . and he only wears those when he's taking out his girl," advised Nino. "You know who she is, right?"

"Of course I know. She's the one who lives in his apartment house," replied Primo.

"Yeah, that's her."

##########

ASPER FONDLED THE CASH CONTAINED IN the front pocket of his pants with his fingers. He was rarely without a wad of bills on him. The ready cash gave him a sense of empowerment. Early on, he had learned of the role currency played in influencing people. Giving someone a double sawbuck made things happen. Twenty bucks in the right hands got him a better seat at an event, an umbrella out over his head by a doorman, and immediate seating in a crowded restaurant. The one thing it couldn't do was bring back his late brother. Today was Jasper's birthday, and he stood alone at the bar of the James Brothers Saloon, drinking heavily to ease his depressed state. The date was an annual reminder of his late twin brother. Jasper called over Eustice, the new bar manager, to join him . He was in need of conversation to help beat the blues.

"Join me for a drink, Bob. What are you having?" he asked.

"Scotch on the rocks."

"Brenda," called out Jasper. The bartender promptly walked over to where the two men were stationed. "Give Bob here a black on the rocks."

Brenda smiled at Eustice without letting on how well they had gotten to know each other.

"Sure. Are you having another one for yourself, Jasper?"

"Yeah, give me another. I got business later, but what the hell. Keep them coming."

The two men chatted amicably until it was almost time for Jasper to leave for his appointment with Silky. "Bob, I gotta go see somebody soon. When Spanky comes by tell him I said that he should wait until I get back." Jasper then put his arm around Eustice. "By the way, you're going to be my right-hand man pretty soon."

Eustice was taken aback by Jasper's candidness. The slight slur in Jasper's speech was an indication that drink had begun to loosen his lips. "Do you have a ride?"

"Yeah, they're coming by for me."

After checking the time, Jasper guzzled down his drink. "Ahhh, what the hell. . . . Brenda, give us another round. I got time for one more." Halfway into his new drink, Jasper began to really open up. "Do you believe what that big dumb bastard did?" he asked.

"Who are you talking about?" asked Eustice, puzzled as to who Jasper was referring to.

"Q-Ball Otto," answered the bar owner, swilling down his drink.

"What did he do?"

"You don't know?"

"I got no clue. . . ."

"He was the one who set up the Mouse."

"Set up the Mouse?"

"Yeah, Otto betrayed us. . . . So you know what? Now he's missing in action . . . him *and* that prick he was in bed with." Although in the dark, Eustice just nodded as if he understood. He didn't want to interrupt the flow of conversation. "I wanted to kill them both myself for what they did to that kid," admitted Jasper.

"Who is this other guy you're talking about?"

The question posed by Eustice seemed to have a sobering effect on Jasper. Now realizing he was talking too much, Jasper shifted direction. "Let's just drop it," he said curtly. After a moment, he broached another line of conversation. "When are you gonna part with that ring?"

Brenda refilled their glasses before Eustice could voice an answer. When she left them, Jasper revisited his interest in the wolf head ring. "So answer me; what about the ring?"

"I don't know, Jasper. I really like this ring a lot," replied Eustice, who held up his hand to admire it.

Seeing the ring only made Jasper more aggressive. "It took me killing a guy to get a ring like that," declared Jasper with the utmost seriousness. "Did you have to clip anybody for yours?"

"No, I got mine in a pawn shop," Eustice reminded him. "Did you really take a guy out just to get the ring?" he then asked, pushing the envelope.

"Not exactly, the ring belonged to some prick in the National Guard who thought his stripes meant something. Ahh, never mind about that," added Jasper, halting his loose tongue. "Just remember, stay in line and you'll be my right arm moving ahead, something that blabbermouth double-crossing son of a bitch Spanky could never be."

Eustice, who had a higher tolerance for drink than Jasper, was thrilled to be getting so much information on tape. "I appreciate the faith you have in me," said the undercover.

"In time, you'll know how everything operates . . . the works. And at that point, you'll really be making coin with me."

"By the *works*, you mean the Palsy-Walsy Club?"

Jasper did a double take. "You can be a pretty bright boy when you want, can't you, Bob?"

Eustice shrugged before answering. "I have my moments."

"Remember something, bright boy, talking about certain things can get us both killed," warned Jasper.

Eustice assumed correctly that he was referring to his organized crime ties. "I thought those guys didn't get involved in the drug business," he said.

"Where do you think my shit comes from?"

"Spanky said something about Upstate New York or Canada. . . ."

Jasper snickered before responding. "Bingo, you can give that bigmouth prick a star at the top of his paper. The old man has family up there."

As Jasper spoke on, his words continued to be memorialized on tape. It was now fairly certain that Jasper would either be put away for a very long time or play ball for team law enforcement once he was taken into custody and charged.

##########

PRIMO SLOWLY PULLED UP TO THE FRONT OF THE James Brothers Saloon. There seemed to be an air of sneakiness about the way he came to a halt. He braked gently enough for the cousins not to feel anything. Primo turned to Nino in the passenger seat, giving him a serious look. Nino returned the gaze. It was an exchange between men committed to a mission of murder.

"He should be coming out any minute."

"I'll finesse this hump into the front seat," said Nino. "I'll tell him that I got a bum leg and need to stretch out in the back."

"What if he doesn't want to get in the front?"

"Front or back, he'll be gone inside an hour."

"Are you gonna use the wire?" inquired Primo.

"I'm thinking of it. Do you remember if he's got a big neck?"

"He's not a small guy," replied Primo. "It'll be work if you go with the wire."

"Then maybe I'll shoot him when we get to Red Hook," advised Nino.

"Just don't light him up in my car whatever the hell you do," said Primo, not wanting to soil the interior of his vehicle.

##########

JASPER LOOKED AT HIS WATCH and realized it was nearing the time to be picked up. He stared down at his drink and made his announcement to no one in particular.

"I gotta go," he said, pushing his drink forward without finishing it. He then straightened to his full height and headed for a visit to the men's room. Eustice rushed outside to light his cigar and signal the surveillance teams. After a couple of puffs, he returned to his drink, arriving seconds before Jasper emerged from the restroom.

Jasper went outside to see if his ride had arrived. The alcohol he'd consumed didn't lessen his visual ability. An unpleasant thought suddenly occurred to him after seeing that Silky's strong-arm men had come to pick him up without their boss. The prospect of entering a vehicle with Primo and Nino without Silky being present didn't seem to be a prudent thing to do. Although he had no concrete reason to feel threatened, he nevertheless was uncomfortable taking a ride with Silky's goons at night. Jasper felt compelled to take steps in order to ensure his own protection. He knew that an outright refusal to go wasn't a consideration, s was bringing along someone to watch his back. The bar owner resorted to loing the next best thing. Standing outside in the drizzle, he placed his hand lramatically to his head in an animated fashion, making it appear as if he forgot something.

"Oh, shit. . . . I'll be right back," he shouted to the men in the car. "I forgot my umbrella."

After reentering the bar, Jasper went directly down into the basement, where a six-shot Colt revolver was taped underneath a card table. Removing the weapon, he placed it in the side pocket of his sport jacket. Then, for a fleeting moment, he had second thoughts.

"What the hell am I doing?" he asked aloud. "Silky is too shrewd a customer to short-circuit a money machine like me!" His trust in Silky soon evaporated after further discussion with himself. "But then again, you never know." In the end, Jasper opted to keep the gun in the pocket of his sport jacket. "Why take a chance?" muttered Jasper as he headed upstairs to find an umbrella.

########

MARKIE AND VON HESS were parked opposite the James Brothers Saloon as usual. The sergeant radioed Agent Leardi, who was parked with another agent a block away, that Eustice just came outside and lit a cigar. He further advised that a black sedan containing two men were waiting in front of the bar.

"Do we know who the two men are?" asked Leardi."

"I haven't got a clue," replied Markie. "Get ready to roll"

########

PRIMO TOOK LONG DRAGS ON the cigarette he was smoking. It was something he tended to do when anxious. He wasn't comfortable being double-parked for too long a period. Doing so ran the risk of creating police interest. Since both he and his cousin were armed with guns, the last thing he wanted was to be pulled out of the vehicle and searched by the law.

"Where the hell did Jasper go now, Nino?" asked the impatient Primo.

"He said he forgot something. To tell you the truth, he looked stewed to me," pointed out Nino.

"Who was that other guy?"

"What other guy?" asked Nino.

"The guy who was outside smoking the cigar when we were pulling up. . . ."

"How should I know?" replied Nino.

Primo flipped his cigarette butt out the driver's-side window when he saw Jasper finally exit the bar. "Here he comes," he said. "He went back for his umbrella."

Nino got out of the car to greet Jasper as he approached his vehicle. Jasper noticed that Nino walked with an exaggerated limp.

"What happened? Did you trip over your snake?" asked Jasper, trying to appear at ease.

Nino smiled when Jasper got close enough for him to smell the alcohol. "That'll never happen. I always strap the big guy to my thigh," replied Nino. "Do me a favor; sit in the front."

"That's alright; I'll ride in the back," Jasper answered, reluctant to have Nino sit behind him.

"No, sit in the front," repeated Nino. "My bum knee is acting up on me with this rain, so I gotta stretch my leg out on the back seat."

"No, you go in the front," answered Jasper. "You can put the seat all the way back."

"Will somebody get in the friggin' front already?" injected Primo, losing patience. "Just sit in the front, will ya, Jasper? He's been crying all night about his knee."

"What do you want from me?" asked Nino, pretending to be protesting. "I have to stretch my legs out across the back seat. If I go back in the front, I'll be crippled all night."

Jasper relented. "Alright, I'll get in the front," he said. "Where's Silky?"

"He's waiting for us at the Villa Benito. We're all going to dinner."

Hearing this further alarmed Jasper because he was aware that Friday was Silky's regular date night.

"How come he made the meet for tonight? He's always with his squeeze on Friday night. . . ."

"She's with him," answered Primo.

The two assassins were determined to keep the conversation cordial. Primo commented on the smell of alcohol that now permeated the interior of his vehicle.

"Jeez, what's the occasion? You smell like you fell inside a bottle of hooch."

"I had a couple of drinks for my birthday," replied Jasper.

"It's your birthday?" asked Nino in a lively voice from the rear seat. "Happy Birthday, Jasper!"

Primo offered the same good wishes with equal enthusiasm.

##########

THE LAW ENFORCEMENT OFFICERS commenced their rolling surveillance as soon as Jasper entered the sedan.

"They're heading downtown on Third Avenue," radioed Markie to the federal agents. After a block, he provided the feds with a description of the vehicle and a plate number

"Got it," replied Leardi. "We'll travel along the next avenue. Let us know if he turns, and we'll pick him up."

"He's coming your way," advised Markie after Primo signaled a left turn. "He just turned on Ninth Street toward Hamilton Avenue," later conveyed Markie.

"Okay, Al, I got it. We'll pick him up on Ninth Street and get behind him," advised Leardi. Several minutes later, the agent posted Markie. "He's heading into Red Hook, Al."

"Copy, I'll go to Van Brunt Street and pick him up there if he goes that far," said Markie.

The law enforcement officers followed the vehicle to where it came to a halt in a desolate area on Conover Street.

##########

PRIMO SLOWED UP THE CAR TO make an announcement. "I have to take a leak," he said.

"*Now* you gotta tap a kidney?" asked Nino.

"What do you want from me? I'm busting over here. I'm going to Conover Street and make a pit stop."

309

Conover Street after business hours was a rarely traveled commercial roadway. The lack of lighting and remoteness of the area caused Jasper's antennas to immediately rise. He became convinced that foul play was afoot when Nino seemed to be fidgeting in the back seat. Jasper put his hand on the gun inside his jacket pocket, silently cursing himself for being such a fool. Adhering to the adage that he who hesitates is lost, Jasper moved to withdraw the gun from his pocket. He had trouble freeing his weapon due to the small size of his pocket. This obstacle afforded Nino the chance to loop a wire over Jasper's neck. As the realization of assassination set in, Jasper fought frantically for his life. He finally tore the revolver from his pocket. Using his left hand he tried to wedge his fingers between the wire and his neck. Primo was quick to spot the gun in Jasper's hand. He quickly reached across the seat in an effort to wrestle the weapon away from the man being strangled. With bulging eyes, Jasper managed to pull the trigger before he was relieved of his gun. The shot was deafening to those inside the vehicle. The wayward bullet entered the dashboard.

Primo, enraged over the damage to his new car, began smashing Jasper's face with the Colt revolver he had taken off him. The blows sustained by Jasper were severe enough to make his face swell to distorted proportions. The scent of gunpowder now mixed freely with that of the booze. When the garroting was completed the cousins took a moment to catch their breath.

"Shit, look at what you did," said Nino disapprovingly. "Silky's not going to like his faced messed up."

"Screw his face! Look at my dashboard!" countered Primo.

"So you'll get the hole in the dashboard fixed. But for right now, we got a bigger problem. . . . What are we going to tell Silky about this jerk-off getting banged up?"

Primo thought for a moment before responding. "We'll tell him that Jasper put up one hell of a fight. Besides, he had a gun, didn't he?"

"Yeah, maybe if we show Silky the gun, he'll believe us."

"C'mon, Nino, let's do what we gotta do and get out of here." Primo quickly tore Jasper's pants pockets and removed his wallet, watch, and ring. He put the victim's gun in his own pocket to later show Silky. "C'mon, let's dump him in the street."

THE SURVEILLANCE TEAMS HAD SECURED POSITIONS far enough away from Primo's car to avoid detection. Although the investigators had their binoculars trained on the target vehicle, they were still unable to clearly determine what was going on inside the car. The first radio communication came from the feds.

"Can you see what they're doing?" transmitted Leardi.

"We can't tell much of what's going on from this end," replied Markie. "Maybe they're waiting for someone to show up," conjectured the sergeant. "Where are you guys parked?"

"Not too far away. We can see the car, but with this rain, forget about it. How is your vantage point?"

"We're okay. We're behind a dumpster. We can see them sitting in the car, but that's about it."

The authorities didn't have a long wait before a firecracker-like sound could be heard in the distance.

"WHAT THE . . . ?" shouted Von Hess. "The inside of the car just lit up with that pop!"

"It's a hit!" declared Markie excitedly, recognizing the sight of a muzzle blast from a gun.

"They're getting out of the car, Sarge," said Von Hess, who was still looking through his binoculars. "I can't believe this; we caught them right in the act. It looks like they're pulling a body out of the car!"

The sergeant alerted the federal agents as to what had just occurred. "Let's move in," said Markie. "We'll take the driver."

"We're rolling," replied Leardi. "We'll get the passenger."

Markie removed the snub-nosed revolver from the holster he carried on the side of his body. "Watch your ass on this one, Ollie."

The two teams converged on the unsuspecting assassins simultaneously. Markie and Von Hess pounced on Primo, while the federal agents focused on Nino.

"POLICE! DON'T MOVE!" screamed Von Hess as he drew down on Primo. "Put your hands on top of the dashboard!" Leardi issued similar instruction to Nino at the point of a gun.

The killers were taken completely off guard. Stunned, all they could think to do was comply.

"Spread 'em, *Jack*," Von Hess barked at Primo.

Primo's hesitation in complying resulted in Von Hess swatting him upside his head with his pistol. Now paying attention, Primo spread out against his car. The killer allowed himself to be disarmed of two guns and handcuffed by Markie. Agent Leardi answered Nino's disinclination to cooperate expeditiously by punching him in the midsection with the barrel of his gun. The blow dropped Nino to his knees with the wind knocked out of him. He was then easily relieved of a gun and handcuffed. In all, the killing wire and three firearms were recovered. Primo and Nino were placed in different cars for transporting. The prisoners looked at each other through the backseat window of their respective vehicles with dour faces.

Markie looked down at Jasper, who was lying belly down in the gutter with his face in a puddle. The drizzle had now changed to fat plopping raindrops. Ripples could be seen as each raindrop struck a puddle. The sergeant took Jasper by the shoulder and turned him over to take a look at his face. It wasn't a pretty sight to behold, even for Markie. Since there had been a shot fired, Markie looked for a bullet hole in Jasper. To his surprise, he found none. A closer inspection of Jasper's body made it evident that the homicide victim had been garroted. Markie instructed Von Hess to check Primo's car. After doing so, Von Hess reported back.

"The bullet we heard must have been a stray shot. There's a bullet lodged in the dashboard."

"Well, I guess this really puts the lid on things, Al," said Leardi.

"I'd say that's about the size of it," agreed Markie. "Ollie, give a call over to the Seven-Six squad. Tell them that they caught a homicide that's already been solved for them."

"How do you want to handle the prisoners?" asked Leardi, joining the detectives.

"We might as well just transport them to the Seven-Six Precinct and interview them there with the precinct squad. This homicide is their case."

"You aren't going to take this over?" asked Leardi, surprised.

"No, this is for the local squad. Our case is solved," answered Markie. "Jasper killed Cornell Mathis, and now he's dead. So that's that. Let's try to work with he precinct squad to try and break these two bozos. Maybe we can clear up ome homicides, and you guys can try to gather some information relative to he narcotics piece."

"Without Jasper, it looks like the end of the trail for us as well, unless these wo got something to say," said Leardi.

"It'll be interesting to find out *why* Jasper got clipped," said Markie.

"We still have a couple of other things to do, Sarge," Von Hess reminded him.

"Yeah, I know, Ollie. There are some loose ends to tie up. But before I forget, 'll notify Lieutenant Wright. He'll want to post the chief right away."

"We'll have to notify Lieutenant Darkenlove that she can clear the Mathis homicide," noted Von Hess.

"Yeah, that's right. The Mathis homicide was Pearlie's case."

"We should also probably take a trip out to Staten Island, right, boss?" asked Von Hess.

"Yeah, we should be the ones to break the news to the Mathis widow. And we have to get that ring from Eustice and return it to the old man down south."

33

The Clock Runs Out

SILKY WAS SHELTERED FROM THE RAIN by the oversized black umbrella he held over his head. Trying to minimize the damage to his soft red suede loafers, he was careful to avoid the puddles as he walked. He wasn't traveling far, just to the corner medical office a short distance from his social club. The purpose of his visit was to see his longtime physician, a man who was a habitual gambler.

The receptionist looked up over her glasses at the visitor who entered the office. Without speaking, the two acknowledged each other with a polite smile and nod. Silky passed through a white door that separated the waiting area from the work areas unannounced. When he came to the private office of Doctor Chukwuma Abebe, he tapped lightly prior to entering. The physician, a middle-aged man of average size, was with a patient. Startled by the intrusion, the doctor's mouth dropped open. He removed his glasses, placed them atop his desk, and concentrated on his visitor.

"What do you say, Doc?" asked the gangster.

"Excuse me, but this is an emergency case," explained the doctor, turning to his patient. He abruptly curtailed the consultation. "Don't worry; everything will be fine. Make an appointment out front to see me next week after the test results come back."

After Doctor Abebe saw the patient out, he returned to shake hands with Silky.

"What's the count?"

"The count?" asked the puzzled medico.

"How many did you croak today?"

The physician smiled tolerantly. "Here," said Abebe, reaching into his pocket for a vial of pills. "Take one twenty minutes prior to engaging. The effects will last approximately two hours."

"I know the routine, Doc."

"Have you been taking your regular medicine, Settimo?"

"Sure I have."

"You must heed what I tell you. Your health is nothing to take lightly," warned the physician.

"Don't worry about me. I take my medicine like a champ, Doc. I rely on those pills as much as these weenie stretchers you give me."

The doctor nodded approvingly. "Very effective, Viagra. Keeps you up, up, up!" said Abebe, jabbing his finger toward the ceiling each time he said the word *up*.

"Are you coming to the game at the Bridgehorn Hotel tomorrow night? I'll have the boys hold a seat at the table for you."

"Who will be playing?"

"A flock of pigeons from Houston," replied Silky. "They're back in town this weekend. You remember those guys; you cleaned up that time you played with them."

"Yes, I remember them!" said Abebe excitedly. "Those men were *very* poor card players." The doctor was now clearly very interested. "It will be regular poker . . . no wild cards, right?"

"We don't entertain that crap; it'll be straight poker all night. The game starts at the regular time," advised Silky. "We'll put out a spread and have plenty of booze. What's your drink again?"

"Remy Martin, as I remember. They ran out last time."

"Yeah, I heard about it. The boys said you put it down like you was a sink. Don't worry; this time we'll have all you can handle."

"You got any tips for me if I go to Belmont Park Sunday?"

"Just one, Doc: all gamblers die broke."

##########

AN IMPORTANT FIGURE IN SILKY'S LIFE was his beautiful mistress, Eva. A former prostitute, she contributed heavily to the image he wanted to maintain. Having her at his side over dinner represented evidence of his virility in a macho world where proof trumped talk. In return for her agreeability, the much younger woman was well compensated. She lived rent free in the apartment house Silky owned, was given plenty of spending money, and never had to worry about working for a living. The gangster's expectations were relatively simple. Eva had to be available when he called, never embarrass him when in the company of his friends, and comport herself in a way that made other men desire her. From Eva's standpoint, being the other woman was far better than being a wife. Cooking, cleaning, and raising a family was not on Eva's to-do list. Having known what it was to hustle in order to make her way, she appreciated the limited labor that came with satisfying the libido of an aging sugar daddy.

"I thought my steak was a just a little tough tonight," Eva said after returning to the apartment.

"Mine was fine. Why didn't you say something? I'd have made them take it back."

"It wasn't terrible, just not as good as usual."

"Whatever," commented Silky. "Go on inside and get ready. I'll be there in a little while."

As Eva prepared herself, Silky popped a pill and sat at the kitchen table smoking his last De Nobili cigar. As he waited for the pill to take hold, he tore apart the now-empty cigar pack. To amuse himself, he set fire to the cellophane wrapping after placing it in the ashtray. Staring blankly as if in a trance, he watched it burn out. Then he did the same with the cardboard packaging and the matchbook cover. The burning of these items seemed to hold a strange fascination for him, as it did with many men of his ilk.

"What, are you turning into some kind of pyromaniac?" asked Eva loudly after emerging from the bathroom clad only in a bathrobe.

"Relax. I'm just killing time."

"Don't be too long. I'm waiting."

"I'll be there in a few minutes."

"And put out that cigar! It stinks up the apartment!"

Minutes later, one of Sinatra's easy listening tunes could be heard coming from the bedroom. For Eva, the crooning of Ol' Blue Eyes provided the mood for what was to follow. The singer's soothing voice also served as a cue for Silky to get moving. The gangster took the hint. He rose from the kitchen table and began undoing his pants as he proceeded to the bedroom. After a moment or two of robotic foreplay, Silky flipped his lover over onto her knees. Rather than the sensual pace set by Sinatra, the mobster's jackhammer execution was more n sync with Rossini's energetic *William Tell* Overture. All that was missing to complete the scene was her Lone Ranger's shout of "Hi-ho, Silver! Away!"

Silky rose at the crack of dawn. He slipped out of bed quietly, not wanting to wake up his girlfriend. The mobster proceeded to the bathroom, where he smoked as he shaved. After showering, he removed clean underwear and socks from the bedroom dresser. The oversized, baggy white boxer shorts he wore drew attention to his pale, spindly legs.

After dressing, the mobster put on a pot of coffee and took a seat at the kitchen table. As he waited for the coffee to brew, he lit up his second cigarette of the new day. He was debating whether or not to bring home some Italian bread and a ball of fresh mozzarella to his wife. Seconds after inhaling a deep drag, he was suddenly struck by a crushing chest pain. Cognizant of the seriousness of the attack, he knew that he needed to get to the dynamite pills that were in his jacket pocket in the next room. Silky's effort to get to his feet resulted in his collapsing back into his chair. His second attempt to rise caused him to fall to the floor. The noise made by the tumble stirred his girlfriend from her sleep. She raised her head a few inches from the bed.

"Silky?" she called out.

Silky was able to muster enough strength to inch himself over to the closest wall, where he was able to lean against it. The notion that he might be nearing the closing of his days began to consume him. With Judgment Day being the one thing Silky feared, religion suddenly became of paramount importance. All of his skullduggery *and* those murders! How could he possibly expect to be absolved of these wicked acts without some outside help to run interference? Silky saw a priest's general absolution as the only angle to escape eternal damnation. He was determined to hang on until a man of the cloth arrived. Unfortunately, the stress connected to his anguish only accelerated his expiration.

"Stop fooling around and come back to bed," called out Eva.

Receiving no response, she got out of bed to investigate. She was startled to see Silky on the floor.

"Silky! My God, what happened?"

"My pills . . . in my jacket . . ."

"I'll go get them," she replied, rushing off to the next room.

Silky let out a groan when she returned with a glass of water and his Viagra pills. He knew he was a goner at this point. "Get me a priest." His words came out feebly.

"Don't you want your pill?" asked Eva, trying to be helpful. Silky never responded.

Two police officers were the first to arrive at the apartment. The officers jotted down the information they received from Eva for use in their report.

"He has a wife on Long Island someplace, but he stays by me a lot," she explained.

"Are you a relative?" asked one of the officers.

"Oh no, we're more like . . . good friends."

The mistress turned to look down at the dead man on the floor. He seemed so small that she could hardly believe that it was really Silky. One look at his pallid face would convince anyone that he was on the journey to where people go when the hourglass runs out. Still, Eva sought further confirmation. Verification came from one of the cops.

"Is he really gone?" she asked, hoping her assessment was erroneous.

"I'd have to say so, ma'am," replied the older officer. "The ambulance should be here shortly."

She bit down on her lip once, realizing that life as she knew it was now going to change. The sad truth was that, to the best of her knowledge, Silky had never gotten around to making those arrangements he had promised. All that she was left with were memories of bony legs, jackhammer sex, and false promises of future security. She turned on the deceased with a vengeance as reality set in.

"Unbelievable! How could this selfish old bastard drop dead on me like this?" she asked aloud. "What am I supposed to do now?"

"I don't know, ma'am," answered one of the officers. Both cops were surprised at her outburst.

"You have to get him out of here. I don't want him found dead in my apartment."

The officers spoke to the EMTs privately when they arrived. They agreed to pronounce Silky dead when en route to the hospital as opposed to at the apartment.

"Are you going to be alright?" the older officer asked.

"I'll be alright," replied the kept woman, now realizing that she was attired only in flimsy sleepwear. Not the bashful sort, she felt no awkwardness. "Can I get his jewelry and money?" she asked the cop in the sweetest of voices.

The older officer wasn't amenable to the idea. "You aren't a relative, are you?"

"No. . . . I'm a *good* friend."

"Does he live here with you?"

"No, he just stays over a lot. He's married."

"I see. We have to voucher *all* his property and hold it for his wife. She can claim it later."

After Silky's body was removed, it was Eva's turn to collapse. With her back against the wall, she slid down into a sitting position on the floor where Silky had been. Her head lowered between her legs, she was deep in thought. Where was she ever going to find another Silky?

##########

AT THE PRECINCT, THE BASILE COUSINS WERE PLACED in separate offices. The squad detectives who had caught the case of Jasper's homicide had all the evidence they needed thanks to Markie and Von Hess having been eyewitnesses to the crime. Their case being solved, the squad detectives had no problem stepping back to let Markie, Von Hess, and the two federal agents grill the prisoners. Each prisoner was allowed to make the one phone call he was entitled to. Not permitted to communicate with each other, the cousins were unable to strategize. Through the night, each man repeatedly dialed the same cell phone number until someone finally answered the ring. Primo was the first to get through.

"Silky?"

"No, this isn't Silky. Who is this?"

"Who are you?" asked Primo after verifying the number he had dialed. Primo was stunned to learn he was speaking to a police officer. "Is Silky busted?" he asked.

"Who is this?" asked the officer.

Seeing that there was a problem, Markie took the phone from Primo. Once he learned that Silky was no longer among the living, he updated Primo. Without even the name of a lawyer to call, the prisoner shook his head in disbelief.

Questioning the cousins individually led to unearthing no pertinent information. As a last-ditch effort to gain the cooperation of the cousins, Markie decided to try talking to both men at the same time. He felt that cooperating might not seem such an awful option if it were packaged in the form of a buddy system. His idea worked. Each cousin, encouraged by the presence of the other, was more amenable to listening. Collectively, the cousins realized there was just one path to take. They agreed to cooperate with both agencies in return for the opportunity to enter a witness protection program. After filling out the appropriate papers, the two cousins admitted their involvement in every crime they participated in, including their role in the murder of Lemon, Buster, Otto and Jasper.

Throughout the night, Markie, Von Hess, and the federal agents were told of crimes involving Silky and his crew. The only person the cousins didn't seem know about was Cornell Mathis. Although unable to provide specifics, the cousins did convey that Silky had relatives in Canada who were rumored to be into drugs. The information provided by Primo and Nino ultimately facilitated the clearance of numerous unsolved organized crime–related cases. Between the two informers, the authorities were also privy to a wealth of intelligence concerning the Guarini organized crime family.

After giving their statement to the district attorney's office as to what had occurred, Markie and Von Hess had traveled as far as they needed to. Markie passed the baton to other members of law enforcement to pursue their own interests.

"Let's go for a shot, Ollie," suggested the sergeant after going off duty.

"Where do you want to go?"

"Let's go to Fitzie's. He'll be there."

"Okay, just one," agreed the detective. "I guess we earned it. Maybe we can get Fitzie to recite that poem about the artist who turned to drink. He still does it, right?"

"Yeah, he still does it . . . that is, when he's not broadcasting the blow-by-blow of one of the big fights."

34

Winners and Losers

CHIEF OF DETECTIVES HARRY MCCOY resided quietly in a one-bedroom apartment in Stuyvesant Town, a residential development on the East Side of Manhattan. It was Saturday morning, his day off, when the phone rang, interrupting his breakfast of coffee, juice, and oatmeal. It was Lieutenant Wright notifying the bachelor of what had transpired the prior evening. Learning of Jasper's homicide came as a bit of a disappointment. McCoy was looking forward to having Jasper face the news cameras in handcuffs.

"That's too bad. A perp-walk would have made for great optics," said the chief. "Who killed him?"

"We *caught* a couple mob guys in the act of whacking him," advised Wright.

"You did?" asked the delighted McCoy. "Beautiful!"

"And we got the shooters to cooperate."

"Even better, did they say why they killed him?"

"They had no idea. All they knew was that they received the order from Silky Seggio."

"They've been trying to nail Seggio for years. . . ."

"Yeah, I know, Chief. But Seggio is dead too."

"He got clipped? What's going on out there . . . a war?"

"From what I'm getting, he died of a heart attack."

After hanging up the phone the chief began humming one of his favorite tunes. He spent the day cleaning his apartment. Late in the afternoon he went to the Strand Bookstore to pick up a secondhand book to read. That evening, after dinner, he made himself an Irish coffee. He sat comfortably in his brown leather recliner with his legs up. He reached for the newly purchased book on his end table. Quite content, he began reading *The Informer*, a novel by Liam O'Flaherty. After reading several chapters, he wanted to know more about the author. His research left the chief in a soured state after discovering that the novelist was a founding member of the Communist Party of Ireland. In response to learning this, he rearranged his bookcase. He buried O'Flaherty's work behind a framed autographed picture of Joyce Kilmer, the hero poet who was killed in action during the First World War. By the following morning, McCoy was over his snit. Rising early, he couldn't wait to get to headquarters to see his friend the police commissioner.

Commissioner Randolph had just sat down at his desk to check his messages when the chief tapped on the door to his office. Randolph could see by the look on McCoy's face that he was bringing good tidings.

"What are you so happy about, Harry?" asked the commissioner. "You finally found yourself a wife?"

"I got something good, John," announced the chief, ignoring the remark. "I cracked the Mathis case."

"Which one was that again? Refresh my memory, Harry."

"Mathis was the National Guardsman who disappeared thirty-something years ago."

McCoy apprised Randolph of the details of the now-solved mystery and the subsequent developments. When he completed his account, there were now two happy men in the office.

"Outstanding! Beautiful, Harry . . . just beautiful!" said the commissioner. "We actually witnessed the murder of the man responsible for killing Sergeant Mathis?"

"We were right there on the spot."

"It's the kind of stuff the public laps up. Give it to our friends in the press so they can play it up."

Commissioner Randolph telephoned the mayor on his cell phone. After hearing the facts, the mayor congratulated the commissioner on his good work. He then mentioned to the PC that he was on his way to a conference in Europe. He neglected to tell him that he had his wife, kids, and golf clubs with him.

##########

EUSTUCE SEARCHED FOR HIS NAME ON THE LIST of those slated for promotion. When he realized that his name wasn't there, he crumpled the paper and threw t to the ground. While his performance in the Mathis case had been laudable, it didn't warrant a promotion to second grade detective this time around. The powers to be felt that a transfer into Agent Leardi's C-9 cocaine group at the Drug Enforcement Administration Task Force would be enough of a reward for a ob well done. Once beyond his disappointment, Eustice put things in perspective. Working in the DEA was the next best thing to getting upped a grade. The position came with benefits, one of them being assigned a take-home car. Eustice was allotted a Checker Cab to serve as his means of transportation. The cab would be his to use until a new case created the opportunity to confiscate a more suitable vehicle. When in the mood for mischief, Eustice would toy with the public. He would ride home in his cab with the on-duty light on, slowing up for people who hailed him for a ride. After making it seem as if he intended to pick them up, he would suddenly change his mind and speed away. He got a hoot out of looking into his rearview mirror to watch the reactions of the irate people.

Working for the feds granted Eustice the freedom to self-initiate a narcotics investigation anywhere in the city. Once established, Eustice reached out to Brenda, the former bartender at the James Brothers Saloon. After convincing her that he alone had rescued her from getting in trouble, the two got reacquainted. Brenda was soon signed up as a DEA confidential informant. She eventually learned that her friend Sandy was also an informant. It made being a snitch easier for both of them.

########

SPANKY'S DECISION TO COOPERATE WITH THE GOVERNMENT came with an unanticipated price. Once made aware of his criminal activities, his father-in-law had the ammunition necessary to convince his daughter to leave her husband. Even Spanky's mother-in-law had to go along with launching a campaign to oust Spanky from the family. With Jasper dead, Spanky ended up serving an abbreviated sentence.

Spanky was relocated to South Dakota, where he lived under the new name of Elmo Basquette. He earned his living driving a tour bus. While at work, he came into contact with a widow from Rapid City who was taking a tour of Deadwood with a visiting relative. While stopping at the well-maintained grave of Wild Bill

Hickok in Deadwood's Mount Moriah Cemetery, Spanky overheard the two women conversing. The widow mentioned the large insurance payout she had received after the accidental death of her husband. Still being a handsome man, Spanky seized the first opportunity to engage the woman in conversation. Fortunately for him, she was receptive to his small talk as well as to his suggestive advances. After getting her number, the former drug dealer pursued her diligently. In time they grew close enough for Spanky to convince the widow to join him on a weekend jaunt to Las Vegas. To Spanky's delight, she agreed to experience the Ride-Em Ranch. At the conclusion of the trip, she felt so connected to him that she urged Spanky to move into her home in Rapid City. Soon after, they made it official and married. This union enabled the former drug dealer to secure the financing he needed to launch his own sightseeing enterprise. As the business grew, the couple began taking Vegas jaunts on a regular basis. It was their favorite getaway destination.

##########

THE BASILE COUSINS WERE CALLED UPON to work for their freedom. They testified at numerous federal and state criminal proceedings against organized crime figures they had interacted with over the years. Their knowledge of the Guarini crime family doings was considered invaluable to the authorities. As a result of their cooperation, a number of mobsters were placed behind bars.

After serving their sentence, the cousins, like Spanky, entered the witness protection program. They relocated to Madison, Wisconsin, under the assumed names of Alex and Jimmy Altimore. The cousins opened up a small business called Altimore's Pizzeria. The enterprise did well once the cousins figured out a cost-effective way to transport New York City tap water into their new home state. The secret to making New York City pizza was in the water.

Socially, the cousins frequented the bar at a Best Western, where they mingled with the locals. Being something of a novelty, the cousins drew the attention of two women whom they later got seriously involved with. With hardworking girlfriends of integrity in the mix, the duo transformed a small pizzeria into Altimore's Italian Gardens. The cousins went on to marry without ever sharing tales of their days in the Brooklyn underworld.

########

WHEN THE DETECTIVES RAIDED THE HOME OF VITO THE BLADE, they found him cooking himself potatoes and eggs. After being taken into custody, the elderly assassin sat at his kitchen table rear-cuffed. Although he remained silent, his outward appearance spoke volumes. His piercing eyes conveyed pure disdain as he watched the law intrude upon his sanctuary. After finding an illegal handgun in his barbershop, the authorities focused their attention on his apartment. The elderly cutthroat had little choice other than to take these infringements without protest. He waited patiently, hoping that they would soon complete their search.

The joyous outburst of those tasked with searching put an end to Vito's fantasy hope. The first roar of triumphant discovery was when the law came upon Buster and Q-Ball Otto in their cellar grave. Vito was shocked to see that they knew exactly where to look for the bodies. He figured correctly that they must have gotten their information from Primo or Nino, perhaps both. To Vito's further dismay, the police continued digging until they found an additional body underneath the cement in another part of the cellar. Their finding was later identified as the assassin's wife, who had become problematic due to her Alzheimer's. Vito began to wonder if they'd dig up the yard and find the others. But at this point, what did it really matter? His life as a free man was over.

In prison, Vito was received with great respect by fellow inmates. No one came close to topping the whopping body count that the elderly hit man had amassed. Ever the survivor, the assassin went on to consider his life sentence to be a gift. Being with those of his ilk twenty-four-seven wasn't too shabby an arrangement at this point in his life. He played cards every day, told mob stories to those with an interest, provided counsel regarding the rules of mob life, and wasn't burdened with many of the frets connected to old age. He ate regularly, slept well, always had company, and received medical care when needed. Vito's advanced age protected him from being bothered by other inmates because humbling him would prove little. When the grim reaper made a house call to the cell of Vito the Blade, the prisoner was nearing his eighty-ninth birthday. A correctional officer found him curled up in a ball on his bed. Vito's exit came peacefully in his sleep. It was a nice way to go and more than he deserved.

LAS VEGAS LUCY'S COOPERATION AGREEMENT WITH THE FEDERAL GOVERNMENT went sour soon after she began telling the feds what she thought they wanted to hear rather than what actually was true. Her chicanery was ultimately her undoing. She failed to take into consideration that the information she put forth to the agents would be later verified or disproven by their conversations with other informants. After it was ascertained that some of the information provided by Las Vegas Lucy was total fabrication, her value to the government became worthless. Exposure as a perjurer revoked her agreement.

Banished to a jail cell, she began serving her full sentence. It took money to make incarceration bearable. An avenue of relief arose when a correctional officer seemed to take an interest in her. The officer, who worked overnight, was someone she was able to compromise though flirtation. Eventually he became amenable to smuggling items into the prison for Lucy in return for nocturnal favors. Another inmate, seeing this as a good thing, decided to move in on Lucy's intimacy with the officer. It eventually came down to a physical confrontation in which Lucy blindsided the competition with a vicious attack from the rear. The impact of repeatedly banging the assaulted woman's head on the ground caused her death, thus sealing Lucy's fate. Lucy saw only one solution in order to evade the years of incarceration she was facing. She hung herself in her cell.

##########

WHEN JOHNNY BLONDELL GOT WORD THAT Jasper had been murdered and Silky was dead, he wasted no time in packing a bag with his belongings. Unsure of where he stood in the mix, he wasn't about to wait around to find out. He was going on the lam until the smoke settled. The only stop he made before absconding was to the James Brothers Saloon. He squeezed into his travel bag several bottles of the finest whiskey. He then went behind the bar to salvage whatever money that was in the register. It was just when he had his hand in the till that Scratchy the bartender showed up at the bar.

"What are you doing, Johnny?"

"Didn't you hear about what happened?"

"No, what happened?"

"Jasper got whacked."

"Whacked?" asked Scratchy. "Says who?"

"Never mind who. I got tipped."

"Oh shit. What do we do now?"

"What the hell do you think?" asked Johnny. "I'm taking what I can and tearing out. If you're smart, you'll do likewise."

"Why do I have to book? What did I do?"

"You saw what happened to Mousey, didn't you?" asked Johnny. "Now it's Jasper who gets it, and my best friend all of a sudden drops dead. . . . Well, I'm not sticking around to find out why."

"But I didn't do anything. Why should I go?"

"Then stay and take your chances. Me? I'm splitting."

Scratchy now began wondering if he should be doing the same thing. "Where are you going?"

"I'm thinking maybe Texas or Florida."

"So you think it's all over for everybody here?"

"C'mon, you know it is."

"You want company?" asked Scratchy. Johnny paused to look at Scratchy. "I know where Jasper and Mousey had some shit stashed."

"You do?" asked Johnny, now showing interest.

Scratchy looked at the older man seriously. "I saw them, but they didn't see me. Are we partners?"

"Okay, Scratchy. Show me where the shit is."

"Are we partners?" repeated the bartender.

"You got a deal."

"C'mon, then, follow me."

The two men went down to the cellar. Johnny watched as Scratchy removed a box that was secreted under the floorboards behind the boiler. Scratchy opened the box and discovered a kilo of cocaine and 36,000 dollars in cash. Had he known how much cash was there, Scratchy would have never shared the information with Johnny Blondell.

"Bingo!" said the wide-eyed Johnny.

"What's the plan, Johnny?"

"We're going to Florida. I know some people down there who can help us move this shit."

After splitting the found money, Johnny and Scratchy made their way to Fort Lauderdale, where they soon began selling coke. Scratchy unwittingly sold coke to an undercover cop. When Johnny was notified by Scratchy that he was in police custody, he asked Scratchy where he kept his money.

"Why do you want to know?"

"You need a lawyer, don't you?" replied Johnny.

Once Johnny got his hands on all the money, he took off, leaving Scratchy in Florida high and dry.

Lots of people wondered whatever happened to Johnny Blondell. Probably the last place anyone would think to look was the Dominican Republic.

35

Perfume or Liniment?

MRS. MATHIS-JOHNSON WAS CONDUCTING AN INSPECTION of her house before her guests arrived. When the doorbell rang, she checked her watch for the time. Before answering the door, she looked out the front window to see who it was. Surprised to see the detectives, she adjusted her clothing and felt the points of her spiked hair. Satisfied that all was in order, she opened the door.

"Oh . . . hi," she said. "I wasn't expecting you, gentlemen. Come in. I *am* expecting friends from my book club," she explained. "We meet monthly for lunch. What brings you gentlemen here?"

"We have some news for you," advised Markie.

"I hope it's about Arthur's ring. He's been complaining that you still have it."

"We didn't forget him. In fact, it'll be in the mail today. He'll get it tomorrow or the day after."

"You should call him and let him know. He'll be glad to hear that."

"Here is the picture you loaned us of Cornell," said Markie, handing her the photograph.

"Thank you," she said in a subdued voice.

"We just figured that you would want to know how things went down."

"Went down?" she asked in a puzzled way. "What do you mean?"

"Bring Mrs. Mathis-Johnson up to speed, Ollie."

Von Hess was used to being called upon whenever Markie didn't feel like talking. As usual, the veteran detective rose to the occasion. "Well, one of the first things we did after we last saw you was to conduct a thorough search of the armory. . . ." began Von Hess, carefully choosing his words.

Mrs. Mathis-Johnson listened attentively as Von Hess articulated the case facts. The former Marine's military bearing presented him as clearly alpha.

When Mrs. Mathis-Johnson placed her index finger to her lips while listening, Markie took this be a sign of attraction. At the conclusion of the briefing, both detectives were surprised to see that there was no emotional reaction coming from Ms. Mathis-Johnson. There were no tears, nor did she exhibit any signs of relief.

"Do you know why he was murdered?" she asked.

"No ma'am. We have nothing concrete in terms of why."

"But it was definitely those two who did it?"

"No doubt about it. It was the two privates who reported to your husband that weekend at the armory. Both of them are now dead."

"How did they die?"

"One died of natural causes, and one was a homicide victim."

"He was murdered?"

"Yes. It was an organized crime thing."

The eyes of Mrs. Mathis-Johnson suddenly widened. "Cornell was mixed up with organized crime?"

"No ma'am, not at all," assured Von Hess. "Nothing suggests that."

"I didn't think so," she said. "So you have no idea *why* they killed Cornell?"

"There was probably a disagreement of some kind. Most likely the similarity to Cornell's stepfather contributed to the conflict. But we have no way of knowing that for sure."

Mrs. Mathis-Johnson nodded her head understandingly. Voices could be heard at the front door. It was the company Mrs. Mathis had been expecting.

"It's the girls," she said.

"If you don't have any further questions for us, we'll be leaving," said Markie.

Stepping between six visiting woman, the detectives made their way to the door. Once back in the car, Markie decided to have some fun with Von Hess. "She had her eye on you, Ollie."

"Who did?"

"The grieving widow," replied the sergeant.

"C'mon. . . ."

"What, are you kidding? Didn't you see the way she was looking at you?"

"I didn't notice. Besides, to get me off the reservation, it'll take the lure of perfume, not liniment."

Markie and Von Hess next went to see Eustice at his home. They went there or the purpose of picking up the wolf head ring.

"He's still asleep," advised Mrs. Costello." I'll get him up," she advised.

"Please, if you don't mind," said Markie.

"I can't tell you how much he loves his new job with the federal task force. He's a new man."

"He is?"

"He's been very happy. You have no idea. . . . It's like he's been reborn."

"Why, that's wonderful."

"It really is remarkable. The only negative thing is that his work hours are eally unpredictable," advised Mrs. Costello. "The new assignment keeps him out all night at least once a week," she added. "But I guess you can't expect everything. He keeps telling me that he'll be getting a luxury car assigned to him at some point this year." The detectives nodded agreeably, not venturing further into that topic.

When Mrs. Costello left the room to fetch her husband, Markie and Von Hess ooked at each other, shaking their heads. After a few minutes, Eustice emerged from the second floor attired in a lightweight red bathrobe. Judging by his bloated facial appearance, the investigators surmised that he was hung over. Mrs. Costello remained upstairs, leaving the three men alone to converse in private.

"Hi, Sarge, what's up?" asked Eustice, fingering the grit out of his eyes.

"We came to pick up the wolf head ring," said Markie. "We have to mail it to the rightful owner."

Eustice, who had grown fond of wearing the ring, came up with an excuse not to return it. "I think the feds want me to hang on to it, boss. The target in this new case I'm on noticed it. It'll look funny if all of a sudden I'm not wearing it anymore," he lied.

Markie didn't like Eustice's excuse or his thinking that he could play one agency against the other.

"Cut the bullshit and get the ring," ordered the sergeant, his patience exhausted.

"But Sarge . . ."

"Don't 'Sarge' me! Look, Eustice, you did a good job on the case we worked," said Markie. "I'll give you that. And I got no problem with you milking the DEA for what you can get. But I'm going to give you a piece of sound advice: don't press your luck with me."

"What do you mean, boss?" the detective asked, sounding as innocent as possible.

"You know what I mean, so go stroke someone else. Get the ring before I stick one up your ass."

Realizing that Markie was prepared to write up a formal complaint caused the detective to back off. Eustice knew that a written reprimand on his record could be used as an excuse to short-circuit a future promotion. The task force detective saw it prudent to retrieve the ring from his bedroom dresser forthwith. He returned to hand the ring over to Markie without speaking.

"I'll wait in the car," announced Markie. The decision to leave the room was a cue for Von Hess to *talk* to Eustice.

Once Markie was out of the house, Eustice immediately vented to Von Hess. "Just who the hell does that son of a bitch think he is?" he asked. "My ass was the one on the line working undercover . . . not his! I could probably get *him* bounced back to uniform *if* I beef loud enough to the feds."

Von Hess responded with the levelheadedness he was noted for. "You can do what you want, Eustice. But let me ask you something: do you want to see a promotion someday?" asked the senior detective.

"Of course I do. Why the hell do you think I'm doing all this . . . for shits and giggles?"

"No, I think you're doing it because it's to your advantage."

"So what if it is?"

"Let me clue you in, pal. You'll never get promoted if Markie blackballs you to Chief McCoy."

"Are you telling me I got no chance for grade without Markie behind me?"

"I'm saying that if the sergeant knocks you to McCoy, you'll have no shot at all."

"What are you talking about?" asked Eustice, skeptical of what he was hearing. "Markie hasn't got that type of pull. He's only a sergeant for Christ's sake."

Von Hess got tired of fencing with the undercover detective. "You can be pretty cute, Eustice. But in some things you really aren't all that smart."

"Huh? What the hell are you talking about?"

"Do you honestly think you've fooled anyone?" asked Von Hess. "You padded expenses, pocketed money when gambling, and did all the other shit that goes along with running amok. Need I go on?"

Eustice took the offensive. "I've done nothing illegal, immoral, or unethical."

Von Hess shut him down. "Look, Markie doesn't miss a trick. He only chooses to overlook. He can paint a picture that reflects you as a contamination to McCoy's *pristine* detective bureau. The sergeant even knows all about that barmaid you're playing around with."

Eustice gasped at hearing this. "C'mon, Ollie . . ." he said timidly.

"Look, I'm no boss," said Von Hess. "You can do whatever you choose to do. I'm just wising you up. If and when the hammer drops, don't say you weren't warned."

Eustice looked at Von Hess seriously. "Did Markie say he was going to do something?"

"Listen to what *I'm* telling you. Once your integrity comes into question by the bosses, it's over. There is no value to a rotten apple. Think about that."

After Von Hess left the house Eustice went to bed. It was definitely better to sleep than worry.

36

Finders Keepers

FISHNET WAS DREAMING THAT TWO German shepherds stood alongside his bed growling menacingly. Each hound began to push forward its snout in his direction while snipping at him viciously. Feeling threatened, Fishnet started throwing crisp jabs at each dog, with each blow just falling short of the intended target. Stretching to make contact, his second barrage of punches came close enough for Fishnet to feel the moistness of one animal's nose on his knuckles. Desperate to hit home, he lunged forward fiercely in a dramatic effort to strike one of his targets squarely. This thrust resulted in Fishnet crashing his fist into the television that hung down alongside his bed. The stinging pain emanating from his knuckles abruptly woke him from his sleep. Realizing that he had been dreaming, the former detective began to massage his injured hand to alleviate the discomfort.

Fishnet's room at the facility faced a large center courtyard with park-like trimmings. He became distracted from his ache when, glancing out the window, he observed over a dozen people milling around an unoccupied wheelchair. Fishnet could tell by the way people paired off to chat that something unusual had occurred. After noticing that Hope was among the crowd, he made his way outside to find out what all the fuss was about.

"What's all the commotion?" he asked.

Hope pointed to the empty wheelchair. "They just took the poor man away."

"Who are you talking about?"

"The old man with no bottom teeth," she replied, referring to the man Fishnet had nicknamed Old Buzzard. "This was his chair," she added, pointing to the empty wheelchair.

"Where did they take him?"

"They took his body downstairs to the refrigerator."

Instead of dwelling on the fate of Old Buzzard, Fishnet thought of how funeral parlors traditionally gave a few dollars to whoever helped transport a body to their vehicle.

"You know something, Mr. Fish-Hook, life is mysterious. We never know when we'll be called home, so we must always be prepared."

"Yeah, very mysterious," agreed Fishnet.

The former detective transported himself to the mythical world in which he reigned supreme. As the ultimate master in control of the action, he envisioned himself as a brilliant scientist hard at work in a castle dungeon. Attired in a long white apron, he stood over the human specimen who was strapped to an operating table. After admiring his handiwork, he placed the needle and thread atop a nearby table. He had just finished sewing Hope's lips together. Watching his victim's agonizing efforts to undo the stitching with her tongue made this an exceptionally pleasurable fantasy for Fishnet. It came to an end when Hope heard the former detective release a short maniacal giggle that she mistook for weeping.

"Don't you fret now; the poor soul is in a better place," said Hope, referring to Old Buzzard.

"He knew his condition," injected another assistant who was standing nearby. "He should have never let himself get so upset."

"That's true," agreed Hope.

Fishnet, now back, wondered what triggered the old man's agitation. "What got him worked up?"

"He lost his money," advised Hope.

"Did you say money?" asked Fishnet, his eyebrows lifting.

"He lost a thousand dollars," Hope advised. "Imagine his having that much money on him in here."

"His son must have given it to him when he came in to visit from New Jersey," conjectured the other assistant. "What a terrible shame to lose so much money."

"Well, you know what they say about money; it's the root of all evil," said Fishnet with a straight face.

"Now, isn't that the truth," agreed Hope.

Fishnet let out a fake cough, using it as an excuse to make his departure. "It's a little breezy out here for me. I think I'll go back inside and say some prayers for the departed."

Hope noticed the redness on Fishnet's knuckles. "Mr. Fish-Hook, what happened to your hand?"

"It's nothing. I banged it accidently. Maybe I'll soak it later."

Fishnet headed directly to the dead man's room. He wanted to get there before anyone else thought of searching there for the money. After checking under the bed, he rifled through drawers and checked beneath the mattress, inside the pillowcase, and everywhere else imaginable.

"The bag of bones probably stashed the money up his rear end," Fishnet declared bitterly. He paused for a moment to think. "Hmmmm, he might have just dropped the money," he uttered in a low voice.

Fishnet returned to the yard with his bible in hand. Looking out at the expansive area, he called upon his police training. He decided to conduct a spiral search. He began at the edge of the yard and made his way to the center by walking in a wide spiral inward. The former detective stared down at the ground as he walked. He wasn't overly concerned about drawing attention to himself, figuring that anyone looking would dismiss him as someone who had forgotten to take his medication.

As luck would have it, Fishnet came upon the money in a grassy area beneath a thick bush. The bankroll, which was kept together by a rubber band, had been partially hidden beneath blades of high grass. The discovery was similar to locating a hard-to-find golf ball off the fairway. Fishnet immediately sat himself down close enough to the money to retrieve it and place it between his legs. He then began pretending to be reading his Bible. In actuality, he was discreetly inserting the bills within the pages of the good book. This was Fishnet's first score posing as a man devoted to performing good deeds. Copping the money came as naturally to him as pocketing cash found in the apartment of a dead person who lived alone. Since Old Buzzard was dead, there was no official follow-up concerning the missing money. Fishnet was elated to have some ready cash at his disposal.

The weeks preceding Fishnet's discharge were used to prepare for his masquerade as a righteous man. He spent lots of time in front of a mirror esting various gestures to use in his presentations. He wanted to see how he would appear to others. He polished his tone to improve his auditory pitches.

Fishnet's focus was interrupted whenever he noticed Wayna Garcia. The young CNA had begun to smile at him, a gesture that he considered to be encouraging. To the young assistant, Fishnet had evolved into an interesting reat. He was a bad boy who enlivened her otherwise mundane workday. Fishnet stood apart from the popcorn and movie sort of man she was accustomed to.

Aware that his looking like Clark Gable had a certain appeal for those with an affinity for the old-school movie star, Fishnet did his utmost to capitalize on the resemblance. Shaved clean, he left only a neatly trimmed Gable-like mustache. To the impressionable Garcia, who finally came to realize who Fishnet resembled, the actor lookalike came close enough to the genuine article to be sexually desirable.

"Why don't you take a break, sexy?" said Fishnet as Wayna stopped by his room to say hello.

"I can only stay a minute or two," said the assistant, smiling wryly at Fishnet. "You're looking very handsome today," she said. "I like your mustache like that."

"I'm glad you like it."

"I finally figured out who you remind me of."

"Who?" asked Fishnet.

"Clark Gable."

"I've heard that before."

Fishnet began staring at the assistant, making obvious what was on his mind. She looked away shyly. Being visually seduced was something that she had experienced before but never with the intensity of an older man. The moment caused her face to redden.

"I thought you were supposed to be a Holy Roller," she commented softly.

"God loves a cheerful giver, so one must share and pass the sugar," he answered. The smirking Fishnet tapped his Bible to emphasis his point.

"You are too much," exclaimed the assistant, shaking her head slowly. She felt herself succumbing to the temptation before her. "Where in that book did you get that from?"

"The Old Testament," he quickly shot back.

"You are so bad. . . ." she repeated, shaking her head as she left the room.

"It might have been the New Testament," he shouted at her back.

Years of working on the street had provided Fishnet with the uncanny ability to recognize someone who was susceptible to his sexual overtures. He saw a definite place in his life for Wayna. He soon drifted off to where they frolicked in the waters of South Africa's Boulders Beach under the curious eye of hundreds of braying penguins. Pleasant atmospheric music could be heard coming from somewhere in the distance as ocean waves broke crisply. He took the young nursing assistant in his arms, his hand gently freeing one of her breasts from the confinement of the bikini top she wore. This was one daydream that went without interruption. The next time Fishnet saw Wayna Garcia, he couldn't resist expressing his gratitude.

"I had a wonderful dream about you, Wayna," said Fishnet.

"You did?" she asked.

"You were great. Thank you."

Wayna said nothing. The bright redness in her face said it all. He equated her reaction to being enthusiastic about his advances.

"How about we go pray someplace?" asked Fishnet as he stared into her eyes.

Wayna thought for a moment before responding. "Where?" she asked, swallowing hard.

"Follow me to my chapel," he answered, leading her to a remote sink closet where mops and buckets were kept. She was destined to become Bonnie to Fishnet's Clyde.

37

Love, Marriage, and Homicide

MARKIE STOPPED OFF AT FITZIE'S to have a drink. As soon as he walked in the bar, he noticed the local bookie sitting in his regular seat. As usual, neither man acknowledged the other. Markie assumed his position at the far end of the room. Alley smiled broadly and waved as soon as she saw him. She brought him his regular libation without his having to ask. Witnessing the gleam in her eye gave the sergeant great satisfaction. Nobody lit up like Alley when she was happy.

Markie noticed the man exiting the restroom. There was something about him that Markie distrusted. Perhaps it was because he was known to be dating a financially secure woman many years his senior.

"Hello, Sarge," greeted the man, smiling as if they were great pals. He then extended his hand to shake.

"Hi," replied Markie, rising from his seat to face him. He accepted the man's hand in his.

As they shook, the man's free hand patted the side of Markie's waist in a friendly fashion. For the sergeant, this was revealing behavior. It indicated to him that the man was a smooth operator who was trying to establish if he was carrying a gun. After a few pleasant words, the man went on his way.

"Alley, did you see that guy who just said hello to me?" said the sergeant. "Don't trust him."

"Why?"

"Never mind why; just watch yourself around him. I don't have a good feeling about him."

"What did he do?"

"He didn't do a thing. I just got a feeling about him"

"He's really a dear, luv."

"All I'm saying is to be careful."

Allie wasn't sure whether or not to tell Markie about *Little Creepy*, the strange little man who had been annoying her at work. Since Alley wasn't one to cause problems, she never bothered to mention to the sergeant Little Creepy's vulgar advances toward her. She thought it best to spare Markie, who undoubtedly would confront Little Creepy over his behavior. Her decision would later prove to be an unfortunate one.

##########

IT WAS A QUIET DAY AT THE OFFICE WHEN MARKIE told Von Hess about his plans to marry.

"I'm thinking about getting married," Markie advised, looking for a reaction from Von Hess through the corner of his eye.

Von Hess did a double take before responding. "I think getting back with Florence is a great idea," said the detective, erroneously assuming Markie was talking about his first wife. "Lots of people remarry their first wife after getting divorced.

"It's not Flo I'm talking about."

"Not Flo?"

"I'm talking about Alley."

Von Hess stiffened. "Are you serious?" Von Hess couldn't see the advantage of Markie's aligning himself with Alley officially.

"Yeah, I'm dead serious."

"Your mind is made up on this?"

"I've flipped-flopped long enough. I'm ready to make it happen."

"Are you intending to have big wedding?"

"I don't exactly relish facing the expense of a big party, but since Alley was never married, it'll be her call. She's entitled to the white dress, the whole bit. It wouldn't be right for me to deny her that."

"You got the scratch to pay for a time?"

"I'll have to take out a pension loan." Von Hess just nodded without replying.

Their conversation was interrupted by Lieutenant Wright who entered the office.

"Saddle up," announced Wright abruptly. "You're hitting the trail."

340

"What's up, boss?" asked the sergeant.

"Chief McCoy wants you to work on a homicide that took place in the subway on West 14th Street. This job comes straight from the police commissioner's office."

"Somebody important must have gotten taken out," remarked Markie.

"Important enough to get the police commissioner off his can," said the lieutenant. "The victim was an off-duty cop from Philadelphia."

THE END